FAIREST

MAIRI MACMILLAN

One More Chapter
a division of HarperCollins*Publishers* Ltd
1 London Bridge Street
London SE1 9GF
www.harpercollins.co.uk
HarperCollins*Publishers*
Macken House, 39/40 Mayor Street Upper,
Dublin 1, D01 C9W8, Ireland

This paperback edition 2026

1

First published in Great Britain in ebook format
by HarperCollins*Publishers* 2026

Copyright © Mairi MacMillan 2026
Mairi MacMillan asserts the moral right to be identified
as the author of this work

A catalogue record of this book is available from the British Library
ISBN: 978-0-00-875944-5

This novel is entirely a work of fiction. The names, characters and incidents portrayed in it are the work of the author's imagination. Any resemblance to actual persons, living or dead, events or localities is entirely coincidental.

Printed and bound in the UK using 100% Renewable Electricity
by CPI Group (UK) Ltd

All rights reserved. No part of this publication may be reproduced, stored in a retrieval system, or transmitted, in any form or by any means, electronic, mechanical, photocopying, recording or otherwise, without the prior permission of the publishers.
Without limiting the exclusive rights of any author, contributor or the publisher of this publication, any unauthorised use of this publication to train generative artificial intelligence (AI) technologies is expressly prohibited. HarperCollins also exercise their rights under Article 4(3) of the Digital Single Market Directive 2019/790 and expressly reserve this publication from the text and data mining exception.

To everyone who has taken a chance and made a change.

PROLOGUE

I push through the drunken smokers huddled in the doorway of one of the oldest pubs in Glasgow, slamming open the door next to the station entrance on Glasgow's busiest street.

Every table is covered in empty glasses, everyone's attention fixed on the TV screen. No one in here will remember seeing me. I take a moment to scan the room, my senses reaching out for any trace of my prey. The barmaid glances up at me, then, realising I'm not going to be buying a drink, returns her attention to her phone.

'Anyone come through here?'

'Not anyone you're looking for, Hunter,' she says, looking up. There's something in her tone that makes me realise she's lying. She lifts a glass to wash it, then realises her mistake as her hand tightens around it. She screams as it cracks, cutting her deep. Never lie to the Kinfolk.

'Which way did he go?'

She stares, but when she swallows and breaks my gaze,

her eyes dart to the door leading to the back rooms. I go through it, moving swiftly along the corridors at the back of the pub. I check the sigil temporarily etched on the palm of my hand, hoping that I was mistaken about the identity of the Kin I'm hunting, but I'm not. There's been no trial, only claims made by the King that Matt killed one of his own in cold blood which has been upheld and a hunt called. I've been sent to ensure he faces judgement but it's getting harder for me with every hunt to dispense that justice in good conscience. The Unseelie Court is growing increasingly fickle, as if the scales of justice are not just a metaphor and something is weighing far too heavily on one side.

As long as I'm the Huntsman, I'm duty-bound to carry out my task. I console myself with the knowledge that at least I can grant him a clean, swift death. Although, if he eludes me until dawn, the hunt will end and the creatures of the Wild Hunt will pursue him instead. They never fail and their kills are neither swift nor painless. Not something I'd wish on my worst enemy, and the man I'm hunting is far from being my enemy.

Matt has only one chance at survival and that's to reach sanctuary. He'll be safe there – a prisoner, but safe. I need to find him. I need to know what happened and decide about his guilt for myself. If he's innocent … well, that will be just one more reason why I must ensure I become the next king. Sooner rather than later.

I pause for a moment, my hand on the door handle as I gather my senses around me. I can smell fear. I shift my perception away from the human world to that of the

Underworld, watching as the door in front of me changes from reinforced steel to a scratched-up but solid, wooden, latched doorway. Behind me, the noise from the pub fades, replaced by a fiddle and clarsach playing folk music. A woman's voice starts to sing as I push the door open and step outside – not into the tunnels that run under the huge glass-roofed station that exists in this time and space in the human world, but onto a narrow lane that leads to the bustling Alston Street. It's the only notable street in Grahamston, a former village now swallowed up by the station in Glasgow's city centre.

I look right and left, heading north past the market stalls and entertainers out on this bright, wintery Saturday afternoon. Here, the Kinfolk who notice me pause, watching me. I can almost hear the sighs of relief as I pass by and it becomes clear that it's not them I'm after.

I hear the click of a door up ahead and the sound of feet pounding up the stairs inside the building. I run towards it, the Kinfolk in the street stopping and staring at me all desperate to know who I'm after.

'Which door?' I ask a cobbler, an elf who hasn't paid any attention to my approach, ensuring that his attention is fixed on the soft leather shoe on the last in front of him. He looks up, feigning surprise for only a second before I step towards him, drawing on the power of Cernunnos, the god of the hunt that my family has embodied for centuries. The cobbler holds my gaze, before his eyes slide away.

'Why do you need us to tell you?' he asks, but I see his hands tremble. He knows who I am, he's just choosing not to cooperate. 'He's as good as Kin to you.'

'You know why. He's killed Kin. The Court demands his presence. Justice must be served.'

'Aye, but whose justice?' he mutters.

All around me, there's a collective intake of breath. I can't afford to take my eyes off the cobbler, but I know the majority of people in the busy street have stopped to watch my interaction with the elf.

'He went into the theatre,' a female elf, probably his wife, says, stepping out from the shoe shop.

'Breagha,' the cobbler hisses.

'If he killed Kin, he should face justice, Tormod. Let the Hunter do his job.'

'There's no justice under the Rialis,' I hear him say before she hushes him.

I've already turned and am striding down the street towards the theatre when I hear the door to the shop slam behind me, and I shake my head. I can no longer disagree with what Tormod said, and my resentment towards the Rialis goes up another notch. Still, Chris Riali is dead, and according to the King, Vincenzo, Matt Muir killed him and has been condemned by The Unseelie Court for the murder.

An entire block is taken up by an imposing theatre building, its ornate façade adorned with four marble statues representing various Arts. The once-grand façade is now cracked and grimy, the arched windows are dark and the statues weathered into ghostly shapes. All four have signs of the Blight's black fungus creeping over their surface, smothering their faces.

At the corner, spreading up from underground is another small patch of Blight. There are scorch marks beside it where someone has tried to burn it off, but it hasn't worked – fresh spread is visible within the burnt area. It's the first I've seen of it so close to the city centre, and it worries me. Where Blight takes hold, everything around it withers and dies, consumed by its relentless hunger. And the longer Vincenzo Riali remains as King, the faster the Blight spreads.

The stench of fear and panic grows the closer I get to the theatre doors. No one tries to stop me as I push them open and pause as they slam shut behind me. In the empty auditorium, I have only taken a few steps down the aisle when the lights flash on and Matt leaps up onto the stage, racing to the wings and disappearing. I stop for a moment to smile before I sprint down the aisle and vault onto the stage. I land on my feet, the smell of sawdust, paint and musty fabric hitting me as I push past the curtains and into the backstage corridors. I've been here before and there's only one exit although more than once my prey has assumed that this would be a good place to hide.

Around the next corner, I hear a door slam open and I speed up. Matt isn't far ahead of me when I run through the fire door, out onto the lane, and with a short burst of speed, launch myself at him. He grunts as I tackle him to the ground, the lane around us emptying of the few Kinfolk unfortunate enough to be here.

I pull a knife from my ankle sheath and press it against his throat, pushing up with my arms to look down at him. His head thuds back on the cobblestones then he shakes it, resigned to his fate.

'You should have headed for the river right away,' I say, satisfied that I've got him.

'I wanted to see Rose before...' he turns his head to the side. 'Although stupidly, I thought the fact that I was innocent would be enough that no hunt would be called.'

I hold my hand up for him to see the sigil with his name underneath etched onto my skin and he pales.

'Are you?'

'I didn't kill Chris. I swear.'

'He was in the bath when he died.'

Matt snorts. 'I'm not the only Kinfolk who originates from the water, Cillian. And it wasn't being in the bath that caused him to bleed out.'

No, the two deep wounds on his forearms were the cause of that – the first far deeper than the other. Matt is right, there are far more hallmarks of suicide here, but Vincenzo is insistent that Matt is responsible and a hunt has been called so there must be something in Vincenzo's claim.

'Besides,' Matt continues, 'Chris was my best friend.'

'Really?'

He shrugs. 'Used to be, at least.'

'Until you moved on to my sister?' I snarl.

He hesitates for a moment. 'I love Rose. And Chris... He was struggling. Especially those last few days. He wasn't himself. You're right, we'd been growing apart for a while.'

Matt isn't lying, but for the Court to instigate a hunt there must also be truth in Vincenzo's statement – the Kinfolk cannot lie to one another without consequence. But I'm not an arbitrator, my duty is simply to hunt and Matt's name is on my palm.

'I'm not going to face the Court, Cillian. There's no point. Vincenzo holds too much sway there and he's already decided I'm guilty. If I'm going to die, then I'd rather it was by your hand.' He looks up at me, and if I wasn't convinced he was innocent before, I am now. 'Do it, Cillian. Here and now. Just tell Rose I love her. Please. To be honest, I expected you to kill me long before now for daring to touch her.'

'The thought had occurred to me, yes.'

I press the knife to his throat, watching as his blood beads up and starts to trickle down to the cobblestones. I've made my decision.

Later, as I wash the blood from my knife, my palm now free of the mark, I can no longer deny that I, too, am losing faith in the Court. I've fulfilled my duty, but things have changed recently. Something is very wrong, and I want no part in murdering the innocent. The Unseelie Court might be the court of darkness, of things the human world fears, but we have our own honour, our own sense of justice. We need change.

The Unseelie Court needs a new king. And it will be me.

CHAPTER 1
NIAMH

FOUR YEARS LATER

Sussurri. It means 'whispers' in Italian. It sounds sort of romantic, but somehow I don't think anything being whispered inside the walls of the Sussurri nightclub in Glasgow is of the romantic variety. More like drug deals or discussions about where to hide a body.

Maybe you shouldn't judge a nightclub necessarily by the state of the ladies' bathroom, but this whole place reeks and the last stall door has been locked the entire time we've been in here. The rhythmic thuds and occasional moans leave no doubt about what's happening inside. The lighting is so dim even the shadows have shadows, and I'm sure there are things moving in them. Things that are huddled in the darkness, watching us. Waiting.

'This isn't one of your family's clubs?' I ask my best friend Rose, my sense of unease growing by the minute.

'Fuck, no,' she says, attempting to get soap out of an

empty dispenser. 'You know my darling brother Cillian would have dragged me kicking and screaming back home long before now if anywhere we'd been to this evening had been family owned.'

'Would that have been so bad?' I look around. 'It is his engagement dinner tonight, after all.' The Hunters own several pubs and clubs in the city and we normally go to one of those. Elliots is a cosy wine bar round the corner from our flat. And their club in Anderston, The Three Graces, has multiple levels, each with a different vibe. None of them wholesome or anything, and I'm convinced there's at least one level that Rose keeps me well away from. But at least they're not sleazy like this place.

'Well, he should have let me bring the plus-one I asked for and then I might have turned up.'

I sigh, although I can't deny that the fact Cillian had expressly forbidden me from going to the meal had upset me. He probably didn't realise I'd heard him, but his words had left no doubt that under no circumstances was I to show my face tonight. I guess my presence wasn't exactly welcome, and for years now, he's kept his distance from me. But it's not been possible to stay completely away from one another. And no matter how hard I try to ignore him, the way my heart races and my breath catches when I'm in the same room as him seems to block everything else from my thoughts and senses. At well over six foot, he's impossible not to notice. And his dark brown hair is a little longer than most men keep theirs, flopping over his eyes when he moves his head; his milky-blue eyes such an unusual shade that they're almost mesmerising.

The intensity of Cillian's gaze is hard to avoid and the way he looks at me – it scares me. Although whether that's because I'm actually scared of him, or because I'm scared that one day I won't care about any of the things that scare me – that I will turn my back on every principle I hold dear, in exchange for a few stolen moments with him – I don't know.

I shake my head. Yeah, not going to happen – from either perspective. And nope, I'm not going to think about any of those times when he was kind, looked out for me, and I simply ... misunderstood. Not in the short term, but in the long term certainly. Now, we avoid each other whenever possible, although there is just something about him that... No, Niamh. Stop. For so many reasons. He's too old. He's your best friend's brother. He's possibly ... *definitely*, not always on the right side of the law. And I'm going to be a fully qualified lawyer by this time next year.

I've seen some terrible things happen to people. Seen too many people get away with cruelty and selfishness. I want to make a difference. Fight for some kind of justice. Maybe one day get justice for my parents' deaths. I push away the familiar grief that always threatens to consume me when I think about all the things they've missed out on. All the life they had taken from them.

Still, I'm worried that a key part of our non-attendance tonight involved us thumbing our nose at Cillian's fiancée's family by coming to their club instead – even if we are accompanied, as always, by Rose's bodyguard. Well, not in the bathroom but he's in the club somewhere, most likely near the door waiting for us to finish up in here.

The Hunters are rich. Crazy rich. They're very traditional, not to mention paranoid. But—

I catch a glimpse of movement behind me in the mirror, turning when I can't see what caused it. But there's nothing. I look back in the mirror and see a shadowy figure staring at me from the far corner of the room. I turn because it sort of reminds me of Vittoria, then huff out a breath when I see there's no one there. She's at her engagement dinner, not hanging around here. I knew I shouldn't have drunk that bottle of Stox earlier. It's been all over the news recently; apparently, it's causing people to hallucinate more than usual. It's a craft beer brewed rather ironically by monks living in a monastery on the edge of the Highlands. I check the mirror again, and the figure is back, but disappears before I can work out who it actually is. I shiver, cursing the Stox and wishing we were anywhere but here.

'Maybe we should go home?' I mutter when I notice the woman beside me staring at my reflection. I give her a half-smile but she frowns, shaking her head and muttering as she pushes away from the sink and heads for the door.

'Absolutely not!' Rose insists. 'We've got the whole night to ourselves, avoiding the most boring dinner party in the world where I'd have to pretend to like that bitch who's got her claws into my brother. So, no.' She turns to face me and gives me a hug, our skin clammy where we touch. I push her away and smile. Even if I'd rather be anywhere else, I certainly don't regret the company. It's worth the risk of being caught. I suppress thoughts of facing her brother's wrath.

I frown at her, then pull the thin straps of the sequinned

dress I'm wearing back into place and attempt to tug the hem down. I knew I shouldn't have let Rose persuade me to borrow it from her. It's way more revealing than anything I own – including most of my underwear. Something that doesn't seem to concern Rose, ever. Well, they do say that opposites attract.

The dress is cut much lower at the front than anything in my wardrobe and I notice my necklace has twisted around. I flip it back so that the stone is nestled in my cleavage, which one of Rose's push-up bras has significantly enhanced this evening. It's warm to my touch, flickering in the light that briefly illuminates the dingy bathroom when another three women squeeze inside.

My mum gave me it years ago, a family heirloom, she'd told me – a plain gold oval with the central deep red heart-shaped stone garnet – a constant reminder of her love for me. I brush away the pang. Almost four years have passed, and I still think about my parents every single day. I squeeze the necklace briefly in my fingers and— What was that? I peer into the corner of the room and there's a door with four empty screw-holes where a sign presumably used to be. It's ajar, the opening deep in shadow, but I'm sure there was movement inside just a second ago.

'We're safe, don't worry,' Rose assures me. 'The Rialis own this place and I'm sure the *lovely* Vittoria isn't going to let anything happen to us. My brother would not be happy, and she wouldn't do anything to jeopardise her chances of him fucking her. Or marrying her. She's very keen on that. It's the closest she's going to get to being queen. Can you imagine what their kids will be like?'

Queen? I sigh at Rose's hyperbole. She often exaggerates when she's been drinking. My cheeks heat at the image of Cillian that flashes into my mind. I can certainly picture him as a king. He's older than us, thirty to our twenty-two, and he's been the subject of almost every single one of my fantasies since the day I laid eyes on him when Rose and I were first-year law students.

Now we've graduated, and in the autumn we'll start our professional training, but no matter how hard I try, I can't shake my ridiculous crush. Is it still a crush when you're carrying so much guilt that you can barely utter his name? At least it's been an easy secret to keep. After all, what would a man like Cillian ever see in a girl like me? He's made that very clear.

God, I was so stupid ... I really thought... My cheeks heat even after all this time. Ever since that day after my parents' funeral, when he made it clear that he was choosing Vittoria and not me, I've avoided him whenever possible. But he'd been so kind when they died and I'd thought ... I'd thought he cared. That I wasn't imagining things. Cillian's such a mess of contradictions, though. Like the first time I went to a party at Cernunnos, their house, and he kissed me then left me alone in his room, feeling awkward and confused. And I know he told other guys to stay away from me, but I don't even know why – it's not like he wants me.

All he's ever seen me as is Rose's naïve friend. I've heard Vittoria talk about me behind my back, her vindictive nature coming through. She's definitely not a girl's girl. Now, when I'm around him, I struggle to work out how to actually speak, never mind what to say. It's ridiculous. I shiver and consciously stop rubbing my thighs together.

Rose smirks at me. 'Come on, let's go to the VIP section.' She grabs my hand and leads me around the dancefloor to where two broad security guards, dressed in all black, smile at her and lift the red velvet cord to allow us to pass into the exclusive area.

'I thought you and Vittoria hated each other?' I whisper as we take the only two empty spaces at the bar, either side of a barely dressed blonde who downs a shot then picks up a large glass of red wine and slides out from between us.

'We do, but she's not going to risk anything happening to me in one of her family's clubs.'

'She won't even be here tonight, will she? I mean, it's their engagement dinner so presumably they will be going … somewhere afterwards?'

Rose pats me on the shoulder. 'I'm pretty sure I can guess what their plans are afterwards, but we're safe here. Look, Sean's right there.'

Everything about this club just feels off. It's gritty but not in a fun way. The bouncers barely glanced at our ID, and I wonder if the dusting of white powder on the edge of the bar in front of me might be worth a small fortune.

'I thought you said her family was crazy?' I say, strongly suspecting that in this case, crazy actually means criminal.

'Oh, they are. You know how totally fucked up my family is, but Vittoria's? They're next level. Like "mess with us and you die" crazy. Losing Chris…' She trails off. Four years ago, there had been a string of unexpected deaths, and we tried not to remind each other about them. My parents. Vittoria's younger brother, Christopher Riali. And Matt Muir – Rose's boyfriend and Chris's best friend. I never really knew what had happened, too lost in my own grief to really care as much as I should have. Something I regret now. But Rose refuses to talk about any of it. Her way of dealing with emotion is to pretend it simply doesn't exist.

'But this is business. Family business. They won't jeopardise that,' she says, attracting the barman's attention rather expertly for someone who has drunk as much as she has tonight. Not that I'm judging or anything. I've had more than I usually do, but I'd like to think I'm pacing myself. 'Rose,' I say wearily when she orders a couple of shots and two bottles of Stox.

'Oh, come on, Niamh. Take a walk on the wild side for once.'

We turn in our seats, leaning back against the bar and observing the various other occupants of the VIP section. Most of the men are in expensive suits, which reminds me of something she said.

'Their marriage is ... what ... business? But—'

'Oh, come on,' she scoffs, making a face at me. 'You don't actually believe they're in love, do you?'

'I can't say I've given it much thought.' *Liar*. I've given it a lot of thought. 'But why would they be together if they don't love each other? It's been years.'

The look of pity Rose gives me makes me wonder if I've hidden my crush as well as I thought. She can't possibly know, though ... can she? I swallow my shot and take a long draught of the Stox. This will definitely be the last alcohol I drink tonight.

'Cillian is young to ... to be in sole charge of all our business interests,' she says, her gaze on a group of three guys in the far corner who are glancing over at us occasionally, too. I groan inwardly. 'And it's not been easy for the Rialis since Chris's death. Vittoria can't inherit his businesses. Mostly misogynistic crap, but that's Vincenzo and his associates for you. And Vittoria is furious. Marrying Cillian is the only way to have any say in the future of everything her family has worked for.'

Rose grins as something brushes against my legs. I freeze, slowly looking down into a pair of sparkling black eyes, which disappear as soon as I see them. Bloody Stox. We should really go home soon.

Pouting, she smiles over at the men, blowing them a kiss from her raspberry-tinted lips, which look good against her auburn hair and green eyes.

'But if they're going to be married, shouldn't you at least try to be ... friends? I mean, you'll see her at family events, right?'

'No one needs a friend like her, Niamh. She's a fucking m—'

She stops short, blinks at herself and takes a deep breath to get her anger under control. Not for the first time, I wonder how she's going to manage as a lawyer with that temper. Her gaze shifts back to the men.

'Time?' she demands. I check my watch.

'Twelve-fifteen.'

'Okay,' she says clapping her hands together, gleefully. 'Three hours and forty-five minutes left to drink, dance and see what else the night brings.' She winks at me.

'Rose...' I sigh.

'Oh, don't be such a prude. You know sex is *fun*, right? You'll end up a dried-up old maid, living with a houseful of cats, or even worse, settling for dull, predictable sex with some nice but boring guy who doesn't even know that a clit exists let alone where to find one.'

I stay silent, not wanting to have this conversation with her. It's hard to argue, in one way – she might be right about the cats, and honestly, I would be okay with that. But I've also witnessed every one of Rose's highs and lows over the past four years.

Since Matt died, she's not had a serious relationship, but has more than made up for that with casual ones. I've hugged her, held her hand, binged nineties and noughties romcoms and talked to her for hours and hours after she's been dumped or ghosted or ignored. Not to mention that twice I've had to buy pregnancy tests when her period was late and she practically stopped functioning until we had the negative result in front of us.

And it's not like I don't ever date ... it's just ... not a priority right now. Not until I've secured my first job and have a decent salary. And yes, preferably find a guy who knows where a clitoris is. Someone who is able to distract me from Cillian. Not to mention someone who sticks around for a second date.

Once I'm settled, there'll be time to have fun. With the added advantage that I won't have to deal with immaturity. Supposedly. Maybe that's part of the appeal of my recurrent fantasies about Cillian. He's definitely mature, and far from boring, in a dark and dangerous kind of way. I'd happily bet that he could find the clitoris on a first attempt.

'Come on!' Rose yells, hooking her elbow through mine and steering me towards the dancefloor. 'Let's see if we can find at least two guys who look like they're capable of giving decent orgasms.'

I sigh and allow her to drag me out onto the dancefloor.

CHAPTER 2
CILLIAN

'A toast,' Vincenzo Riali declares, standing up with a glass of Cristal in his hand, pointedly ignoring the empty seat between myself and Alec Carruth. 'To my beautiful daughter, Vittoria, and my future son-in-law, Cillian. May the Rialis and the Hunters thrive once more under your combined leadership. Although, let's hope that happens later rather than sooner.'

We're in an elegantly decorated private dining room in The Angel's Share, one of Vincenzo's Michelin-starred restaurants, and no expense has been spared. Alongside the Rialis and my family, Vincenzo has taken it upon himself to invite the six other Kennards who, like Vincenzo and myself, are the heads of the ruling Kinfolk families. We are all who remain of the original twelve that formed The Unseelie Court, thanks to the Blight.

Two Unseelie Kin disappeared in the first wave of the Blight which also destroyed the whole Seelie Court, and a further two have since disappeared, all of their homes, businesses and seats at The Unseelie Court choked by the creeping, fungal Blight. Although the fact that this happened directly after them challenging Vincenzo has not gone unnoticed.

Soon, the number will become seven once the Hunter and Riali Kin are brought together with my marriage. I glance at the others around the table. Alec Carruth, whose Kin work predominantly with stone, has come alone. Beside him – representing smiths of all kinds – his rival, Thomas MacGowan, sits with his silent wife. At the far end, I've already heard Robert McLoughlin trying to persuade Duncan Webster to invest in his latest start-up, but no one here is foolish enough to trust anything that a representative of Lugh suggests – they've all been caught out by the trickster once too often in the past. The final two Kin, the Kelsos and the Macphersons, refuse to even speak to McLoughlin and Vincenzo has wisely placed them all as far away from each other as possible.

With the exception of myself and my fiancée, everyone around the table stands and raises their glasses to us, their expressions falsely congratulatory – I hate Court politics but it's a game that must be played if I'm to restore the Court to its former glory. I paste on a smile and glance down at my phone, wondering where the fuck my sister has got to. Surely, she isn't planning to not turn up tonight of all nights? This is a historic union, not to mention it being the next step in my campaign to replace Vincenzo as King of The Unseelie Court as soon as I possibly can. Unfortunately, the only option is to do this with his daughter, Vittoria, as my queen. A dark price I will have to pay.

'Will this marriage mean that another root of the Tree of Life is killed by Blight?' Carruth asks.

'Both bloodlines will survive,' Vincenzo insists, refusing to face the underlying issue, as usual.

Thomas MacGowan shrugs. 'So much is gone already. Only our eight twisted roots remain. The tree itself is long dead. I doubt anything we do will help.'

'We shouldn't be simply accepting this. We should be fighting it, trying to restore our world to what it was,' I say.

But Vincenzo laughs. 'You will learn what battles to fight, Cillian. Once you are king, you too will see that the Underworld is dying. But we have done well in the human world. That is where our future lies. Why fight it?'

'Surely the *Craobh na Beatha* is worth saving?' I argue. 'Our power lies within it. As the years pass our powers fade, our people fade. Fewer are born, more die. And the Blight destroys more and more of the Underworld itself.'

The Kelsos shrug and look away, taking long draughts from their glasses, and I can't decide if they have ceased caring or if it's guilt about their own inaction. They're the largest of the families, but also the most secretive, living their lives in the shadows of the Underworld.

But not even they know why the Blight happened and how it started. There are few alive today who witnessed it, but a hundred years ago something poisoned the *Craobh na Beatha* – the Tree of Life that grew in Glasgow's Necropolis – the city of the dead, east of the city centre which is the most important site that links the Underworld of the Kinfolk and the human world. As well as linking the two worlds, the Tree also housed both The Seelie and The Unseelie Court chambers. Now only The Unseelie Court remains, housed in the partially withered roots of the great tree. And where the tree itself should be, there's simply nothing.

I'm surprised when Murdo Macpherson speaks. 'I was out in the far reaches of the forest yesterday. The Blight has choked up several streams to the north and large areas of woodland are dying. I can understand why Cernunnos's Kin are worried.'

'Humans have polluted that area with a smelting factory,' Vincenzo points out. 'What can we hope to do to prevent the destruction the humans wreak?'

But I blame Vincenzo, if not for the Blight itself, then certainly for his failing to stop its spread. I know he has shares in that smelting plant and considers his profits more important than the Underworld. It wasn't until four years ago that I began to research exactly how Vincenzo was profiting from the Blight. Matt warned me then, and I've watched Vincenzo carefully ever since. He simply brushes off all reports of the Blight's destruction and refuses to act. And it's spreading from the trees and the land to the Kinfolk themselves – while he grows rich.

Only last week, two foresters were found, their bodies twisted in agony, riddled with sores that oozed a black, tar-like substance. But he refuses to allow any investigation, quietly disposing of the corpses and fencing off the land now destroyed by the creeping black mould. Given that he's not even willing to break with tradition enough for his daughter to inherit in her own right, his inaction should come as no surprise, and it's time I ensure his reign comes to an end, soon. The future of the Underworld might depend on it.

I meet my fiancée's gaze – it's been two weeks since we announced our engagement. For four years I've tried to find another way, but on the night of my sister's graduation party, I realised there was none and proposed. Or, my decision was made when I set eyes on Niamh Whyte again. I've avoided my sister's best friend as much as possible over the years. The woman is a temptation I can't afford to give into. Until I marry Vittoria, Niamh will always be there, tempting me to relinquish my quest to become king. I've worked too hard, waited too patiently, to give it all up for a human but seeing Niamh at that party, I knew I wouldn't be able to resist her for much longer.

With Vittoria's eyes on me, I push my phone into my pocket and turn to face her. She glances pointedly at my pocket and rolls her eyes. I lean forward, my hand snaking around the back of her neck and draw her towards me to kiss her. Her blood-red lips are ice cold as our tongues tangle, fighting for control. I refuse to allow her to win even this small battle, just as she will never let me win if she can help it. She pulls back, pressing a red-tipped finger to my lips and smiles seductively.

'Later,' she whispers, running the finger down over my lips and chin before pulling it away with a flourish, smirking at the others around the table like the dark queen she aspires to be.

Conversation flows as freely as the champagne, but for the most part, I allow my mind to wander. I deal with the other Kennards when I have to, but as my job is to administer the Court's justice, I've found it easier to keep my distance. I can't avoid the Rialis, though. They own a wide range of hospitality-related businesses around the city. The seat they occupy at The Unseelie Court is that of the great sea god Llyr, and with the sea as their element, it was only natural that they gravitated towards providing the humans with its fruits. Sustenance, and the promise of pleasure, have always been the simplest ways to entice humans, which offers endless ways for us to control them. It may just be coincidence, but as the Riali empire has expanded, the Blight has spread.

My phone vibrates with a text from Rose's bodyguard, Sean. I open it despite Vittoria's frown. It's a photo and it's not just of Rose. She's on a dancefloor, with Niamh, and it takes me a moment to tear my gaze away from the young woman who has tormented me for the past four years.

Niamh attracts me in a way I'm not sure I fully understand. She's wholesome and good – the opposite of the women I'm usually drawn to – but at the same time, something about her calls to the darkest parts of me. Whenever I'm in the same room as her, the hunter within me rises to the surface, hyper-aware of her, watching her, stalking her like prey – even if it's only with my gaze. More than once I've had to leave her presence to stop me killing every other man in the room and claiming her as mine.

But that's a desire I can't afford to indulge, not least because if she saw me killing anyone, she would go to the authorities faster than my sister moves between men. She's human and knows nothing of my world. Plus, she has an overdeveloped sense of justice that has motivated her since the moment we met. She's determined to fight for fairness, a concept at odds with the ever-changing vagaries of The Unseelie Court, where justice is determined by Vincenzo's latest whim or the strange unpredictable power that lies within the Court chamber itself.

My own ambition is as much of an obstacle. Marrying Vittoria is my chance to become king and take a different path, not only giving our people the chance to survive but also thrive. I refuse to let the Blight destroy us.

Normally, Niamh is the exact opposite of my sister – she dresses modestly, doesn't drink too much and is careful not to give any man foolish enough to wander into her vicinity the wrong idea. Except that tonight, she looks anything but innocent. My cock hardens at the sight of her slender, toned body barely covered by a sequinned bodycon dress, her breasts pushed up into an impressive cleavage. The dress leaves little to the imagination and it would be so easy to slide a hand up her skirt, to part her thighs and slip her underwear to the side, to see just how turned on she would be. An ache inside me wishes I could be there.

The more I stare at the photo, however, the more I see beyond my lust. They're both smiling, but I can see the strain on Niamh's features, the way she's looking to the side, tension in her body as if poised ready for an attack. Because deep down, despite all the human laws we choose to abide by on the surface, and all the security that's in place around her in the club to theoretically keep her safe, she still understands what she truly is.

Prey.

Or I could bind her to me forever by promising to fulfil her heart's desire if she accepted. I've heard stories of humans being granted the most amazing voices, exceptional dancing talent, the ability to play a musical instrument with more skill than any other living being – but there's always a catch. One woman could only ever sing and lost the ability to speak. Another danced herself to death. And yet another played the fiddle with such skill that everyone who heard her was instantly entranced, but as soon as the music stopped all memory of the music and the musician was gone.

What am I tempted to offer Niamh? Is there anything out there that she would be unable to resist? I doubt it. She's not so easily tempted. It doesn't stop me wanting her, though. Over the years, my thoughts have strayed to her with a disturbing regularity, and in those fantasies, my sister's best friend is far less sweet and innocent than she is in reality. Most of the things I want to do with her – *do to her* – I'm sure have never crossed her mind.

I refused to allow Rose to bring Niamh tonight. It's bad enough being around her the times we've met in the human world, but downright dangerous to bring her here, to Vincenzo's restaurant in the Underworld. Like most humans, Niamh isn't aware of the presence of the Kinfolk around her all day, every day, but if she was and if she witnessed the way we operate, the things my family does to manipulate humans, her moral code would send her straight to the authorities. And they might actually believe her. It's a quality that will make her a fantastic lawyer – and utterly wrong for me. Her friendship with my sister is just another way in which Rose tries to rile me up every single day.

'Looks like your sister is enjoying herself,' Vittoria says, looking at my phone over my shoulder. 'And at Sussurri. Really?' She shakes her head and exchanges a look with her father.

My phone vibrates again with a text from Sean:

> She's insistent on staying. Want me to risk causing a scene?

'News of your sister's whereabouts?' Vincenzo asks.
'Yes, her bodyguard.'
'Such a simple task,' he says. 'I hope you're going to punish him severely for his failure.'

'He has many other useful qualities,' I say, taking a sip of my whisky as I consider Vincenzo's lack of empathy for the Kinfolk he employs. I know my sister, and she doesn't make Sean's life easy. Given that he's the only man who has been even remotely able to keep an eye on Rose, while also managing to keep his hands off her and his dick out of her, I'm not willing to dispose of him yet. But his coat is on a very shoogly peg after tonight and if anything happens to her, he won't be breathing for long. I text him back.

> Time to take Rosebud and her friend back to their flat.

Rose detests the nickname, insisting that it demeans her. But if she's going to act out like a child, I feel justified in using it.

> On it.

'No!' Vittoria, looking at the messages says suddenly, her expression cold, jaw set. 'Leave her be. I'm sure she has a good reason not to make the effort.'

'Very well,' I say, although dressed like that in a place like

Sussurri, Rose and Niamh are really fucking far from being safe in the way I'd like them to be. But I'm not ready to push things yet.

'Rose will be fine in Sussurri,' Vittoria assures me as if reading my thoughts. For all her faults, she wouldn't lie to me, not about this. If Kinfolk lie to one another, there are harsh penalties to pay, and I'm sure my fiancée would never risk that. Especially as we never know what it might be as Court magic decides. The loss of her voice – or her magic? A visible mark of shame? She would never risk any of those, so my sister should be safe.

'I'm sure she will,' I say, and we exchange a look. She realises the significance as well as I do. Rose partying in a Riali-owned nightclub instead of being here is a giant 'fuck you' to our marriage. The two of them have never liked one another, and while I tend to agree with Rose's opinions about Vittoria, our family has a lot to gain from this marriage going ahead.

Vittoria places a hand on my chest and leans in close to me and whispers, 'But I expect you to make it up to me later.' She nips at my ear with her teeth before sitting back and sliding a hand from my knee to my crotch. And if she notices that I'm already hard, she doesn't comment on it. Thank fuck.

I text Sean to leave Rose be.

'Well, I for one am looking forward to the big day,' says Alec Carruth, changing the subject back to our wedding. 'My father didn't enjoy socialising, and I've kept myself hidden away in the darkest depths of Ayrshire for far too long, but now that I've seen what I'm missing, I'm looking forward to coming into the city far more.'

He gestures around the opulent room and Vincenzo preens. The Rialis have always been susceptible to flattery – it's a flaw. To be honest, I wasn't expecting Alec to attend. His lands lie south-west of Glasgow and until recently his father was the Kennard and showed no interest in making connections with the other Kinfolk.

'Are you planning to wear white?' Alec asks Vittoria.

'Of course,' she says sweetly, but her expression is tight and I hide my smile at the way he has managed to piss her off without giving her grounds for a challenge. 'Everything will be very traditional, *Alec*.'

The way she says his name makes me certain he's going to pay for that comment, but he's smiling back at her, oblivious. I can't bring myself to anticipate what my life is going to be like married to her.

'It's tragic, in a way, that the eight Kinfolk families of The Unseelie Court will reduce even further, but this way at least both our bloodlines will live on,' Vincenzo says. 'It'll be a day to celebrate when your oldest son fully unites both families – although I hope that is a long time away.'

I'm sure he does, because he'll be dead. Come to think of it, that would require my death, too. Let's hope it is many, many years in the future.

'So few Kinfolk females, nowadays,' Vincenzo continues, shaking his head sadly. 'The Blight took The Seelie Court in one fell swoop, but it's killing The Unseelie Court just as surely.'

'Like I said earlier,' MacGowan puts in, 'the pollution in

the human world is having an effect. The Seelie Court thrived in the light, in fresh, clean air. We've only survived because of our links with the darkness, and even death.'

'Oh, Thomas, you're making it sound like a battle of good and evil,' Carruth says, pouring his friend another glass.

'It has certainly reduced the number of women born at all levels of society. Only two women in this generation. You're fortunate Vittoria has chosen you, Cillian. Soon, only your sister, Rose, will be available.'

I clench my fists.

'At least from your perspective, Cillian, it means there are potentially fewer rivals for the position of king in the future,' Vincenzo says, laughing. 'Although, I'm not planning on giving up my position anytime soon.'

In order to become king, a Kennard must marry the daughter of another – and there's a growing fear that in the next generation, no females will be born and every Kin of The Unseelie Court will die out – if the Blight doesn't overcome it first.

'Uncertainty doesn't encourage anyone to breed,' points out Thomas MacGowan. His family has always been a powerful one, working with metal to form weapons and ammunition. Their products are bought by both humans and Kinfolk, and perhaps one of the few universal truths is that everyone wants to be able to defend themselves – although it's certainly convenient that those same weapons can also be used to attack.

'Then we must work together to ensure stability,' Vincenzo insists. 'You two should set a good example and have as many children as possible, as soon as possible.'

I glance at Vittoria, but her face is unreadable. I struggle to imagine her as a mother, though I have few objections to the process of making her one. We've been lovers on and off for years, although 'lovers' seems too pleasant a term for it. We both know what we want and we both know how to get that from each other. No part of our relationship bears any resemblance to love.

'Well, Cillian, we had expected Rose to be here, but we'll give you your gift, anyway. Although it was really for the two of you,' Vincenzo says.

Vittoria smiles, her eyes bright with excitement as her father gestures to a couple of his men.

'You know, if your sister insists on being difficult, perhaps it's time to marry her off, Cillian,' Vincenzo adds. 'There are a few possibilities for suitable husbands who should be able to keep her in line. Alec here is still young enough to marry her.'

I tense at the gall of this man, thinking that he can tell me what to do with my sister. I'll be the one to take over *his* Kin. He gets no say in mine. And Rose will not be marrying a man twice her age.

'I certainly wouldn't mind taking her off your hands,' Alec smarms. 'She's a pretty little thing. Feisty.'

Barely a second has passed before I'm out of my seat, my hand around the older man's throat as I pin him against the nearest wall. Our chairs clatter to the floor behind us, echoing in the sudden silence.

'No.'

'Sorry, I'm sorry,' he sputters, his hands gripping my wrists.

I let him go, stepping back and righting my chair before sitting back down. The room holds its breath as he brushes the front of his suit and sits back down – a little further away from me this time. Picking up his whisky tumbler and swallowing a mouthful, he stares at me. I stare back. The audacity. He's already been married. He's two decades older than her. How does he even think—

I know my sister's reputation, although few are foolish enough to even allude to it in front of me. Our mother died when Rose was only three, and I often wonder if Rose would be different now if she had lived. Rose's adolescence was uneventful, but the loss of Matt caused a change I couldn't have predicted. She's become increasingly reckless with her decisions, unemotional and manipulative. Qualities that make a good hunter, but not ones I'd want my sister to possess.

Before our relationship crumbled entirely, we'd come to a compromise. Her bodyguard would accompany her everywhere to ensure her safety, especially in the presence of the men she chooses to become acquainted with. This in exchange for her prioritising academic success. Rose is a smart young woman, she just lacked a female role model – until she met Niamh. And for the past four years, she's lived up to her side of the bargain. Bloody typical she'd pick tonight to publicly throw her rebellion in my face.

The door to the private dining room opens and two of Vincenzo's hard men enter, dragging a third between them.

'Ah,' Vincenzo says. 'Your gift.'

'I don't understand,' I say, looking at Vittoria. 'I've never seen this man before.'

'You haven't, but your sister certainly has,' she practically crows, grinning dangerously.

One of the men pulls a phone out of his pocket and holds it in front of the man's bloodied face to unlock it. He taps on it briefly then hands it to me.

If what Alec just said was enough for me to choke him, what I see on this guy's phone is enough to murder him several times. Or torture him for weeks.

'Not just me you have issues with, then, Hunter,' Carruth jibes. 'Good to know.'

I barely hear him, but I do turn the screen away from the rest of the room because anyone who sees those photos of my sister isn't going to be seeing anything else as long as they damn well live.

'Did she let you take these?'

I can almost see what's left of his brain working, trying to decide whether I'll hurt him less if he says she consented or not. But then I swipe to the next photo and it's clear that there was absolutely no consent given or received.

I grab his head, bring my knee up to meet his face and glory in the feel of teeth and bone breaking. He falls to his knees, and I let him go, waiting as he spits out blood.

'I'm sorry,' he mumbles, though his broken jaw. 'I didn't know ... didn't know she was your sister.'

'You shouldn't be fucking doing that to anyone,' I yell, wishing I was on bare ground rather than inside. There's only so much power I can draw from dead wood and inside a building with a steel frame.

I'm not keen on him being shackled, it's unsporting – like shooting fish in a barrel. In other circumstances, this would have been a good opportunity to remind the other Kennards who I am and what I'm capable of. But there's nowhere for this guy to run and it's not the same without the chase, without the hunt.

And then, as I begin to feel the Huntsman's power build inside me, Vittoria moves towards him. I just catch a single glint of a knife before she steps back and I watch the last breath gurgle out of his sliced throat. Blood soaks the carpet at our feet as we watch the man die.

'Sorry, darling. Couldn't resist. You were taking so long and ... well, maybe it's a girl thing, to get so ... upset when a man does something like that. I just couldn't stop myself.' She presses herself tight against me. 'Besides, it's so ... exciting when a hunt is interrupted. You always need to find another outlet for all that energy. And I may as well use it to my advantage.'

I say nothing, simply glare into her eyes as I try to get my instincts under control. If the others weren't here, maybe I would take her up on her offer but I can't. She smiles at me and I see triumph in it, as if she thinks she's bested me but it's not a situation that I'll let go unchallenged for long. I step away from her and drop into my seat.

'To later,' I say lifting my glass from the table and draining it as Vittoria smirks back at me.

With his body discarded on the floor, our party returns to their seats to continue the celebrations, as if nothing ever happened. But the power of the hunt still heats my blood, and my resentment at Vittoria taking away my kill grows as I force myself not to think about Rose and Niamh alone in the club.

CHAPTER 3
NIAMH

As we dance, I notice three guys watching us from the bar. They're smartly dressed and about our age. Rose smiles at them.

'Come on!' she yells over the music, dragging me closer to them before the music changes and one of my favourite songs comes on. I love to dance. Rose smiles at someone over my shoulder and I jump when hands land on my hips and I twist around to see the tallest of the three behind me.

'Sorry,' he says, immediately removing his hands and holding them up, palms towards me. 'I thought you'd realised I was there?'

Aye, right. 'With my back to you? Hardly.' But okay, he let me go and is apologising. It's worth giving him the benefit of the doubt. Plus, he's cute. He's not darkly handsome like Cillian Hunter, but at least this guy seems to want me. And he can smile.

'Your friend smiled at us,' the guy says, still trying to

apologise, 'and she seems to want to dance. I thought you would, too.'

I look over at Rose, who has her arms wrapped around the neck of one of his friends already, while the other is grinding against her back, keeping her body trapped between them.

'Rose is way too drunk to know what she's doing tonight.' I don't know why I'm saying that to this guy – hoping he'll tell his friends so they don't get their expectations too high, maybe? Rose is a lot less uptight about sex and the number of sexual partners she has than I am, but she's too drunk to consent right now and she's not leaving my sight with any guy who I'm not sure understands that fully.

'She likes dancing,' the guy says, shrugging and tilting my chin with his finger so I'm facing him again. 'And that's all they're doing right now.'

'It is,' I agree. And then deciding that maybe Rose is right, and I am just way too uptight, I decide to take a risk and smile. 'I like to dance, too.'

'Rob,' he says, smiling down at me as he places his hands back on my hips and we move together to the music.

'Niamh.'

'The Irish spelling?' he asks.

'Yeah, still pronounced *Neev*.'

'Nice.'

I smile back at him and move to the music, conscious of how close our bodies are. He's not pushing it any further, though. Just dancing with me. Close but not *I'm-imagining-you-naked* close.

Am I up for this? I'm not sure, but Rose is now happily grinding herself up and down the bodies of both of his friends simultaneously so why not? I step in closer and wrap my arms around him. We dance, talking occasionally before he leans in slowly. His gaze never leaves mine and I could say no or turn away at any time. But I don't. I close my eyes when I feel his breath whisper across my lips and ... push him away.

'Unlucky!' His friend mocks from beside us, where he's still grinding against Rose, only now he's the one in front of her and his other friend is behind.

'That's Ed,' he says, jerking his head towards the guy in front of Rose.

'Sorry,' I mutter as Ed smirks at him, then pulls Rose in closer to his body and covers her mouth with his, snogging her right there on the dancefloor. The third man moves her hair from her neck and trails his lips from the back of her ear down to her shoulder. She shudders between them. Ed's hands are... I don't even want to guess where his hands are. I can only assume that if Cillian were here, that guy would not be smiling for long. Then he spins her around by the shoulders and she kisses his friend just as deeply. I sigh.

'Want to sit down for a while?' Rob asks.

'Sure,' I say. 'All of us?'

'I'll speak to them,' he assures me. He pulls Ed briefly away from Rose and I look away swiftly at the sight of his obvious erection tenting the front of his trousers.

I move beside them and jerk my head at Rose. 'She's had too much to drink to—'

But Ed holds his hands up in surrender. 'Just dancing here. Nothing else.'

I bite back a sharp retort to keep it that way but end up rolling my eyes at Rose's giggles. I turn to see the third guy's hand slide slowly down over her hips as he kisses her neck. Or is that her ear?

'We're going to sit down for a bit,' Rob tells him, and he nods, turning back to the other two and leaning in. I follow Rob across the dancefloor. He must have the luck of the Irish because just as we reach the first booth, the group sitting there start to push themselves out one by one.

'Yous leaving?' Rob asks.

'Aye, yous can have it,' a big guy with shaggy brown hair says, slapping him on the back after eyeing me up and down. He nudges Rob and gives him a thumbs-up, making me roll my eyes.

Rob slides in on the opposite side, but moves round beside me while Ed drags Rose into the same side of the booth as me, fixing his mouth to hers as soon as he's dragged her far enough up over his body. He slides his hand over her hip to cup her butt, touching my thigh in the process, and I squirm away closer to Rob. If it weren't for the table, I'm sure she'd be straddling his lap by now. Rob and I look at each other before he puts him arm around me awkwardly.

'This okay?' he asks, pulling me against him, but when he doesn't do anything more, I nod. It's not really okay. I definitely don't feel what I should if I truly wanted Rob. But given that the one man – the only man – I've ever felt anything differently for is currently sitting in a posh restaurant on the other side of the river, celebrating his engagement to one of the most awful women I've ever met, then maybe I should put my childish notions aside and simply have some fun. Rose does. She's told me before that Matt was the *one* for her, and with him gone ... well, let's just say she's not waiting for the *one* anymore.

'Here we go.' The third guy returns from the bar with five bottles of Stox and sets them down in the middle of the table.

'Oh, but we can't—'

He holds a bottle opener out for me to take. All the bottles are still sealed, shutting down my argument against drinking them. Rose takes it instead and opens her own bottle, chugging it before grinning at me across the table.

'Come on, Niamh. Live a little.' She holds the bottle out and after a pause, I clink mine against hers, then take the bottle opener and open it.

'Frank,' the third guy introduces himself, once he's sat in the booth with us.

'Niamh.'

'Cute, yeah?' Rose grins at me.

'Hey!' Ed complains, pulling her mouth back to his.

I watch Rose kiss Ed then Frank, before they get up and lead her back onto the crowded dancefloor. Rob shuffles closer to me and I turn my head, meeting his lips, which are warm and soft, and eager but— An image of Cillian fills my thoughts and I pull back.

'I'm sorry, I...' I get up quickly, stand and face him, my heart racing. 'Drink?'

He shakes his head. 'No, thank you. Why are you running away from me?' He sounds ... kind.

'I'm not. I just ... I can't do that. Not tonight. Sorry.' I push away from the table and don't look back as I seek out Rose.

I find her, still hemmed in by Ed and Frank, a vacant, dreamy look on her face as she catches sight of me.

'Hey,' she says. 'Get me a double vodka and orange?'

'Rose...' I shake my head.

'Don't be judgey, Niamh, just get me the drink.'

'Yeah, Niamh, just get her the drink,' Ed says, nuzzling her neck, his hands sliding up her body, until they come to rest, cupping her breasts.

'Fine,' I snap, rolling my eyes. She's a grown-up. She can tell them to fuck off herself if she wants.

I head to the bar, where the barman glances over at me and holds up a finger telling me to wait. I nod back, sighing, and turn to check on my friend, now shimmying between those two creeps, and take a few breaths to calm myself down. Sometimes, I could kill her. Rob is still over at the booth, watching me, although he's got his phone in his hand.

'Here you are.' The barman hands me a vodka-orange and a glass of tap water. 'Is that all?'

'Yes, thanks.'

The barman is hesitant as I pay, his gaze sliding over my shoulder, and I turn to see that he's looking at Rose.

'This for her?' he asks, nodding at the vodka-orange, and for some reason, he looks nervous.

'Yeah, against my better advice,' I say, 'but apparently that makes me boring.'

I pull a face, expecting him to laugh. Instead, he swallows and leans forward.

'Maybe it's time to call it a night?' he whispers.

'Oh, it definitely is,' I agree. He stares back at me blankly for a moment, then someone calls him over and he goes to serve them, glancing back, before focusing on the next customer. There's a man in a suit standing at the end of the bar watching me, frowning. Jagged white scars reach from the corners of his mouth towards his ears. I've never actually seen anyone with a Glasgow smile, allegedly a rather old-fashioned punishment amongst gangs of an earlier era, but this guy is probably old enough and looks dodgy enough. Sick of men being weird, I lift the two drinks up in a toast and smile at him facetiously. He stares back, then abruptly turns towards the till, pulling a cash envelope out of his inner jacket pocket and starting to push the larger notes into it.

I pick up our drinks and walk around the edge of the dancefloor.

'Rose!' My tone is sharper than it needs to be. 'I think we should finish these then leave. Sit down for a minute.'

She pouts but follows me back to the booth where I put the drinks down.

'But I'm having fun.'

'I can see that.'

'Oh, don't be like that,' she slurs. I'm sure Rob wants to have fun with you.'

He lifts an eyebrow.

'But Niamh never wants to have any fun,' Rose slurs. 'She's too uptight. Hell, she barely even drinks. I bet that's just water.'

'So what?' I put the glass to my lips and drain it.

'Chug, chug, chug,' Rose chants and then tips her own glass to her mouth and downs it in one. 'Woo-hoo!'

The lights flicker in the club signalling that this will be the final song. Ed and Frank reappear, moving towards Rose like a couple of cockroaches, their hands outstretched.

'Come on,' Rose urges me. 'Last dance?'

I shake my head, as she levers herself up and stumbles. Ed catches her, and she giggles, leaning into him. The smirk on his face makes my blood run cold.

I rise to push myself out of the booth, but my legs feel weightless and I wobble. I grab hold of the table to steady myself, but I can't seem to stand up, and sink back onto the seat. I see Rob's mouth moving but can't work out what he's saying. My ears are buzzing and I'm hot all over. Too hot, burning up from the inside. And as I look around, everything's getting fuzzier. I'm thirsty again. How can I be thirsty again, even after all that water? The music is pounding, the lights flashing, and yet it feels like it's all at a distance.

I glance at Rob, but his back is to me and he's waving to the others. Ed seems to be fully supporting Rose's weight now. Oh god... The drinks. The barman's apologetic look.

I need to do something. And soon.

I check that Rob's still not looking at me then slide my hand into the bag on my hip until my fingers close around my phone. I'm not sure if the three guys we're with are in on this or not, but I'm not going to take any chances.

I pray that it looks like I'm unconscious as I keep my phone under the table while I type in my password and find my messaging app. There's only one contact in my phone that can help me, or at least, help Rose. Cillian. He put his number in my phone the night my parents died, in case I ever needed him.

Well, I need him now.

> With Rose at Sussurri. Drugged. Help.

CHAPTER 4
CILLIAN

If I'd hoped I'd get shot of Vittoria once the meal was over, I was mistaken. And now I need another plan. Reluctantly, we leave Vincenzo and the other Kennards drinking together at The Angel's Share, which I hope doesn't result in disaster. I want to go and drag my sister and Niamh out of Sussurri, but I can't as long as I'm with Vittoria, and she seems determined not to let me out of her sight.

'We're not going to your house?' She pouts when we pull into the private car park outside the former mansion where my club is located.

I capture her hand and draw her towards me, kissing her hard on the mouth before letting her go. 'No, I have something far more special planned here.'

I'm gratified at the hitch in her breath and the slow smile that slides across her face. There are so many possibilities open to us in the exclusive Underworld area of this club, and while I'd prefer to bring someone far more submissive here, the fact that Vittoria will fight me at every turn might provide the distraction I need from Niamh tonight. Plus, I'm going to make her pay for killing that man earlier – the Huntsman inside me is still desperate for blood.

The Three Graces lies on Grace Street – the name a sly dig at the pretentiousness of the clientele who frequent it. They choose to associate it with ancient Greek myths and legends when, in fact, it's merely a statement about the number of levels the club has – only two of which exist in the human world.

Rose has suggested several times that we tailor the branding to catch all the New Agers who are obsessed with anything that can loosely be described as pagan, druidic, or even Celtic. And if they happened to witness any of the actual supernatural aspects of the club, they would likely just accept them and come back more often. Three is a magical number, appearing as the maid, the mother and the crone, the Celtic triple goddess, and the three faces of the Morrigan, to name only a few. Even amongst the Kinfolk so many stories have been lost to time. Particularly the stories of powerful women – other religions may have a lot to answer for there.

There's a queue at the door – always a good sign – and I notice Jamil, one of our newest bouncers, checking the ID of a group of smartly dressed and painfully young-looking girls. I see the flash of fear that crosses his features when he notices me just as the last of the young women disappears inside the building. He's a large man, a good four inches taller than me and with a lot more bulk, but he's human and wise to look nervous – especially if he has something to hide.

'They all had driving licences, Mr Hunter. I checked carefully,' he says as we reach him.

I nod at him, my suspicions evaporating as I realise he's just concerned that I might be there to see if he's doing his job properly.

'Good job,' I say. Given some of what goes on in the lower levels of this club, I'm insistent that the city's laws are observed carefully on the upper two. The last thing I need is for the polis to have a reason to poke around with a warrant – I could use the *Guth Dorcha* to make them forget, but it's easier just to avoid the situation arising in the first place. Jamil nods back and turns to open the VIP door that's next to the main one. He holds it as I usher Vittoria in ahead of me.

'You know that paying your staff is more than enough. You don't have to pretend to be nice to them, too,' Vittoria says as I key in the security code and allow her to precede me into a private staff corridor.

'Staff loyalty is an important business practice, darling. The Rialis should try it some time.'

'The threat of a hideously painful death if they fuck up or betray us works just well, Cillian, and requires a lot less effort,' Vittoria says. 'And how many human staff are you relying on now? You should keep the jobs for Kinfolk. It involves far fewer explanations – not to mention bloodshed, if someone sees something they shouldn't.'

'There are ways to make sure no one sees anything they're not supposed to, Vittoria,' I say. 'Or do you find Glamour and the *Guth Dorcha* a challenge?'

Kin make use of our different powers to control the humans we come into contact with, as well as the lesser

Kinfolk. Glamour is the most frequently used – the ability to make something look like something else. Levels of ability vary, from straightforward alterations in appearance that last only a short while and are easily broken, to more complex spells that even other skilled practitioners would find it difficult to undo – that is if they even realise that they're there. The *Guth Dorcha* is the voice of darkness – or forgetting. It works best when combined with physical contact, but it's not always necessary.

I push open a door that takes us back out into the main area of the club and out onto the mezzanine, from where we can observe the upper bar. There's a small dancefloor downstairs, which is currently packed.

'Another busy night.'

'Yes,' I agree. There's a hen night in – a group of about ten women wearing pink sashes and enough bling to rival the disco ball. One of them, presumably the bride, is wearing an extravagant tiara and currently dancing with four men, two of whom are grinding against her while a friend tries unsuccessfully to pull them off. I swallow, a chill spreading through my bones. If that was my future wife, I'd be wading through the other dancers and those two would be lucky to ever find their balls again. Vittoria presses herself against my side and moves her hand over my chest.

'If that was me, would you stop them?' she asks, her hand slipping lower to palm my cock. I won't deny that the woman has talented fingers and before I can stop her, I'm hard. And yet, despite her standing right beside me and being the one with her hands on my cock, it's not her I'm thinking about.

It's Niamh's long, pale legs wrapped around my waist

that I envisage. Niamh's wide blue eyes that I want to stare into as I make her mine. Niamh's long, ebony hair that I can almost feel wrapped around my fist as I force her to take me deep between those rose-red lips. There's something about her innocence I crave control over.

Vittoria's smirk when my thoughts cause me to harden even further has me covering her hand with mine and removing it from my aching balls. I'm sure she thinks she's wholly responsible for my rock-hard cock, and I don't want her to suspect anything different.

'Would you want me to?' I ask, twisting her arm behind her back and pulling her roughly against me before taking her mouth in a brutal kiss. I pull back when she bites me and laughs.

'Of course, darling. There's nothing sexier than a possessive man.'

What neither of us says is that until we're married, we're both free to see other people, sleep with other people. Something I have happily done all my adult life – until that bloody graduation party. Since then, Niamh has occupied every sordid thought, although anyone paying attention to my choice in women over the past four years would quickly recognise that each and every one has had a striking resemblance to that one woman.

Besides, I simply don't care enough about Vittoria to do any such thing, and she knows it. Not to mention the fact that she'd be pissed as all fuck if I interfered with her sex life. Although I imagine she'd enjoy the feeling of multiple men fighting over her, and I can picture her bathing in the blood of the men I'd defeated.

She'll make a formidable wife. For as long as we survive each other. And no matter how much I might crave someone else, only marrying Vittoria will make me king.

We head down the spiral staircase to the wine bar. The seating is designed primarily for the more adventurous couples. The upholstery, luxurious black velvet, and pillars topped with gilded ornaments are designed for indulgence. Unlike upstairs, this area isn't overlooked and gives the impression of privacy, although there are carefully placed cameras everywhere and the recordings from those have provided much of the material we've needed over the years to ensure that various influential customers remain under our control.

Vittoria is correct. We'll never trust humans in the same way we trust other Kinfolk – even our enemies – and we ensure that we have iron-clad ways of getting what we want from them. From there I lead her towards the back of the building, pausing in front of a studded wooden door. I place a hand flat on the surface, feeling the wood heat beneath my palm and a set of carved symbols appear. I read the ancient letters of the Ogham inscription aloud and the door pulses, shifting in its reality before it opens, not into the narrow basement staircase of the human world, but into the foyer of my club in the Underworld where fantasies are indulged.

The worlds exist on top of one another, but time functions differently in each, meaning that there are only certain times and places where you can move between the two without some kind of magic. Some areas have changed in one world but not the other. Glasgow's Underworld includes an extensive series of tunnels and underground features long since covered by the modern human city.

Kinfolk are able to move easily between worlds using the thin places. Some are permanent, while others appear and disappear on a whim. A rare few can be conjured using a particular type of magic.

Humans can also pass between worlds, but it's not as straightforward. Human eyes can't see the Underworld except in exceptional circumstances, or when it is shown to them by one of the Kinfolk. Certain things, rituals you might call them, are required, but are far easier when they are with Kin. And often they are lured through with extravagant promises like I would offer Niamh if I thought she was corruptible.

Humans should never make a deal with the Kinfolk – they simply don't understand the danger. But if they do ... then we are restricted only by the limits of their desires.

Those desires take many forms, but the lowest level of The Three Graces, focuses on sexual fantasies. It's not a sex club, but it does cater to those who seek desire in whatever form they can dream up if they are foolish enough to make one of those deals.

Vittoria pauses outside a door when we hear the crack of a whip, followed by a groan of pain-tinged lust but I stride on and, as soon as she realises where I'm headed, she follows.

The door at the end of the corridor houses my favourite playroom. As soon as we've entered, any sense that she'll go along submissively with what I want disappears. I walk forward, stopping at the foot of the four-poster bed and turn to face her. In turn, she saunters towards me, and I'm surprised to see a smile play along the corners of her mouth.

'This is ... exceptional,' she breathes, her gaze moving from the blood-red satin sheets covering the bed, to the black velvet drapes that can be used to enclose the bed simply by tugging a single satin cord. 'And so romantic.'

I almost believe her as we stare at the flickering flames of the black and red candles on display. Most of this was my idea, but I did tell the Kin responsible for setting up the room to add her own flourishes where appropriate. She knows both me and Vittoria well, having spent time pleasuring us both, together and separately, so I trusted her to know what our darkest pleasures are.

'Wax play?' Vittoria asks, waving her hand through the flames of the bottom row of candles.

'Whatever you wish,' I say, watching as she tilts her head to one side and takes the central candle from that row then stretches out her other arm in front of her. She angles the black candle and we both stare as she moves the candle down the length of her arm from her elbow to her wrist, the heated wax dripping smoothly onto her tanned skin. I smile at the sight of her skin reddening, and the way the wax hardens, as does my cock.

She sucks in a breath. 'I'm sure the red will look good on you.'

'On me?'

'You don't think you're going to have all the fun, do you? There's nothing quite like the fear in a man's eyes when those hot drips of wax get closer and closer to the soft, sensitive skin of his—'

I blow the candle out.

'Spoilsport.'

I unfasten my jacket and slip it off. Wandering back to the door, I hang it on a hook on the mahogany coat stand. Everything in this room is dark, from the wooden furniture to the soft furnishings to the various toys sitting in plain sight or hidden away in drawers.

One of those drawers scrapes open and Vittoria chuckles, the leather whip and cat-o'-nine-tails that she holds in either hand dark against her skin. She swishes the cat through the air a few times, then cracks it once at her side before repeating the same with the whip in her other hand.

'What I'm wondering, Cillian, is why you've never brought me here before.'

'This is my workplace, Vittoria.' I loosen the bottom of my shirt and shrug. 'But now, I've decided it's time to explore your limits.'

'Why now?'

'It's a celebration or our engagement. Besides, you'll be part owner of this club soon. You should understand what we offer.'

She takes a step towards me, flicking her wrist so that the whip cracks between us. Another step and it strikes the floor just in front of my feet. At the third flick she angles her wrist and the leather strap wraps around my body. I grab onto it at my waist on the side nearest the handle and pull her towards me. It wouldn't be difficult for her to let go, but she doesn't, allowing me to pull her right up against me.

I thread my fingers through her hair and pull her mouth to mine. Our kiss is violent and rough until she places her hands flat on my chest and pushes me backwards. I let myself fall, my knees catching the edge of the bed. I lie still, staring up into the depths of her brown eyes. She looms over me, her long black hair tumbling forward in glossy waves that brush against me as she lowers her mouth to mine.

I can't deny that as much as she antagonises me, Vittoria is beautiful. Where Niamh is pale, Vittoria is tanned, her skin flawless, her voluptuous breasts peeking from the bodice of her dress, tantalisingly close to spilling over, begging to be kissed. I fight the urge to run my hands over the sleek black satin that covers her otherwise toned, slender body.

'Not fair,' she says. She nudges my knees apart and steps between them but it's when she places one knee up on the bed dangerously close to my groin that I begin to worry. As she leans forward her angle shifts, and she grinds my cock and balls between her upper thigh and my pelvic bone. A wave of pleasure mixed with pain envelopes me as I grow harder beneath her weight. I capture her long hair in my hand, and twist it roughly before pulling her head back, exposing her throat to me. I see a flash of pain cross her face as I pull more tightly, relishing in the moment of control I have over her.

'Mercy!' she says coyly, and I laugh.

'No. This isn't a game.'

'Isn't it?'

I shift one leg, straightening it and taking her feet from under her, use my weight to flip her onto her back. Her mouth opens in a silent scream that she quickly covers up before she even makes a sound.

'Cillian,' she sighs as I angle her head upwards, twisting

her away from me. My lips connect with her throat, sucking and biting as I kiss up to her jawline before pressing her hips into the bed with mine. She'd worn the satin dress with buttons down the front tonight, the one I'd bought her specifically for this evening. I planned to tease her by unbuttoning it ever so slowly but the desire to remove it now overwhelms me. Using my free hand, I roughly pull at the small buttons. She scowls as the top one pops off and plinks onto the floor ad I expose her lace bra.

Her breasts are firm, her nipples dark and they'd be perfect topped with the black wax. Given she's already teased me by pouring wax over her arm, I know she'll willingly let me drip wax over her naked breasts, maybe even down her inner thighs. She arches her back as I kiss down the soft skin that lies between her perfect breasts, then circle each nipple with my tongue before sucking each one into my mouth. And then I bite.

Her cry of pleasure lets me know she's turned on, but I think it's the first time I have ever truly shocked her and my time in control is over. For now.

She rolls me violently onto my back, the two of us only just remaining on the surface of the bed. Straddling me she starts to unbutton my shirt, leaving my tie in place, then she places her hand over my heart and presses her fingers down. Her nails are sharp as they rake over my chest, and the pain sends a chill of unexpected desire down my spine.

I grab her wrist, squeezing my fingers tight around it and she eases off on the nails with a sigh.

'Oh, Cillian. Sometimes you're just no fun.' With one swift movement, she tightens my tie, choking me and I see the fire light up her eyes as she takes control. But I am a Hunter and my instincts kick in. I push her off me and flip her over pulling up her dress, and running my thumb along her underwear before she can stop me. The hitch in her breath and the wetness I feel sends a guttural groan from my throat. While we might dislike each other, our pleasure should at least appear mutual. Pushing her down onto the bed, I undo my trousers with one hand and line myself up to take her. Her teasing, the thwarted hunt, and my thoughts of Niamh, have driven me over the edge. This will be rough, brutal, and when I've found my release, she'll be screaming my name and begging me for more. This is about me, not her, whatever she might think.

A particular chime from my jacket pocket commands my attention, just as I place my hands on her hips, ready to fuck her. I freeze.

'Ignore it,' Vittoria says as I feel the frustration radiate from her. Any other night and I might be tempted to do as she says, but something is telling me not to.

Pushing back off the bed I move to find my phone.

'Honestly, Cillian. Surely, you're not going to let a message interrupt us.'

Her seductive smile falls flat as I read the message.

'What's going on?' Vittoria asks.

'It's Niamh.'

'Niamh? Rose's friend? Why the fuck does she have your number?' Vittoria spits out. She's still lying half-naked on the bed, her cheeks flushed from heat and now anger.

'I have to go.'

'But—'

'My sister's in trouble, Vittoria.' I'm already getting dressed, my erection having vanished as soon as I read Niamh's message. I lift the phone to my ear. Sean doesn't answer, so I try again. 'Aiden, meet me at the car. We need to head to Sussurri. As fast as possible. Rose is in danger.'

'Cillian? You didn't answer me. Why does that girl have your number?'

I put my phone back in my pocket and face Vittoria. I don't have time for her pettiness. Surely, she understands that I won't ever leave my sister in danger. 'Does it matter? Rose is in trouble. I need to go to her. Now.'

Vittoria sighs as though this is all very tedious. 'I can get security to take a look, but she's probably just trying to ruin our evening, Cill. And you can't just bring me here and then leave.'

'You should know,' I tell her, 'that I will always prioritise my family's safety. When you're my wife, I'm sure you'll appreciate that.'

Vittoria's lips thin, but she buttons her dress back up, tutting at its loss when she reaches the top one and moves from the bed. Slamming the door behind us, she follows me as I stride up the stairs and out of the Underworld. I hear her on the phone behind me. She's speaking Italian, so I don't get more than the occasional word. But as I reach the main door. She speaks to me.

'Security found Sean unconscious in the bathroom with a nasty head wound.' She shrugs as I round on her. 'We can hardly put cameras in the bathrooms. Rose and her friend were dancing with three guys most of the night, but they've lost sight of them now. Guess they left together.

Again, Cillian, this might not be anything sinister. Your sister—'

I take a step towards her, forcing her back against the wall. My hand captures her throat and I begin to squeeze, all trace of desire replaced by fury.

Defiantly, she holds my gaze, and her hand curls around my wrist. 'Let. Me. Go.'

I hesitate only for a moment before I release her, then start moving again. I'm just wasting time with Vittoria. She's not going to help me with Rose. Or Niamh. Rage fills me as I imagine what might be happening to them now. My sister at least has a chance of defending herself – as long as she's conscious. But Niamh? The thought turns my stomach.

'Where are they?'

Vittoria hesitates. It's brief but noticeable. 'They can't find them on the cameras, but they haven't left the building,' she assures me.

'Don't let them leave,' I yell, and she gives me a short, sharp nod as she lifts her phone to her ear. 'She's my sister,' I grind out through gritted teeth. 'You of all people should understand.'

Jamil holds the door open for us and we step out into the not-quite-darkness of the summer night where Aiden is waiting in the limo. It feels at odds with the anger rushing through me right now. I clench my teeth.

What if I'm too late? For Rose. For Niamh.

CHAPTER 5
NIAMH

'I've got you, *bella*.' Rob's voice is soothing, comforting, almost. I know I should fight him. Try to get away. But I can't. I force my heavy eyelids open and see Frank swing Rose up into his arms. Her head lolls back over his arm, her body limp. Then my world tilts as Rob does the same with me. I close my eyes and try to remain relaxed, hoping he'll think I'm out of it, too.

'I'm going to have such a good time with you. You can pretend all you like, but I know you know exactly what's happening,' he whispers into my hair and my stomach plummets. Still, it's better that he doesn't realise I'm aware of what's going on, so I keep my eyes firmly closed, hoping that this is all a nightmare, and when I open them again, none of it will have happened.

Someone else's rough hands grip the tiny straps of my dress and with a jerk they're ripped free of the bodice and a large hand runs over my breasts, one finger circling a nipple, before Rob jerks me away.

'What are you doing?' Rob snaps.

'You don't want at least a look? Maybe even a taste.' It's Ed's voice, and his hand returns to grab my breast, squeezing it hard and causing me to yelp before he yanks down the top. A cool breeze runs over my heated skin, and my nipples pebble despite me hating everything about this.

'Stop, for fuck's sake,' Rob hisses. 'We need to get them out of here. I don't want to die.'

'It's only the Hunter girl that we're not to touch,' Ed says. 'We can do what we want with this one. There's a storeroom near the exit. I'm sure no one would notice if we all had a shot before we take her to the warehouse.'

His hand slides back over my bare skin, but once again Rob shifts me away.

'No, Ed. We take the Hunter girl back home, then you can take this one to the warehouse and she'll be ours for as long as she survives. Just like we were promised.'

Panic roils in my belly. Oh god. How is this happening? There's CCTV in the club, at all the doors. The Rialis are surely going to make sure Rose isn't assaulted in their club? But then I remember the smartly dressed man with the Glasgow smile emptying the till, the worried look on the barman's face, and I realise someone in the club must be behind this. I can only pray Cillian bothers to read my text in time and it's not too late.

Then I remember, he's with Vittoria. A Riali. Are they behind this? Have they found a way to keep Cillian occupied? Or worse, Cillian knows. He didn't want me there tonight. Maybe he really is as ruthless as he's rumoured to be, and now that he's engaged, he's getting rid of any potential ... distractions.

Doors bang open and damp air hits my bare, sweat-coated skin, rousing me a little more from my semi-drugged haze. We're in a dark alley behind the club. A car door clicks open, then I hear the rumble of an engine.

'Can I touch her now?' Ed asks.

'No! For fuck's sake, Eduardo,' Rob says. 'Dump her in the back, Franco. I'll sit with them.'

Eduardo? Franco? And earlier ... *bella*? I lift my head even though it's like moving through treacle. The guys are all dark-haired, vaguely tanned, despite the Scottish accent that marks them as second, third, or even fourth generation, Italian.

Italians. Like the Rialis. Like Vittoria.

'Gentlemen?' That one word almost causes me to weep in relief. Not the word. The voice. Cillian. He came. He's here. I force my eyes open to see him standing in front of his familiar limo, his foot resting on the bumper, arms folded, two people flanking him. I recognise one as Cillian's driver, Aiden. The other is Vittoria. 'I sincerely hope you were about to bring my sister and her friend home to me.'

Rob turns, his body tense, and I feel him swallow.

'Hand them over,' Cillian orders, his sharp, compelling tone striking fear deep inside me, let alone what effect it's having on my abductors. I can't do anything but stare at the man I hope will be our saviour. Right at this moment, he looks anything but. Dark and dangerous. An avenging angel. I blink a couple of times as the shadows in the lane deepen. My skin prickles as a chill brushes over it, and although I can't see anything move, it feels like everything around me is shifting somehow. Everything feels so confused.

But more confusing still is the shadow looming behind Cillian. The shadow of a huge, horned stag surrounds him, making him seem like some kind of monarch of the glen, powerful, majestic and utterly in control. For a second, his smart black suit is gone, replaced with what looks like a leather tunic, trousers and boots. He lifts his head, and I see not only that but a cloak covering his shoulders and head, huge antlers an integral part of the hood. Four small, dark creatures poke their heads out from under the car. I frown as one catches my eye, and then they're gone as if they were never there. I'm more drugged than I thought. Before my addled mind can find an answer, he speaks again.

'Now.' Cillian's tone is icy-cold. Dead, almost. 'You're going to hand the girls over, tell me who you're working for, and then you're going to get down on your knees and beg for your lives.'

Their lives? What?

Frank steps forward, handing Rose over to Aiden who puts her in the limo. Cillian jerks his head to one side and Aiden takes me from Rob. He's careful to pull my dress, arranging it so that it's covering me, and I let my head rest against his chest, somehow managing not to weep with relief.

I force my eyes open again, watching the scene from a different angle now. Rob and Frank are on their knees in front of Cillian, but Ed is still standing, sneering at him. I don't miss the way he glances repeatedly at Vittoria before slowly turning his gaze back to Cillian.

'You're a fool!' Ed says. He laughs and looks Cillian up and down. 'You know, I know what she likes in bed, how she fucks, the noises she makes. *Scemo!*'

For a horrifying second, I think he's referring to me, even though I'm pretty sure nothing's happened. But Cillian is shaking his head slowly, a smile of contempt on his lips.

'And yet she's choosing to marry me,' he says. 'You're not quite the stud you think you are. Especially since you have to drug your victims first...'

I let out a shaky breath. They're talking about Vittoria. But is Ed really stupid enough to say that to Cillian's face?

My eyes widen as Ed takes another step towards Cillian, his hand going behind his back as if reaching for a weapon. But before he can bring it out, Cillian punches him, twice in quick succession. The first catches him under his chin, snapping his head back, the second lands in his stomach and he falls to his knees with a sickening groan. A swift kick to his chest has him toppling awkwardly backwards, landing on his back with a loud cry, with the sickening sound of his head cracking on the cobblestones. His body goes limp, but Cillian isn't finished yet. He rears up and grabs Ed's head and with a sharp snap, he twists it to the side. Ed doesn't move again.

Bile rises in my throat and I squeeze my eyes shut. That didn't just happen. It can't possibly have happened. And yet ... I've always known that the Hunters lived their lives too close to the edges of the law. And that both Cillian – and Rose – have a ruthless streak. But this...?

Now, across the alley, Cillian's eyes meet mine, and in them I can see victory.

'Cillian!' Aiden's shout startles me, and I jerk in his arms finally able to move enough to look back towards where Rob and Frank are kneeling. Both men have pushed themselves to their feet and are scrambling past the limo clearly hoping to reach the road and get away.

Cillian is after them in an instant, whirling around in pursuit. Aiden puts me down and goes to assist him. I watch as Cillian barrels into the two men, tackling them to the ground. He stands, dragging them both up with him and I see the shadowy figure around him once more, like the presence of some ancient hunter. Cillian is somehow bigger, larger than life, his fists flying as he takes on Rob while Aiden takes on Frank.

And suddenly, I understand. Cernunnos – the name of their house – the Celtic god of hunting. Except it's not just a name, is it? Cillian *is* Cernunnos. I press my hands over my ears, hoping to drown out the sound made by his fists pummelling flesh as I struggle to make sense of what my senses are telling me. None of this can be real. It's impossible. What is real, however, are the cries of pain from Rob and Frank.

I scream as Frank twists away from Aiden and heads towards me holding a large knife. But he's quickly grabbed from behind by Aiden, who snaps his wrist, sending the knife clattering to the ground beside me. I stare at it for a moment, just out of my reach, as the fight continues to rage. Frank gives Aiden a Glasgow kiss, and Aiden howls and grabs his nose, blood pouring from between his fingers as Frank whirls once more and leaps for me.

I don't even think, I simply react, and somehow the knife is in my hand, and I watch in horror as I sink it into Frank's throat, his hot blood pouring onto me. I scream again as his body collapses onto mine and starts to shake uncontrollably. I'd push him off, but my fingers are still wrapped around the handle of the knife which is still embedded in—

Aiden pulls Frank's body off me, the knife ripping his throat further open. Then he dumps him onto his back beside me. He is very, very dead. I've gone from judging Cillian mere moments ago, to being a killer. Just like him.

'You okay?' Aiden has to ask this twice because I'm simply staring at him, and finally I manage to half-nod, half-shake my head. Behind him, Cillian catches Rob under the chin with an uppercut. There's a vomit-inducing sound and Rob slumps to the ground.

'Make sure he doesn't get away,' Cillian orders, striding towards me. 'Are you hurt?' he asks, kneeling beside me.

'Not really,' I whisper as I see Vittoria lean over Rob. There's a flash of silver, a brief gurgle then an unnatural silence descends on the lane.

I sit up cautiously, staring at the bodies on the ground beside me as dark liquid pools around both Frank and Rob. I feel sick. I can't think. Can't speak. Can barely breathe. But what I definitely don't do is close my eyes. I'm afraid that if I do, I won't ever open them again. My heart's beating so fast and so hard that I'm sure the others must be able to hear it.

'Vittoria,' Cillian says, pushing to his feet and turning to look at Vittoria standing over Rob's body, knife in hand. 'What the actual fuck? I had questions.'

'I knew you wouldn't let any man who wanted to hurt your sister live. Besides, it would have been a waste of time.

He wasn't going to answer,' Vittoria says, glancing down at them and poking Ed's body with the toe of her shoe.

'He was a lover,' Cillian states.

'Not a memorable one.' She shrugs. 'I'll get people on it. We'll pull the CCTV but some of the other Kennards have been causing problems recently, although we don't know who, which is exactly why my father invited them to celebrate our engagement. Keep your enemies close—'

'That's why I wanted them alive to answer my questions.'

Vittoria walks up to Cillian and places her hand on the side of his face. She leans in to kiss him, and I can see that the top button on her dress is undone, missing, even. I wonder if my message caught them in the middle of something. My insides tighten, I have no right to be jealous, he's not mine and never will be. She pulls back from him, her piercing eyes coming to rest on the scene around us.

'Right now,' she says, 'you've got a more immediate problem, Cillian.'

He looks at the bodies discarded on the cobblestones.

'Clean up? That won't be a problem.' He pulls out his phone and is about to use it when Vittoria sashays towards me.

I swallow, her gaze holding mine as she slowly gets closer.

'Not that,' she says, squatting down beside me then reaching forward and gripping my chin with cold, hard fingers. 'She killed him. This little human killed Kin.'

'Fuck,' Cillian mutters and I pull my eyes away from Vittoria's cold stare and meet his. I expect it to be reassuring, but I'm very, very wrong.

CHAPTER 6
CILLIAN

How the fuck did Niamh manage to kill a man? Kin, no less. Why the hell did she have to pick up a knife? All she had to do was just lie there like the victim she was and we wouldn't be in this situation. But of course she wouldn't. She might be quiet, innocent, but one thing I've learned as I've watched her over the years, is that she's no pushover. The girl has backbone. She's just not obvious about it.

I know what Vittoria is going to say, because she's right. The Court will order a hunt as soon as it's informed. No human can be allowed to kill one of us and live. Self-defence or not, that isn't important. It's not easy to accomplish and the fact that she did without even really trying just proves the danger she poses to all of us. What the hell is going on tonight? Dammit, why did Vittoria kill that guy? I want far more answers than I'm sure I'm going to get now.

'You need to deal with her,' Vittoria states as I stare down into Niamh's slightly unfocused blue eyes. 'You can't just ignore that she's killed Kin.'

Niamh frowns at the words as she succumbs to the pull of whatever drug has been forced on her, crumples back down to the ground and finally goes limp. Could she not have done that five bloody minutes ago? My head snaps up, and I glare at Vittoria. As a woman, how can she be so callous towards an innocent victim? Does she honestly expect me to do this? But she's despised Niamh since the moment she laid eyes on her – which has only got worse after her brother's death.

Aiden crosses to Niamh and lifts her up in his arms. 'Surely you can't be considering this, Cillian. She's the victim here. She's the one who texted you. She saved Rose's life.'

'She's a human who killed Kin, Aiden,' Vittoria inserts. 'The Court—'

'He was going to rape her. Probably murder her. I think she's justified.' I shake my head.

'But you know the rules, Cillian. You have no choice. It's your sacred duty as the Unseelie Huntsman.' Vittoria's voice is unwavering. 'I've already notified my father and the Court. You should be summoned soon.'

The door from the club slams open and Sean staggers out, sees the bodies on the ground and pales.

'Where's Rose?'

'In the limo,' Aiden says far more calmly than I'd manage right now.

'Is she...' Sean swallows and no matter how furious I am with him right now, I can't ignore the guilt in his expression, nor the fear.

'She's unconscious,' Aiden says. 'But I don't think they...' His gaze flits to Niamh and my fists clench. I swear to the gods, if these assholes have harmed either of them, I will dedicate my life to seeking out Bran's Cauldron just to bring them back so that I can torture them to death over and over and over again.

With a last furtive glance at me, Sean hurries over to the car, opens the door and reaches in to check on Rose.

'We should get her home and get the doc to take a look at her as soon as possible. Can you—' I stop and draw in a breath, not wanting to ask. 'Does it look like they hurt her?'

He shakes his head. 'Not on the surface, but—' He stops and my gaze shifts to Niamh. There might be no outward signs of what happened on Rose, but Niamh is a different story. Her dress is torn, and it's been ruched up her thighs until I can see her lacy underwear. Her dress is now also soaked in blood. There are a number of finger marks that look like they'll bruise. Aiden has covered her up as best he can, but I didn't miss the bare skin of her breast and the dusky pink of her nipple when the thug now lying dead at my feet shifted her in his arms as he faced up to me.

What is it about this woman that I can't seem to ignore? I've tried to keep my distance from her, but I'm no saint. My memories of her skin beneath my fingertips, smooth and warm and perfect, flit through my thoughts. I can still remember the taste of her lips, the tiny sighs she made when I kissed her. There's no way for us to be together, no matter what regrets I have. I can't become king with her by my side and not only that, but I'd destroy her. Although now, seeing her lying there, covered in the blood of her enemy – it makes me wonder if maybe she is strong enough to withstand me. Either that, or her proximity to me has just destroyed any goodness within her. It's sure to be one of the two.

'What does it matter?' Vittoria says. 'Cillian will do his duty and kill her anyway.'

What the fuck? The three dead men failed to abuse and maybe even kill Niamh, but Vittoria is going to make sure that she dies anyway? Except, Vittoria isn't wrong. Niamh has killed Kin and The Unseelie Court would certainly condemn her to death, no matter the justification. I don't have a choice.

Is she gloating? Surely, she can't suspect that I have feelings for Niamh? Vittoria has never cared about any of the other women I've fucked, just as I haven't cared about her men. Niamh and I have never even slept together, so...

But if she does suspect something, then this situation has played right into Vittoria's hands. No, I'm sure she doesn't know. If she did, I don't think Niamh would have survived this long.

There's something missing from the scenario in front of me and I'm not going to rest until I have discovered exactly who is behind Niamh and Rose being drugged and almost kidnapped. But first I have to try to work out a way to keep Niamh alive. Maybe the Court will understand?

No, there are no exceptions to a human killing Kin. Regardless of whose fault it is.

'You need to take Rose home.' I say to Sean.

'What about ... this one?' Aiden asks.

'I'll take care of her.' I ignore Vittoria's glare and lift Niamh's unconscious body into my arms. We've been here before, the first night we met, when I was already a disillusioned twenty-six-year-old, she only a day or so over eighteen. But the effect she has on me hasn't reduced at all during that time. If it wasn't for Vittoria's presence, I'd take her home and put her safely in my bed just like that first night, to sleep off whatever she's been given and then keep her there. Safe and protected and most importantly, mine.

She's not an innocent eighteen-year-old anymore. She's very definitely a grown woman, with at least some experience, I assume – despite the many times I've sabotaged any relationship she tried to have. And there are still eight years and my sister keeping us apart. Not to mention my engagement to Vittoria and my need to become king. With Niamh, I can't have the future I deserve. And neither can The Unseelie Court. This is bigger than me. Vincenzo is corrupt, and all the Kinfolk are suffering because of it.

Rose cares about justice but she has no desire to lead our Kin. Plus, until she's married, her position will be precarious, and she would be someone for the other Kinfolk to fight over.

'Well, we can't stand here gossiping all night, gentlemen,' Vittoria says, gesturing at Niamh. 'Aiden...'

She's got a bloody cheek assuming she can give orders to my man. I'd never presume to order around hers, but – Aiden immediately looks at me – at least mine are loyal to a fault.

'You want me to take her, boss?' Aiden asks. 'Clean-up will be easier if we leave the body here.' But I see the way he looks at her with sorrow in his eyes. He doesn't want to do this anymore than I do.

'It's for the best,' Vittoria agrees.

'No!'

Aiden freezes after only taking a couple of steps towards me.

'We're taking her with us,' I say. 'Open the boot.'

'Cillian!' Vittoria hisses. 'You can't let her live. And it's not just about tonight. That first night we met her, that was when Rose and Matt got together. She was playing the poor little innocent and then within weeks Chris was gone, Matt was gone... It all started with *her*.'

'Don't be ridiculous, Vittoria. Chris's death was—'

'No! I don't want to hear it, Cillian. If it wasn't for that girl, Chris would still be alive.'

What the hell is she on about? What the fuck does Niamh have to do with Chris's death? Matt was blamed for that. I hunted him down. So how does Vittoria figure Niamh into it? But she can't be lying or there would be a sign. The palm of my hand starts to tingle and my heart sinks as I look at my hand and find a sigil there, with Niamh's name beneath it.

'A hunt has been called?' Vittoria asks, although it's not really a question. 'Looks like it'll be another disappointing kill. How frustrating.' Vittoria and I stare at each other for a long minute before I shake my head.

'Not here,' I say. But there's no getting out of this situation. I have to act. I could kill Niamh now, but ironically Vittoria has given me another option...

'She's guilty of a crime against The Unseelie Court,' I say. 'I'm taking her to the woods. I'm not going to be denied a hunt and a kill twice in one night.'

'You're really going to...' Sean begins, eyes wide.

Annoyance flashes over Vittoria's face, then she tilts her head to one side, considering.

'She deserves the chance to try and outrun me. The chance to reach sanctuary. Even if we know she won't succeed.'

'I'm not sure a mere human deserves that, Cillian,' she says, moving towards me and running a finger down the side of Niamh's face. 'What is she to you?'

'Am I not supposed to offer the same justice to all, Vittoria? Each of us have both just killed Kin, too.'

'Oh, Cillian. We all know it's not the same. We were saving your sister – a member of one of the Kinfolk families who sit in The Unseelie Court. She's nothing, a nobody, a human who killed Kin to save herself.'

'The Unseelie Court is supposed to be just, Vittoria.' I don't point out that there's a growing sense of dissatisfaction with her father's rule. A feeling that Vincenzo is using the Court for his own benefit. She must have heard the rumours just like I have. She just doesn't care.

She laughs. 'Well, it doesn't matter anyway, does it? She's a human, and as the Huntsman, she should be no match for you. And you'll be back in my bed before morning.'

She's taunting me, testing me and unless I want to risk making my feelings obvious, I can't argue with her. If it was any other human, she would be absolutely right. Fair or not, Court decisions always prioritise our own people over theirs. No matter what. After all, it's not like the human world would be lenient with any of us if they discovered our existence.

'It does seem ... disloyal to kill her when she saved Rose,' Sean points out.

'Boss?' Aiden prompts. He's opened the boot and I lower Niamh inside.

'I'll drop you and Rose off at Cernunnos, then take Niamh out to the woods.'

Vittoria smiles wickedly, and moves towards me, pressing a hand to my chest and trailing it down. When she reaches my belt, she lifts her hand and places it flat on the side of my face, kissing me.

'I wish I could watch you hunt her down, Cillian. See that moment when she realises who you really are and what you're about to do to her.' The malicious glee in Vittoria's eyes shrivels any arousal I might have felt, had she been talking of anyone other than Niamh. She curls her arms around my neck, staking her claim on me. 'I'll arrange the clean-up here.'

'See that you do,' I snap as Aiden folds one of the rugs we keep in there and places it under Niamh's head, covering her body with another. He looks sideways at me as I pull a gag, cable ties and duct tape from a bag I keep stashed in the car. Every touch of her skin makes my senses tingle and I wish I was doing this for other, far more pleasurable reasons.

Aiden's expression is blank and I wonder if he'd help me if I asked him to, or consider it an act of treachery and refuse. But I can't leave Niamh unrestrained in case she wakes up when I'm driving and somehow draws attention to herself. I have no idea what she's taken and therefore no idea when she'll wake up.

I almost pray that at least one of the old gods is looking out for her tonight. But that's ridiculous. She's not Kin. And the gods abandoned us long ago.

I hide her presence in the boot using Glamour and I'm about to close the boot when Vittoria comes to stand beside me.

'I still think it's odd that Niamh had your number,' she murmurs, but I detect the hint of an edge to her voice. 'Are you in the habit of texting your sister's friends?'

I sigh, with emphasis. 'Fuck's sake, Vittoria. I can't remember why she has it. Perhaps I gave it to her because Rose is so obstinate about answering her phone. And'—I close the boot hard—'it seems I was right to. Given that my sister almost died at the hands of some random thugs.'

Vittoria lifts an eyebrow at my barely concealed accusation, and the fact that Niamh and Rose were in one of the Rialis' clubs.

'Those responsible are already dead, Cillian,' she says. 'As you suggest, just a few chancers. I doubt they even knew Rose was sister to the great Cillian Hunter.'

There's definitely an edge to her tone now that's impossible to miss. I frown, noticing Aiden react to her words, too. And while Vittoria is a viper, only out for her own gain and always determined to come out on top, I realise I've been counting on her wanting this marriage as much as I do.

When Vincenzo either dies or abdicates, there are currently only two likely choices to rule The Unseelie Court – Vittoria's husband or Rose's husband. And there is no way Vittoria will allow my sister to take the role she has always coveted.

'Cillian,' Vittoria steps in close to me, sliding her hand inside the lapel of my jacket, the warmth of her touch moving through the silk of my shirt.

She presses against me, her hips tight against my groin. I push my leg between hers, cup her arse with my hands and pull her flush to me, taking her mouth as I slide her up and down on my thigh. She gasps, her fingers popping open two of my shirt buttons before her hand slips under my shirt and she runs her palm over the smooth muscles on my chest, teasing one nipple with her fingernail. I catch her hand by the wrist, pull it free, and whisper, 'Later.'

'But, darling.' She pouts. 'We've already been interrupted once. And it is our engagement night. Why not kill her now and be done with it?'

'No,' I state, but I put my hands around her slender waist and whirl her around, pushing her roughly up against the side of the limo. I kiss her deeply, desire stirring again, despite my hatred, until she captures my bottom lip with her teeth. She nips it, drawing blood, which I wipe away with my thumb. I run my hand up her thigh, hitching her dress up and sliding a finger into her underwear. I have no intention of fucking her, but teasing her reminds me I have the power. I swipe my finger through her folds, toying with her clit until she lets out a moan.

'And waiting will give us the chance to take our time and make it memorable, my sweet. Besides, like you said. It's important for me to handle this myself.' I whisper against her hair as I insert my finger inside her and pump it slowly. Once, twice, three times before I remove it and leave her empty and wanting more.

Frustration, anger, flashes across Vittoria's features but she tampers it quickly.

'Fine,' she agrees, but I don't think I've ever heard her

utter a more reluctant word. 'Take her to the woods, but I want the heart when it's done. Bring it to me.'

For one moment I consider taking Niamh through to the Underworld, to a tall tower in the darkest, thorniest woods and keeping her locked up there, trapped and helpless, unable to escape, forever waiting for my arrival. She would lack for nothing. Except her freedom.

'I'll bring it over in the morning,' I say curtly, as the memory of Niamh's body pressed against mine rushes through me. I've never forgotten the feel of her, no matter how many times I've been with other women, no matter how often I've tried to forget her, in the intervening years. The choices I've made throughout the last four years threaten to suffocate me. Niamh could have been mine. I could have given up my role at Court, acted on every impulse I've felt towards her, brought her into our world bit by bit. Corrupted her sweetness, her morals and ethics, piece by piece. But I chose not to. I chose to leave her alone. And in the end, all I've done is condemn her.

The urge to make my feelings a present reality rather than a distant memory is nearly overpowering, but I can't allow any of these feelings to show. I want to lift her out of here, feel the welcome weight of her in my arms, untie her and take her in the back seat of my car, but I can't.

'One last thing, Cillian,' Vittoria says. She places her fingers on Niamh's face. Niamh's eyes flicker open, widening in fear when she looks up as Vittoria whispers, 'What happens in the darkness, stays in the darkness.'

I feel the power flow from Vittoria into Niamh, even as Niamh tries to move away from Vittoria's touch.

'What have you done?' I yell pulling her hand away as Niamh's eyes close.

'This way she won't remember anything, won't know who you are or why you're there. You'll just be an anonymous monster set on murdering her in the woods. You don't need to worry that she'll think you've betrayed her. It's the least I can do to make this kill easier for you.'

I step away from her before I add Vittoria's body to the ones needing to be cleaned up in the alley and get in the car. I feel her gaze on me as I drive out onto the main road and head out of the city. Vittoria was right, it will be easier to kill Niamh if she doesn't know who I am. At least this way Niamh won't die believing that I betrayed her.

'What happens in the darkness, stays in the darkness,' I whisper, already mourning the loss of everything we've shared. The kisses, the comfort. And for a moment, I wish I could use the spell on myself and stop this pain threatening to drown me.

CHAPTER 7
NIAMH

'What happens in the darkness, stays in the darkness.'

Cillian whispered this four years ago, right after the first time we kissed. And now Vittoria is using those exact same words. When Cillian said it, they sounded comforting. Now, I fear it might mean that no one ever finds my body. It was clearly meant to accomplish ... something. And it was equally clear it didn't, which might be a problem if he finds out.

I open my eyes to darkness. My head is thumping and when I move it, rough fabric chafes the side of my face. There's something stuffed in my mouth and tied in place, and cable ties dig into my wrists. My hands are bound behind my back and searing pain shoots through the shoulder I'm leaning on.

I take a breath and choke on scrunched-up fabric. Breathing in through my nose works a little better and I calm down a little. Then there's another moment of panic when I realise my feet are also bound and I'm unable to stretch out in any direction. Have I been buried alive? A moment passes and I hear an incessant droning noise of a car engine and realise I must be tied up in the boot of a car.

Memories of earlier slowly re-form in my mind and my heart starts to pound. The club, the alley, Cillian ... the vision of the stag, the hunter god, around him. Three dead men. I stifle a sob. What did I do? Did I ... did I kill a man? They said he was Kin. What does that mean? Did I kill one of their family? But that doesn't make sense. They killed the others. Would they really kill their own blood? I know Cillian is dangerous, but would he go that far? Am I fated to end up the same way? Although surely if Cillian was going to kill me, he would have done it in the alley to save time? My thoughts are running a thousand miles an hour as I try to process what happened this evening. Rose! What happened to her? Panic sets in, I hope she's not still in danger.

No, Rose will be fine. I saw Aiden put her safely in the car. At least one of us is all right. A sense of betrayal nearly suffocates me. If it wasn't for me contacting Cillian, both Rose and I would have been victims of those men. I may not know exactly what they had planned, but from the things I heard them discussing... I shiver... I can make a pretty decent guess. The car turns and my head knocks against the side of the boot causing me to gasp in pain. In exchange for rescuing Rose, Cillian has tied me up and trapped me in the boot of his car to take me who knows where. Still, I guess it's better than being dead.

I close my eyes, blinking them open when I feel a soft touch on the side of my face. For a moment, it feels like I'm not alone, but I must be. The space is too cramped for there to be anyone else in here. I swallow down my panic. I'm not usually claustrophobic but my senses have been dulled and my anxiety heightens at my unknown future.

'She's awake,' a tiny voice whispers, 'and still breathing.'

My heart rate accelerates as the words are followed by something, or someone, pulling my hair and giggling. I thought I was seeing things in the club, not to mention seeing Cillian transform in the alley. Maybe tonight isn't really happening, maybe the whole evening really has been a nightmare. Or maybe I drank too much Stox and now I'm hallucinating. Yes, that must be it. Whatever is going on, I need it to stop.

The car hits a bump and pain rips through me. I'm definitely not imagining that. I need to free myself. If I can do that I might at least to be able to try to run when Cillian stops the car. I struggle, feeling the pain of the cable ties biting into the skin of my wrists.

My brain attempts to scroll through all those social-media videos that I scoffed at and didn't pay attention to. The ones that show you what to do if your arms are cuffed behind your back, or you're cable-tied to a chair. I'm sure there was probably one about being locked in a boot. As it is, I have no clue how to even begin to think about escaping. But I should do something. I *need* to do something.

I close my eyes and try again to steady my breathing. I try to think of a happier time, something to focus on that will help get me through this nightmare. My mind focuses on my mother's advice about Rose the first time I met her.

'Be careful who you trust, Niamh. Not everyone deserves it.'

A lone tear slips out the corner of my eye, sliding down my cheek as my body starts to shake. How could Rose let this happen to me? How could Cillian do this? The last time we were alone together he made it clear that he doesn't want me, and since the day we met, he has done nothing but confuse me, pull me towards him then shove me away.

But I never thought he'd want to see me dead.

And yet, here I am. Tied up. Alone. Frightened. Then it occurs to me that it could be Vittoria driving this car. She saw everything that happened, after all. If Vittoria is responsible for my current situation, I know I won't live to see the dawn.

After what seems like hours, the car finally slows, and my breath catches in my throat. I can't just lie here calmly and wait for ... for whoever has me to open the boot and possibly kill me. I need to do something. I need to escape. Somehow. I try rolling onto my back, but my bound hands prevent that. I struggle against my bindings but I'm too exhausted.

We cross what feels like a cattle grid and then the car comes to a halt, the engine cutting out. My heart stutters in my chest as the door slams and footsteps grow louder. Maybe instead of trying to summon help, or persuade Cillian that he's going to get in a lot of trouble if he doesn't just let me go, I should simply just get down on my knees and beg for my life? Will I even get that chance?

I stop breathing and squeeze my eyes shut as the boot clicks open, expecting to be blinded by light, but when I dare to crack one open, I see the strange, not-quite-darkness of a summer's night, and the steely glare of Cillian Hunter.

If I was hoping for a saviour, I'm out of luck. He's preferential to Vittoria, but the fury on his face reminds me of the night we first met, and the expression on his face when he dragged me out of the cloakroom.

CHAPTER 8
NIAMH

FOUR YEARS AGO

'C*ernunnos*,' I read on the wrought-iron arch over the drive.

'You sure this is where you want to go?' the driver asks.

'I'm sure,' I say, swallowing as the electric gates slide smoothly open and he pulls off Great Western Road into a tree-lined drive that ends at an ornate red sandstone mansion.

Rose told me it's named after the Celtic god of the hunt and given that her name is Hunter, I guess it's a clever choice. I look down at my outfit, which now feels rather shabby. The burgundy trousers were stylish when I bought them two years ago, and the floral top with the sweetheart neckline is pretty, but through the large window I can see that most of the women are in dresses – short, tight, shiny dresses that show off more skin than they cover. I didn't realise I should dress like I was going clubbing – not that I ever dress like that. I'd feel so exposed. I pull off my cardigan and stuff it into my bag. No one needs to see that.

The driver loops round the turning circle and pulls up at the front door of the mansion. And it truly is a mansion. I honestly never believed that people actually live in houses like this. Wow, this girl is rich. I've only known Rose for a few weeks and I know she comes from a different world than me – no way could I miss all the designer labels she wears or the brand-new tech she carries – but this ... this house was built with serious money.

The carved wooden door has been left wide open, music spilling out from somewhere deep within the walls and I breathe a sigh of relief when Rose comes rushing down the stairs with a smile on her face.

'Put it on Mr Hunter's account, please,' Rose says to the driver as I get out. 'Plus ten per cent. Oh my god, Niamh, I'm so glad you made it!'

I smile at her, knowing I had no choice given she'd insisted on sending a taxi for me.

Grabbing my hand she all but drags me inside. My jaw drops. I thought the exterior was grand, but the interior... Well, let's just say that every single thing in it is a valuable antique – worth at least seven figures, maybe priceless. *This* is Rose's house?

'You can leave your things in here for now.' Rose pushes open a small door, almost invisible in the mahogany-panelled walls, with *Cloakroom* on an engraved plaque. Inside, there are rows of coat hooks adorning the walls, and a bench seat with space underneath for shoes. I didn't know people had rooms like this in their houses.

'Butter' by BTS starts to play as I'm still staring around the front hall. The sound of chanting interrupts my thoughts, the noise coming from the same direction as the music.

'Come on,' Rose says, taking my hand. 'Let's go see my friends, you'll love them. Then I'll introduce you to my brother and his friends. They're old. And boring.' She rolls her eyes.

She takes my hand and pulls me into the largest room I've ever seen. It's beautifully decorated, of course, and I catch my breath when I see a grand piano sat in front of a floor-to-ceiling bay window. Despite its size, though, it looks small in the grandeur of this room.

The chanting stops suddenly as people turn their heads in our direction – twenty strangers who look a lot more sophisticated than I think I could ever be. I survey the room, seeing couples sprawled on sofas and standing close together. My cheeks heat when I notice one guy sitting on the piano stool with a woman straddling his lap, her dress has ridden up around her waist, a flash of lace peeking out from underneath. His hands cup her butt as he stares into her eyes. Two men are tucked into the bay window, their arms around one another and their tongues down each other's throats.

'Rose,' I whisper, suddenly shy. I take a step back and she grabs my arm, stopping me from running away.

'You'll be fine. Come on. Let's get you a drink.'

'Does Cillian know you invited a hu— a friend, Rosebud?' A tall burly guy standing at the drinks table turns to face us.

He looks familiar but I can't quite place him. Maybe I've seen him around university.

'You know Sean, don't you Niamh?' Rose says and I shake my head. 'Oh, I thought you'd realised that he follows me everywhere.'

'You know your brother just wants to keep you safe,' Sean says, but at least he smiles. 'Drink?'

'Just a Coke, thanks,' I say jumping when someone presses up against my back and runs a hand down my arm.

'Hey, Matt. Hands off my friend,' Rose says, as I pull away. Being here has me on edge.

'Sorry,' Matt says putting his hands up as if to surrender before moving beside Rose. She smiles and leans back against him, twisting her head to kiss him.

Sean makes gagging noises and reaches for a bottle of Stox. I've never tried it – and given that I'm not used to drinking alcohol at all, trying one with allegedly hallucinogenic properties is not a good idea. Although I can't deny I'm curious.

'See what I have to put up with? Maybe with you around they'll kiss less.' Sean takes a long swig from the bottle and winks at me. 'Might get to see something better drinking this. Want one?'

'No, thanks.'

'Try it,' Rose says. 'You might like it. It's not as bad as people say.'

Sean opens a new bottle for me, and I take a couple of sips, the sharp taste tangy in my mouth. I grimace, 'I'll stick to Coke, thanks.'

'Sure you won't have a splash of vodka with it?' Then he frowns. 'You are eighteen, right?'

'Erm, yes, but no, thanks.'

'Oh, for fuck's sake, Sean. We're in the house.' Rose snaps.

'Yes, and your family makes its money from licensed venues and we're not going to risk losing those licences by being accused of giving booze to underage kids.'

'She's not a kid. She's in my class at uni. And yes, she's eighteen.'

'I ... I have ID. But I just want the Coke,' I mumble, but Rose shakes her head and leads me to sit on an empty sofa, Matt on her other side. I've not met him before, but she's talked about him a lot. They're an interesting couple – her auburn hair, green eyes and curves contrasting with his tall, toned physique and dirty-blond hair. I know they've not been a couple all that long, but I haven't seen her smile like she is now since I met her. A pang of jealousy hits me as I watch them together, him sliding an arm easily around her shoulders, her leaning against him, a small smile playing at the corner of her lips. The way he looks at her ... I'd love someone to look at me, just like that.

'Seriously, though. Did you clear it with Cillian?' Sean says, pulling a chair over beside us. Rose sighs and I frown at him. I expect him to be joking, but his expression is serious.

'Not yet,' Rose says. I frown. She actually has to ask her brother if I'm allowed to come to the party? That's weird. But I guess with all the valuables lying around they need to be careful.

'Rose,' Sean says, the warning clear in his tone.

'It'll be fine. Seriously, Niamh, my brother knows how to suck the joy out of absolutely everything.'

'Be nice, Bud. He has a lot of responsibility on his shoulders.' Matt strokes his fingers up and down Rose's arm and leans in to kiss the side of her neck. She giggles. 'Now, Niamh, tell us what you're studying? What do you want to be when you grow up?'

I glance at Rose. Surely, they'll expect me to be doing the same as her? But it's a big university there's lots of places we could have met.

'I'm going to be a lawyer,' I say, and I could swear there's a sharp intake of air around the room.

Nervous, I start to babble. 'There's so much crime in this city and people's lives get messed up and it's difficult to get justice sometimes.'

Sean searches my face for something, then turns to Rose. 'You have definitely *not* cleared this with Cillian, have you?'

This is getting distinctly weird.

'Rosebud—'

'It's Rose, Sean. I'm not a baby anymore.'

'You let Matt call you Bud,' Sean points out.

'I let him do a lot of things,' she sasses back. 'Fine we'll go visit the boss. Get his approval. Sake.'

'Want me to come?' Matt asks, standing as we do.

'No.' Rose steps into him, kissing him for longer than is comfortable to watch. 'If he's in a mood, he might decide to throw you out.'

'Can't have that,' he says. I turn away awkwardly when I notice his hands start to roam across her body. Intimacy like that has always made me feel uncomfortable. Maybe if

I'd had the chance to experience it, I wouldn't mind so much.

Leaving Matt behind, Rose directs me out of the room and down a number of corridors to another area of the house. 'Does your brother really vet all your friends?'

She takes a deep breath, then sighs. 'Sort of. The city's liquor licences are strict. And our money sometimes attracts the wrong sort of people.'

'Am I the wrong sort?'

'Don't be silly, Niamh. What on earth would make you the wrong sort?'

'Because I ... I don't think we come from the same world,' I say quietly. Her eyes narrow and she searches my face for ... something. Then she smiles and shakes her head, throwing her arm around my shoulders as she leads me back to the hall. 'And your friends seemed upset about me being a lawyer.'

'No one likes law enforcement, Niamh, and lawyers also fall into that category. You'll need to get used to it. And that's not what my brother is worried about. I promise you.'

There's something about her words that reassures me. But even though they make me feel somewhat better, I still feel totally out of place here. By the time we've crossed the hall, the feeling of reassurance has gone, and I hold my garnet necklace for luck. The warm stone calms my nerves immediately.

'Cillian?' Rose calls, pushing open a gleaming dark wood door. The lighting inside is dim, atmospheric and sensual music plays softly. The change of vibe from the airy room with the bay window is extreme. When there's no response,

Rose huffs impatiently. Despite being behind her, I can see that the lighting is coming from a handful of wall sconces, and on the far side of the room, a large, ornate mirror dominates the space.

A tingle runs down my spine as if I'm being watched but when I turn, the hallway behind me is empty, and it's only when I look back that I catch a glimpse of a reflection in the mirror. The most striking woman I've ever seen is staring right at me. Her straight, thick black hair hangs down around her perfectly made-up face and over her bare, evenly tanned shoulders. There isn't even a hint of a strapline. She tilts her head to one side as she observes me with cold, almost black eyes, her bright red lips pursed together as they curve downwards. There's not a single ounce of warmth in her gaze and, together with the heavy black and purple sequinned dress, it makes her appear like an evil queen.

Rose pulls me further into the room, breaking my gaze with the unknown woman. The silence is unnerving. And then I see the figure sitting next to her, though he's shrouded in shadows.

'Cillian? This is my friend, Niamh,' Rose says. 'She's in my class at uni – and in an attempt to make respectable friends like you are always telling me to do, I invited her to my party tonight.'

Aside from the evil queen, the attention in the room focuses on me for what feels like an eternity. I shift nervously under the scrutiny as Cillian puts down a whisky glass and gets to his feet, and it's as though the shadows physically retreat, sliding from his shoulders and slithering down to the floor, then vanishing. I blink, maybe that sip of

Stox has had more of an effect that I expected? My breath catches in my throat as I meet his gaze. His eyes are the oddest shade of blue I've ever seen, giving him an ethereal quality.

I lift my head, and for a brief moment I think I see horns appear either side of his head. Huge, great horns like a stag's antlers, but antlers that are more like tree branches wound through with leaves. I'm startled by the sound of a horn, almost as if signalling the start of a hunt, but no one else seems to notice. I shake my head unable to process what's happening in my mind, but I can sense Rose's impatience growing, her desire to get back to her party, and she propels me further into the room until I'm stood directly in front of her brother.

We simply stare at one another, and it suddenly feels as though it's just the two of us in the room. At well over six foot tall, he commands the space. His hair is that darkest of browns, and I'm caught up in those pale blue eyes, so unlike anything I've ever seen before. And when they meet mine I'm a deer caught in headlights, trapped by the intensity of his gaze. I can't tear myself away. I think Rose has just repeated the introductions and I'm guessing that I should do or say something. But in this moment, where it feels as though no one exists but me and Cillian, I can't catch my breath, let alone form a sentence. Maybe I should have accepted Sean's offer for vodka with my Coke after all.

'Hi!' I manage to say at last, but I'm not sure what to do. Do I hold out my hand to shake his? This feels a little like a business meeting, with him wearing an actual suit in a dark black that seems like a total absence of colour rather than a colour in its own right. His shirt is also black, but open at the neck, and he's not wearing a tie.

I suddenly notice that there are other people in the room, too. Men, also in suits, while the women are in a mix of sharp velvet or silk suits and cocktail dresses. None of them looks older than about twenty-five. Is this how rich young people socialise?

My gaze shifts back to Rose's brother.

She has already told me that Cillian's twenty-six, but the age gap feels much bigger right now. I will never be that sophisticated. Or so dominant. Down the side of his neck, reaching under his shirt, is a tattoo, at odds with the rest of his appearance. I don't want to be caught staring too hard, but it looks like it might be antlers, similar to the ones I imagined framing his head a few minutes before. His surname is Hunter, after all. Maybe he's playing up the link, what with their house being named after that ancient pagan hunting god. Well, he definitely has the body of a god if the way he fills out that jacket is anything to go by. Deciding that it doesn't seem like he's going to shake hands, I curl my hands into fists and put them behind me.

'And this is Vittoria Riali,' Rose says, unenthusiastically, gesturing at the evil queen. 'My brother's'—she pauses—'girlfriend.'

The evil queen, Vittoria, flashes Rose a look of pure animosity.

'Is this some stray you picked up at college to make yourself look good?' she scoffs and glances around the room at the other guests. Some of whom smile back, although most shift nervously, watching Cillian as if to gauge his reaction before deciding whether to join this woman's snideness or not.

'Niamh's hardly a stray, Vittoria,' Rose says, flicking her hair off her shoulder. 'And it's university. Not college. We're going to be lawyers, remember? One day, you might need our help.'

'I doubt it,' says Vittoria dismissively, rolling her eyes at Cillian, whose attention is still solely focused on me. I can't bring myself to look him in the eye again, he's making me nervous. Is this some kind of test to see how long I can withstand his piercing gaze?

'Niamh is planning to specialise in criminal law,' Rose points out, and I reach for her, pleading with my eyes for her to just stop. I don't want these people to know anything about me. *Knowledge is power.* The words whisper through my head from nowhere, but I shiver as if someone whispered them directly into my ear. 'She's keen to ensure that victims and their families are able to access the justice system, no matter their socio-economic background.'

'How very ... noble.' Vittoria says, although distaste flits across her features before she schools them back to haughty disdain. 'Only the very young and the very naïve nowadays believe that's possible.'

There's a titter of amusement around the room, but this is the one aspect of my life where I am confident and I have the sinking sense that if I don't stand up for myself right now, that these people will ... will what? What can they possibly do except look down on me?

'Anything is possible if you put your mind to it,' I counter, more loudly than I intend, and the group falls momentarily into a shocked silence.

'Cute,' Vittoria says, recovering quickly, smiling in amusement as she slides a hand over Cillian's chest, two fingers slipping in between the buttons of his black shirt. But Cillian doesn't seem amused by Vittoria. His eyes are still firmly fixed on me.

'Sometimes, in this world the only person capable of getting justice for you is yourself,' he says. 'With or without the blessing of the legal system.'

With one swift movement he captures Vittoria's hand and removes it from inside his shirt. He tucks it in the crook of his elbow, and I see the dark red lacquer of her nails, perfectly matching the shade of her lipstick. The perfection of her appearance makes me look at my own pale pink nails, and I notice a chip on my index finger. How insignificant I must seem to these people.

'Besides, is anyone ever truly innocent?' he asks me.

'Yes,' I say. How can that even be in doubt? But laughter circles the room and my cheeks flush in the dim light. 'Some people are victims who deserve to be defended.'

'I doubt you can relate, Vittoria.' Rose says.

'Relate? To being a victim?' Vittoria sneers. 'I'd rather have a lawyer who was guaranteed to win.'

'Vittoria.' The warning in Cillian's tone is clear. But if I think this means he approves of me, I'm soon corrected when he snaps at me: 'Surname?'

'Whyte,' I reply, instantly. 'Niamh Whyte.'

'You're ... Irish?' Cillian asks, his voice a rich, velvety murmur that seems to brush against my skin, leaving a trail of heat in its wake. A delicious shiver coils its way down my spine.

'Yes. My grandparents are – *were* – Irish.'

There's an awkward silence as Rose and Vittoria stare daggers at one another while Cillian gives me his full attention. I find it impossible to look away.

'Rose,' Vittoria says with deep condescension, 'why don't you and your little friend go and get a drink? Dance a little. Maybe play some party games. Let the grown-ups talk.'

I feel Rose bristling beside me. 'Why don't you go—'

'Now, now, Rosebud. Let's not be rude to our guests.'

'Rude? That's rich. *She's* so beyond rude, she's—'

'Rose!' His terrifying demeanour is broken for a fraction of a second when he rolls his eyes, then looks at me. 'She may stay. *For now.*'

She may stay? Would Cillian really have thrown me out? I glance around and realise that yes, yes he probably would. And if he didn't want to get his hands dirty doing that, there were plenty of people in the room who would be willing to do it for him.

'Why, thank you,' Rose mutters dryly.

'Just making sure you're safe, Rosebud. We wouldn't want anyone ... unsuitable ... hanging around the house.'

There's a low chuckle from around the room, and the atmosphere shifts. Cillian's sharp eyes meet mine one last time, and I look down submissively. On the back of one hand, curling out from the sleeve of his jacket, I can see the head of a black serpent and as I watch it, it moves. I step back on instinct, bumping into Sean who seems to have materialised out of nowhere. He reaches out to steady me but a low growl from Cillian has him removing his grip instantly.

'I didn't want to intrude on your ... affairs, Cillian,' Rose says. 'But Sean insisted you had to meet Niamh. If you want someone to blame for this intrusion, then blame him.'

With that, she turns dramatically and flounces out of the room. Unsure of what's just taken place, I turn and follow as quickly as I can. But before I pull the door to the room closed behind us, I catch sight of Cillian's reflection in the mirror. His antlers have re-formed. I can smell the outdoors, pine needles and wood, as though there's a forest surrounding us. The faint sound of the hunting horn plays out once more and I suddenly see myself running through the woods, fleeing from the Huntsman. From *this* Huntsman.

My mind is playing tricks on me again. One thing's for certain. I should never have tasted Stox.

CHAPTER 9
CILLIAN

FOUR YEARS AGO

'The girl looks like she'd hide at the first sign of trouble,' Vittoria says as Niamh closes the door behind herself and my sister. 'If that's the future of our legal system in this city, I doubt she'll trouble us much.'

'A future conveyancer for sure,' her brother, Chris, says, laughing as he finishes whatever foul concoction is in his glass.

I disagree with Vittoria about Niamh. It's the innocent, the pure at heart, that don't give up. That find a cause they believe in and don't stop fighting until they bring light to the darkness around them. And while no one person can possibly bring enough light to illuminate the dark depths of my family, someone like Niamh might actually try. Although, it's far more likely that our darkness would corrupt her.

I sit back down on the dark leather couch, and Vittoria

does the same, leaning against me and sliding her hand under my shirt again. I let her trace my nipple with her taloned fingers and shiver in pleasure, hiding my real thoughts, which are on the girl I've just met.

Niamh.

As soon as I saw her standing in front of me, something ... a connection ... slid into place. My mouth curves into a smile and a rush of heat floods to my cock as I think about exactly what I'd like to slide into place, and where. There's something about her naivety and inexperience that attracts me – and I can tell she's not had the chance to experience a real man yet. My desire grows as I imagine her naked in my bed, me keeping her there for as long as it takes to rid her of every last shred of innocence. I let out a breath. Surely she can't be as pure as she seemed?

I've never thought I had a type before – I enjoy women, especially women who will submit to my desires – but Niamh's long dark hair, her delicately pale skin, the faint blush on her cheeks, reminds me of a barely-bloomed rose and has my senses stirring in a way I've not felt in years. She's ... perfect, even if she is nothing like other women I've experienced.

My finely tuned senses heard the beat of her heart, felt how it speeded up in fear as I fixed my stare on her. What I wouldn't give to follow her right now, back her into a quiet corner in my house and force her to acknowledge her weakness in the face of my power. Then I would claim her. I'm sure with a little patience and coaxing, she'd submit beautifully to me, allowing me to show her what her body is capable of. I could sense her arousal, she was intrigued by me, too, although it's clear she doesn't yet understand.

I shake my head, frowning. Did my sister bring her here on purpose to torture me tonight? Perhaps. But one thing I am absolutely sure of, is that one taste of Niamh Whyte would never be enough and my future lies elsewhere. She cannot ever be for me. Besides, I can't let Vittoria think my attention has been drawn elsewhere – that would end badly for everyone. So I focus on the fact that I am the Huntsman and one day I will rule the Kinfolk. That has always been my ambition and I cannot allow it to be derailed by anyone. Especially a human.

But I can afford to be curious, make sure she's suitable as a companion for my sister. I cross the room to speak to Aiden, my right-hand man. He's worked for me since my father died over five years ago, passing the role of Huntsman onto me. He's loyal, which is the main consideration. And while he is both my chauffeur and my bodyguard, he's officially on my books as a 'researcher', since 'hacker' raises too many red flags with the taxman. It shouldn't be too hard for Aiden to find everything we need to know about Niamh – she doesn't give the impression of being aware enough to cover her tracks. It's a pity that some of the old magics are now lost to us. Scrying – a magic that allows you to use one polished surface to look through into any other, read the contents of any screen like a sort of magical CCTV – would have accomplished this much more quickly and without the need for using human systems. But it was considered too dangerous, and the Hunters were tasked with killing anyone caught manifesting the ability.

'Anything?' I ask him, knowing he'll already have started looking when she gave her name.

'Father is Glasgow born and bred. Mother's second generation from Dublin. Married nineteen years. He's a plumber. She works part-time as a receptionist in the local GP surgery. Nothing interesting. They live in a post-war cottage on the south side, near the subway. Niamh is their only child. Went to the local Catholic school. Good grades. School Captain. There is nothing noteworthy about her, not for your purposes. Nor her family. No red flags.' Aiden frowns as he looks up at me. 'Which may itself raise questions.'

'You think so?'

He glances towards the door and shakes his head. 'Nah.'

I nod in acknowledgement, the desire to investigate further slipping away. I wonder what game my sister thinks she's playing this time. Niamh is not the sort of person, I'd have expected her to befriend. Rose is confident, loud, bordering on obnoxious at times. While Niamh looked on the verge of running screaming from the house. I cannot imagine what they have in common – other than their choice of vocation.

Vittoria's brother Chris has been standing nearby, eavesdropping.

'She very wide-eyed and innocent, isn't she. Probably thinks she's going to right every wrong in the city. Pretty, though.' Chris moves to the drinks cabinet. 'Drink, anyone?'

To my surprise, I clench my fists. Him talking of her as some idealistic nobody has me riled up, and I'm not exactly sure why.

'I'll take another glass of wine,' Vittoria says.

'Two fingers,' I say, nodding to the whisky. Chris gives me four, before pouring his sister another glass of red. The room is filled with Kinfolk from the other ruling families and those who work for them – notably, the MacGowan kids and some of the Kelsos – and a few request drinks, much to Chris's irritation. Once he's finished serving, he finally unscrews a bottle of Stox and takes a long swig of the craft beer.

Vittoria's face contorts with disgust. 'Oh, that's rank, Chris.'

He shrugs and finishes the bottle in a second gulp. 'Happy to support Kinfolk enterprises,' he says, before pouring himself two fingers of my top-shelf whisky and downing that just as quickly. 'Even if I still don't understand why the Hunters get to control St Marnox.'

'Because if someone has bested us to get there, we're stuck with looking after them. Consider it motivation for every hunt to end as it should,' I point out.

The conversation moves on, but I notice Vittoria glance at Chris more than once. He downs several more bottles of Stox at speed and I can see the concern in her eyes.

'It's just as well you're Kin,' I point out to Chris. 'A human would be seeing monsters in every shadow by this time.'

'Why bother looking for monsters in the shadows,' Chris says. 'I can see you all right in front of me sitting in chairs.'

'Enough!' Vittoria says, grabbing the bottle of Stox from his hand and taking it over to the drinks tray. She screws the lid on and pours him a glass of water, handing it to him. 'It allows us to control humans, Chris. We're not supposed to get addicted to it ourselves.'

Stox is sold as a craft beer, a branded version of a

substance that we've been using for thousands of years to, under certain circumstances, control any human who ingests it. A perfect system, since it doesn't show up in human lab work. It's not exactly a drug. It's been called different things over the centuries. Fairy food. Magic.

Stox is only one way in which we offer this substance to humans and it's proved surprisingly successful. A putrid, herbal concoction, it has been brewed by monks, ironically enough, for the past seven or eight hundred years – maybe even longer – at St Marnox, a former monastery on the edge of the Highlands, which exists simultaneously in both the human world and the Underworld.

St Marnox hasn't had anything to do with any established church for more than a millennium although somehow no one ever thinks to check. It's an extremely picturesque, thin place, leading to an area of the Underworld which doubles as a sanctuary for any accused Kinfolk fortunate enough to escape me hunting them down. Anyone can visit it in the human world, although it's something we discourage. St Marnox is not under the rule of the King, but The Unseelie Court, and it's considered a punishment for my family that we are bound to ensure the wellbeing of any who evade us during the hunt and reach its sanctuary. Most residents, however, call it a prison as there's no escape, except death or to face trial at The Unseelie Court.

Still, despite Stox's foul taste, and its reputation – or perhaps because of that – it's the most popular drink in the city. I've lost count of the number of licences my family has been granted thanks to the fact that Stox makes humans extremely persuadable. On the flip side, we do get to keep the income from the brewery which is significant and the main reason why my family can afford the lifestyle and status that we've come to enjoy.

'Don't be such a fucking snob, Vittoria. The taste reminds me of home.'

'If you're so homesick, Chris, maybe you should consider spending some time in the Underworld.'

'But it's so much more entertaining here, dear sister. Especially watching you trying to control Dad and get him to make you his heir instead of me.'

A hush falls across the room, as everyone's conversations come to a halt. It's no secret just how much Vittoria desires to rule The Unseelie Court. Her ruthless nature would undoubtedly mean change for the Kin, but her father, Vincenzo, is determined to follow tradition, and it's not just him. When the Blight hit, both The Seelie and Unseelie Courts were ruled by queens, but since then the patriarchy has taken over and rewritten the rules – using this fact as justification why women shouldn't rule the Court. There hasn't even been an Unseelie queen since Vincenzo's wife died almost twenty years ago. There were no other suitable women in that generation, and if he had remarried someone not born of the Court, he'd have had to give up his throne. And the only way Vincenzo will do that is over his dead body. Possibly the only thing we have in common.

I shake my head, leaving Vittoria to have a go at her brother while my thoughts return to Niamh. She's... I'm not sure what she is, exactly, other than lingering unexpectedly in my thoughts.

I wonder how well Niamh really knows Rose. My sister

has secrets, she's vivacious, volatile – and the only reason I've allowed her relationship with Matt Muir to progress is that he seems to keep her out of trouble. I wonder, would Niamh be capable of drawing me out of my own darkness? I stare into the mirror above the fireplace, barely seeing my friends reflected in it. No, the vision in my mind's eye is so much more appealing. Niamh, running from me but looking back. Tempted. Unsure whether to run or surrender—

The sound of cheering from the other room breaks my train of thought. I frown, my sister's party is interrupting the business I need to conduct with the Kin.

'Seven minutes, starting now!' someone shouts, and a door slams shut. I close my eyes and take a deep breath, reminding myself that Rose is no longer a child, despite the game they've chosen to play, and she won't thank me for interfering with her life. A wave of brotherly protectiveness comes over me. If any of the guys here does anything to upset her or harm her, they're going to wish they'd never been born.

'I wonder what poor bastard will end up having to kiss Rose's virginal friend?' Vittoria ponders. I fight to keep my expression neutral as her face twists into a nasty smirk. I have a sudden urge to march down there and take Niamh away from every single last one of them. Most of them are my friends – or Rose's. Acquaintances at least. All Kinfolk, with the exception of Niamh.

'Well, I for one wouldn't say no to solving that problem for her.' Chris raises his glass.

'Have some self-respect. Really, Cillian, I can't imagine why your sister even invited her. She's utterly out of her depth. Poor girl. You should have sent her home.' Vittoria sneers at me.

I tense, about to snap back at her, before remembering that it is not wise to encourage Vittoria's clear, spiteful jealousy.

'Right,' Chris slams his glass down on a table and rubs his hand together. 'Well, I'm going next door to the fun party.'

We all watch as he barrels out the room.

'Go with him, would you?' I ask Aiden, nicely. He might work for me, but he's a friend, too.

Vittoria sits in a dark cloud of silence beside me, before she gets up and goes to stare out the window into the dark garden. I move to stand behind her, putting my arms around her and pulling her back against me.

'You're intrigued by her, aren't you?' she asks.

'Who?' I bluff.

Vittoria turns in my arms and puts her arms around me, pressing her body against mine and capturing my lips in a kiss. Uncaring if there's anyone in the garden who can see us, she runs her hand over my cock, her lips curving when she feels me harden beneath her. She rubs slowly, with frustratingly languid movements, taunting my desire, before she pulls away suddenly. I expect her to take my hand and pull me into a more secluded part of the house, somewhere I can play with her, taking what's mine and forcing pleasure out of us both. To my disappointment, she doesn't.

'I should take my brother home,' she says, moving towards the door. I don't follow her right away, forcing my body under my control before turning to see her check her appearance in the ornate mirror on the sitting room wall. She smiles seductively at me, then leaves the room.

I follow her and watch as she drags Chris from a rowdy game of Spin the Bottle. Another friend helps to keep him upright as all three make their way to a waiting car. Even after what she just did to turn me on, Vittoria's planning to leave. As I accompany them outside, she places her hand in mine, the coldness reminding me of her very inhuman nature. I'd expected her to stay, she rarely turns down an opportunity to fuck so whatever's going on with Chris must be much worse even than it appears. Helping her climb into the car, I shut the door and watch it drive away.

'She won't be so innocent now,' Chris calls back out of the window as the limo rolls down the driveway. 'I made sure she got picked for some "alone time" with Finlay. He's got a rep for breaking in virgins.'

I glower. And as the car headlights disappear into the night, I storm back into my house, yanking open the door of the lounge. My temper spikes when I see Niamh's not in the room. There's no sign of Rose, or Matt, either. Cursing the pair of them I head back into the hall and pull open the door to the cloakroom to meet Niamh's terrified eyes.

CHAPTER 10
CILLIAN

FOUR YEARS AGO

'What the fuck is going on?' I demand as I open the cloakroom door. My blood pressure lowers slightly as I see Finlay standing on the opposite side of the room, his mobile in his hand, while Niamh is facing me, looking ready to leave.

'N ... nothing,' Finlay stammers. 'It was a game. I ... I wasn't going to... Tell him I didn't...'

Niamh turns around to look at him, then looks back at me and frowns.

'He didn't do anything. We weren't doing anything,' she says, quietly, but more confidently than I expected. Behind me, there are footsteps on the stairs and Sean rushes to stand beside me.

'What's happening?' he asks, his gaze flitting between me, Finlay and Niamh.

'This little fucker took one of our guests into the cloakroom to—'

'What? No! It was a game!' Finlay says. 'She was in the circle. She was playing the game. Sean, tell him. I was just supposed to kiss her but she said no and... Tell them!' Finlay's voice has risen a couple of octaves. At least someone here tonight respects me.

I look at Niamh and she looks almost as terrified. Not to mention embarrassed. 'He didn't do anything wrong,' she states clearly. 'I got selected for the game, we came in here and when I said I didn't want to kiss him ... well, that's about when you opened the door.'

I stare at her, but other than the redness in her cheeks, she's not looking distressed.

'You're sure?'

'Yes,' she says nodding, glancing over at Finlay.

'Fuck's sake, Finlay. Why do you think the bottle never landed on her?' Sean says.

Finlay frowns, confused. 'But it did. It landed on me and then her.'

'Sean?' I lift an eyebrow.

'I've been making sure she wasn't picked since Rose ... erm, since Rose went upstairs...' He runs a hand through his hair and shakes his head. 'I just went to check on her. I thought Niamh would be fine for a couple of minutes. I didn't expect—'

'I'm fine.' Niamh cuts in, 'There's really no need for all this fuss. I'm just going to get a taxi—'

'No. Upstairs,' I demand, glaring at her. 'I'm not risking anything happening to you on the way home. Party's over.'

For a moment, I think she's going to argue, but Sean nods at her and smiles and, with a frown, she does what I tell her and leaves the closet, rounding the corner to the stairs. Everyone else in the hall hurries away into other rooms, and the music in both the lounge and the drawing room cuts off abruptly.

My fist catches the side of Finlay's face sending him flying across the hallway. I stride towards him as he starts to pick himself up and kick him back down again.

'I'll take Finlay downstairs,' I say to Sean. 'And make sure he has somewhere to stay tonight.'

'But—' Finlay starts, but I turn quickly, my hand shooting out to grab him by the throat.

'Right now,' I say, 'I'd be extremely careful what I say.' Finlay stares at me for a moment, then nods. I push him in front of me and down the dark, narrow corridor that leads to the basement, his head bowed and shoulders slumped.

I wash my hands in the basement sink before heading upstairs sometime later. Taking out some of my frustrations on Finlay, who I don't think will ever even consider looking at Niamh again as long as he's breathing, has helped.

'Do you think he planned to hurt her?' I ask Sean who was waiting for me when I came out of the secure accommodation where Finlay is staying tonight.

'No.' Sean says instantly. 'He's far more likely to be the victim of shit like that. I can't help feeling that maybe someone else put him up to it.'

'Chris?' I nod. 'Yes, he did say something suspicious.'

I'm sure that Chris rigged the whole thing, but it didn't hurt to put Finlay in his place.

'Well, currently the kid's crying too hard for me to get any sense out of him. But maybe his memory will be better in the morning,' I say.

Both he and Niamh might have claimed that nothing happened in that cloakroom, but I know that was only because I opened the door. Finlay's face was a mask of pure guilt and there is definitely something he's not telling me.

'Call the doctor to come and check him over,' I ask Sean.

'Sure,' he says.

I do a quick recce of the ground floor to make sure there are no other unexpected issues occurring. Thankfully, everyone seems to have found a place to sleep. Blowing out a breath, I head for my own room, trying to block out my returning thoughts of Niamh.

I don't expect to find her curled up on the chaise longue on the upstairs landing. Her eyes are squeezed shut, but her body is far too tense for her to be asleep. I crouch down beside her and put a hand on the side of her face, and she jumps. Her tongue traces her bottom lip and I don't miss that its trembling.

'What are you doing here?' My voice sounds gruff, and I see her recoil, frowning. 'Rose has a spare bed in her room.'

'Oh, um...' she glances over at Rose's bedroom door. 'I think she—'

'Fuck's sake.' I start to stride towards the door, startled when Niamh jumps up and grabs my arm.

'Don't!' Her cheeks are a bright shade of pink and I falter.

My first instinct was to castrate whoever is in my sister's bed, but I know who it is, and Matt's an acceptable choice for her to have made, for now. Even if it is difficult for me to accept that Rose is an adult now and able to decide for herself.

Matt may work for the Rialis – understandable as he's water Kin and they represent the sea god, Llyr, at Court – but for the first time in years, Rose is happy. Despite being friends with Chris, he's always seemed sound.

'Sorry,' Niamh says. 'But it's all she's talked about all week. Seeing Matt tonight, I mean. Not specifically...' She waves her other hand vaguely in the direction of the door. 'I didn't know where to go.'

I look down at where she's touching me, the sensation of her bare skin on mine sending shockwaves through my body. My breath catches and for a moment all I can think of is how much better it would be if she were touching more of me.

She pulls her hand away, as if she's aware of my thoughts, stepping cautiously back out of reach.

'I think they just fell asleep,' she says, gesturing towards the door.

I lean closer, use my heightened senses to listen, then wish I hadn't.

'No,' I tell her. 'They are definitely not sleeping. Come with me. There are guest rooms.'

'Actually, I think...'

I roll my eyes, crossing the hall to first one door, then the other. Fuck's sake, is everyone in the house getting some tonight except me? And Niamh. And, of course, Finlay.

'You can sleep in here,' I say, placing my hand on a door and pushing a tiny amount of magic through my fingers to unlock the charm keeping it secure. I turn the handle with one hand and push the door open, standing aside to let her go in first.

'Where are we?' she asks, looking around wide-eyed.

'My room.'

My body responds when the confusion in her eyes morphs into fear as I undo my tie and slip my jacket off.

'But... I can't... Thanks, but I think I should just go home.'

'What would your parents think if you arrived home at this hour? There's no one here willing to drive you and surely your parents wouldn't want you getting a taxi this late, alone and upset.'

'They would rather I got home in a state than not at all,' she blurts out.

'I'm sure they'd rather you came home in the morning, safe and well-rested. You don't want to worry them now, do you? Next time they might not be so happy about you going out in the first place.'

I shouldn't be playing into all her insecurities like this, but if I'm sure about one thing this evening, given the way things have panned out, it's that I'm damned if Niamh isn't going to spend tonight right here in my bed. I don't trust anyone else here to keep her as safe as I will, and as I don't plan to do anything to harm her, why shouldn't I take the opportunity to indulge myself with her company?

'Did you bring a bag?'

She nods. 'It's downstairs. In the cloakroom.' She bites her bottom lip and stares down at the floor embarrassed by the reminder of what happened earlier. 'I'll go and get it.'

She's out the room before I can stop her, and the

temptation to chase her is suddenly very real, and no matter whether I justify that to myself as ensuring that she's okay, I know that most of my reasoning will be the thrill of the chase. I'll stalk her, tire her out, build the anticipation of the moment when I catch her, watch as she surrenders to me...

I shake my head and sigh. Put away my shoes and hang up my jacket, unfastening my cufflinks, then undo the buttons on my shirt. Sometimes I yearn for the days when I was able to dress more casually, but as I'm now solely responsible for running our family businesses, including both Elliots and The Three Graces, I have to be projecting the right image in public. Rose will contribute more to the family businesses once she graduates but I want her to focus on her studies for now. We need a reliable lawyer on the team as our current lawyer is talking about retiring.

I strip off my remaining clothes, either hanging them neatly over my chair or dropping them in the laundry basket. I usually sleep naked but that's not an option tonight, so reluctantly I pull on a pair of grey joggers. A sharp intake of breath alerts me to Niamh's presence. If I thought she was blushing before, then this is next level. She stares at me from the bedroom door, open-mouthed at my bare chest, and hastily takes a step back, swiftly closing the door.

'Sorry,' she squeaks from the other side of the door. I grin, doubting she's ever going to open that door again voluntarily, so I cross to open it. On the way, I catch sight of my bare chest in the mirror and the way the stark black of my tattoos stands out against my skin tone in this light. I glance back into my room, frowning when I think I might have caught a glimpse of Vittoria's face in the mirror, but there's no sign of anything other than my own bedroom when I recheck the mirror. Fuck me, I'm tired and just want today to be over.

'I'm sorry,' Niamh squeaks again when I open the door. 'I'm in your way. I should go.'

'No.' I reach for her, the smooth bare skin of her arm warm in my hand. I slide my fingers further up her arm, loving the feel of her, but stop when I realise she's staring at me, curious but fearful. She hasn't given me permission to touch her, and without that I won't take this any further. I'd rather my partners were trembling because they want to be touched, not because they don't. 'Please stay. You're safer here tonight.'

'Okay'—she nods, her tone becomes more confident as she says—'but you weren't massively keen on me being here earlier, so what's changed?'

Should I tell her that Chris was setting her up? That should really frighten her, not all the men here know where to draw the lines of consent and most will obey Chris without hesitation.

'My sister shouldn't have abandoned you like that.'

'It's okay.' She shrugs, her skin moving under my touch, and I swear I feel her shiver before she pulls her arm away from my touch. I like that she does. It's just one tiny rebellion. 'She really likes Matt. I don't want to get in her way.'

'Come and get some rest. I'm not going to do anything to you without your consent.'

I smile as her eyes widen and I guide her to the bed, trying to subtly adjust my joggers before she notices just how my body is responding to touching hers. And if I'm responding like this to touching her arm, what would it be like if— I let her go. I'm so very, very tempted. And she's interested, I can tell, but as she looks up at me, her eyes wide and guileless, I'm reminded once again of how young she is.

Even with her consent, I shouldn't touch her. She has no idea about the world my sister has introduced her to, and I plan to keep it that way. What the fuck was Rose thinking inviting her here tonight? She's not one of us, not one of the Kinfolk.

'But I can't—'

'Don't argue,' I say. 'You won't win.'

'What will your girlfriend think if I stay here? And where are you going to sleep?'

'She will understand, and I'm not going to sleep. I have work to do.' I resist the urge to brush my fingers through the hair on her temple. 'But I will make sure no one else bothers you. I have a responsibility to make sure you're safe as long as you're under my roof. I run several prominent bars in town and have a reputation to uphold. The newspapers would have a field day reporting that I allowed a young woman to leave my home at this hour, drunk, only for her to be accosted on the way home. Besides'—I aim for a rueful grin, hoping that will win her over—'Rose would never forgive me.'

'What would the newspapers say about you keeping me a prisoner in your bedroom instead?' Her hand covers her mouth as soon as she finishes speaking, but I grin at her, pleased to see the spark I sense within her starting to burn.

'Not a prisoner. A guest.'

I smile at her and she relaxes. I know fine well I could just order Aiden to drive her home but I'm not going to, and while my body has decided it wants her, regardless of all the reasons why it is a fucking terrible idea, I'm not going to pass up the chance to get to know this woman who intrigues me so much a little better.

'You can change in the en suite,' I say, with a smile.

I sit down on the other side of the bed and pick up my tablet, opening it to tonight's reports from Elliots and The Three Graces.

When she thinks my attention is on my work, she opens her bag, then scurries past me with her pyjamas. The information on my tablet is meaningless since all I can think about is her undressing on the other side of the en suite door. Vittoria and I have been together for so long that I've forgotten what the thrill of lust really feels like. My girlfriend might match me with her power and dark fantasies, but I can't deny the fact my attraction to her has never been as strong as it is for the young woman currently in my house.

The delicate satin camisole and shorts she's wearing leave little to the imagination and from the look on her face, she's wishing she had brought something more demure with her tonight. The thin fabric stretches across her breasts, her cleavage visible and her puckered nipples pebbling into hard points. I've barely said three sentences to her and I'm already imagining all the ways to bring her pleasure. I run my tongue across my lips, barely able to control my want as I feel myself harden. Thank fuck I thought to put loose joggers on, although they'll do little to disguise my full girth and length. Niamh's legs are pale and slender and if I don't push each and every thought of having them wound around my waist while I fuck her until she can't remember her own name out of my head, then I'm going to do exactly that. Right here, right now.

She crosses back to her bag and this time I get a view of her toned buttocks, barely covered by her shorts. I watch her in the mirror, imagining bending her over the chest of drawers, watching as I slide my thigh between hers to part her legs, spreading her in front of me to fuck. How I could bend down and plunge my tongue inside her wet pussy as she begs me for more—

'Why are you doing this?' she asks again, jolting me from my thoughts.

'I told you, and because my sister is being rude, and I feel responsible.'

She stares at me for a long moment.

'It feels like pity,' she says abruptly, and I smile, realising she's found a little confidence.

'It's not. Get into bed.' The building tension inside me is making me lose my cool around her and the sooner she's covered up the better.

She looks at me for a long moment before reluctantly climbing under the covers. I arrange them carefully over her and return my attention to my tablet. After a moment, she turns onto her side, facing away from me. To turn off the light, I'm going to have to reach over her. I should get off the bed and walk around, but I don't. She could turn it off herself, but she doesn't. I lean over, breathing in her delicate vanilla scent. It's such a contrast from the heavy, cloying perfume Vittoria wears. Her body is warm against my chest as I pause with my hand on the switch. Then I click it off, plunging us into darkness.

For the next couple of hours, I read reports, and check figures and place orders, aware of every sound and movement Niamh makes beside me. Dawn is breaking when I rest my eyes for just a moment – and then I'm waking up, Niamh's arm draped across my body, her breath whispering across my abs, her small hand curved around my opposite hip.

She jerks awake, and there's a momentary pause before she tenses and slowly sets about lifting her arm and head from my body. She lifts her head and looks up, swallowing nervously when she finds me staring down at her. As she rolls back onto her side, the back of my hand grazes her breast. Her breath catches, her cheeks flushed, and the temptation to slide my hand inside her top and claim what I want to be mine is almost overwhelming. I'm fairly certain she would submit willingly, and I could satisfy my need to have her, and then move on.

But I don't. If I did that … then there's a chance that I wouldn't stop and, while this young woman is absolutely not a person I expected to appear in my life, that doesn't change the fact that right now, she's here in my bed, tempting me in ways that no one else ever has.

I can't take any risks. I have plans, except that my cock doesn't seem to be getting that message. I put my phone on the bedside cabinet, and slide down the bed, staying on top of the covers. Her head is on her pillow, watching me as I mirror her position, finally letting myself relax.

She lets out a sigh. 'Last night was my first proper party.

I was hoping maybe for my first kiss and instead I end up in bed with… I should have known I'd get it all wrong—'

She breaks off as if just realising what she's said. Well, Chris might have been being an arsehole earlier, but he was right in his assessment of her experience. Except that, what he saw as something to mock, I find … intriguing and, god help me, endearing. She covers her face with her hands and sighs.

'Wow, you must think I'm pathetic,' she says. When I don't respond she slowly pulls her hands away.

'We all have to start somewhere,' I reply eventually. She gives me a wry smile, an embarrassed laugh escaping her perfect pink lips. Before I can stop myself, I roll and take hold of her wrists, pushing them either side of her head against the pillow and lower my face to hers.

'Is that something you still want?' I whisper.

She doesn't say no. She doesn't say yes, at first, either, but her eyes stay locked on mine, her breathing growing shallow, until she nods and a low groan of want escaping her lips, tells me exactly what I want to know.

I thread my fingers through her hair and angle her face up to mine, her garnet necklace slipping round to the side of her neck, warm against my hand.

'What happens in the darkness, stays in the darkness,' I murmur against her lips, then I cover her mouth with mine, and take. The words of the *Guth Dorcha* will claim her memory of her first kiss because she can never know that it was me – even if it's only a stolen kiss. But I will remember.

I will vividly, and achingly, remember.

CHAPTER 11
NIAMH

NOW

Cillian stares down at me for a long moment, then reaches for me. I whimper, pushing myself away from him as best I can, the cable ties around my wrists and ankles biting further into my flesh as I move.

He lifts my head, forcing it forward until his fingers find the knot at the back of the gag, but although he pulls, and twists and curses, it doesn't loosen. He straightens and pulls out the metal handle of a knife. I jump at the loud click as a large blade comes into view in front of my face. And when he leans towards me, I scream, bracing my feet on the floor of the boot, pushing away from him, pulling at my bonds with all my might, despite the fact that I know it won't do any good. There's nowhere to go.

'Fuck's sake,' Cillian hisses, his fingers gripping my jaw and holding my head still, forcing me to look at him. 'I'm not going to hurt you. Just stay still and let me cut you free.'

He's not going to hurt me? Does he think I'm stupid? I shake my head, still trying to shift away from him. Tears pool in my eyes and I blink them away. Not that it matters. He has the control here and I have none.

He straightens, his words gradually penetrating my brain. Cut me free? Okay, that does make sense. I stare up at him, my chest heaving, sweat beading on my forehead, as I manage to stop the pointless screaming into the gag. My heart races and I force myself to breathe in an attempt to keep calm.

'That's a good girl,' he says and deep inside me, heat coils at his words. 'I'm going to lift you out, cut you free. And then you're going to run from me. As fast as you can into the woods. Understand?'

I nod, frowning at him.

'I know you're frightened but...' he whispers, his voice catching. I can't work out what this new expression on his face means, what he's thinking. If this situation pains him, why doesn't he let me go? He pulls the blanket off me, and I shiver when the chill of the night air hits my bare flesh. I glance down, remembering that the straps of my dress have been torn and my breasts exposed. But the stretchy material has been pulled neatly back, the strap pinned into place and, although the situation is precarious, I'm currently decent. I flinch as he slides his hand over my shoulder.

Goosebumps form on my skin where he's touching me, my body reacting to his touch even though it shouldn't. Each brush of his fingers sends sensation coursing through me. The strength in his hand both reassures me and awakens something deep within me, something that I hesitate to explore, fearing that it'll consume me. How is it possible to still want this man, when he's brought me here for one reason and one reason only.

'Bloody hell,' he mutters, putting the knife in his pocket. He leans into the boot, his strong arms sliding beneath me as he pulls me out, lifting me effortlessly. For a moment, we stare at one another, his embrace comforting, his body supportive. Everywhere we touch his heat warms my cold body.

We stare at each other for a long moment, and I can feel his internal debate about what to do, but he snaps himself out of his thoughts and sets me down next to the car.

He's changed into his version of casual clothes – dark jeans, a designer T-shirt. He's not wearing a jacket, but he doesn't appear to feel the chill that sends a shiver through my body. His tattoos are dark against his skin, and I stare at them, remembering how mesmerised I was the first time I saw them. Now I recognise the designs as a mix of Pictish symbols, Insular Celtic knotwork and some more modern illustrations. The double disc on one bicep consists of two perfect circles connected by double straight lines. Within each circle, triskelion spiral, creating a vortex that symbolises the endless cycles of life. The colours he's chosen are bright, far more vivid than anything found on the actual symbol stones, but which seem to make the designs feel modern, alive even. His lower arm carries the image of a curved hunting horn, and I'm reminded of the sound I thought I heard all those years ago, the night we first met.

On his other arm there's a crescent and V-rod, vaguely reminiscent of a cruder version of the Masonic compass and dividers, but it's the black serpent that curls around his lower right arm that catches my eye. Its tail sits neatly in the crease of his elbow before it winds around his arm twice, the head slithering at an angle onto the back of his hand. While it might be clearly a serpent, it's head is reminiscent of a ram, with curved horns on either side. The black body of the serpent is solid enough that it must have been painful beyond what I could endure to have it inked.

He slams the boot closed, picks up his knife and moves it up to my face. My eyes meet his as I struggle to decide what I should do, although realistically, there are no good options. I'm completely at his mercy. He tugs on the fabric of the gag, pulls it away from my skin and slides the knife in between, then with a single easy movement, the gag falls away from my face. I try not to think about how sharp the blade must be or how much damage it could do to my flesh should he decide to use it against me.

'Cillian...' I whisper as his fingers grip my chin and he freezes.

'What? But... How?' He steps back, his mouth open, moving as if he's trying to form words.

'How do you keep doing this to me?' he mutters, his voice cold and controlled, as he slowly kneels in front of me. I whimper as he slides his hand between my legs, running the hilt of the blade up my inner thigh. The cool handle makes me gasp, the threat of danger and pleasure taunting me with what this man could do and how vulnerable I am. I hold my breath, praying he doesn't turn the knife around. As the handle reaches my core, he pulls it away, lowering it and slicing through the thick ties that bind my ankles.

He grabs me by the shoulders, turning me to face the car with one arm clamped around my chest, holding me side-on against him.

'Raise your arms,' he demands, and I do so with some difficulty, my fingers nearly numb. Once again, he slides the knife between my limbs, then, with one smooth movement, the cable ties fall to the ground as his blade slides through them. I stumble instantly, and he catches me again.

'Sorry,' I say, then wonder why the hell I'm apologising to him.

He runs his fingers over the welts left by the cable ties on my wrists, shaking his head as he smears my blood with his fingers. I look around at the small clearing surrounded by dark, menacing trees, noticing the familiar wooden signposting of a Forestry Commission car park. I have no real idea of where we are, but it feels remote.

'What are you going to do to me?' If I sound terrified, it's because I am.

His eyes close and it looks like he's taking deep breaths to gather his courage. But that can't be right. The man in front of me isn't afraid of anything. If the past four years have taught me anything, it's that the Hunters are successful because they're ruthless. I stare at him, everything within me telling me to run, but I don't. I can't.

'I know you don't remember what happened—'

'In the club? In the alley? When I was attacked? When I killed—'

'You ... you remember?'

'You think killing a man is something I'd forget?'

'You shouldn't remember. Vittoria ... she did something.

Used the *Guth Dorcha*. She told me she had taken all your memories of me, of Rose.'

'Would that have made it easier for you to murder me?' I laugh. Surely he can't think something like that is even possible. 'Well, either she lied to you, or this goo doracha thing didn't work because I remember everything, Cillian. The night we met, the way you kissed me the next morning—'

'But you shouldn't ... I... I don't understand,' he says. 'But ... it's too late now anyway.'

He doesn't answer, just continues to stare at me before he shakes his head and takes my hand, attempting to drag me towards the woods.

'Come on,' he says, but I plant my feet and refuse to move, yanking my hand from his grip.

'Why don't you just kill me here? It'll save us both the walk.'

We stare at one another, but he doesn't answer immediately. I take a step backwards, then another and another, before I make contact with a tree and spread my hands back over the bark, steadying myself. It'd been raining earlier in the day, and there's a puddle beside me, still and shiny. I dread to think what would be looking back at me if I looked into it. I doubt my hair and make-up have survived the evening's events.

Cillian moves towards me, still confused, and I'm getting the oddest sense that we're not alone anymore, that we're being watched. But the car park is empty and all I can hear is the soft sound of the wind through the branches. He reaches for me, runs his fingers down the side of my face, then around my jaw and throat. I shiver. No matter how much I try to hate him, my body has other thoughts, and it reacts to his touch in a way that should send me running, but instead anchors me to the very spot where danger is lurking within him.

His hand slides down the front of my chest, cupping one breast briefly and circling the nipple with the pad of his thumb. I gasp as his hand continues its path, sliding down over the angle of my hip, teasing the hem of my dress before his fingers slide around the curve of my thigh. I don't know why but I have craved this man since the moment we met, no matter that I know he's dangerous, to my body as well as my heart. Maybe, if I let him... No, how can I even consider it?

'Run, now,' he says. 'Take your chances in the woods. If you reach the sanctuary you will have both won and lost your freedom. But you'll still be alive.'

'And if you catch me?'

He closes his eyes for a moment and the world shimmers around him. He opens them again, fixes his gaze on me, and reaches over his shoulders behind his back, pulling a crossbow from ... from nowhere.

I risk a glance down the narrow path that leads into the heart of the forest and shake my head.

'What's the point?'

He stares at me for a long moment, then shrugs. 'Probably nothing, but at least you'd have a chance...'

'A chance at what?'

He walks towards me, leaning in when he reaches me, stepping up close until his body is pressed tight against mine. He settles his head against my neck and breathes in before his lips trace a path around my ear and he whispers.

'Please, Niamh. Just ... please, don't make this any more difficult than it needs to be. Take the chance, it's all I can give you. But if you haven't reached the sanctuary by dawn... Wait for me.'

'Why?'

'Because there are fates worse than death. Now, go.'

Shivers race down my spine at his words. I shake my head, refusing to move my feet, and although Cillian takes my arm and tries to pull me away from the safety of the tree, I let my body become dead weight, and wrap my arms around the tree behind me.

'Niamh.'

'No,' I snap. 'I'm not going with you willingly. I'm not going to be complicit in my own murder.'

'If you stay here, I'll kill you. The hunt is your only chance. Run from me, Niamh.' His face changes, his stance changes. He straightens, the pleading look gone. I cringe inwardly. What have I done? He killed a man in front of me a few hours ago. I suspect it's not the first time he's killed even if he's never even set foot inside a court of law – and provoking him like this probably isn't going to help my situation.

Behind Cillian, tendrils of mist are curling around the trees, and even as I watch, the mist thickens, as if someone has pulled a curtain around us. It's still dark, a breeze picks up, bringing the mist closer. And I think I must be in shock, because although it races across my skin, it's barely chilled.

'Niamh. You have to. Before it's too...' He trails off,

shaking his head, then turns his hand palm up. There's a tattoo there, one I haven't seen before and it looks like its pulsing with a fiery light. And underneath it, is my name.

'What? Why?'

'You killed Kin, Niamh. The Court has marked you for death and I am the one to carry out that sentence.'

'But... but I didn't mean to. And both you and Vittoria—'

'We're both Kin. We were protecting Rose. None of this is fair, but it's not the same. Now, go. Try to reach St Marnox.'

'What?'

'I know you're angry. I know you don't believe me, but I never wanted any of this for you. I tried my best to keep you away, to keep you at a distance, but my bloody sister kept you tethered to us. I wish things were different.'

I swallow, unsure where he's going with this. We've only ever had a few stolen moments together, moments he instantly regretted or that I misunderstood. I've always thought I just wasn't right for him, wasn't enough for a man like him.

'There's something about you. Nothing I could do or say would persuade Rose to give you up. Maybe if I'd told her how much I want you, she'd have understood why I couldn't have you around.' He shakes his head. 'But I'm sorry that it's led you here.'

'You ... you want me?' I whisper, looking up at him.

'You know I do. I have done since the moment I met you.'

'But—'

'Come here,' he commands, and my feet have moved before I've even thought about it. He caresses my cheek, his eyes never leaving my face as he looks at me as if learning every detail of my features. He threads his fingers though my hair, palming the back of my head and drawing me towards him. His mouth covers mine and his arms come around me, as our tongues tangle. I close my eyes, getting lost in the feel of him, loving his smell, his taste, the way he makes places deep inside of me tingle because of his touch. As we kiss, the world around me slips away, Cillian's body against mine the only anchor to reality. Slowly, the sounds of the surrounding forest creep into my awareness, leaves whispering and branches creaking gently as they sway in the night breeze, the distant burble of a burn in the distance.

'You should run,' a voice whispers directly in my ear and I jump, turning, but there's no one there; there's nothing except a tendril of mist. It sounds exactly like the voice I heard in the car. I push Cillian back, looking around and seeing nothing but the approaching mist.

'What is it?' Cillian asks. I don't answer, but I push away from him taking a couple of steps towards the forest path. It's clearer than anywhere else, and somehow I know that the mist is there to help me, to show me which way to go.

'He's going to hunt you down and then...' Another voice whispers in my other ear. 'Well, I guess we'll find out.' The voices chuckle and I swallow nervously.

I shake my head. Have the drugs mixed with the Stox messed up my brain? Am I hallucinating? Or is it sheer exhaustion? Or is it plain and simple fear making me imagine voices in the mist. In fact, am I imagining the mist? Cillian doesn't seem to have noticed it. He's staring at me, watching as I get closer to the path that he wanted me to run down.

I look around just in case there are actually people here

that I just haven't noticed before. The mist swirls and moves, coalescing in places, almost as if there are figures obscured by it. I close my eyes and open them slowly. Maybe I'm going crazy? This is a dream and I've imagined the whole night, right?

'He wants to make you his queen.' Another voice speaks as I try to twist away from it. 'But he can't. He wants to be king.'

'You're not one of us. He couldn't be the Huntsman anymore.'

'No! She killed Kin. He's already giving her more of a chance than she deserves.' The last voice carries far more authority than any of the others, but the words sound like they're signalling my death.

'There are thin places in the forest.' This voice, at least, sounds friendlier. 'Perhaps the Huntsman is right. Could she survive the hunt, find sanctuary? She would need to reach the Underworld first.'

'She doesn't know how to move through a thin place.'

I clamp my hands over my ears and squeeze my eyes closed.

'What is it?' Cillian asks. 'What are you doing?'

'There are voices in the mist,' I whisper.

'What mist?' he frowns. 'Niamh?'

'Are you the Huntsman?'

His eyes narrow, but he nods.

'How do I reach the Underworld?'

CHAPTER 12
CILLIAN

'What the fuck are you talking about?' I ask her, even though I know, I just don't understand how she does. She wasn't conscious when we talked about it earlier.

'You told me I might find sanctuary but the voices. They said it's in the Underworld and I don't know how to go through a thin place.' Tears slide down her cheeks as I stride towards her, taking her in my arms.

She's right, there are thin places in these woods, and with help, she could pass through to the Underworld. Even if I took her through now, there's no guarantee she'd reach the sanctuary, and if I hunt her in the Underworld there are so many more dangers to be faced. The Wild Hunt might have to wait until dawn to chase her, but there are other creatures in these woods who are not bound by any such magic. There's no guarantee she would even find the sanctuary. I can give her the words that will allow her entrance but will they allow a human to enter? It's not something I have ever heard of. We simply deal with the humans who cross us, decisively, and move on. None that I've hunted have made it to dawn.

A swift death at my hands may still be her best hope for tonight. Although, it's clear there's something strange going on here. Something that I can't see. Which means that if there's magic, it's been carefully crafted. For her to be seeing and hearing things that I can't – that takes power that no one at The Unseelie Court at present holds. But where else can it come from? The Seelie Court has lain abandoned for over a century.

There is, however, a simple alternative.

'You were drugged,' I assure her, although I'm not convinced that's all that's going on here. 'You're confused.'

She shakes her head. 'No, I heard them, voices in the mist. You're supposed to hunt me down. Although no one seems to know what will happen if I get away from you. If I do, will I end up in the Underworld? Or is it just for criminals like you?' She stops, frowning, and then her lips part in some kind of realisation. 'Oh, that Underworld. Yeah, I ... I guess it's just the drugs.'

I hate that she looks so confused, so defeated. And her words should sting, but they're true. In the Underworld of the Kinfolk, however, I'm not a criminal – quite the opposite, in fact – although the longer I have to enforce Vincenzo's bad decisions, the more I feel my position is being tainted and abused.

'What else did the voices say?'

She stares up at me, a crease between her eyebrows.

'They said you couldn't rule if you— If you're with me. It doesn't matter, none of it made any sense.'

That is dangerously specific, too specific to be drug-addled imaginings. She can't possibly know anything about my place at The Unseelie Court. Rose would never have told her. And yet, it is that very thing that is keeping us apart, that which has forced my engagement to Vittoria.

I pin her in place with my body. She tries to escape my embrace, a blush spreading across her cheeks as she feels my erection pressing against her thigh, but I'm not letting her go until I understand what's happening.

The way she's trembling calls to the Huntsman inside me, the Kinfolk side of my nature that I have always kept controlled and hidden when I've seen her in the human world. None of this helped by Vittoria pre-empting my kill earlier and our interrupted time in the club.

The voices weren't wrong. I did bring her here to hunt, and the way she's pulling away from me only makes those instincts come to the fore. I want her to run. But I'm still not sure that when I catch her, I'm going to be able to kill her. I have wanted her for so long and keeping away from her has only made me want her more. We have what's left of the night, after all. What would be the harm in taking my time. Filling her remaining time with pleasure, rather than an adrenalin-fuelled chase? No, there's a line to be drawn there. There is no way I could do that and then kill her, but neither can I leave her to the tender mercies of the Wild Hunt. Not to mention that it takes away her chance of reaching sanctuary.

I slide a hand up her arm and capture her throat. Her pulse

hammers under my fingers and her breath catches as I tighten my grip. This is when she should be screaming for help, telling me no, kicking me in the balls and running. But she doesn't. And even if she did, she'd be playing right into my darkest fantasies.

Her eyes stay fixed on mine, widening with fear, but also with desire. I run my other hand down her body, round the curve of her arse so she can't help but feel how much I want her.

'Will you let me live if I let you...' Her body trembles as she puts one arm around my neck and pulls my face down to hers, kissing me with a lot more finesse than she did that very first night we met. Her lips are chilled, but when I force them to part for me, her mouth is warm and wet and willing. I kiss her in the exact way I always want to, slow and deep, my tongue tasting her, the desperation in my senses clouding my judgement. I want her. I need to have her.

She whimpers as I move the hand on her arse down over her hip and catch the hem of her dress, pulling it up so that I can slip my fingers inside her underwear. I tear my mouth away from hers, kissing her urgently down the side of her neck, across her throat, my teeth sinking into the curve of her shoulder. She tilts her head back, gasping, and I run my lips up her throat, nipping along the line of her jaw.

Her hand slides around my waist, pauses for a moment, then she pushes it between our bodies, spreading her fingers over my cock, which hardens even further under her touch. I want to drag her to the ground, strip the ruined, bloody dress off her body and thrust inside her. And then do that over and over again until she's shattered around me and I've filled her with my cum, claiming her in the most primitive way a man can claim a woman.

But then I'll still need to kill her.

She pulls her lips away from mine, her breathing shallow and uneven. Her lips are parted, but she closes them slowly, her tongue running along them as she does. I watch as her eyes flicker open, filled with lust, and she stares at me, and I realise it's not fair for me to think of her as pure. I've simply never given her the chance to learn, explore her own sexuality with someone her own age, someone who might have loved her and given her all the normal things I can't.

'Please, Cillian, please don't kill me. I'll not breathe a word to anyone. Ever. I'll just disappear from your lives. You'll never see me again. Please, you can trust me.' She falls to her knees, clasping her hands in front of her.

'That's not possible, Niamh.' I look down at her thinking of what I would much rather be doing with her there.

'I promise you can trust me. Cillian!'

But I shake my head. The guilt would get the better of her, eventually. 'You're too good a person. Too honest. You'd go to the police. Want closure. Be overcome with guilt.'

'No, the things they were going to do to me... They deserved ... he deserved to die, so that he wouldn't do it to anyone else.' She wrings her hands for a moment, then the breath huffs out of her and she sinks back onto her heels, staring at me. 'Cillian?'

I force myself to take a step back and then another.

There's fear in those midnight-blue eyes, but also something else. Curiosity. I shake my head. What the fuck am I thinking? Is she only doing this, only allowing this because she's offering herself up to me in exchange for her life? And while I don't want to kill her, the alternatives, don't bear thinking about.

At least I won't let her suffer. Although in bringing her here and prolonging this, I've already made her suffer more than I should have. Initially, I was stalling for time, hoping I would find another way. When I drove out here with her in the boot of my car, it felt like something was drawing me to these woods, and I hoped against hope that a solution would present itself. But a hunt has been called and a hunt, with everything that entails, will happen.

'What will you say to Rose?'

I shake my head slowly. 'Rose won't remember a thing, she'll think you've just disappeared.'

She swallows and I can almost see her mind whirring, trying to find something else to bargain with.

'She won't believe that. She knows me well enough to know I wouldn't just leave.'

'Rose will understand that you've left to protect her and our family.' I don't add that this is something Rose already knows all too well.

Her face falls, uncertainty causing her to frown.

'Cillian,' she whispers. 'I ... I'll do anything.'

Now that, I almost believe, although when she flicks the torn strap of her dress over her shoulder, then pulls the other one slowly down her bare arm, I realise I've misinterpreted her words. She pauses, and swallows before taking hold of the top of the barely-there dress and starts to pull it down over her breasts. I already know she's not wearing a bra from when I cleaned her up, but the skin beneath her dress is smeared with the blood where it has soaked through.

I should tell her to stop, let her go. But I don't want to.

Niamh is blushing so hard I can almost feel the heat radiating off her skin. I don't want to resist what she's offering, regardless of why. I take her hands off her dress and kiss her again. I cup her breast with one hand, feeling her jerk in my arms as my thumb circles her nipple. I kiss down her throat, loving the way she lifts her head, the upward stretch pushing her breasts eagerly against me.

I kiss across her collarbone, using a nail to flick the tight peak of one nipple before my fingers tighten on it and pinch. She cries out, as all my blood flows from my brain to my cock, leaving me as much a victim of desire as she is. I lift my head to take her mouth again, but pause as I notice her necklace against her pale skin. I've seen it before, a red garnet in the shape of a heart against a gold oval, but I don't remember the delicate filigree tracery on the solid surface of the gold.

I touch the stone with my finger, feeling it pulse. If I didn't know better, I'd think it was made by Kinfolk, although not by any of the artisans I'm familiar with. But that's impossible.

'Where did you get this?' I ask, sliding my palm beneath it and lifting it up.

'My mother.'

'It's pretty.'

No, looking at it more closely, I realise I'm mistaken. The stone didn't pulse, there is no filigree on the gold. I shake my head and let it fall back against Niamh's pale skin. And the moment is gone, washed away in a sea of guilt.

'You shouldn't let me do this,' I say, pulling her dress back up, enjoying the feel of her skin against my hands even as I awkwardly pull the straps back onto her shoulders. Tonight isn't about Cillian Hunter. Tonight, I am the Unseelie Huntsman and I have a duty to fulfil. With every moment that passes, my human persona is slipping away, giving precedence to the Huntsman, making way for my duty to The Unseelie Court.

'I don't want to die. Tell me what it'll take to...' She's staring up at me, no longer at my face, but at just beyond that, to where I can feel the aura of Cernunnos materialising. The god of the hunt wears the antlers of the mightiest, most noble prey in this land that he hunted and killed with his bare hands. He wears its antlers and hide to celebrate his victory, his dominance over nature. I would rather dominate Niamh in any way but the way fate has forced me.

Niamh reaches up as if to touch the antlers, then lets her hand drop. But she can't possibly see them. No human should be able to see the embodiment of. It's simply not possible. Or is it? After all, the *Guth Dorcha* didn't work on her, not when I used it, not when Vittoria used it. But how? Has she spent so much time with Rose that she's become sensitive to our world? Aiden's background check didn't throw up any prior links and everything about her tells me that she's human.

'What does it mean for you to hunt me?' she asks, her eyes wide and terrified.

'The evidence presented to the Court already has established your guilt.' I shrug. 'You get a chance to run. I hunt you down.'

'And if you catch me?'

'*When* I catch you,' I correct. 'When I catch you, it's considered proof of your guilt and I'll ... I'll know what to do.'

'But what?' I can see in her eyes, however, that she already knows.

'I'm the Huntsman, Niamh. Dispensing the Court's justice... It's what I do.'

'Please, Cillian,' she whispers. 'I don't want to die. I saved Rose. Don't you owe me something for that?'

Guilt fills me. I know she's right. What can I say? But the man here in the woods with her is not simply Cillian. I'm the Kennard of my Kin. I sit on one of the eight remaining thrones of The Unseelie Court. I'm honour-bound to keep the Kinfolk safe by sacrificing... her. When I don't respond, tears well in her eyes and spill unchecked as we stare at one another.

I close my eyes, regret filling my entire being. How the fuck did we end up here? This is the worst possible outcome I could have imagined.

Well, maybe not the worst – she could have ended up in the Rialis' hands.

She shakes her head over and over and over, her eyes wide and terrified. 'No. No, please. Don't you... Don't you want...'

'Oh, I want, Niamh. I want very much,' I say, reaching for the crossbow slung over my shoulder. 'I just can't have.'

'You're going to shoot me? With that?' She's held onto her dignity so far, but I can see just how close she is to breaking. But she doesn't break. Her whole body is trembling, but her gaze doesn't falter and I see the sort of backbone she would have had as a lawyer.

'Cillian,' Niamh whispers, falling to her knees in front of me. She doesn't bow her head, she's not giving in to this. She's begging, hoping to appeal to the man she thought was me. I push him away and lock him down to do what has to be done.

I reach for her and haul her roughly to her feet. Then find I can't let go. Her eyes are clouded with confusion, mist swirling around in their depths.

I've looked into these eyes so very many times before, although not enough. I have a feeling that even a lifetime with Niamh would never have been enough. But our time is already up. It has to be.

Can I do what I have to do? Vittoria isn't wrong, it's what The Unseelie Court demands. Humans cannot be allowed to kill Kin. I have no choice. I stare down at her. Her eyes widen as I step back and raise the crossbow. She backs away from me until she's facing me across the clearing. A small path behind her leads into the depths of the forest. Tears are flowing down her face, and I can't break her gaze.

'Cillian?' she whimpers.

'I'm sorry, Niamh. I'm so fucking sorry. I should be down on my knees thanking you for saving Rose and instead—' I break off.

I swing the crossbow into position and brace myself.

I swallow, my hand trembling for an instant, then I get it together. She's only one woman, and there is so much more at stake here. She takes another step back and moonlight falls across her pale face. But no matter how much I deny it, there's something about her. Something I don't fully understand. I nock a bolt with practised precision, raise it and ... pause.

Fuck. I really have found a line I cannot cross.

If she were Kin, she would have a chance to reach sanctuary before dawn. As a human, Niamh is unlikely to even reach the Underworld even though these woods are full of thin places. But without help, she doesn't know how to use them and without the necessary words, she won't be allowed into the sanctuary even if she finds it.

There's a crashing sound from the woods in front of me and we both turn to watch as a huge white stag races towards us from the forest path. It skids to a halt at the edge of the clearing, right beside Niamh. It looks between us, perhaps trying to decide which of us is the bigger threat. Then the majestic animal looks over at Niamh before bowing its head, as if in acceptance of its sacrifice. I settle the stock against my shoulder, metal cold on my cheek as I align my eye with the sight. I steady my aim with a deep breath, my finger poised, ready to let loose the bolt.

'Run!' I yell at Niamh as I release the bolt. She turns and races down the forest path behind her, her footsteps a steady thud on the hard-packed surface of compressed pine needles as I pause, take a deep breath, aim, and let the bolt fly.

The deer stares at me, red blossoming between its eyes as it crumples to the forest floor, the bolt lodged directly between its eyes. I stand still listening to her footsteps recede into the depths of the forest, and a feeling sweeps through me that I struggle to name. And then I realise what it is. Joy. My mouth curves into a rare smile at the thought that she's still breathing. Even if she's running from me and in fear of her life.

I check that it's a clean kill. I'll come back later to deal with the deer, but for now I hide the carcass with Glamour and allow my primal instincts to rise to the surface and prepare to hunt.

I take a deep breath, standing and drawing myself to my full height to ensure I release the last of the Glamour that keeps me from appearing fully human. There's no need for that while I hunt in these dark woods. I'm torn between my instincts, which are revelling in the thought of a hunt, and my sorrow at the fact that it's Niamh I'm hunting.

I listen. She's running quickly. Too fast to keep it up for long. And I know that won't be her strategy – it's not in her nature to run. No, she's a negotiator by choice. That's easy to see, although she's not stupid enough to stand and face me yet. No. She'll hide, watch, try to turn things around and gain the upper hand with knowledge. Then attempt to persuade me to do things differently. It's what she's trained for, after all. But none of that will work against me. I can track her wherever she hides and outpace her in speed. And when I catch her, I'm going to take what's mine.

CHAPTER 13
NIAMH

I don't stop to think. I run.

I neither know nor care where I'm headed, as long as it's away from Cillian – and I'm not sure if it's because I'm worried that he's going to kill me or kiss me. My lungs burn as I run through the dark, twisting forest. The air is thick with the scent of pine and fir, and damp, mouldering earth. At first the path is clear, solid underfoot. But the further I run into the woods, the thicker the layer of pine needles ready to slide out from under me and the softer the ground. Branches scrape my face as I stumble over tree roots and my feet catch in tufts of undergrowth. The pounding of my soles on the spongy ground thuds through my body, ragged breath filling my ears, so very loud in the night air, punctuated every so often with the memory of that one word.

Run!

My heart is racing, a combination of the physical exertion and the fear gnawing at my insides. The events of tonight play in my head. Except, not all of my memories are a nightmare.

Aiden carried me in the alley, Vittoria held my chin as she whispered the words I now know were a spell, but after that, every touch has been Cillian's, every kiss has been Cillian's. I can't forget how his tongue demanded entrance to my mouth, the feel of his lips on my skin as he kissed down my throat and the sensations that ran through me as he touched my breasts. The warmth that pooled between my legs as he took what he wanted from me.

Right before he pulled a fucking crossbow on me.

I slap my hand over my mouth, although I guess when you're running for your life, swearing is acceptable.

The memory of staring at the bolt poised in the crossbow triggers another flight response, and my legs pump harder. It's darker in this part of the forest. The night sky is no longer visible and my breath clouds in erratic puffs as I run. The mist is growing more and more dense, as if each of my breaths is adding to it and it's becoming a living thing with tendrils creeping along the ground that I might soon have to jump over rather than run through.

I scream as one foot slides badly on a patch of mud, stones and rotting leaves and I land on one knee for just an instant before I push back to my feet and carry on, a little less confident, and in a lot more pain. I force myself to keep going, my body screaming in protest. Am I running towards safety or deeper into danger? I'm not going to slow down to find out.

And then, suddenly, I break through the treeline, stumbling out of the woods into a barren landscape of gorse and rough, heather-clad ground. Gasping for air, I collapse onto the damp grass, close my eyes, and let out a shuddering breath. Everything hurts, especially my chest, and I don't feel as if I'll ever be able to breathe normally again. My palms are scraped, my knees bruised, and all my exposed skin is covered in a tapestry of red lines – scraped by thorns and brambles, and bitten by ever-present midges. Do the little bastards ever stop?

I curl into a ball and focus on simply breathing in and out. In and out, with no idea how long it is before I open my eyes. There's a little light now in the eastern sky as I stare back into the dark forest, trying to work out if he's followed me. If I'm still in danger. I shiver and wrap my arms around myself. It's so cold, now that I'm not running. I know in my heart that it's pointless anyway. I won't be able to outrun him forever. He'll catch me and then...

A shiver runs through me as I remember watching as he pulled the crossbow from behind his back like some kind of slasher-movie psycho. I could have sworn it wasn't even there just a second before. His eyes ... they'd been cold, empty. I'd thought he was going to ... I really thought... Panic grips me once more. I can't wait here. I need to keep moving, keep running, to make sure he doesn't catch me. Because he'll kill me if he does. Or will he? I can't quite get my head around that fact. One thing I am sure of is that he didn't want to. He killed the deer, when he could have killed me. He's given me a chance to run. To reach the sanctuary. Wherever that is.

I take a deep breath and try to stand, but my head is still reeling. Instead, I scoot backwards to lean against a tree, my head between my knees, until the waves of dizziness pass. The way he touched me, the way he kissed me, is all I can think about. Why? Why did I let him? But deep down, I know that I would have let him do so much more; I wanted so much more. What the hell is wrong with me?

Cillian is dangerous. I saw that with my own eyes tonight, and yet... And yet, I'm still alive. And it seemed like he was struggling to keep his hands off me. Cillian Hunter, who could have any woman he wanted. I sigh, realising I may just be one of those women. I wonder if he's killed any of the others? Vittoria, at least is still alive. What on earth have I found myself in the middle of?

Gradually, my breathing slows, the cold and the damp from the ground chilling my flesh. The heat generated from running is slipping away and I shiver. New sounds begin to emerge from the soft rustling of the trees and the gentle babbling of a nearby stream – the scurrying feet of small creatures, the tiny chirps of fledglings in their nests, the insistent chirps of the bats flying erratically around the clearing.

And then a steady rhythmic thud emerges, punctuated by the occasional snap of branches, the deep breaths of a seasoned runner. He maintains his pace even over the uneven ground, so I guess I got that wrong. Not to mention everything else about the Hunters. I stare back towards the forest. The sounds are bouncing off trees, making it hard to pinpoint where he's coming from. But there is no doubt that he's coming. He's tracked me down. And if he's the hunter, I can only be the prey.

I roll over, tucking myself beneath the jagged branches

and bright yellow flowers of a late-flowering gorse. My breath catches at the pain when I roll over rough stones on the ground and sharp gorse spines pierce my bare skin, catching on the fabric of my dress and leaving red scrapes across my body. I pull the worst of them out, keeping my movements as small as possible so as not to give away my position. I hold still as the footsteps slow and Cillian comes into view at the edge of the clearing.

He looks around, stares upwards at the moon in the sky above us. I blink at the sight of the antlers visible again behind his head. Maybe none of this is real? But the pain of the needles reminds me that this is happening.

He strolls into the middle of the clearing, his expression grim.

'I know you're here, Niamh. I can smell your fear.'

I swallow, trying not to breathe as he brushes a speck of something from the lapel of his jacket. At least his hands are empty, no sign of either the crossbow or the knife. He stares upwards, stretching his spine, cricking his neck from side to side.

'It'll be so much easier for you if you just come out,' he says.

But maybe I can stay frozen forever and he'll get bored and go home. Yeah, like that's going to happen. A man like Cillian isn't going to give up and let someone like me win. Part of me wants to crawl out from my hiding place and beg again for mercy. But I've tried that already, offered him the only thing I have left to give, and he didn't take it.

Tears run down my face, I can't give up – can't surrender to this man without a fight, even if I know I won't win. I have to at least try and find this sanctuary. I wipe the tears from my face as carefully as I can, but when I look back into the clearing, he's staring directly at me. And he smiles.

I don't think. I just react and roll in the opposite direction from him, pushing to my feet as soon as I clear the gorse bush and racing away as fast as I can with the thick undergrowth pulling at my limbs. It slows his progress as much as it does mine until there's another path in front of me and I run and run and run.

I'm not sure if what I can hear is my own thudding footsteps, my heart beating or his. But it's not long before I sense him behind me, his breath on my neck. A large hand grabs me, and I'm yanked backwards. My feet leave the ground instantly, but as I fall, he twists us both around so that he hits the ground first, his body cushioning mine.

He grunts as his back slams against the ground and instinctively I roll off him. But he anticipates the move, shifting his hips to roll with me and my back slams onto the ground instead. He moves over me, his weight pinning me, even as I try to scramble out from under him. He grabs my wrist, trapping it against the ground above my head. Then he grabs the other, placing it in the same hold. Panic floods through me as I buck and roll and fight, but it's hopeless, nothing works.

But I refuse to give in, even when I realise that it's not a gun in his pocket pressing into my inner thigh. I continue trying to throw him off me, increasingly conscious that those movements are only serving to arouse him more and more. I try to bring my knee up, determined not to make his conquest of me easy. But he barely makes a move before I've exhausted myself and my body grows still, trapped beneath his, my movements subdued, limited to the rapid rise and fall of my chest. The ground is cold underneath me, leaching the last remaining heat from my skin.

'Please,' I whisper when he pulls back. His erection presses into my core, and I move against it, seeking ... something. I writhe underneath him, cursing my body for always responding to his in ways that I find confusing and arousing.

'Please, what?' he asks. 'What is it that you want?'

I try to find an answer. What do I want? Right here, right now, I want him. He's proven himself in the most primal way, chased me down and captured me and now I want him to take me, make me his. Forever. But I shouldn't want that.

'Earlier ... I would have let you... But you didn't. And now... Please don't kill me. I don't want to die,' I say instead.

His expression hardens. What did he think I was going to say? That I wanted him to fuck me? Just saying the crude words in my head reminds me that we don't see this act in the same way.

'That's it? Your only request?'

I nod and he tightens his grip on my wrists. I whimper as the welts reopen, covering his fingers with fresh blood.

'So, I can do anything else I want to you, so long as I don't kill you?'

'Y-yes.' Why does that sound so much more like a promise than threat?

'You don't mean that.'

'I do,' I whisper. Maybe I do mean it. I've kissed other guys over the years, but each and every one of them has simply disappeared out of my life as soon as things looked like they might go further. Not that any other man has ever made me want this the way Cillian does. But how can I want him to do that when he brought me out to kill me? Maybe in my own way, I'm just as messed up as he is. I stare up at him, and he gazes down at me confusion in his eyes.

'Niamh,' he whispers. 'I want you just like this. Scared and restrained so I can do whatever I want to you – your pain bringing me pleasure. That isn't something you should want.'

'Why do you get to decide what I want?' I glare up at him. 'My mother told me to stay away from you. And Rose. That people like you were different.'

He looks at me for a moment, then laughs.

'And how right she was.'

'But what I want, that's my choice to make, not anyone else's.' I shift my hips against his erection, his groan making me feel powerful despite the way he's restraining me. He bends his head to trail a line of kisses from my ear along my jawline. I shiver, pressing closer to him. Our lips meet again, hungrier than before, our hands tearing and pulling at clothing, seeking out bare flesh to touch.

I part my legs, and he pulls my knee up so that he can nestle more easily between my thighs. He gazes down at me as he slowly, methodically grinds himself against me. Those shadowy antlers are visible again like some kind of aura around his head.

'Who are you?' I manage to ask between breaths. This can't be real. Slowly, I pull one hand from his grasp and lift it to brush my fingers through the place where the antlers seem to be. They brush against a solid surface. Impossible. It's the drugs or my exhaustion or else this really is a dream. 'What ... what are you?'

'Niamh?' He sits back on his heels and takes my hands in his, pulling me up. Movement draws my attention to his wrist, and I watch as the tattoo of the snake takes form beneath my fingers, writhing around before the head and upper body twist around my finger and it hisses at me, baring its fangs, and then strikes. I yank my arms out of his hold and scream.

What the actual hell?

Cillian jerks in surprise, the serpent disappearing back into the flat ink of the tattoo as we stare at it. He moves back a little, and as his weight lifts, my adrenaline surges and I kick my foot up as hard as I can, not caring where it lands. His face creases in pain and a strangled 'oof' escapes his lips. Then I'm rolling out from under him and scrambling away. Off and running again. And this time, I'm determined not to let him catch me.

The feel of the serpent coiling its head around my finger. The pain radiating from the two puncture wounds. What the hell is he? Or is it me? Am I the one going mad? I keep running and as I run, I send up a brief prayer to St Jude – he loves a lost cause.

CHAPTER 14
CILLIAN

'Ugh.' I roll over, agony radiating out from where she kicked me. Fuck, I was utterly unprepared for that. I didn't even consider she'd have the strength, so it's going to take me a few moments to recover. As I wait for the pain to subside, I study my tattoos. The serpent on my left wrist and the tattoo of Cernunnos on my chest were completed when I took over as head of my Kin – alongside the hunting horn on my other arm. They mark a sign of leadership and power, and the pigmentation is so strong because it's made from plants found only in the Underworld.

But why and how did the serpent embody like that? It's never come alive before. And it certainly shouldn't have been able to bite a human. But the way Niamh stared at it earlier, she definitely saw something, and that should just not be possible – unless she's been consuming large quantities of—

'Fuck,' I mutter, realising she and Rose had been drinking all night and if Niamh has consumed large quantities of Stox, together with whatever drug – possibly one from the

Underworld – that her attackers gave her, it might explain why the *Guth Dorcha* didn't work, why she seems to be sensing more, seeing more, than I would expect a human to. Or maybe I'm clutching at straws right now, trying to come up with reasons as to why she deserves to be saved. She's defying all my expectations, maybe she could have a chance. Could I take her through to the Underworld, lead her to St Marnox and give her the words she needs to claim sanctuary?

By the time I'm back on my feet, Niamh has crossed the clearing and reached the edge of the forest on the opposite side. She disappears into the dense treeline as I pick up my pace again, determined to find her once more. There are thin places nearby, and Kinfolk only heard of in myths and legends are ready to trap and kill the unwary who wander through them and I'm now convinced that if any human is going to find one and be capable of stepping through, it'll be Niamh.

As I run, I can't stop thinking about the endless possibilities of what might happen to her. What if I'm too late?

I have to accept that there's already a greater power guiding the events of tonight. The white stag appearing just as I was making that final choice to shoot her was no coincidence. Perfectly positioned in my eyeline, I had a clear shot, and I realise it could provide me with a heart to present to Vittoria if necessary. Proof that I have followed through on the demands of being Huntsman and proving that I am worthy of becoming king.

My first priority, however, is to find her. By the time I reach the point where she disappeared into the woods, a thick mist has descended, making it impossible for me to see more than a metre in front of me. Despite my heightened hearing and sharp senses, the mist deadens any sound, too, making my progress much slower than I'd like.

Niamh saw the mist before I did, which concerns me. As Huntsman I should always be one step ahead of my prey. Her knowledge has given her power, something which I'm not comfortable with. At least it's now finally revealing itself to me, but Kinfolk magic is definitely protecting Niamh. I take a deep breath in through my nose, close my eyes and let my senses guide me – my Kin have little in the way of actual magic beyond Glamour, the *Guth Dorcha* and the speed and strength of Cernunnos, but my tracking abilities in reading my surroundings will help me search for her. After all, I have hunted in these woods more times than she has ever been here.

I have hunted all my life, been the Court's Huntsman for almost a decade since my father's untimely death. This is the way I prefer to hunt – the prey I prefer to track down is exactly the one I'm after tonight. Not deer or other wildlife. No, I prefer to leave them to go about their lives for the most part. The chase that really appeals to me, that gives me pure satisfaction, is when my wits are pitted against another person, be they human or Kin. And tonight, there's the added dimension that I'm pursuing a woman I desire, a woman I'm sure will submit to me willingly the next time I catch her.

The mist grows thicker and thicker the deeper I go into the forest. I stop when I reach a fork, trying to decide which path to follow – both obscured by the mist. I take a step towards the left, but the coiled serpent inked around my wrist tightens. I turn to the right and it relaxes, assuring me I'm heading in the right direction and that someone is definitely using Kinfolk magic to help Niamh escape. A few steps further on, I can smell the slightest trace of her vanilla perfume and hear a whisper that might be her breath in the distance.

As I move ever closer to finding her, I'm reminded of Vittoria's view that Niamh's appearance in our lives marks the beginning of so much upheaval for us. At first, I dismissed this as ridiculous, but now I'm wondering if she has a point. Is there more to the situation than just the simple fact that she met my sister on her first day at university? The timing is certainly interesting.

I've always considered it to be Chris's death that cemented my doubts about the Rialis' rule and their increasingly selfish decision-making. I believed Matt when he told me he was innocent, I just never understood why Chris would kill himself, although I do understand Vincenzo wanting to cover it up. But now, I'm beginning to wonder if Vittoria is right, and it was meeting Niamh that triggered everything. That something in that meeting was always destined to change the course of our lives? But that's ridiculous. She has no prior connection to the Kinfolk world. Aiden has double-checked.

But since that night, I have lost faith in Vincenzo's rule and his lack of interest that something, possibly the Blight, is destroying the integrity of The Unseelie Court. There's been so many cases where justice fell in the Rialis' favour for no apparent reason. So many Kinfolk I've hunted down for reasons I didn't agree with, my sense of duty to The Unseelie Court being stretched impossibly thin at times.

Maybe it's more than a coincidence. Could there be something else at play? This evening was supposed to have been about cementing the future of the Riali and Hunter families. And what have I done instead? I've chased another woman – a human, no less – through woods bordering on the Underworld, and then managed to lose her. But there's Kinfolk magic on her side. Perhaps even enough to protect her from me, or from the Wild Hunt if she finds a way herself into the Underworld and to the sanctuary.

I take a few deep breaths, trying to make a decision. I remember the way her necklace glowed, patterns reminiscent of Seelie magic forming on its surface. I shake away the thoughts. It's just wishful thinking. If she was Kin, then I could marry her without giving up my role as Huntsman. But Niamh is human – there is nothing to suggest otherwise.

Up ahead, I hear voices and speed up my steps. In front of me, the mist has thickened even further and it's clouding my senses, suffocating me. Its source must be magical. Every step feels like I'm pushing through a barrier. It doesn't hurt, but I don't feel good doing it. I stop for a moment and turn around. Behind me, the mist is clearing, the earthen path appears more visible, the tree roots separate to form a route away from the overgrown, dense vegetation I've been pushing my way through. Letting out a frustrated growl, I turn around and force myself through the mist, determined that it won't stop me reaching my prize.

And then the atmosphere around me changes, the mist

still there, still solid but ahead of me I can see the faint shimmer of a thin place. I pause, trying to work out whether to go through or not, but if Niamh has, I need to follow. I place my hands on the shimmering doorway and pass through. Almost too late, I hear the sound of running water and pull up short on the bank of a stream. In front of me is a shallow fording point, the only visible way to cross.

'You're a stubborn man,' a female voice says. 'But you'll want to watch your feet.'

I take a step back as an old woman appears in front of me, as if formed from the mist itself. She's seated next to the ford, on the other side of the stream, a basket full of washing and a large wooden basin beside her. I know her.

'Careful now,' the *Bean Nighe* warns, flapping a large white sheet. She has an old worn plaid shawl draped around her head and shoulders, leaving her arms bare to do her washing. Panic claws at my throat as I consider what might have happened to Niamh if she passed by this washerwoman – the *Bean Nighe*, the washerwoman of death.

'Where is she?'

'Gone.'

My heart stutters in my chest.

'Gone?'

The *Bean Nighe* looks up at me and smiles, a dark and menacing toothless grin that sends a chill down my spine. 'Ah, well, that's unexpected.'

'What?'

'You're concerned whether the Whyte girl got herself wrapped up in my sheets aren't you? Odd when you brought her out here to kill her.'

'Did I?' Why am I putting my motives in doubt? The old woman might be Kin, but she's nothing like me. She's from a world beyond the Underworld. A world reached only through death. She knows more about how The Unseelie Court functions than I can ever hope to, and if she passes on the fact that I wasn't going to do my duty—

'She didn't, by the way. You passed her, reached this place first. But she will cross the stream.'

My heart starts to beat again. Confirmation that Niamh is still alive is probably the best thing that's going to come out of this interaction. The washerwoman is a harbinger of death. She's not the only one in the Underworld, but she is the one I know of who is more than just a harbinger – she can *cause* death, too. Her washing may make her look innocent, but her cloths are shrouds and if one touches you, you're marked for death. And not a quick death either. That would be too convenient. You won't know when or where but fear will follow your every step until you go mad, begging for an end as she draws her power from every second of your fear. Even as Huntsman, I am not immune to her deadly tricks and despite the distance between us, I know she could condemn me to death if she wanted to.

'Here?'

But the *Bean Nighe* doesn't answer.

'I thought you and the Riali girl were getting married, going to unite two of our remaining Unseelie Kin, bringing our numbers down to only seven Kin left at Court.'

'That's the plan,' Confused by her change of subject, I nod, mindful of keeping her on side.

'And you hope to be the next king?'

'If I'm acceptable to The Unseelie Court, yes.'

She looks up at me, her paper-thin skin almost translucent. Why is she telling me this? She nods and returns to her work, scrubbing a sheet in her basin, then dunking it in the stream to rinse it. My patience is wearing thin as I'm aware the longer I'm caught up here, the further Niamh will be from me – however much I don't want to anger the *Bean Nighe*. I need her permission to cross the stream, otherwise I'm not going to be able to catch up with Niamh on time.

'And try to stop the Blight?' she asks.

'If I can, yes. Vincenzo lets it continue unchecked.'

'I predict identical twin boys. One to rule each family in the next generation.'

An image forms clearly in my head, two boys who grow quickly, handsome, strong. But then they smile at me and as their lips curve upwards, their mouths open and Blight pours from inside them, covering them, devouring them until there is nothing left. She smiles at me and I try not to recoil at the sight.

'No?'

'I'm the Kennard of the Hunter Kin, *Bean Nighe*. I don't base my decisions on other people's visions.'

'Maybe you should.' She smirks at me, squeezing the water from her sheet and flicking it up before returning it to the murky waters below.

'Are you going to let me pass?'

'You're welcome to try your luck,' she taunts, repeating the move as I watch her. She's seated next to a fording point. Any attempt to cross is likely to result in me being touched by the sheet, and if I'm going to die, it's not going to be because

I got taken down by a washerwoman – even a Kinfolk one with ties to The Unseelie Court.

'There are questions you could be asking, Huntsman,' the *Bean Nighe* says, continuing with her task.

'Would you answer them?' I challenge her.

'Yes.'

'Honestly?'

But she just laughs. I look along the stream, into the darkness but I can feel that dawn is close. Fuck it. I may as well try asking questions. The *Bean Nighe*'s reaction may give something away, even if her answers don't.

'What will happen to her?'

The *Bean Nighe* chuckles. 'Silly boy, that is a question that no one can answer yet.'

'Where is she?'

'She still has time to reach sanctuary.'

'But she's not Kin, she cannot enter.'

The *Bean Nighe* looks around at the quiet, mist-filled landscape. 'Strange things happen, Cillian. Many humans find their way into the Underworld and whether or not they should be able to do so, the fact is that they do. Niamh has already found a way into the Underworld. Human ... or not.'

'You helped her to pass through?'

'Not I.'

I should have known the *Bean Nighe* would only speak in riddles. 'Then how? And why did the *Guth Dorcha* not work? She remembered everything.'

The *Bean Nighe* just laughs. 'You know already, Cillian. You just keep forgetting. There's more magic in this world than Unseelie magic.'

I frown at her. 'But The Seelie Court is gone, destroyed by the Blight. The only magic left is ours.'

'The Tree of Life can be healed when its roots are strong. A king should know this.'

I frown at her, shaking my head. 'Nothing has worked to reverse the Blight.'

She pulls another sheet from her basket and dumps it into the water. 'Nothing that the Rialis have done. Nothing ... yet. Now, I have work to do, Cillian. Niamh is heading this way and I don't want you scaring her off. Life and death is an ongoing process. You need to stop believing what you think you know. The Rialis hide truth in their lies and lies in their truth.'

'Will she be safe there?'

'The rules of sanctuary apply to all who have the right words to enter. She is safe inside its walls, from you as well as others who would harm her.'

'She's a human who killed Kin. She'll never be able to leave. The Court will find her guilty.'

'Then it's just as well your family have been tasked with the duty of overseeing the sanctuary, isn't it? Enforcing the rules. As the only Kinfolk able to enter you'll be able to visit her. If she wants to see you. But it's time to stop dawdling here. Someone wants Niamh dead. Someone wants her alive.'

'And I need to work out who?'

'No, you need to work out why. You're not listening, Cillian. Only a fool doesn't listen when death itself speaks. Now, you have a fiancée waiting for you to return to her with a trophy. Go back.'

And with that she flicks her wrists, the sheet held in her

gnarled fingers flaps up into the air, and I back away to avoid it touching me. Then she's gone, the stream has disappeared, and I'm back in the human world. Her magic has returned me to the car park. I blink, not used to being at the mercy of someone else's magic. There's no hint of the mist anywhere.

Ahead of me the sun appears over the horizon. The hunt is over. My palm tingles and I watch as the sigil and Niamh's name disappear. My heart sinks as I come to terms with the fact that I didn't reach her in time. I failed. The Wild Hunt will be called and... I shudder, knowing the consequences of my failure.

I pray that the *Bean Nighe* was telling me the truth, and Niamh has somehow reached St Marnox. Maybe she'll be safe. For a while, at least. If not... No, the *Bean Nighe* couldn't lie about that. Niamh will reach the sanctuary. Now I just have to hope she stays there. I sigh, realising there's little hope of that in the long term but I'll do what I can to persuade her to delay it as long as possible. But first, I have a delivery to make.

I open the boot of my car, retrieve my hunting kit and set to work cutting out the deer's heart.

CHAPTER 15
NIAMH

I head deeper and deeper into a wall of thick mist. I can't see anything in front of me, but somehow I manage to keep running without falling or bumping into anything. Around me, the sound deadens and I slow to a standstill, unable to run any further. I can't hear Cillian chasing me. I can't hear anything at all, other than my heartbeat pounding in my chest.

'Niamh!' I turn at the sound of my name, a woman's voice calling to me through the mist. Even as I identify the direction it's coming from, the mist begins to thin, and I cautiously make my way towards it.

'Hello?'

I'm lost on a mist-covered moor, and yet a woman is calling my name. I'm definitely in the middle of a drug-induced nightmare. Or I'm dead. Maybe that was the Underworld the voices mentioned. I pinch my arm, and it hurts. Hopefully not dead. Ahead of me a patch of mist shimmers. It's roughly the size and shape of a normal doorway, but there's no walls, no frame, nothing but this endless mist around it.

The sound of a running stream reaches me moments before I find myself on its bank. It burbles over a bed of uneven rocks, some worn smooth by the passage of time, others still jagged and uneven, as if only recently been sheared off by some force of nature.

Across the shallow water, sits an old woman with a large wooden basin beside her. She's got an old-fashioned washboard in one hand and is humming a tune under her breath as she rhythmically dunks her washing into the water before rubbing it on the board. The large white sheets flapping in and out of the water make me think of death shrouds.

'Hello, Niamh,' the old woman says, and for a moment the voice is familiar — she sounds just like my mother. But one look at her weather-beaten face and I can see it's not her.

'Hi,' I say, wondering how this old woman knows my name. I look up and down the stream. Where has it come from? Where has she come from? There's no sign of any houses or even a bothy nearby.

'I thought you would make it here faster,' the old woman says, giving me a sly grin. She has a kind voice, but her toothless smile causes me to take a step back. Her appearance reminds me of something from a fairy tale. What is she talking about? I was never even supposed to be here.

'I'm not supposed to be here at all,' I say. I'm supposed to be at home, in my bed, with Rose in the room next door. This morning, we were supposed to be going to the gym, then meeting friends for lunch. I want that life back, not whatever this is.

'Maybe not. But none of us could have foreseen what happened.'

'What are you talking about?'

The woman smiles again. Behind me, a flock of crows fly up into the sky, reminding me that I'm not alone out here and Cillian could be stalking me, closer than I think.

'There's a man—'

'Isn't there always?' The old woman chuckles.

'He's coming after me. You should go. Hide.'

'I do not fear the Huntsman.'

I take a step back. What the hell is going on? I wonder again if I'm dead.

'You know Cillian?'

'I do. And despite what your mother might have thought, you have nothing to fear from the Huntsman, either. At least, not in the way she thinks.'

I stare at her, confusion crossing my face. 'He brought me here to kill me.'

'No, he was never going to do that, Niamh. He might have thought it was the right thing, but he's worked it out. He believes that you have killed Kin and there is no choice except death, but he's wrong.'

'I thought it was because Vittoria ordered him to.'

The old woman shrugs. 'Vittoria instigated the hunt, certainly, and Cillian is duty-bound to obey. He thinks he has no choice but to marry Vittoria and was willing to give up—' She smiles at me again. 'Well, I'm sure you understand.

Try to be patient with him. In his own way, he tries to do the right thing.'

I definitely do not understand, and am only able to stare at her, open-mouthed.

'He told me that if I didn't reach sanctuary before dawn, that if he didn't capture and kill me, something worse would come after me.'

'He was telling you the truth. Follow the stream to the loch. In the middle of the loch there is a monastery. Ask for sanctuary there. *Thoir fasgadh dhomh* – give me shelter.'

'But I want to go home. I have a life—'

'You will have no life if you are dead, Niamh. Seek sanctuary for now. Only the Court can resolve this when it's strong enough, and until then, the only sanctuary is at St Marnox. No harm can come to you within its walls.'

'St Marnox? But—'

'Good, you know of it? Then you will recognise it when you see it. Hurry, before dawn breaks.'

'I will but—'

The old woman lifts the item she is washing from the basin and dumps it into the stream. I step back as she then pulls it from the water and flaps it, water droplets flying out from it in all directions. I turn and cover my face to stop water splashing me, but when I look back, she's gone.

I'm tired, panicked, and running for my life. Last night I was drugged, threatened with death and then chased down by a man who seems to both want and not want me at the same time. Apparently, my life choices right now are limited. I laugh to myself, I guess listening to the advice of an old woman washing clothes in a stream is as good a choice as any right now.

She told me to follow the stream, but should I cross it or not? This may be the only fording point for miles. Deciding that the fact that she met me at a crossing point is probably significant, I make my way cautiously across. The mist is clearing faster downstream, so I head that way. And by the time the stream widens out into a large, still loch, with an island in the middle of it, the mist has all but gone. I'm in a glen surrounded by hills on every side – odd, given that I don't remember going up or down any hills as I ran. There's a change in the air, and behind me I can sense the darkness starting to be burned away by the dawn. I have to reach the island.

There are buildings on it that I recognise from the logo on the beer it produces – and from the Stox bottles, of course. St Marnox.

Do I do what I've been told and head towards the sanctuary? Or do I keep going with no clue where I'm going or even where I am? Cillian said that something worse would come after me if I didn't reach the sanctuary in time. I stumble, and a stone digs into my foot. My shoes are splitting at the seams, hardly surprising given that they're meant for dancing rather than for running through a forest.

Beside me, the water in the loch is getting lower, almost as though it has a tide, and up ahead a line of shingle is now exposed, forming a causeway between the shore and the island. Behind me I hear the howl of ... something, and whatever it is, I don't want it to catch up with me. Another howl echoes and

I take off, running as fast as I can towards the causeway. My heart is thudding in my chest, and every breath is painful by the time I reach the island. As I take my first step onto the island itself, a painted wooden sign reads *St Marnox* and warns of crossing only when the causeway is fully visible. I risk a glance behind to make sure nothing has followed me, surprised that the causeway has already disappeared beneath the surface of the loch once more. There's no sign of Cillian, nor of any of the howling creatures. For now, anything chasing me will either have to wait until the water retreats again or find another way to cross the loch. I'm safe, I hope, even if it's just for a little while.

I sit down to catch my breath and look around. The island is mostly flat; grass stretches from shore to shore, not a smooth, well-manicured lawn but harsh, uneven, tufted grass interspersed with patches of purple heather. In places, rocky outcroppings break up the plant life, and a small flock of sheep is watching me, looking puzzled as they graze. I relax, it's the first sign of wildlife I've seen in hours, apart from the deer Cillian shot, and there's something calming about the presence of these animals. They seem peaceful, which steadies my nerves.

To my right, the buildings follow the shoreline, graceful stone arches and columns appearing a little too grand for the remote spot. Close by, a wooden jetty juts out into the loch, but there's no sign of any boats on the water. To my left, is a small graveyard full of haphazard rows of weathered stones and monuments. The brewery logo shows the buildings in ruins, but this place is far from desolate. It must have been restored since the original design was created.

The main buildings have been constructed from

weathered sandstone. Rain has etched channels onto every surface and many of the carvings are worn beyond recognition. But generally, it looks well-maintained. The grounds are neat and cared for. Overall, the island feels safe. And inhabited.

Having taken in my surroundings, I start up towards the entrance to the sanctuary. There's nothing on the sign to state that it's a brewery, but I only have to close my eyes and breathe in to smell the scent of hops.

When I open my eyes, St Marnox looks like it does in the drawing, half-ruined and crumbling in places. Then I blink, and it's restored to its current glory once more. I shiver, thinking of all the strange visions I've been subjected to over the course of the last twelve hours. They haven't been real, surely? Cillian chasing me? His tattoos coming to life? I look at my finger where the serpent bit me. The two small puncture wounds are definitely there. And the old woman? Clearly, some things I never thought I'd believe in might actually be real.

'Hello?' The voice startles me. A monk wearing long brown robes with his hood pulled up steps out of a shadowed doorway in the monastery wall. 'Are you lost?'

'Not exactly,' I say. 'I was told to come here.'

I tremble as I walk towards him. I shouldn't be feeling this vulnerable, surely? It's a monastery. He's a monk. A holy man. He watches as I approach, but it's only when I'm in front of him that he brings his hands forward and lifts the hood from his face.

'This is no place for a woman.'

The monk has ginger hair, thick but short, a neatly

trimmed beard and an Irish accent. His face is pale, with patches of sunburn visible on his skin. He looks to be around thirty, and tall enough that I have to look up to meet his eyes. I'd prefer to say his expression was blank, but in reality, there's a definite hint of suspicion there.

The door behind him creaks open, and another monk appears. The first one doesn't react at all to his fellow monk approaching, but I watch his progress. His hood is down, and he's older, scarred where someone has slashed him across the face and down his right cheek with a knife. They're old scars, well healed, and the diagonal one has left only a very thin stripe. The other is wider. He's not an unattractive man – the scars might make him seem more dangerous, but his salt-and-pepper hair gives him an air of distinction that I'm not sure he'd have had as a younger man.

'Who is this, Brother Declan?'

'She hasn't said, Brother Dominic,' Declan says. 'Yet.'

'I... My name is Niamh.'

The two of them exchange a glance, and my heart sinks. The old woman's words come back to me. *Ask for sanctuary.* And those strange words.

'Niamh Whyte,' I say and, feeling like I've just stepped into some kind of medieval fantasy realm, I add, 'I am seeking sanctuary.'

'Sanctuary?' Declan says. 'And what makes you think we would offer such a thing?'

'This is a monastery. You're monks...'

But Declan merely smiles. 'That is how we appear to the ... public, yes.'

'Then it's just a brewery and you're just playing at dress-up? It's not Halloween.'

Declan shrugs. 'All part of the St Marnox branding. Such an enchanting idea, don't you think? Wholesome. A selection of craft beers brewed in a medieval monastery by monks.'

'Stox is far from wholesome,' I point out.

'We can't control everything about our image,' Declan says. 'However, we don't get many visitors and the robes make it easier than having to decide what to wear every morning.'

As Declan speaks, Dominic moves closer to me. I have to force myself not to step away from him, sure that if I show any sign of weakness that he'll use it against me. He stops too close to me and lifts his hand as if he's going to touch my face, but then he freezes and sniffs.

'You smell like Cillian Hunter.'

I step back. I smell like Cillian? That's not a weird thing to say at all. 'He ... he was hunting me.'

Dominic moves so fast, I don't have the chance to evade him as he reaches for the strap of my dress and looks at where it has been ripped then fastened with a safety pin. Then, he grips the front of my dress and squeezes. He lifts his hand and looks at it, then shows it to Dominic. It's covered in blood.

'What did you do?' Declan asks. Nothing happens for a few moments. I don't know if I should just turn and run? But where to? I'm stuck on an island. Why did I follow the guidance of a random old woman in a forest? What was I thinking? Well, I guess I wasn't. God, the whole thing's ridiculous. I'm cold and tired and probably delirious, given the visions I've been seeing.

Declan tilts my chin up with a single finger, forcing me to look at him. 'No woman has ever outrun the Hunter before. Did you bribe him to let you go?'

I shake my head. The Hunters' businesses are supplied by this brewery. I can't work out whose side these men would take, so it's probably best not to tell them any more than I need to.

'You don't look like one of his ... *toys*,' Dominic says, sounding intrigued by the idea that Cillian might have hurt me. What sort of man – let alone a monk – refers to women as toys? Aren't they supposed to be respectful or ... I don't know, something? But they clearly think I'm one of Cillian's girlfriends, and despite the way he kissed me, that is one thing I am not.

I have no idea what I am to him. He's spent the last few hours hunting me down to kill me. And while he was attempting to justify that on the basis of me having killed a man, without a proper trial surely even his Unseelie Court couldn't justify killing me for it. Plus, he's marrying Vittoria Riali and I'm not the kind of woman who goes about stealing other people's men. Both Dominic and Declan continue to stare at me with near-blank expressions, clearly expecting an answer.

'I'm not one of Cillian's...' I can't bring myself to say it. 'I'm not anything to Cillian. I'm his sister's best friend.'

'And why has he sent you here? To us?'

I swallow again. Should I explain that it wasn't really Cillian who sent me here? I stare at Declan for a long moment, then shift my gaze to Dominic. Deflection, however, is something I've been studying for the past four years, so I answer his question with a question.

'Will I be safe here?'

'All who are granted sanctuary are safe within these walls.' Declan speaks with a tired acceptance, but Dominic's fists clench as if he is anything but happy about that fact.

'You didn't answer his question,' Dominic points out. My breath catches as I wonder if they'll take my avoidance as a lie. 'Whatever story you're trying to invent in your head right now, stop. *Why* has Cillian sent you here?'

But Declan puts a hand on his arm. 'Dom,' he says, stopping him. This time I follow my instinct and back away.

'Some men ... attacked me. In a nightclub, with Rose, Cillian's sister. And these men, they tried to—' I stop, not really wanting to put the whole thing into words. 'They drugged us and—'

'Did they hurt you?' Declan asks, sounding deathly calm.

'They didn't get a chance. Cillian came and—'

'What happened to the men?' Declan's voice is like ice, and between him and Dominic, they look like avenging angels. Except that they're far too late, the sounds and smells of the events of last night will haunt me forever.

'Cillian killed one, and Vittoria another. Then, I don't know what happened. There was a knife on the ground. And then it was in my hand. One of them ... he fell onto it.'

Dominic gestures at me. 'Hence, the blood on your dress?'

I nod. 'Vittoria said that because he was Kin, I had to die. Then Cillian took me into the woods and—'

'You killed Kin?' Dominic says.

'I didn't mean to,' I assure them. 'I don't know how it happened. He attacked me and then I was holding the knife and...'

The two of them exchange shocked looks.

'It is not often I agree with Vittoria Riali,' Declan says. 'But you escaped from the Huntsman, so we may be able to help.' He looks at me expectantly.

I've seen Gaelic written and tried to pronounce it before, so it's unlikely what I remember is anywhere near correct, but I manage to form sounds as similar to the old woman's words as I can manage. 'Hor fasgah yov.'

Dominic lets out a long whistle and turns to look at Declan, whose brow furrows.

'Doesn't ... aren't you obliged to give me sanctuary?'

The two men step aside and gesture towards the door behind them.

'If you can open the door, then sanctuary has been granted,' Declan says.

I walk up to the door slowly, realising that there's no handle. I look back at the two men, but both are standing with their arms folded, waiting – most likely for me to fail. I place both my hands on the warm wood and lean forward until my lips are almost touching the door. As soon as I whisper the words again, the door swings open.

'Welcome to St Marnox. I'll show you to your room,' Declan says. 'But it's not a free ride, for any of us. You'll need to earn your keep.'

Dominic chuckles, and the sound fills me with dread.

'Doing ... doing what?'

'We'll find you an appropriate task,' Declan says. Dominic smirks, looking me up and down.

'I can think of—'

'Dominic!'

'If she's willing, what's the problem?'

'I'm not!'

'No one will touch you without permission, Niamh,' Declan assures me. 'We are bound by rules towards the other seekers.'

'Seekers?'

'Of sanctuary.'

'I'm not the worst, Declan,' Dom says. 'You know that. There's never been a woman here before. It's going to draw attention—'

'You can't harm another in sanctuary, or you'll forfeit your own place, Brother Dominic.'

He turns to me. 'Dominic does have a point, though. Seven men, living together in this ancient monastery out here on this ... barren moor, with no other female company...'

'But I thought you said...' He's trying to scare me. Seven men? At that moment, I realise I've simply had enough. I straighten my spine and look up directly into his face.

'Will they be willing to answer to Cillian if anything happens to me?'

A smile teases the corners of Declan's mouth.

'So, you're not Cillian's, but you are Cillian's?'

'Yes.' I nod. Nothing else in this place makes sense, so why should I?

'Now, that's more like it,' Declan says, stepping aside. 'Come inside and we'll get you settled.'

I'm shaking as I follow Declan through the door into the cool interior of the monastery, grateful when Dominic doesn't follow.

CHAPTER 16
CILLIAN

I can't decide whether I am disappointed or relieved that I lost the hunt. Relieved that I didn't have to kill Niamh, certainly, and I hope that the *Bean Nighe* is correct and she's reached St Marnox. Once I've dealt with Vittoria, I'll call and check.

By the time I'm on my way back to Glasgow, I want nothing more than to sleep and figure this all out when I'm rested. I grip the steering wheel until my knuckles turn white. What started off last night as an engagement celebration has turned into a disaster. A human killing Kin? It's happened in the past, but not for decades, and I can't believe Niamh is the one who committed murder. As soon as I've delivered Vittoria the heart, I'll figure out what to do about Niamh.

The metallic smell of blood and musty earth fills the car as questions run through my head. How the hell did Niamh get to St Marnox? The *Bean Nighe* claimed it wasn't through her, so who? There was magic behind the stag and the mist tonight. I need to find out whose magic it was and work out why they are doing this. What's so special about Niamh? And why have they enabled her to find sanctuary in the Underworld?

I keep my speed legal and an eye out for the polis, explaining why I've been deer hunting in an Armani suit is not something I want to get into, and I'm too exhausted for my magic to be reliable. Dealing with the carcass, however, at least served one purpose – to help rid me of some of the frustrated desire still coursing through my veins. I didn't have to bury the deer, I could've left it to rot in the woods, but I didn't want an animal missing its heart to make the news and for Vittoria to become suspicious of the gift I'm presenting to her. My future as king is important now, more than ever.

The Glamour I've cast on the heart to make it look human should more than satisfy Vittoria. I barely pass another car on the road into the city and stop off at Cernunnos. Our housekeeper isn't best pleased at being woken just after five a.m. – but her job is to sort out our problems, and right now cleaning my ruined suit is essential, and it gives me the opportunity to shower and change before I see Vittoria.

I detour into the city centre to check behind the Sussurri premises, making sure Vittoria's security did their jobs, even if they did a piss-poor one inside the club last night. They have, and there's no sign of anything from last night, not even a single drop of blood on the cobbles. Then I cross the Squinty Bridge, heading for Vittoria's flat south of the river in Kingston, fighting my desperate need to go to St Marnox and see Niamh. I tell myself I just want to make sure she's okay, but I know my desire is much more primal than that.

By the time I pull into Vittoria's visitor's parking space, I'm ready to deceive my fiancée. I have to be convincing, because one thing I am sure of is that if Vittoria realises that Niamh is still alive, she'll not rest until she isn't. And even though Niamh should be safe within the walls of St Marnox, I'd be a fool to underestimate Vittoria's vindictiveness.

I glance up at Vittoria's flat. The bedroom light is off, but the one in the lounge is still on. Has she waited up for me? My thoughts have been so consumed by Niamh that I don't remember whether I promised to come as soon as I got back or not.

Much as I don't want to admit it, the events of tonight have only made me realise how much I've been denying my feelings. How strong the pull towards Niamh Whyte really is. I close my eyes and take a deep breath. I want Niamh. I was so close to taking her, I felt her desire and her fear, and now I've got a taste I want more. I want *everything* from her. But no one argues with the *Bean Nighe*. I'm furious that I lost the hunt, but like Niamh, I don't want to die.

I ring the buzzer for Vittoria's penthouse, knowing I need to play this carefully. I look up at the camera, the realisation that neither of us has keys to each other's homes summing up our relationship. I'm buzzed in immediately, although when I reach the top floor, I wait longer than I expect at the main door and have lifted my fist to hammer on it, before it's pulled open and I'm face to face with my fiancée, who is looking well-rested and coldly beautiful.

Before she's even looked at me, her focus falls to the cool box I'm carrying.

'You've showered?' she asks, finally looking at me.

'I stopped at Cernunnos. Didn't think you'd want me showing up at your flat covered in blood.'

It takes an effort for me to keep my expression neutral in the face of the sick, twisted smile that curves her mouth, an ugly contrast to Niamh's gentle smile, and an image of her fearful face replaces Vittoria's almost immediately. I rub my hand across my stubble, an unfamiliar response twisting my guts. I push it away. I never feel guilty.

'That's hers?'

'You asked for a heart.' It's dangerous, sometimes fatal, to outright lie to any of the Kinfolk, but I don't owe Vittoria the whole truth. Niamh's life depends on it.

'I did. Come in.' Vittoria holds the door open for me, and I enter. I spot my reflection in the antique mirror she has hanging in her hallway. It's out of character with the rest of the modern penthouse, but it's such a piece of exquisite workmanship that the fact it doesn't fit in here doesn't really matter.

Vittoria leads me into the ultra-modern kitchen. The gleaming white and shiny stainless-steel surfaces contrast with the darkness of their owner. I hold out the cool box, and she claps her hands in delight before reaching for it.

'Thank you!' she says, her blood-red nails curling round the handle as I hand it over. I watch as she practically skips over to the sink.

'Have you slept?' I ask. Every muscle in my body is

screaming for rest, while Vittoria is positively buzzing with energy.

'Yes, I wasn't sure how long you'd be,' she says. She turns and smiles at me, but I can't find it in myself to smile back. Her energy exhausts me further. Exhaustion is slowing my every movement, but there is no fucking way I'm sleeping here today. I'm not convinced I'd wake up in one piece.

'What day is it?' While I don't think I spent long in the Underworld, it can be unpredictable how much time passes relatively between the worlds. There are ways of controlling this, but they take focus and concentration. Even the time spent talking to the *Bean Nighe* could have resulted in this not being Saturday morning as I expect.

'Saturday.' Vittoria frowns at me. 'You've been to the Underworld?'

'Yes, but not intentionally,' I reply. 'But someone seems determined to fuck me over this weekend.'

'Aww, poor darling,' she pouts. Thankfully, her attentions return to the cool box, any concern about my evening and the hunt long gone. She doesn't even ask me how I killed Niamh, her sole focus is on the fact I delivered the prize to her, not the lengths I went to to get it.

She places the cooler in the sink and opens it, then peers in and ... giggles. It might be the first time I've ever heard her do that. It sounds anything but amusing.

'It's bigger than I thought it would be,' she says.

'You've seen a lot of human hearts?'

'A few,' she confesses, lifting it out of the cool box and holding it up in both hands to admire. 'But none as pretty as this one.'

I watch as brilliant-red blood oozes from the heart down Vittoria's arms, the sticky liquid coating her hands as she cradles the organ. She runs a taloned finger over the surface, tracing the outline of it. I hide my emotions as she beams at her prize. Where smiling implies joy, her features show evil. A dark, stagnant evil.

'Goodbye, *Fairest*,' she says with glee as she dumps it unceremoniously in the sink. Blood drips from her fingers, and she turns and cups my face, smearing blood over both my cheeks. Leaning in, she pulls me towards her, kissing me deeply. The feeling of her tongue entering my mouth and the smell of the metallic blood has my insides churning.

'Fuck's sake, Vittoria. The blood,' I say, pushing her away. She pouts and turns back to the sink.

'Actually,' she says, eyeing the heart with sickening glee, 'I might keep it instead. The end of an era, so to speak.'

'The end of an era?' I query, as I search for something to clean the blood off my face, concern that Vittoria suspects more than I think she does begins to gnaw at me.

She doesn't face me, but shrugs.

'She appeared in our lives just as everything turned to shit, Cillian. Consider it symbolic. And maybe it'll stop you being so distracted.'

'Distracted?'

Now she turns, her expression way too innocent, and a chill runs right the way down my spine. Has she fucking known all along?

'Surely this will be a wake-up call for Rose? That it's time for her to fully support her family.'

I pray to the old gods that that's all she means.

'I'll find a suitable container,' she says, pulling open the door to a cupboard. 'Then I'll ask around, find out the best way to preserve it. For posterity.'

I shake my head and frown. I'd much rather she disposed of the evidence now. 'Why?'

'If it wasn't for her...' She trails off, shaking her head as she slams a box on the counter and lifts the heart out of the sink into it, seals it, then stores it in the fridge. I stare into the sink as she throws a tiny piece of stray flesh into the waste disposal and presses the power switch, smearing blood over it as she does so. I flinch – the grinding loud in the morning stillness. Vittoria stares gleefully as the little piece gets pulled into the machinery.

'What did you do with the rest of her body?' she asks as she washes the blood off her hands.

'Buried somewhere it won't be found,' I say, as she tosses me a clean cloth. I use it to wipe my face. Then she pours bleach onto the cloth and wipes down the sink with the thoroughness of someone well-versed in cleaning crime scenes.

'One problem, all gone,' she says, turning to face me, pouting when I don't close the gap between us. 'Oh, you're no fun this morning, Cillian. Anyone would think someone had died.'

She laughs and my guts twist into knots as I think about the fact that I'm supposed to marry this woman, be tied to her until death do us part. It's not the fact that she doesn't care about the death of another woman, it's the fact that she's taking such pleasure in the death of an innocent.

'My sister isn't going to be happy.'

'Is she ever? You know she hates me.'

She goes to pass me, and I step into her, pushing her back against the fridge. The one in my sister's flat is covered in a collection of ridiculous fridge magnets, which Rose and Niamh buy whenever they go on holiday. Most of the surface is now covered in a clashing, gaudy ensemble of moulded magnets, few of which are even used for the purpose intended. There's one from Paris that I bought when I went with them once – although 'with' is doing some heavy lifting there.

Neither Rose nor Niamh know I'd followed them there, watching as they explored the most romantic city in the world, and making sure that every man who even looked in Niamh's direction understood fully that she was not his for the taking. The one guy who ignored me, got as far as sending drinks to them in a pavement café. Sadly, he hadn't survived his trip to the bathroom, and neither of them even realised that they'd walked over his unmarked grave when they explored Père Lachaise cemetery the following morning.

Vittoria's fridge is magnet-free, clean and clinical, and she smiles seductively up at me as I press my body into hers, pinning her in place against the surface.

'Don't you care that an innocent young woman is dead?'

Vittoria laughs. 'You really believe she's innocent? She killed Kin, Cillian. And after all these years, undoubtedly Rose has led her astray—'

My hand shoots up around her throat and squeezes, cutting off the cruel words. She might not be wrong. Rose was always wild, but when she lost Matt, her behaviour grew even wilder, and now she moves easily from one guy to the next, leaving a trail of broken hearts and empty balls behind her. Do I like it? No? Is she any worse than me? Also no.

'She's not like Rose,' I say.

'They must have had something in common. Why else would they be friends? Unless she was just interested in your family's money.'

'She's not interested in our money.'

'Everyone is interested in your money, Cillian.' Vittoria slides a hand up the side of my body, hooking it around the back of my neck and pulling my face down to hers. 'She's been happy to live rent-free with your sister for the past four years, after all. Accepted gifts from her, worn clothes that she can't afford, partied in venues that wouldn't even look twice at her if she tried to get in. She's been using your name, your influence, for years.'

Worry nags at me again. Vittoria has been paying a hell of a lot more attention to Niamh than I realised. Her lips whisper over mine, her fingers tighten in my hair, her other hand slips between our bodies to palm my cock. And despite it all, I feel ... nothing.

'Rose is better off without her. We're better off without her. She was so desperate for you to notice her, to fuck her. It was embarrassing.' And the way Vittoria looks at me right that second – I know I've been an utter fool.

'She's gone now,' I say, a chill creeping through me. Vittoria knew. For four years, I've thought she didn't suspect anything, but right now I suspect she knew everything.

'Good.' As her lips touch mine, a red veil descends over me, and my fingers grip more tightly around her throat. Vittoria gasps, but she's thrumming with excitement beneath my fingers. Her pulse racing, her breathing shallow. I close my eyes and kiss her. Her lips are cold and taste like poison, inspiring a single tremor of lust within me. When she reaches for my belt and yanks it open, expertly popping open the button fly and covering me with her hand, I close my eyes, breathing in through my nose as my body reacts. She rubs along my length, knowing me too well not to be able to provoke a reaction, and I groan.

'Come to bed. You promised to make up for last night's rude interruption. I was just thinking about how we could put some candles to good use...' she says, taking my hand and pulling me towards her bedroom just as my phone rings.

I'm so full of frustration, at Vittoria, at Niamh, at the failed hunt. I could fuck her to relieve some of my stress, but it won't solve my problems. In fact, it would just cause more.

'Don't answer,' she insists. But I ignore her, stepping back and checking my watch.

'It's Rose, I have to. She'll have questions that I need to answer so that there's no confusion.'

'But I want you,' Vittoria pouts, her red nails tracing down the front of my shirt, her hand searching beneath my waistband as she palms my cock, stroking it steadily, causing my mind to reconsider, just for a moment. 'You've already made me wait once.'

I place a hand over hers before I move her sharp nails away from my tender flesh and answer the call. 'I'll be right over, okay?' I tell Rose, and end the call.

Not wanting to arouse her suspicions, I pull Vittoria into my arms and kiss her hard.

'You're just going to leave me, again?'

'My sister is my priority. Family comes first.'

Vittoria laughs, then stops, clearly realising I'm serious. Her lips twist into a snarl. 'How is she?'

'Other than the fact I'm about to tell her that she got her best friend killed and I'm not sure she's ever going to forgive me, I'm sure she's just fine.' I sigh, knowing that the pain I'm going to cause will help keep my deception running.

'Forgive you?' Vittoria leans back as I rebutton my jeans, a tiny frown forming between her eyes. 'But Cillian, darling, surely she knows it was her fault in the first place? You have to make sure that she starts to accept responsibility for her actions.'

'For her actions?' I stare at Vittoria, trying to work out just how her mind works. How exactly does she figure that any of this was Rose's fault?

'Your sister has always been difficult. If she had been where she was supposed to be last night, then none of this would have happened.'

The callous disregard for Rose's safety sparks something inside me that it's been years since I listened to. How can Vittoria think of becoming a part of our family when she cares so little about my sister?

I shake my head. In my world, the game is played for family and family alone. And you don't just let them get hurt because they make a stupid mistake or an even stupider decision. I stare at my bride-to-be, realising that Rose's little acting-out episode was exactly the right thing to do. This marriage will be a disaster.

'I'm sure Rose had a very good reason for choosing not to attend last night. And we both have to respect that,' I state.

Vittoria pauses, then looks at me, quickly hiding the surprise on her face, and changes tack.

'You can't possibly be justifying it. It didn't look good. She's mocking you, Cillian. Disrespecting your decisions. She makes you look weak.'

I reach for her, threading my fingers through her hair, forcing her to look up at me as she presses against my body.

'It would be a mistake, Vittoria, to think I'm a weak man. My family is the most important thing to me and you're not a part of that ... yet.'

I walk away from her and out of her place. Something smashes against the closed door as I leave.

CHAPTER 17
NIAMH

I wake to what I think might be late afternoon sunlight shining through a narrow window – a welcome change from the thick mist. The room Declan showed me to was tiny, but much warmer than I expected and with a small en suite bathroom. It's not going to win a tourism award anytime soon, but after the events of last night and me running through the woods, I was grateful for the chance to shower and sleep. He also gave me a T-shirt to wear that was too big, but anything is better than my blood-soaked dress.

I smile at the faint sound of birds singing. Even though the window is open, the room is hot and airless, the ancient stones trapping the heat. There's an old-fashioned lock on the door, operated by a heavy, cast-iron key. A huge deadbolt gives me an extra sense of security.

I wonder how Rose was this morning. Did she wake up in her own bed, safe and oblivious to the events of last night? I try to push down the anger that gnaws at my gut, unable to decide if I'd be in a better or worse situation if I hadn't called Cillian last night.

Worse. Definitely worse. If those men had loaded us into their car and driven us who knows where. I'm certain I wouldn't be alive to tell the tale. And despite Cillian promising Vittoria that he was taking me into the woods to kill me, somehow I'm still alive. I wonder if he's still looking for me? Except that I know he's not. He was very clear that the hunt ended at dawn. He knows that I'm either here or ... or wherever my body would have been left if the Wild Hunt had got me. If he had wanted to kill me, I'd already be dead.

Even tucked up in bed with a room that locks, I can't help but feel on edge. Despite Declan's reassurances that no harm will come to me at St Marnox, I don't feel all that safe. And if Cillian comes here, what exactly will happen? Worse still, what if Vittoria finds me?

Climbing out of bed, I stretch my aching limbs and wander to the small window, looking out into the sunshine. I lean against the ledge and sigh, I clench my fingers around my necklace, feeling a sense of relief from the familiar weight in my hand. The things I've seen over the past twenty-four hours should be unbelievable. The Kinfolk, the Underworld, how can these be real? And yet ... there's something on the edge of my consciousness, telling me that it's all true, but when I focus on it, it slips away, as if it were never there.

Out on the water, a small head peeps up from beneath the smooth surface and disappears in circles of ripples. It's gone before I can see it properly. The waters of the loch are clear and an intriguing shade of greenish-blue, sparkling in the sunlight. The head bobs up again, closer to the jetty, and then I realise it's a man swimming.

He reaches the jetty and pushes himself out of the water, landing easily on his feet on the wooden boards. Naked. I gasp, turning away from the window and pressing my back to the wall. I take a deep breath and peer cautiously back out. He's got a towel wrapped around his waist now, and he's standing looking out over the water, his back to me.

I don't think it's Declan or Dominic. This man is taller and looks younger. He's tall, broad-shouldered, his upper body tapers athletically to a slender waist and muscular legs. I watch his muscles tense and loosen as he stretches a little before he turns and looks up, right towards my window, and I'm hit with a jolt of recognition.

Except it can't be. He's ... he's *dead*.

A chill seeps through me. Have I got everything wrong? Maybe Cillian didn't shoot the deer. Maybe that bolt was aimed directly at me. Was everything from the moment I turned and ran into the mist last night actually me entering the afterlife? Is that what the Underworld is? Am I ... am I dead? I let my head drop forward, misjudging the distance to the glass, and pain shoots through my forehead.

'Ow!' Shouldn't the afterlife be free from pain? Rubbing the sore spot on my head I squint in the bright sunlight. The man finishes drying himself, drops the towel and leans over to pick up his discarded robe. He pulls it over his head before he walks back towards the monastery. As he draws closer, I'm more certain than ever that it's him.

Matt. Rose's dead boyfriend, Matt.

I race to the door and pull it open, then realise I can't go downstairs dressed just in the T-shirt Declan gave me to sleep in last night. But I need to talk to Matt.

Footsteps echo on the stone stairs, and I duck back into my room, only to jump when someone knocks on my door. I open it to see Brother Declan, carrying a robe similar to the ones the others wear.

'Thank you for letting me stay here last night,' I tell him. 'I'll try and repay you once ... once I get home and get my credit cards and—'

'You think you can leave?' He stares at me in confusion.

'Well ... yes,' I say, confused. 'Can't I?'

'No,' he says, as if there's not even a discussion to be had.

'But—'

'Not unless you're willing to go through the Court. It's the only way out.'

I stare at him, a chill running through me.

'The Court? But ... but... Please ... I need to leave.'

'You can stand trial in The Unseelie Court, but given that you killed Kin, I don't think you'll enjoy the result.'

'The what? What's The Unseelie Court? And ... it would have been self-defence, if I'd even meant to do it. Which I didn't. He fell on me and the knife, I didn't mean to kill him.'

Declan rests his hand on my shoulder. 'I don't think it'll matter.'

'But it should.' I have never wanted to clench my fists and stomp my feet more than I do right at this moment.

He nods in sympathy, but his answer doesn't change. And he doesn't answer my question about The Unseelie Court either. If only I could rewind my life and just refuse to go to that nightclub with Rose. Then none of this would be happening. Everything would be all right.

'So, unless I agree to go to this Unseelie Court, then I'm a prisoner here?'

He pauses for a moment before he speaks. 'You sought sanctuary here. Do you really not know where you are?'

I shrug. 'No, not really. I mean, I know where St Marnox is, but that's not what you mean, is it?'

'All of us here, we've each been accused of committing a crime. Our accusers had enough evidence to take to The Unseelie Court, and the King, that's Vincenzo Riali,' he says and I nod. 'If either the Court itself or the King is convinced, a hunt is called. The hunt is considered as a sort of trial. If you're captured and killed, then it proves you were guilty.'

I scoff. 'Like a witch-hunt?'

'Quite,' he agrees. 'Those lucky enough to reach here can go back, face a proper trial. Those of us who remain here, know we would never be acquitted by The Unseelie Court – either because we really are guilty, or because it suits the current king to believe we are. Much as we all dream of justice, the Court isn't like it used to be, and we have to accept that the Riali family controls it completely now. We all managed to outrun the Huntsman, or got here before the hunt began, to seek sanctuary. We're safe here. St Marnox exists in the human world, obviously, but the part that sits in the Underworld – only those granted sanctuary and the Hunters can enter here. And only the Hunters can leave.'

I gasp. 'Cillian can come here?'

'Yes, but he can't harm you within these walls. And he won't. Once you reach sanctuary, the Huntsman's duty ends.'

'Can Vittoria?'

'No.'

Confusion clouds my thoughts. A million questions running through my mind. Humans, Kinfolk, the Underworld, Vittoria's family controlling the Court? None of it makes sense. It feels as though I've stepped into the pages of a story.

'Nothing you're saying makes sense. None of this can be real—' Except I already know that's not true. Everything I saw last night was real.

'There's so much more than you can even imagine, Niamh.'

I think for a moment, then decide to focus on the most immediate matter.

'What's stopping me from leaving?'

'The only exit leads directly into The Unseelie Court. There's a *geas* on all of us.'

'A *geas*?'

He tilts his head to one side, observing me. 'It's kind of Celtic curse. A magical bond placed on us – one that imprisons us here. If we swim to the far shore, we will simply end up back here on the island. If we go through into the human world and try and leave that way – well, I wouldn't recommend trying that. When you were granted sanctuary, it came with this consequence.'

'A consequence no one told me about.'

'Whether you were aware or not, you asked for sanctuary, and it was granted.'

'But the causeway—'

'Appears and disappears when it wants to,' he says. 'Any other questions, or can we go and eat?'

'Just one. What are the Kinfolk? It means family ... in Scots.'

Declan nods, tilting his head to one side as he thinks. 'Yes, and no. The Gaelic is *Cinneadh*, or "clan" in English, I suppose. But that word has other connotations among the humans. And the concept for us is so much more than the English conveys. It is family, but a family through so much more than blood.

'The Kinfolk have always been here, Niamh. Before humans, back into the mists of time. They go by many names, come in many guises,' Declan tells me. 'The wee folk, the guid folk, the gentle folk, the fae, fairies, even – although that one's been so twisted that it bears no relation to what we really are, how powerful we really are.'

I stare at him. Despite all the things I saw last night, to hear him say them so matter-of-factly... 'Those aren't real.'

'They're not?'

I shake my head, but even as I look at him, his appearance changes. His shoulders broaden, and his face changes, becomes more rugged. His eyes grow darker, and his hair and beard grow longer, thicker, bushier, plaited in places and threaded through with intricately carved wooden beads. He's just as handsome, but in a different way.

'How are you doing that?'

He shrugs, 'I have more than one form and can change between them. Human eyes see me through a magic called

Glamour that means you see what I want you to see. We're all different.'

'What are you?'

'Not completely human. I'm one of the many types of Kinfolk who lived originally in the Underworld. We spend our lives in the mountains, mining for precious jewels and metals.' He sighs as if he misses it.

'The Underworld,' I whisper. The voices in the mist last night mentioned it and suddenly I remember that growing up my parents told me stories about another world, one which overlaps the one I know. It exists in the same place, but not, and these two worlds connect at certain points, known as thin places. Sometimes, the unwary or the foolish find these places and pass through – usually with disastrous consequences.

Is that what I've done?

And the stories weren't just about a place, but about people, too. Kinfolk. How could I have forgotten? Every detail they told me about the magical powers each Kin held was so elaborate and intricately described I thought they must have read it in a story, or in a book about folklore. Were they actually telling me something true? That the Kinfolk I thought they'd made up to entertain me, might really exist? I loved those stories. How did I forget them?

With every piece of information Declan tells me, I feel more questions coming, and then more answers unlocking in my memory. But there's still more I want to find out from him about the Hunters, about this place, about my future.

Somewhere in the depths of the monastery a bell tolls, and Declan shakes his head.

'Enough,' he says. 'It's dinner time. Put this on, and I'll take you downstairs to meet the others. You must be hungry.'

'Starving.'

'As well as meeting the other seekers, you will also begin your duties shortly. Dominic and I have discussed it, and we agree that while you are here you must cook and clean to pay your way. It's what will make you most useful, but also keep you safe. You must also mind your own business. There are secrets here. Don't dig. You'll only get hurt. Understand?'

'But I have questions about this Underworld you're talking about. Given everything I've been through in the past day, you owe me. And just because I'm a woman doesn't mean I should get stuck with the cooking and cleaning. Is there nothing else—'

'You know how to operate a brewery?'

'No.'

'Then there's nothing else. And believe me, your tasks are going to earn you the most popularity points with the rest of the Seven. We owe you nothing. You've been granted sanctuary here, just like us.'

'The Seven?' I swallow the lump in my throat as I follow him out of the room.

'There's currently seven of us here. And now you, *Gléigeal*. For now you will be in charge of the domestic chores the rest of us despise.'

I roll my eyes, but I know nothing about breweries and cooking and cleaning is at least in my skillset whether I think they're being sexist or not.

'How long have you all been here?' I ask not really expecting him to answer.

'Remember what I said about not asking questions,' he says. 'Besides, time moves differently here.'

'All right, then. Can I ask what Glay-gyal means?' I do my best to copy his pronunciation.

'It's Irish. It sort of means Snow White,' he says and chuckles. 'One woman, seven men, hiding somewhere beyond the enchanted forest. Hair like ebony, lips like blood. And you're so very, very pale. I don't remember it all now. Life here is far from being a fairy tale.'

'I don't think there are many monks in fairy tales.'

'Monks?' Declan chuckles and looks down at his robes. 'Aye, we certainly live like monks. Not by choice, though. And certainly not for a higher purpose.'

I had never truly believed the story that the brewers here were monks. It always feels wrong somehow that they, of all people, make a product that causes so many problems in the city. According to the people who sell it, it's not the product but how it's misused that's the problem, and that's down to the customer. Which sounds just like the kind of excuses business owners would make to maintain their profit margins or whatever.

Brother Declan leads me through the building, our footsteps echoing against the flagstone floor. We descend a spiral staircase with me clutching the iron handrail to avoid tumbling around the twist. The door at the bottom opens into an internal courtyard surrounded by cloisters similar to those along the water's edge. In the centre of the neatly mown grass is a huge stone Celtic cross engraved with interlaced knotwork and what looks like four figures carrying staffs or spears.

On the far side, Declan pushes open a heavy wooden door, smooth and polished from generations of hands touching it. There are metal studs all over its surface and an old-fashioned latch mechanism that appears still fully functional. And then I'm following him down a short, cool corridor, and the smell of food grows stronger with every step. My stomach growls.

'Be careful with the Seven, *Gléigeal*. Some of us have been here for a very long time and we've seen no women here but you.'

'You never have women here?'

'Only the Hunters can come here.'

'Why? Isn't that a bit of a contradiction?'

'One might think so,' he says. Then laughs. 'Do you argue over everything?'

'Mostly,' I say. 'I'm training to be a lawyer.'

'Then you should understand the contradiction. The Hunters do their job for the Court, but if any of the accused reach here and claim sanctuary, then it is up to the Hunters to ensure they are protected until they are ready to face the Court.'

'You make them sound almost noble.'

'It may not follow human standards, but yes, the Huntsman is a noble man. Far more so than our current king.' He shrugs. 'But be careful. We are all guilty of something here. Well, most of us, at least – even if that is simply pissing off the Rialis.'

'Guilty of what?'

'Many of us here have killed, *Gléigeal*. These are not men to be trifled with.'

'What about Matt? Why is he here? Rose thinks he's dead.'

Declan frowns a little, then tilts his head to one side. 'You don't know?'

I shake my head. 'I just heard that he died. I didn't ... I didn't ask Rose too much about it, she was too upset.'

'Matt killed Christopher Riali.'

'What? No.'

Declan pushes open the door to the refectory, and several more monks follow us into the room, all of them moving almost silently. They move past us, their heads covered by the hoods of their robes, leaving their faces in shadow.

'We have a visitor?' one says, his deep voice sending a shiver down my spine.

'Yes, Brother Salvatore, this is Niamh,' Declan tells him.

'Niamh? That doesn't sound like a prostitute's name.'

My breath catches, and I cough.

'Sal—' The warning is clear in Declan's tone, but Sal ignores it and takes a step towards me, reaching out to touch my hair.

At that, I turn and run straight into another hooded figure standing in the doorway. I didn't even hear him coming. He flips back his hood, and I look up into Declan's face and scream.

'Going somewhere?' he asks. 'I don't think that's allowed.'

How can Declan be standing in front of me, blocking the exit? I turn, and sure enough, there he is, behind me. I turn back.

'Let her go, Lachlan,' Declan says, sighing. 'Niamh, this is my twin brother. Lachlan, meet Niamh. Cillian Hunter sent her here. I'd say touch her and die, but in all honesty, I think you'd be more likely to find yourself in Cillian's basement being tortured for all eternity if you dare to.'

'She's Cillian's?' Lachlan asks, and I notice that Sal, too, looks a little less cocky.

'I don't belong to any—' I begin, but Declan cuts me off.

'You'd better hope you do, Niamh. You have a much better chance of surviving this place if you belong to him than if you don't. Believe me.'

'Why is she here, then, if not for us to—'

'Enough, Sal. She is a fellow seeker.'

'Really?' That single word turns my blood to ice, and when Sal throws back his hood, I'm struck dumb by his appearance. He's a beautiful man, with black hair, deep brown eyes and olive skin, the planes of his face smooth, as if carved from solid marble. But there's a darkness in his expression, a tense, coiled evil that gives the impression of a fallen angel rather than a saint. 'She's pretty. I am surprised the Huntsman let her go and did not simply keep her locked up for his own private use.'

He tilts his head to one side, observing me carefully. 'I don't even get to touch her just a little bit? Not even if she asks me to?'

I swallow, fear and indignation filling me from top to toe. The way he talks reminds me of the men in Sussurri. A shot of rebellion surges through me. I've just spent four years studying to be a lawyer. If anyone should be able to get the Court to do what they want it to, it should be me. Part of my law course has involved regular mooting, taking part in competitive court cases, and I'll draw on everything I've learned to face this man down now.

'If you harm me and have to face the Court, what will happen to you?' I ask Sal.

'They will likely kill me, little one.' He steps closer to me, and I refuse to flinch, keeping my eyes fixed on him as he circles me. Then he stops and frowns. 'You ... you're human. What could you possibly have done?'

'I killed Kin,' The room falls silent at my words. 'Someone tried to do to me what you're suggesting. His two friends fared no better.'

'He's not going to harm you, little one,' a fifth monk says, stepping through another door that might lead into a kitchen. 'Now, can we eat? Is the dick-measuring contest over? The lasagne is getting cold.'

'Lasagne? Again?' Lachlan rolls his eyes.

I don't think I breathe as Sal holds up his hands in surrender, then moves gracefully across the room, his robes brushing against me as he passes to take the farthest seat on the left of the table. Declan pulls out the chair on the right-hand side for me, and I sit down. Declan and Lachlan sit at either end with Duncan beside Sal. The two other monks take the seats either side of me, lifting their hoods as soon as they are seated. Dominic is one, the other is a handsome mixed-race man, who nods at me but remains silent.

That leaves an empty seat opposite me, which is filled by the seventh monk hurrying in. I get a strong whiff of salt water and seaweed as he sits down, and judging from his build and height, I'm pretty sure he's the swimmer. Matt. I hold my breath as he lifts his hood and lets it drop. His skin is far more tanned than I remember, his hair bleached an even lighter blond by the sun, but the man in front of me is most definitely Rose's dead boyfriend.

'Matt?' I'm filled with excitement for a split second when I think how happy Rose is going to be when I tell her that Matt is alive, but then I realise that that's probably not how this is going to play out. He's here, I'm here – and Rose is alone, likely thinking that we're both dead.

'Hi, Niamh,' he smiles at me. 'Surprised?'

'Hi,' is the only thing I can think of to say. He watches me, his eyes full of the intense curiosity I remember, but he doesn't ask any questions, nor does he volunteer any further information.

'I'm James.' The man beside me holds out his hand for me to shake. He has a tattoo that stretches from the back of his hand to where it's covered by his sleeves, but I recognise the top of it – the staff and serpent of Aesculapius.

'You're a doctor?'

'I am.' He nods, but Sal laughs.

'He used to be a doctor. He's barred from practising in the human world.'

James's hands clench into fists, his knuckles paling with the force, and I feel an urge to cover his hand with mine.

'I'm not guilty of what they accused me of,' James insists, and starts to push himself to his feet, which only makes Sal laugh harder.

'You think you can take me? With those hands as soft and weak as a—'

'Enough,' Declan barks, and there's a sudden silence.

Matt makes a face at me. 'As you may have noticed, Sal

likes to make his boring existence here more interesting by pissing off everyone around him. He's harmless, really. He's being particularly annoying today because it's his turn to make dinner tomorrow.'

'Actually, here's the new deal. You'll all keep a safe distance from our newest seeker, and in return, Niamh will be responsible for the cooking and cleaning, allowing the rest of us to work in the gardens and the brewery.'

'Fine,' I say, like I have any choice. But I promise myself it won't be for long. That I'm going to work out how to get back to my real life.

'Please tell me you know how to cook more than pasta?' Matt asks, pushing his lasagne around his plate. I look down at my own plateful and sigh.

'Lots of things.'

Matt grins at me, and I feel a pang. Rose would give anything to be here right now to see Matt again.

'Good,' Dominic claps his hands together, and we make it to the end of dinner with no further drama. I look back at Matt, who is now intent on eating, any hint of a smile long gone from his face and only the same brooding sadness I so often see on Rose's face left. In the time he's been exiled here, he's aged a lot. He's been working out to keep his body much the same, but his face is etched with sorrow. He'd just lost his friend, Chris Riali, four years ago when he… well, I guess he disappeared as he's obviously not dead. I hadn't liked Chris, but I know his death affected the Hunter family more than I've ever understood. Perhaps Matt still being alive is connected? But here, surrounded by all these strangers, is neither the time nor the place to ask.

Was it connected to my own devastating loss? I hadn't been around for Rose during that time as much as I should have because of what happened right before Matt's "death". Too busy mourning what happened during a trip I'd taken to Edinburgh with him and Rose to be fully present for my friend.

CHAPTER 18
NIAMH

FOUR YEARS AGO

'Are you sure this is all right with your friend?' My mum asks, her brows creased with worry. 'It's already kind of them to pay for the hotel. I don't want you to feel like you owe them anything.'

'Rose says they'd be spending the same, whether I go or not,' I assure her. 'Her brother wants her to be safe at this law conference and he's happy she's not staying by herself.'

That is definitely stretching the truth. I haven't even seen Cillian since the morning I woke up in his room after the fateful Hunter party. I'm not even sure how I'd react if I did see him, especially after what happened between us.

'Please be careful about accepting gifts from people, Niamh,' Dad says, kissing the top of my head. 'Relationships can get complicated when there's an imbalance. And you know what we've always told you about those gifts that come with consequences.'

'Cautionary fables,' I say, laughing. 'But I'll be careful. The money thing worries me, too. That's why I was supposed to be the one driving. Then, at least, I was contributing something towards the arrangements rather than just sitting back and taking everything for granted and it's you two who are getting in the way of that.'

I smile to make sure they know I'm not making a dig at them.

'Aunt Mary's death was unexpected,' Mum says. 'We need to make sure her house—'

'It's fine, Mum. I understand. Really.'

'Is Rose driving instead?' Dad asks.

I pause before answering. 'She has a driver.'

Mum's eyed widen. 'Just be careful, darling. That family has a reputation. I know you like Rose, but rich people are different.'

'I will. I promise,' I reply, convinced that it's an easy promise to keep. I stand and watch as they reverse out of the driveway, waving as they head off. We live on an ordinary street in an ordinary suburb of Glasgow, so I frown when I notice an unfamiliar BMW do a U-turn in the road and drive off without signalling. Sighing at the lack of respect, I turn around and go to check my overnight bag.

I'm not really planning on leaving the hotel except to go to the conference itself, but it's my first time staying somewhere fancy, and I'm going to make the most of the facilities.

Fifteen minutes later, a horn beeps twice outside and I head for the door. Sean is already waiting when I open it. He takes my suitcase to stow in the boot.

'Looking forward to the weekend?' he asks.

'Yes,' I say.

'Even playing gooseberry to those two?'

I shrug. 'I really don't mind. Seeing them together gives me some hope that there are nice guys somewhere out there. And besides, I have you to talk to.' I grin at him, expecting him to smile back, but instead his mouth is set in a grim line.

'Don't say that in front of Cillian,' he says.

I frown. It feels like a warning, but why would Sean care. I can't imagine Cillian has told anyone about what happened between us the night of the party.

'I mean, I'm working,' he says a moment later. 'He pays my salary.'

'Oh, yes, right.'

He pauses at the passenger side before opening the back door for me instead, and I wish I hadn't said anything.

We pick up Rose and Matt from Matt's house, before setting off on the hour-long journey. Rose had insisted on sneaking a bottle of champagne for the ride to keep us entertained, and I catch Sean's eye in the mirror, but he keeps his mouth shut.

'That looks expensive,' I point out. And Rose smiles impishly.

'It's Cillian's. He won't even notice it's missing,' she assures me.

～

The hotel is on the Royal Mile, right in the centre of Edinburgh, and despite me constantly expecting to be asked to leave because they've realised I don't belong there, I love it. Rose has booked a suite, and we both have our own bedrooms, in addition to a lounge area. I didn't even know hotels had rooms like this. And though I'd hoped the hotel would have facilities I could use, the pool and spa are even more gorgeous than I could possibly have imagined.

Following a fancy dinner in our suite, I decide to head to bed early. The antics of the day's travel and the champagne bubbles making me feel tired. I leave Matt and Rose curled up watching a romcom, with Sean half-watching from a chair near the door. I fall asleep quickly, until an annoying buzz from my phone by the bed wakes me from a deep sleep. The room is pitch-black when I open my eyes, and my mouth is still dry and tastes gross, despite the fact I didn't drink much last night. I debate switching it off and going back to sleep, but something makes me answer.

'Hello?' I murmur.

'Is this Niamh Whyte?'

'Erm, who's calling?'

'This is Sergeant Nevin calling from Ayr Police Station.'

'What?' I sit up and for a moment, my heart stops and I wonder what sort of trouble Rose has got herself into.

'We've tried your house, but you weren't there. Can you tell us your location and we'll send our officers to come and speak to you?'

'Erm, yes, but... Why?' My mind runs through a very short list of possibilities and lands on the most likely. 'Has something happened?' Then I realise that Ayr is the largest town near where my parents were headed.

'This isn't really a conversation for over the phone. Can you tell us where you are, please?'

I then think about all the things you're warned to do if scammers call you asking for information like this. But I don't do any of them. For some reason, I know this is genuine. I give the woman on the phone the name of the hotel.

'I'll come downstairs and meet you out the front. I don't want... I don't want to make a fuss in the hotel.'

She's quiet for a moment. 'You haven't done anything wrong, Miss Whyte.'

'I'd still prefer to come downstairs. I'll be outside in ten minutes.'

I quickly get dressed but don't even make it to the door of the suite when I realise Sean is sitting on the sofa, reading something on his phone.

'Going somewhere?'

I swallow, not sure what to say.

'What's happened, Niamh?'

'The police called. They want to speak to me. Outside.'

He stands up and takes a step towards me, all trace of friendliness wiped from his features.

'Why?'

'They didn't say. Just that it wasn't something to discuss over the phone.'

His brow furrows, eyes narrowing as his gaze sharpens, lingering on me a moment too long. 'Is this something that happens often?'

'No, I don't... I don't know what it's about. I should go.'

He nods slowly, his lips pressing into a thin line, and a

flicker of something cold glints in his expression. 'Text me once you find out.'

'Yeah, sure, okay.' I hurry from the room, wincing when the door slams behind me.

The sky is pitch-black, and the early-morning air is chilly. I hover inside the entrance to keep warm until I see a police car pull up outside.

A uniformed police officer gets out the passenger side.

'Miss Whyte?' she says as she moves towards me, and I nod, rubbing my arms against the cold. I'm dressed warmly, but the chill is coming from inside me. She smiles at me, and the sympathy in that smile is so clear that I know before she tells me that it's bad. She holds up her warrant card as she introduces herself. 'I'm Constable MacDonald. Sergeant Nevin asked us to come and pick you up and drive you through to Ayr. Why don't you take a seat in the car for a minute while we have a word. Do you have anyone with you right now?'

I think of Sean, but after his reaction just now, I don't want to involve him until I know what's going on.

'Not really,' I say. 'I just ... just want to know what's wrong.' The woman holds the door open for me and closes it before getting in the other side.

'Hi, Constable Armstrong,' says the police officer who's driving, introducing himself. He's an older man, and after turning to say hello he turns away as if giving us privacy.

I stare at the woman as she starts to talk, barely hearing the first few sentences through my panic.

'Your parents own a red Renault Megane is that correct?'

'Yes.'

'And they were travelling south from Glasgow down the coast road towards the village of Maidens?'

'Yes, my aunt ... my mum's aunt died earlier today ... yesterday ... and they went to make sure the house had been locked up properly.'

The woman smiles that same practised, sympathetic smile before taking a deep breath and reaching for my hand.

'Niamh, I'm so sorry to inform you—'

I don't really hear the rest over the blood rushing through my ears and the thudding of my heart in my chest. This can't be right. It can't be true. There must be a mistake. Phrases lodge in my brain: 'Died on impact.' 'Didn't suffer.' 'Nothing anyone could do.'

But there is, I want to scream and shout. *You can tell me you're wrong, that it's some other Renault Megane with a licence plate just like ours in an area I know they were travelling to.*

'I know this must come as a massive shock, Niamh. We'd like to take you back to the morgue at Crosshouse, just south of Glasgow, and ask you to help us identify their bodies. Is that okay?' The officer pauses with a concerned expression. 'Are you sure there isn't anyone we can call for you?'

'No, there's no one.'

The two officers exchange a look.

'If you're sure?' she says, 'Do you need to go back into the hotel and collect your belongings?'

'I'm sure. And, no, I just want to go.'

We've only just pulled out onto the Royal Mile when my phone rings and Sean's name lights up the screen.

'What's going on?' he asks, sounding guarded.

'There's ... there's been an accident.'

'What's happened? Do you need help?'

'My parents—' I break off, not sure if I can say the words that will make it all seem so real. But it is real. I have to get used to this. I grit my teeth and take a breath. 'My parents have been killed in a car accident,' I say. 'The police are taking me to the morgue at Crosshouse.'

There's silence for a few seconds before Sean replies. 'I'm so sorry, Niamh.

'I'll get Rose. We'll come with you. I'll—'

'No, I ... I need to do this myself.' I'm not sure why I'm insisting on this, but Sean's suspicion earlier, his warning me off... That coupled with what my parents said to me before I left for the conference... No. I need to be alone right now, because I know I'm going to fall completely apart. 'Thanks, Sean. Bye—'

Sean is still talking as I end the call, but he doesn't call back. I take a deep breath and feel the first hot prickle of tears in my eyes as I sit staring down at my phone.

'Everything all right?' Constable MacDonald asks, concern etched on her face.

'No. But...'

She smiles sympathetically at me. 'We'll try to support you, however we can.'

'Thanks' I say and turn to stare out the window at the dark fields of Scotland's heart as tears slide down my cheeks.

If they're really gone, then I have no one. And that scares me more than anything else.

CHAPTER 19
CILLIAN

FOUR YEARS AGO

It's not the first morgue I've walked into, and I'm pretty sure it won't be the last, but when I see her sitting on a hard metal seat in the waiting room, a polystyrene cup of coffee cradled in her hands, I'm very glad I came to this one.

'I'm here for her,' I inform the receptionist, nodding towards where Niamh is sitting alone.

'Miss Whyte?' she asks, smiling sympathetically when I nod. 'If you can just wait a moment.'

My fingers curl into my palms, the nails biting into my flesh as I take long, steady breaths and fight to control my anger at being told what to do. The one place I don't want to lose it is within the human legal system. Slow and pathetic as it is.

'Thank you,' I say, not moving a muscle as the receptionist eyes me warily and slides the glass window closed before she goes over to speak to Niamh. Niamh jumps when the woman speaks to her, then stands up and stares at me.

When our eyes meet, I know I did the right thing coming. I know her parents weren't keen on her being friendly with Rose. I'd considered going round to speak to them, do my best responsible-older-brother act to persuade them that Rose posed no risk to their daughter and that a friendship with her could potentially unlock doors for Niamh, but every time I was about to do so, something happened to distract me and now eight weeks have passed and I never will.

Niamh's eyes never leave mine as she nods, and I'm buzzed through the security door.

'Niamh,' I breathe, memories of when my own parents died stirring for the first time in years.

'You didn't need to come,' she whispers, tears welling in her eyes. 'How did you—?'

'Sean,' I say. Sean alerted me to the fact that she was sneaking out of the hotel room to meet with the police, and after Aiden had verified the accident, I decided to come and see what the situation was first-hand.

'Of course,' she murmurs, looking down at the ground.

'I'm so sorry, Niamh.'

She nods at me, and we turn as two police officers approach.

'Miss Whyte and...?'

'Cillian Hunter,' I say.

The woman nods while her colleague stares at me, fascinated. The police have never, will never, have anything concrete to charge me with. Evidence has a habit of disappearing or eyewitnesses simply forget or recall widely different versions of events involving Kinfolk. That is, if anyone even sees anything in the first place.

We're ushered through to a small office and I catch Niamh's eye to make sure she's okay with me listening in. I might feel as though I've known her forever, but we've only met once, and I want her to feel comfortable with my presence. In the claustrophobic room, they go through the explanation of how Niamh will need to conduct the formal identification. Her whole body tenses. She's tough but I can see through her bravado to the broken-hearted soul inside. I'm usually the one causing pain to others, so I'm not sure why I want to be the one to soothe hers now. And yet I find myself reaching for her hand. Her fingers slip into mine with a familiar ease, and when she glances at me, her lips slightly parted, my chest fills with an emotion I can barely contain.

Despite the mortuary assistant insisting only next of kin are allowed into the morgue, I stand my ground. No way am I letting her go in alone. Following my own parents' passing, I know more about the process anyway. We follow him to a room lit by cold blue lights, which reeks of antiseptic-covered death. Niamh rubs her arms, and I move closer, wishing I'd had someone to comfort me when I lost my father. She leans back against me, and I don't resist the urge to wrap my arms around her.

Niamh stares at the two covered bodies laid out on trolleys, her body suddenly leaning more heavily against mine as the tech pulls the sheet down until she can see her mother's face. For a moment, I think I recognise her, but I'm certain we've never met. Slowly, Niamh reaches towards her, then stops.

'Yes, that's her.' Her voice is barely above a whisper. 'Can I touch her?'

'Carefully,' the tech answers, 'but please don't move the sheet.'

I allow Niamh to step away from me so she can trail her fingers down her mother's cheek ever so gently a couple of times. Then she swallows and nods, and the tech re-covers her mother's face. I put my arm around her shoulders as she turns to identify her father.

Tomorrow, I'll ask Aiden to hack into the police records and find out exactly what happened. I'll also make sure to check any available traffic-cam footage myself. They'll put out an appeal for dashcam footage, though it may take a few weeks to get much response, if any. Theirs was a common car, and there's probably no reason for anyone to have noticed it. The road is a quiet one, rarely with more than one vehicle on it at a time, but not so quiet that any at all are noticeable.

'You can confirm the identities of David and Rhiannon Whyte?' the tech asks. Something shifts in the air, and I look around, expecting to see some sign of the Kinfolk, but there's nothing. Odd. Perhaps just the presence of so much death is triggering parts of my brain. Maybe even for humans, naming the dead can have a special significance.

In the end, Niamh doesn't say anything, just nods her confirmation.

'Is there anything else I need to do right now?' she asks the tech, and I have to admire the way she's managing to compose herself.

'Not for me, but check with reception,' the man says. 'I'm so sorry for your loss.'

She nods. Fuck, I want to pick her up and take her away from this awful place. An overwhelming need to protect her floods me, sudden and unexpected. This young woman, who I barely know, has the power to make me want to remove her pain. Abruptly, she turns away from me and moves towards the door.

'Niamh,' I call after her as she pushes through the door into the corridor. She takes a few steps before she stops and looks back. Her lips are pressed into a thin line, and her eyes glisten with unshed tears.

'Let me take you home,' I say. For a moment, I think she's going to refuse, then she sighs, the adrenaline that's kept her going for the last hour or two deserting her.

'Thank you, and thank you for coming, you didn't have to.' She still doesn't meet my eyes. And I wonder if she's waiting for me to take her hand again. But I daren't. Not here, because once I touch her, I'm not going to want to let her go.

'What do you need me to do apart from that?'

'Nothing, it's fine. I don't even know what needs to be done,' she says, staring down at the ground.

'I'm taking her home,' I say to the receptionist. I can see her hesitation but the darkness in my eyes has her shrinking back in her seat.

'They'll send Family Liaison Officers round tomorrow to discuss the arrangements and sort out counselling, if necessary. You can help her by seeing if she knows who her family solicitor is. Do you have contact details?'

'She'll be here,' I say, handing her my card, and she smiles politely and staples it to the rest of the paperwork.

'My condolences,' she says as we leave.

'Thanks,' Niamh mutters, but her blue eyes are glazed, and when I steer her over to my car, she's trembling.

'Come along, let's get you home,' I say, but it's as if I haven't spoken. Niamh stares straight ahead, over the roof of the car even after I open the door for her.

'I don't want to go home,' she says. 'I don't think I can stand it—'

A sob erupts from her chest and her hand covers her mouth as if to hold back any more signs of emotion. She reaches for the door handle but I cover her hand with mine and turn her to face me, cradling her against my body. Her tears are silent but her body shakes with her sobs. Damp heat blooms through the fabric of my shirt and I press my cheek to her hair, breathing in her light floral scent and wishing I could take this pain away from her. She clings to me, as my hands skim over her back. I ache to pull her closer but she lifts her head, her eyes red-rimmed, her lips parted as if to speak.

Instead she pushes me away, opens the car door and gets in, the door thudding behind her. I sigh and get in my side.

'I'm sorry,' she says, not looking at me. 'If you wouldn't mind driving me home, I'd appreciate it.'

'I meant Cernunnos. You can stay with Rose for now. You should try to sleep. You must be exhausted.'

'But—'

'It's easier for me this way.'

She nods, but remains bolt upright, staring out the window throughout the journey.

By the time I pull into the driveway at Cernunnos, I am deeply regretting not dragging Aiden out of his bed to drive me to the morgue. Instead, I've had to sit beside Niamh the whole way home while she sat straight-backed in the passenger seat, pretending that her life hadn't just fallen completely apart.

'It was supposed to be me in the car tonight,' she whispers as I pull into the garage and kill the engine. I knew that. Rose had mentioned that Niamh was going to drive them all to Edinburgh, but I am eternally grateful to whatever changed their plans. Although it doesn't necessarily follow that they'd have had an accident – different road, different drive, too many variables.

'Then I, for one, am very glad that it wasn't.'

She turns away and stares out the window before whispering, 'I'm not.'

I reach for her hand again and squeeze it. 'I doubt your parents would have wanted to lose you, Niamh.'

'Yes, I guess,' she says, frowning. 'But ... I don't know what I'll do without them.' She turns to face me, tears slipping down her cheeks, and it reminds me of the last time I saw my sister cry. She was much younger – only twelve – but otherwise the circumstances were similar. Our mother died when Rose was only three, and I don't think she remembered much about her death. But I'd never forget the way she just fell apart when Dad was killed.

Officially, it had been a car accident, but in reality, it had been a hunt gone wrong. And my first duty as Huntsman was to track down and kill the man who had murdered my father in cold blood. Feelings I've suppressed for years rise up and threaten to overwhelm me. The anger about what had happened, the pain of every thought of them, leading to a huge gaping rupture where my heart should be.

'Come on, you can stay in a guest room and I'll bring you a pair of Rose's pyjamas. You can get changed and get into bed.'

'I don't want to be a bother,' Niamh says instantly.

'It's not a bother.' I don't tell her that I want to keep her close, she'll wonder why I'm so invested, especially given she's so much younger than I am. I don't want her to think my motives are anything but genuine.

'Here, give me your phone. You can call me if you need anything during the night.'

'Oh ... okay,' she murmurs, handing it to me. I put in my number and hand it back as I push open the door. I go to leave, but she reaches for me and when her warm hand touches my arm, a jolt of desire rushes through me. I step back on instinct, and she quickly removes her hand as though by touching me she's scolded herself. 'Cillian...'

'What?'

'I just wanted to say that I'm sorry. You must think—'

'You're sorry?' I look at her. Her being sorry is definitely not what I want.

'You shouldn't have had to drive all that way...'

I tilt my head to one side, considering.

'You think that you can make me do something that I don't want to do?' My tone is harsher than I intend, and she tries to pull back, but I don't let her.

'Let's get you inside.' I lead her inside and up to one of our guest bedrooms. Leaving her to get settled, I speak to our housekeeper, then find Aiden to inform him of his latest, and urgent, task to find out everything possible about the accident. A short while later I find myself pausing outside her door on the way back to my own room. I should keep walking, but something about her calls to me. Though I am not the person she should be turning to.

I knock softly on the door. 'Niamh?'

'Yes?'

I push open the door. She's sitting up in bed, a steaming mug of tea beside her. Our housekeeper will have brought it up, but it remains untouched.

'It's supposed to be relaxing,' I say. 'Drink some more.'

'I'm fine,' she murmurs.

'Niamh.' My tone is sharp, but it's enough to jolt her from her dwam. 'Drink the tea.'

She keeps her eyes on me, wide and scared, as she reaches for the mug and drains every drop.

'It'll help you sleep,' I say more gently. 'It's been a really tough day.'

She relaxes slightly, her gaze still on mine.

'Things will never be the same again, will they?' she asks quietly.

'No, they won't,' I tell her.

The truth might hurt, but right now, it's all I've got for her.

'Stay with me,' she begs and I'm unable to refuse. She's wearing a pair of Rose's pyjamas, and I wish instead that I'd offered her one of my T-shirts. When she thinks about tonight, I selfishly want it to be me she's grateful to, not my sister. I sit down beside her, on top of the covers once again and fighting the temptation to offer her comfort in a more physical way. Sex is always seen as an antidote to death is it not?

'I can't believe they're gone,' she whispers and turns to face me, burying her head against my chest just like earlier. I tip her chin up with one finger and look down into her tear-filled eyes, fighting the urge to take her mouth and more if she'll let me. But she's hurting, vulnerable and no matter how much I'm drawn to her, she's just not mine to take. I cradle her head against my chest and kiss the top of her head, holding her as she cries. She falls asleep soon after, but I don't leave her side for the rest of the night.

CHAPTER 20
CILLIAN

NOW

I call Rose from the car straight after leaving Vittoria's. I have to call five times before she answers.

'Sorry,' she says groggily as soon as the call connects. 'I keep falling asleep.'

'I'm sorry about what happened last night, Rose,' I begin. 'But I'm also totally fucking furious about what you did.'

There's silence for a moment before she says, 'What did happen? Sean won't tell me anything.'

'How the fuck should I know what happened? You're the one that bailed on my engagement dinner, pissed off my future in-laws and got yourself in so much fucking trouble—' I stop, taking a deep breath to calm myself down. 'You need to wake up and get a grip, then tell me everything you can remember.'

'Well, that won't take long,' she says. 'Nothing. I don't remember anything. Where's Niamh?'

'She's not in her room?' I already know the answer to that, but the idea that, maybe, whoever protected her last night might have simply returned her to her normal life with no memory of what happened is a possibility. A slight one, but a possibility nonetheless.

'She's not.' Rose's tone is flat. 'And Sean is insistent that only you know why.'

'Sean's an idiot.' I roll my eyes. Sometimes I think I pay him too much. Could he not have said something else; something that didn't throw me quite so much under the bus? I don't want to lie to my sister, but the less she knows, the fewer questions she'll ask and the easier it'll be for me to avoid that. I change the subject back.

'Why, Rose? Would one dinner have been such a hard thing to do?'

'How can you even ask that? You know why! That woman is poison. I just ... I don't want this for you, Cillian. I don't want you to have to marry her just because you have to. We're Hunters. Is that not enough, why do you need to be more?'

I pinch the bridge of my nose and sigh. 'I'm coming over,' I tell her, not wanting to have this conversation over the phone. Aiden takes my security seriously, checking regularly for bugs and other tapping devices, ancient and modern, but when you want to discuss treason ... it's best to at least limit the number of locations and devices involved.

It's not long before I'm in Rose's sitting room and we both have a cup of strong coffee in our hands. I've drawn the curtains and opened the door onto the balcony, so that the summer sunshine floods the room, the sunlight catching on the tiny strings of mirrors hanging from the wind chime I gave her last year. I'd gone to Italy with Vittoria, and somehow the tinkling of the chimes reminds me of her — definitely not what I need right now.

'Cillian?' Rose says quietly and I look up at her. 'You're scaring me. The last time you did this...'

She trails off and I realise she's right. It's a different house — she was still living in Cernunnos when I had to tell her that the Court had called me to hunt Matt. Like me, she doesn't believe that he murdered Chris, but whatever Vincenzo said to the Court was convincing enough for them to order the hunt. Matt begged me not to tell my sister the whole truth but it's a deception I often regret, given the devastating effect that one piece of news has had on her life. At the time I thought Matt was just another boyfriend. If I'd realised how deep their feelings for each other went...

No, it wouldn't have changed anything. That night I had chosen to let Matt try to reach sanctuary at St Marnox, but he knew there would be no subsequent trial, no coming back. After all, he was accused of murdering the king's son, by the king, and a hunt had already been called. He knew his future would be spent as a prisoner at St Marnox, and he wanted her to be able to move on with her life and be happy. If I hadn't already believed he hadn't murdered Chris Riali, that would have convinced me.

'Did you ... did you hunt Niamh last night?' Rose asks me, her eyes wide. She's staring at me, barely breathing.

'Yes.'

'Cillian!' She stares at me, her mouth opening and closing as if she's trying to work out what to say. 'How could you?

What the hell has she supposedly done? Niamh would never, ever... Cillian, tell me you didn't.'

'The less you know, the better. Keep trying to find her, Rose. Report her missing. Do everything that you would do if you were innocent.'

'I *am* innocent, Cillian.'

I don't reply. Much as I love my sister, there is an anger clawing at my gut because it was her behaviour that led to this.

'Cillian?'

'Do everything that you would if you woke up to discover your best friend missing. Although, maybe don't run to the polis right away.'

'Missing?'

I wonder what more to say. If I tell her the truth, there's a chance she'll try to see Niamh. And then ... the possibility of her finding out that I've been lying to her about Matt hits me. What an absolute shitshow this is turning out to be. Mentally, I curse my sister and decide the risk of her visiting St Marnox is too great. Besides, Rose created this problem. I don't owe her an explanation and certainly not one that might increase the risk to Niamh.

'In this world she's missing. For now.'

'Someone like Niamh doesn't just disappear,' she points out.

'Her parents died four years ago, Rose. She's never really got over the trauma of losing them. Apart from one close friend and a handful of acquaintances, she's kept to herself. You'd have no idea she might be considering—'

'No, Cillian. I know her. She's just graduated with a first-class degree!'

'Well, perhaps the strain has been too much for her.'

'No, no one who knows Niamh would believe that.'

'We never really know how other people are feeling, Rose.'

'No, Niamh would never... And what the hell is she supposed to have—'

The lounge grows darker despite it being late morning, and the middle of summer. I shiver, the shadows growing deeper around the edges of the room as I push to my feet.

'What's going on?' I ask, looking around, but my sister is acting as if nothing happened.

And instantly the shadows are gone, and the room is bright, sunny, warm.

'Stop trying to change the subject, Cillian. You've done something to my best friend. Did you really kill her? Just like you killed Matt.' Rose's eyes are glassy with tears, with grief. 'And for what? To appease a family whose rule has brought the Court all but to its knees? Why? Why would you do this?'

'Because ... I have a duty,' I snap. Does she really believe I wanted to do this?

'Then give it up! What are you going to sacrifice for your duty next? Me? Niamh loved you, did you know that? She thought I didn't know, but I did.'

My heart seems to turn over in my chest, pulsing as though it might burst as Rose's words register. My thoughts focus solely on the wild, impossible truth of it as a rush of heat floods my veins. Niamh loves me. My pulse thunders in my ears and I clench my hands into fists so that Rose can't see them trembling.

'I did not know that, no.' My voice is flat and hollow in an effort to conceal what I'm really feeling.

'And I know you cared for her in your own sick and twisted way.'

We stare at each other, both breathing heavily.

'When did it start? At the party? Where did she sleep that night, Cillian?'

'I don't know what you're talking about.'

We glare at one another, but Rose isn't giving up.

'Anyway. You abandoned her, as I recall, so that you could go fuck your boyfriend!'

'Really? I'm not stupid, Cillian. You think I don't know that you watch us when we're out. Make sure that any guy, no, make that anybody at all, who gets too close to Niamh, suddenly finds a reason to abandon her. Do you know what that's done to her?'

'What do you mean?'

She laughs as she lets her head fall back onto the cushions and turns her head away from me, towards the window.

'How can you not see it? She's stuck exactly where she was when she first met you. Pretty much. Every time she gets close to someone, something *happens* and they suddenly ghost her. Or leave the country or—'

'What do you mean "pretty much"?'

'Oh, for fuck's sake, Cillian! You weren't watching us all the time. There were a couple of guys who got past your security safeguards. Although you didn't exactly leave her with the cream of the crop, so I'm not sure exactly what happened, but—'

'Who are these guys?' My muscles tense.

'I wouldn't tell you even if I could, because I don't want to read about them floating face down in the Clyde in the morning papers. If I'd told you about them, the poor bastards would have had to cross busy streets just to avoid her, because whatever you'd have threatened to do to them if they tried to have a relationship with her would have put each one of them off taking the risk.'

I clench my fists to stop myself yelling at her. The fact is, nothing she's said so far is untrue. But I never expected to feel such guilt.

'I was simply keeping unsuitable men away from her, making sure that she was safe.'

'Safe? From who, Cill? Someone who *might* fall in love with her? One day give her a home, a family, children? All the things you're going to give to Vittoria and at the same time make sure Niamh never has with anyone! The biggest danger to Niamh Whyte was always you and now you've proved it.'

'Rose—'

'No, Cillian. Just leave. I have nothing else to say to you.'

My breath hitches, the flicker of disbelief rapidly giving way to a sense of outrage. My hands curl into fists as her words sink in but this situation is not all on me.

'You should have come to the party. Played along. This marriage – if I become king—'

'Why the hell do you want to be the king of a dying Court? Vincenzo isn't all that old, he could have decades left and Vittoria will have locked you up in her basement and murdered you long before then.'

My lips twitch in a smile. 'She could try.'

'Why, Cillian? Why?'

Why? Because with every passing day I become more and more convinced of the necessity to hasten Vincenzo's exit from this life. But that's not something I'll ever say out loud. Although, there's not many capable of hunting me down – even for treason. But there's always a chance that Vincenzo would be arrogant enough to try.

'Get out. You've taken everyone I loved from me, Cillian. I don't want to hear any more of your justifications. What you did was wrong.'

Rose glares at me, and I almost consider telling her that Matt's safe at St Marnox, but I can't. It would jeopardise his safety and Niamh's. Plus he wanted Rose to move on with her life. Though she doesn't seem to be doing that. As a Hunter, she can go there, visit them, but the fact that they are prisoners there will just not change. I take a deep breath, my path becoming clearer. For Rose's sake I need to do something. Make sure the corruption in The Unseelie Court is stopped and at least give Matt the chance of a fair trial. And if I'm lucky maybe that will even work for Niamh, too. Even though the only way I can see to achieve that means cutting me off from her forever. 'Vincenzo will not be King forever,' I promise her. She's silent, knowing full well that it's true, no matter how big a grudge she holds against him and how impossible it might seem right now for Vincenzo to be gone. Even though his family are nothing if not tenacious, only arriving at The Unseelie Court less than a century ago, but quickly rising to power within it. Their Kin back home in Northern Italy were also powerful, so it was no great surprise. And, thanks to the Blight here, we were in need of powerful families to help hold the remnants of the Court together.

'Being more powerful can never be a bad thing, Rose,' I say softly, almost believing it myself. 'But despite our power ... the Kinfolk are fading, the Blight is weakening us. A union between the Riali and Hunter families would give us more power, me more power. Maybe one day with me as king, we can stop it. Maybe even start to reverse it.'

She scoffs. 'With Vittoria as Queen? Please, Cillian. A Court with hatred and evil at its heart is no foundation to rebuild the Kinfolk on. The Blight would continue to spread – it benefits the Rialis more often than not.'

'Rose—' I break off, knowing she has a point, but this is not something that we should be focusing on right now. I have other priorities. And if I could tell Rose what those were, she would help. But I can't. All I can do is tell her enough to hope she allows me to get on with what I need to do. Or, at least, not get in my way.

I leave Rose's flat, my sister's words still running through my head, and head to my office at The Three Graces to figure out the cause of last night's commotion and why those men tried to abduct her and Niamh. Vittoria has sent over the surveillance footage as she promised, but there's not much there. I'm watching it for the third time, when my phone rings. Declan.

'What the fuck were you thinking?' he barks into the phone when I pick up. 'What the fuck am I supposed to do with her?'

'Declan—'

'She turned up on our doorstep this morning, and frankly, being the only female, she's already getting—'

'She's mine.'

His sudden laughter makes me close my eyes and take a deep breath. And then another. Anger churns deep in my gut and if he's not careful, I'll be driving straight up there and wiping that smirk I can see so clearly in my head off his face with my fists.

'You might want to come and make that clear in person, Cillian, before Sal gets any ideas.'

'Tell every single man under that roof that I will tear them limb from limb before choking them with their own dicks if they so much as lay a finger on that girl.'

'She doesn't look like a girl from where I'm standing. She's all woman, Cill. And you've sent her here. Sal is already—'

'I meant what I said, Declan. And if you can't control them, I'll come and personally drag every single one of you in front of The Unseelie Court...'

'Even you can't break the rules of sanctuary, Cillian,' Declan says quietly, and I fight to control my reaction.

'For Niamh, I will bloody well try.'

I can almost hear him shaking his head. 'Only we can opt to go in front of The Unseelie Court to be tried, and you can't harm any of us within the walls. Now, tell me, why is she here? She found this place, right as dawn broke. And she knew the words.'

I don't answer, unsure whether I should explain that, however she got to St Marnox, it was nothing to do with me.

'Cillian?'

'I didn't,' I admit. 'Although I would have, if I'd thought it possible. I hoped...'

There's silence on the other end of the phone.

'What?' I ask after a moment.

'I'm trying to work out whether she lied to me or not. If she did...'

If she lied to him, there's nothing he can do about it as long as they're both inside the sanctuary.

'I imagine that technically she didn't lie, and you either heard what you wanted to hear or you made assumptions. She's going to be a hot-shot lawyer, Declan. They're a lot like the Kinfolk in terms of principles.'

'Aye, you're probably right.' He blows out a breath. 'I'm impressed. Maybe she does have a chance in hell of surviving this place.'

'She's just my sister's friend, Declan. She better fucking survive.'

'Just your sister's friend,' he says slowly, and I can hear the amusement beneath his words. 'Maybe if you tell us in person that's all she is, then we'll believe it. But there's seven guys trapped here. Some of us haven't seen a woman in decades. And Sal was quite right in suggesting that she might be useful to us.'

'Shut up.' Rage is coursing through me, my heartbeat

pounding in my ears as thoughts of them taking what I have so carefully kept for myself all these years sends me into a spiral.

'I'm just yanking your chain,' he says.

'Well, as long as you're enjoying yourself.' My words are said through gritted teeth.

'Oh, I'm in a great mood, all seven of us are fecking overjoyed about her arrival. As you can only expect, she's not getting a free ride and we're delighted that she's taken over the cooking, the cleaning and the laundry.'

'She's worth more than that, Declan. She has a brain.'

'Yeah, you said. But we don't need a fucking lawyer here, Cillian. Or someone to do the accounts. Domestic chores are the Seven's least favourite. It'll be the easiest way to get them to accept her and want her to stay.'

'She's not your servant.'

'No, but she is stuck here, so she'll be whatever I tell her to be, Cill. If you don't like it, find a way to get her out. The rest of us here work. If she doesn't, imagine the level of resentment that's going to build. And when resentment builds, bad things inevitably start to happen. And, I'm just putting this out there now before you come in here threatening to cut off bits of my anatomy, but I'm not going to stand in her way if she does show an interest in any of the others. In fact, I believe she's gone to the loch with Matt. It's a beautiful summer's evening here. Very romantic. And you know how he loves to swim. Naked, of course.'

'You might want to rethink your priorities, Declan. Keep this up and a lawyer's going to be exactly what you need.'

I end the call, but I can hear his laughter as I get in my car, and head for the monastery.

CHAPTER 21
NIAMH

By the following evening, I decide that I've done a reasonable enough job for my first day as cook. I've just finished wiping down the surfaces when I see Matt passing the window. It's been another beautiful day and the evening is still warm. If I needed proof that this place is an alternative version of the Highlands, it's the weather. I dry my hands, and head for the jetty.

Matt has already reached the end of it. I'm thankful I'm behind him when he bends down and strips his robe off over his head, then dives into the water. I pause, feeling like a peeping Tom, watching him when he's naked, but he's in a public place. It's hardly my fault.

I've reached the end of the jetty before he surfaces, and I'm impressed with how long he can hold his breath. He turns, noticing me, and swims back. I focus on keeping my eyes on his face as he approaches.

'You coming in?' he asks.

'Isn't it cold?'

'Refreshing.' He grins. 'Absolutely Baltic. I'm freezing my balls off in here. But it's good. I like to swim.'

'I don't have a swimsuit.'

'Neither do I,' he says, laughing and pushing himself off the dock to float on his back. I roll my eyes, then look away, but can't help the way my cheeks heat. Thankfully it's not long before he rolls over and swims off again. I lose sight of him, then suddenly he's shooting up, out of the water at the side of the jetty, soaking my robes.

'Matt,' I chide, but I'm not overly bothered. My robes are hot, the cool water a welcome respite. I'm tempted to join him, but I compromise by sitting down on the edge of the jetty, pulling my robe up to my knees and dangling my feet in the water. I yelp at the first contact, but manage to keep them submerged the second time and lean back on my elbows, as the orange hue in the sky grows more pronounced.

'You make that look easy,' I say when he returns to the jetty and pushes himself out of the water. Although it's not really a push, it's almost as if he's catapulted straight out of the water, to land on his feet on the wooden planks.

'It's just practice,' he says, but there's something about the way he says it that makes me suspect it's not strictly true. I frown, turning to look at him, then immediately look back out over the loch.

'Robe,' I instruct, shutting my eyes.

'Sorry,' he says, and I open them again to see him wrapping it around his waist and sitting.

'I was hoping we could talk.'

'Okay... What about?' he asks, picking up a small stone from the planks and throwing it into the water. We both watch as the ripples circle out from where it lands. 'As long as I'm not going to end up with the Hunters after me.'

'Just for talking to me?'

'Have you met Cillian?' He rolls his eyes and I laugh, then see him narrow his eyes. 'Are you two—?'

'No!'

He lifts an eyebrow. 'I know he's obsessed with you. I also know you slept in his room the first night you met him. He doesn't just let anyone sleep there. In fact, as I remember, Vittoria never slept over.'

I go still with this information, unsure how to process it. 'Did Rose ever know about that? Me sleeping in his room.'

'Not sure, but I wasn't going to start mouthing off about what I saw Cillian Hunter doing in his own house. Especially given why I was there.'

'He didn't approve of the two of you?'

Matt pauses for a moment, then shrugs. 'He didn't love it ... but he didn't kill me either. And he could have done. Court-sanctioned removal of the dangerous guy who's fucking his little sister. Every protective big brother's dream.'

'Court sanctioned?'

'Cillian was sent to hunt me by the Court, instead he let me come here. He must care for you, too, to not kill you after killing Kin. Or was he actually outrun by a human?'

'I'm not sure. There was...' I stop, deciding it's probably best not to share any more information than I have to. Cillian was pretty set on hunting me through the forest, and it didn't feel as though he'd let me go by choice.

Matt nods, hesitates, then says, 'Has Rose ... has she met someone?'

I'm not entirely sure what answer he wants, but the last thing I want to do is hurt him with the whole unvarnished truth. 'No one special, not yet.'

He nods again, and I can't work out if he's pleased or upset by this news.

'She graduated, though?'

'Yes. Cillian blackmailed her into studying by—' Nope, not something Matt needs to know. 'So, you knew about all of this – the Underworld, the Kinfolk, everything.'

'Niamh, I'm one of them.' Matt stares at me. 'Even after all these years, you didn't know?'

'Over the past couple of days, I seem to have discovered that I do not, in fact, know anything at all.' I shrug.

'You'll get used to it. Although they make most humans forget,' he says, shooting me a sidelong look. 'So ... back to you in Cillian's bed.'

'There was nowhere else to sleep.'

'Uh-huh. There were plenty of people on the sofas and curled up on the floor in both the lounge and the drawing room.'

My cheeks heat. 'Nowhere else that Cillian approved of. There were a lot of couples ... doing couple stuff – including you and Rose, apparently.'

Matt grins at me.

'Cillian said he had work to do, so I slept in his bed, while he ... worked.'

'Right.' Matt's lips twitch and he breaks out into a peal of laughter that I can't help joining in with.

'I guess I was a little naïve and trusting.' I sigh. 'But nothing happened. Well, nothing much.'

'Nothing much?'

I shake my head but can't stop my cheeks from heating.

'And, since then?'

'Nothing important,' I assure him.

He makes a face at me, shaking his head. 'Cillian Hunter, eh? There's much more to you than meets the eye. Nothing like setting your sights high.'

'Matt, he's marrying Vittoria Riali. Their engagement dinner was what started all this—' Then I remember that what's keeping me safe here is that all the men think I belong to Cillian. And I guess that all of them are assuming in what way I belong to Cillian. 'He was supposed to kill me.'

'That's kind of his job, Niamh. But sometimes, he makes good choices, so I suppose there's hope for him. And he's put off marrying Vittoria for all this time.'

I can't think about what-ifs. I've been told several times that Cillian needs to marry Vittoria to achieve his goals. That doesn't leave any place in his life for me. I refuse to be someone's dirty secret. I have too much self-respect for that.

'Anyway, you're supposed to be dead,' I say, changing the subject.

'I may as well be.'

'That's ... that's not true. If Rose knew you were alive she might not—'

'No, Rose shouldn't waste her life on me. I'm never getting out of here. She deserves more than I can offer her.'

'Matt,' I reach for him and squeeze his arm gently. I think of how much Rose has changed since he disappeared. And it worries me. Her behaviour, her attitude to me, to relationships. She needs him.

He sighs and looks away.

'I was accused of a murder I didn't commit,' he mutters.

I nod. 'I know. Vittoria's brother. Chris Riali.'

'How do you—' He pauses. 'Did Cillian tell you?'

'No. Declan,' I tell him. 'But if you're innocent, can't you just go to this Court everyone keeps talking about?'

'Well, I could. But Chris's dad controls the Court, and I'm not willing to bet my life on me getting a fair trial. St Marnox is the only option – unless things change. And now you're stuck here, too.'

'Seems like it,' I say vaguely, knowing that I'm going to do everything I possibly can to get out of here. 'But if you didn't kill him. Tell me what happened.'

He sighs. 'Chris had been acting strangely for, I don't know, a week or two, maybe. He'd had problems with drugs and alcohol—'

I recall the first time I met him at Cillian's house. He seemed a little off the rails then. 'Yeah, that was obvious.'

'But when he died, his father, Vincenzo ... he made Chris out to be some saint.'

'I suppose I can understand that.'

'It was me who found Chris ... that night. He'd been drinking, heavily. Cut his wrists in the bath, bled out. I tried to save him. I really did.' Matt stops, takes a breath. 'I called for help, called his family. But when they arrived ... they just decided I'd killed him. I was covered in his blood, after all. Vincenzo wanted to avoid the shame of his son dying by suicide. So, he blamed me.'

'Wow. That's so twisted,' I say, though not shocked. And Cillian agreed with the Rialis? He ... hunted you down?'

'He didn't have a choice, Niamh. He hunted me, he even caught me and could have killed me on the spot ... but he didn't. He gave me the chance to reach here instead. Because he didn't believe Vincenzo either. But it's been years, and this life... It's barely worth living.'

'But at least you're alive,' I say.

'I have to live every day without Rose. Not able to see her, talk to her. Cillian tells me a little when he's here—'

'Cillian comes here?'

'Yes, anyone can go to the human side of St Marnox. But only the Hunters can enter into the monastery in the Underworld. It's what makes this a sanctuary.'

'So, Rose could come here, too?'

'I ... I suppose she could.'

I feel conflicted, not knowing if Cillian knows I'm here and what that could mean for me.

'So, how often does he come?' I ask.

'Rarely,' Matt says, then is quiet for a moment. 'You know, while I've been here, I've had a lot of time to think. What do you know about your parents' deaths?'

The question takes me by surprise. 'That they died in a car crash. An accident. No other cars were involved.'

Matt is staring at me, waiting for me to say more, I think, but what else is there to say? Certainly nothing relevant.

'That's all you know?'

'It was dark. The road was wet. It's a bad bend. There's been plenty more accidents there since.'

'Fatal ones?'

What exactly is Matt getting at?

'I ... I assume so. But... Look, what does that have to do with Chris's suicide or with you being accused of murder?'

'Nothing, you're right. Forget I said anything. Come on, we should get out.'

But a sudden chill in the air makes me shiver. For weeks after my parents died, I was constantly looking over my shoulder, feeling like I was being watched, followed even, and I have the same prickling feeling on the back of my neck right now. I push myself to my feet beside Matt, looking all around, as I sense, but cannot see, something coming towards us. Suddenly, Matt is falling back into the water, and I find myself staring into the furious face of Cillian Hunter.

'Cillian. What do you think you're—' I only take a single step towards the edge of the jetty, to try to make sure Matt is all right when Cillian grabs my hand and pulls me back against him. I struggle but he's stronger.

There's a thud on the jetty behind me and Cillian growls, lifting his head to stare at Matt. I try to turn, but he won't let me.

'Go inside,' Cillian orders Matt.

'I'm not going to let you hurt her,' Matt says. 'You need to calm down.'

I push again at Cillian's chest. 'Let me go.'

'Why? So that you and Matt can finish whatever it was you were doing?'

I look up at him and shake my head at his hypocrisy. He's the one who has someone else. Him, not me.

'We were sitting chatting on a jetty overlooking a loch,' I tell him. 'What did you think we were doing?'

Matt sniggers behind me, and I see Cillian's lips curve upwards.

'That's not going to stop me taking exactly what I want from you. And you'—he glares at Matt—'you seem rather amused for a dead man.'

'We're not going to touch her, Cillian. In fact, Lachlan suggested that she might be able to help us. You know, if any of us decide to face the Court.'

'You want her help as what? A lawyer?'

Cillian is still holding me way too tight, but his muscles are relaxing, the tension draining from him with every passing second.

'Go!' he says to Matt again.

'You going to be all right, *Gléigeal*?'

Cillian's grip on me tightens. 'He has a pet name for you?'

'Declan gave it to me. He said it meant Snow White. You know, out here with seven guys and at least one of them is some kind of mountain man. One that isn't quite human.'

'His twin, Niamh. There's two of them. And the rest of us have secrets, too,' Matt points out, and he's grinning now. 'Let me guess, Cillian. Sal told you where she was.'

'Declan, actually.' Cillian's tone is clipped. 'But he reminded me of Sal's somewhat predatory nature.'

Matt sighs. 'You should know better than to let him rile you up,' he says, pulling on his robes and letting them fall into place. 'I'm off. Don't do anything I wouldn't do.' With that, he heads towards the monastery, whistling.

'Are you all right?' Cillian asks, letting me go and looking me up and down.

'Fine,' I say dryly. 'I mean other than being held prisoner, and having to cook and clean for seven men.'

'That's all they've asked you to do?'

'Why does it matter, Cillian? It's not like you want anything else from me. No one does.'

He's shaking his head. 'That's ... that's not...'

I push at him once more and this time he lets me go. I turn away, moving past him to walk up the jetty.

'Where are you going?'

'To my room, to shower.'

'No, not until we've talked.'

'Cillian, I'm hot.'

'Then take off your robe. Get into the water.'

I roll my eyes. 'Why so that you can hurl more accusations at me for—'

But instead, he leans over and catches my robe with his hands, pulling it up and over my head. I squeak as I grab for my T-shirt so that he doesn't pull that up as well.

I stand, watching as he drops his jacket to the wooden boards, followed by his dark dress shirt. I swallow as he toes off his shoes, then undoes his belt and removes his trousers, folding them neatly and placing them on top of his shirt. I stare at him, mesmerised once again by the smoothness of his skin, the firm curve of the muscles in his arms and torso. I've seen his tattoos before, but I'm still drawn to reach out for the largest one, the one of Cernunnos. The image is larger than my hand and I can feel his heart beating through my fingers. Then he grins a wicked grin.

The next second, I'm hitting freezing water.

'You bastard,' I yell, spluttering back to the surface. Baltic doesn't even begin to cover it. I tread water as my body adjusts, ducking to the side as Cillian dives in beside me. I swim away from him, but strong fingers grasp my ankle pulling towards him. He wraps his arms around me, his mouth on mine before I can even wipe the water out of my eyes.

He lifts me, so that my chest is level with his and my legs automatically wrap around his waist. My T-shirt rides up onto my hips and there's a hard bulge in his underwear, pressing against my most sensitive parts. But he doesn't try and kiss me again. Doesn't do anything at all.

The last time we met, this man was hunting me, and now I'm letting him do this. I want him to do this. I'm not sure what I'm doing right now, I only know that after everything that's happened, I'm not going to turn this down. I've wanted Cillian Hunter since the moment I met him, and strangely I believe he wants me too. He circles his hips, grinding me against him and leaving no doubt what he wants from me right now. Behind him the crumbling stone walls of the monastery are falling into shadow as the sun sets. I shiver as the breeze hits my shoulders.

'Cooler now?'

'Why are you here?' I want to know what has happened to suddenly make him think I'm his to take. Every time I think he might want me, he pulls away. He's gone from occasionally kissing me to flaunting his relationship with Vittoria in my face for four years. Yet here he is, again, confusing my feelings and ripping my heart out with every touch. 'You were going to kill me.'

He closes his eyes for a second, shaking his head before

opening them again. 'I have a duty, and if you hadn't made it here... The Wild Hunt... Many choose a quick death at my hands once they know they won't reach sanctuary.' He swallows. 'I failed in my duty that night. I couldn't pull the trigger.'

'Except you did.'

'To shoot the deer. And now you're safe here. Vittoria is convinced that you're dead and the hunt is over.' He holds his hand up, showing me his palm, now free from the strange symbol and my name.

'So now you can run off here to see me whenever you feel like it and then go back to your life with her?'

'No. That's not ... I'm not going to ... I wanted to make sure you were okay,' he says. 'I know they can't harm you, but that's not to say that one of them wouldn't ... that you wouldn't choose to—'

I pull back. 'So, you're *really* here to make sure that I haven't decided to ... what? Fuck any of the seven men you sent me here to live with?'

'Sal—'

'—was hoping I was a prostitute,' I finish.

His jaw tightens. Sal should be very grateful that magic is stopping Cillian from harming him, because I'm not sure anything else could.

'And then I find you here with Matt—'

'My best friend's boyfriend. Cillian, I don't know if you've noticed but up until now, no one has ever been interested in me for longer than a few minutes – a day at most. Even you – you come along, kiss me, occasionally even sleep beside me –

but then you're off again, making it clear that you're not interested. That you don't want me, that I'm not enough for you.' I slap my hands on his chest to make him let go. I should have known better. This won't be leading anywhere. Cillian will do what he always does, what any guy I meet does – go so far and then disappear completely. And you're probably right. No one sticks around. No one ever wants me enough to—'

'Niamh, how can you think that? Say that? That isn't it at all.'

'Really? Because for years, *years*, Cillian you've kissed me, sometimes even comforted me. But you've always been gone by morning, made it clear in public that I was nothing to you, thrust Vittoria in my face. Yeah. I get it, I'm the dull little virgin. And nothing more. Too stupid to understand that you were just being nice, for her sake. And—'

'That's not why. That's not why at all,' he insists, his blue eyes piercing me. 'Niamh.' My hands are resting on his shoulders as we stare at one another, and suddenly he cups my head and pulls me towards him, his lips crashing into mine, kissing me as though I'm the reason for his existence. The warmth of his mouth sends shivers down my spine as our tongues tangle together, dancing in a rhythm that feels so right. The muscles in his shoulders harden under my fingers as he pulls me closer against his body. Then we break apart gasping.

He drops his forehead to rest against mine, and for a moment we just breathe.

'Then why?' I whisper. But he doesn't seem to want to answer that.

Instead, he shakes his head. 'You have to know that you are infinitely ... desirable, *Gléigeal*.'

'Stealing Declan's term of endearment for me?'

'It fits. It's mine now,' he promises. 'If Declan uses it again ... it'll be the last word he utters. I've been selfish, *Gléigeal*.'

'What do you mean?'

He kisses me again, his tongue pushing its way into my mouth, seeking acceptance as his kisses get deeper and more urgent. His hand pulls at my wet T-shirt, removing the fabric stuck to my body as he slides a hand under the material. He presses it against the small of my back, his mouth moving across my lips, down the line of my jaw before he drops kisses down my neck, and I shiver. I cup his head with my hand and force him to still.

'Cillian?'

Now he looks at me steadily. 'Rose is right,' he says. 'I've kept you for myself, pushed other men away from you. Then abandoned you to be with Vittoria. My only excuse is that if she'd ever realised how much I wanted you, then she would have—'

'You want me?' I know he does, I've probably always known, but it matters, hearing him say it out loud.

He adjusts his hips, letting me feel exactly how much he wants me. The hardness of his cock brushes against me as he guides my body in a slow rhythm, the thin fabric between us creating a delicious friction against my most sensitive spot. I wrap my arms around his neck and he lifts me so my legs tighten around his waist while the cool waters of the loch heighten every sensation and leave me wanting more.

'From the first night I saw you, I've been drawn to you. It's as if you were meant for me. But I have a duty to my family, to The Unseelie Court and I thought the best thing, the *right* thing was for me to marry Vittoria. You've made me feel things I couldn't let myself feel. And I can't leave you alone. No matter how hard I try, I can't get thoughts of you out of my head. I want you, Niamh. I always have.'

I stare at him for a long moment, the weight of his words and the feeling of his body against mine reflecting everything he just said, but what does it mean?

His arms encircle my waist, and I can feel his hand move further down to my buttocks as he pulls me closer, removing any gap between us. I'm flush to his abs, and I can feel his erection pushing against me.

I capture his lip between my teeth and gently pull, before I kiss him back. 'And I want you,' I breathe. 'I want whatever you're willing to give me.'

'I want to give you everything.' His thumb strokes me, and I gasp as I feel him rub slow circles over my clit. It's not the first time he's touched me but it's the first time he's touched me when he knows I want him like he wants me. And it feels different. And even if it's just for tonight, here in the Underworld, Cillian Hunter can be mine. But first there's something I need to know for sure.

'What did you mean when you said you kept other men away from me?'

CHAPTER 22
NIAMH

TWO YEARS AGO

'We're halfway through uni, and I never seem to meet anyone,' I moan to Rose, stirring my Porn Star Martini.

'You meet plenty of guys,' she says.

'No one that sticks around for longer than five minutes.'

'What about Martin? You met him at the Cathouse, and then he turned up for a date at Elliots.'

'Yeah. He did,' I say. 'And then he bailed.'

'So, what did you say to him?'

I shrug. 'Nothing bad. We were just chatting and then he went to the bathroom and never came back.'

'What *exactly* were you talking about beforehand?'

'Uni ... and stuff.'

'Did you tell him what you were studying?'

'Erm ... maybe.'

Rose sighs. 'You have to hold back on that information for a while. No one wants to date a lawyer. Especially guys you meet in a club.'

'But—'

'Actually, there's a guy in one of my classes—'

'Philip?'

'Yes. He's not completely boring.'

'We've already met,' I say. 'We had coffee, and then he ghosted me. Have you not noticed he doesn't sit near me in lectures, that if I happen to sit anywhere in the vicinity of him, he actually gets up and moves.' I bite my lip. He's not the only guy who seems to go actively out of their way to avoid me, either. 'What am I doing wrong?'

Rose sighs and looks me up and down. 'We could try a makeover?'

'I want them to like *me* and want to spend time with *me*, Rose. Not whatever they think I'm going to be like because of what I'm wearing.'

'You dress like a nun, Niamh. I'm not sure that your clothes really give guys an accurate picture of who you are right now.'

I sigh. 'Maybe once I'm qualified and earning decent money I'll invest in a new wardrobe.'

'Did you listen to what I said earlier at all? No one wants to date a lawyer. Everyone thinks that somehow when they're with you, they're going to do something that you think is evidence of them committing a crime, or you're going to see something you shouldn't and have them locked up forever.'

'That ... can't possibly be true, can it?'

Rose sighs. 'Okay, why don't we try something? I've got a spare outfit in my bag. Nothing too revealing,' she assures me before I start to object. 'It'll suit you. Come on. You've got nothing to lose, right?'

She winks at me and hands over a bag from a designer store nearby.

'Rose, I can't accept—'

'Yes, you can. Now come on, drink up and I'll get us another round while you change. The bar isn't open yet so no one will see you.'

The cocktail goes down easily, its sweetness barely making it feel like I'm drinking alcohol, then I down the accompanying shot of prosecco.

'Right, fine,' I sigh, standing up and heading downstairs.

It's weird walking through the closed bar. I don't usually come to this part of The Three Graces as there's no dancefloor, and the clientele are usually older. Late twenties at least.

The bathrooms are in the far back corner, a long wooden screen separating the short corridor they are located on from the rest of the club. I push open the door to the ladies', wincing at the loud squeak the door makes as it swings slowly shut.

Standing in front of the large mirror, I put the bag Rose gave me on the counter and remove my cardigan and blouse. I wrinkle my nose. Rose is right about the energy I'm giving off – uptight, prim. I start by fixing my make-up, putting on a little more blusher, making my eyes a little smokier. I'm leaning forward to apply a deep red lipstick when I hear footsteps approach. And suddenly the door crashes open.

I grab for my clothes, holding them in a ball in front of me so that whoever it is sees as little as possible.

'We're closed.'

The voice is entirely devoid of emotion, sending shivers down my spine.

'Sorry,' I squeak. 'Rose Hunter ... said I could come in and—'

For the first time in ages, I set eyes on Cillian Hunter as he steps out of the shadow of the doorway. He's wearing a sharp, tailored suit and his dark hair has been perfectly styled. I catch sight of his jawline with just a hint of stubble and I'm reminded of his beauty. How is it possible for one man to look this good? He stops short of entering the bathroom when he sees me, his eyes running the length of my body, stopping and frowning when they settle on my chest and he sees I'm only wearing my bra.

'Niamh?' he says, his voice catching in his throat. He looks directly into my eyes and I'm lost in their icy-blue glare for a moment, unsure what to do, whether to move. He has the power to make me speechless and I feel insignificant and childish under his gaze. He clears his throat.

'I don't think you should be in here,' I say, finally finding my voice.

CHAPTER 23
CILLIAN

TWO YEARS AGO

The moment I swing open the door to the ladies' bathroom, I knew I should have asked a female staff member to follow Niamh inside. But the last thing I expect is to see her standing half-naked. It takes me a moment to compose myself, she looks so serene standing there in the white lacy bra that she's not been quick enough to cover up. I almost want to laugh at the sight, but I can't, because she's so beautiful, ethereal, that for a second, I forget to say anything.

'Get dressed and go back upstairs,' I bark at her when I eventually recover my composure. I don't want to be alone with her in here anymore, the space is closing in around me and despite it being a long time since we were face to face, let alone have spoken to each other, I can't trust myself to be a gentleman.

There have been so many nights over the past couple of

years when I've thought about what I would do to Niamh to make her mine, and the pull to do so, right here and now is almost overwhelming. Her doe eyes stare at me innocently, waiting for me to leave, but all I can think about right now is bending her over the vanity counter and taking what I want. How I'd push her breasts out of her bra and play with her nipples until she moaned with pleasure. How I'd flip her skirt up, slide my fingers into her panties to feel her slick wetness, ready and waiting for me to be the one to fill her. How I'd slip one, then two fingers inside her, pumping slowly at first before going faster, teasing her to find her release.

My thumb would tease slow circles over her clit, until she was writhing, breathless, crying out my name as I push her over the edge. Then I'd drag my fingers from her and watch her suck them, so she could taste how sweet her pretty pussy is. And then I'd fuck her, hard, as we watch in the mirror. I can almost feel how tight she'll be, how she'll take every inch of my cock until I'm seated to the hilt. I groan quietly at the thought, the desire overwhelming as a light sweat pricks at my temples. I've never wanted someone so much, never mind someone I cannot have.

She's breathing heavily, and I wonder if she's thinking the same things as I am. I doubt it. She's too innocent to imagine being fucked in a club bathroom. I barely look at her as she quickly, tearfully re-dresses, then hurries out. I adjust myself, the painful ache of my cock straining against my trousers and turn to follow her upstairs. By the time I reach the main level, I find Vittoria talking to Rose, who glares at me as I approach.

'Well—' Vittoria begins, then stops, her attention firmly

fixed on someone just ahead of me. I hadn't taken in what Niamh had put on, lost in my own thoughts, but now I can see she's changed out of her usual demure tops and is wearing something my sister must've given her. The barely-there top leaves almost as little to the imagination as when she was stood in her bra just a few minutes before. I'd love nothing more than to bend her over and spank her for showing off so much of herself. Men won't be able to look away, and I ball my fists at the thought of the unwanted attention. The attention I don't want her to have.

Vittoria steps towards me and winds her arms around my neck. 'We'll leave you and your little friend up here to enjoy your drinks, Rose. Porn Stars? How … inappropriate.'

I grit my teeth as Vittoria laughs, although it comes out as more of a cackle. I try not to flinch at the sound.

She lets go of me. 'I should go, darling. Don't want to be late for the event. I promised my father I'd hostess at Sussurri tonight, so I won't be finished until close.' She strokes a red fingernail down my cheek, making me shudder, and not in a good way. 'Walk me out?'

As reluctant as I am to leave my sister and Niamh, I can't stay with them. I don't think I could hide my responses, and Rose would ask questions I've no intention of answering. I smile tightly as I wind my arm around Vittoria's waist and lead her away before my sister decides to murder her.

~

I spend the night watching both girls carefully. I know my sister finds it easy to pick up then quickly drop men, but when she's in our clubs, I do at least try to weed out some of her more inappropriate choices. But Rose is confident, sure of what she's looking for in a man, so it's not her I usually focus my attention on.

By late evening the dancefloor is packed and both girls have switched from cocktails to soft drinks, which is a relief. There's been no shortage of interest from guys, and I'm not surprised given the lack of clothing they both seem to be wearing. Although they've danced with multiple partners, most haven't lasted more than a few minutes. The bouncers I employ have all been under strict instruction to remove anyone who gets too close. All strictly hush-hush, though, so Rose doesn't realise what's happening.

I'm seated in a booth overlooking the dancefloor. It allows me to keep an eye on the bar and the patrons. And tonight, it gives me a great view of Rose and Niamh. Unfortunately, Niamh's been dancing with the same guy for at least an hour now and he's sticking way too close to her. Too close for me to give him a friendly warning to leave her the fuck alone.

I watch as he helps her on with her jacket. She smiles at him, and he tucks her under his arm as they say goodbye to Rose and the guy she's with and head to the door. It's never got as far as this before with Niamh. Every time I've watched them both in my club, she's never actually got to the point of potentially leaving with someone.

And tonight will be no different.

I retreat to my office and watch on the CCTV as one of the bouncers pulls Niamh's companion aside as he tries to follow her out. She is waiting outside, her jacket tight around her as she huddles from the chill of the night air, oblivious, as her gentleman friend is directed back into the building and towards my office. I've given the bouncer strict instructions to watch her.

In the low lighting of my office, high above the dancefloor of The Three Graces, I explain more than once to the young man that Niamh is not his to take. When he finally understands, I leave Aiden to escort him out via a back door as I bind my grazed knuckles with a clean bandage and watch on the cameras as she checks her phone. Ten more minutes pass before I see her shoulders slump and she orders an Uber.

CHAPTER 24
CILLIAN

'So, all this time, and...' says, Niamh, when I finish confessing what I did to keep her to myself. 'How did you even think you had the right to ... to make decisions for me like that, to control my life like that? It's ... wrong, what you did. You made me ... you made me doubt myself, Cillian.'

I shift uncomfortably. I'm not proud of my actions, denying her the kind of happiness, or fun that she was reasonably entitled to with other guys. But then, I've never been reasonable. I look into her eyes, and that's when I see a hint of amusement there.

'Wrong,' she repeats, 'but also kind of ... hot.'

My eyes widen as I take in her words. 'You're not angry?'

She considers. 'Oh, I'm angry, yes. But the knowledge that you were watching me, because you wanted me. And couldn't stand to see me with anyone else... It's ... I'm not sure I believe it. That I could really make someone like you—'

'Want you so much that I couldn't even stand to be in the same room as you in case I fucked up and revealed to the world just how obsessed I was with you?'

'Why?'

'Because you're beautiful, and there's something about you I just can't resist.'

I shift Niamh on my hips, and her breathing deepens as she stares up at me. I smile and press my erection against her. It's sweet the way that makes her blush, and suddenly everything inside me is demanding that I truly make her mine. I'm not going to deny myself – either of us – any longer. How could I have even considered for a single second killing this woman? As the evening breeze cools the last of my temper, and the sweet smell of the honeysuckle growing by the loch reaches my brain. Looking at Niamh now, knowing that after this, after tonight, I will never marry Vittoria Riali.

'I thought about you the whole way here,' I say. 'And then when I saw you with Matt...'

She blinks up at me, and my mouth curves into a slow smile as she whimpers as I move my body against hers. She's not wearing underwear, so only the fabric of my boxers is stopping me from entering her. But she doesn't stop me, doesn't say no, and she definitely isn't trying to get away. Then she moves her hips, grinding against my erection once, twice and then a third time.

'I don't want Matt.'

Her mouth opens in a silent 'O' as my body reacts – as I grow harder and tent the fabric of my boxers. I don't have to push her away anymore. Instead, I can strip her innocence away, piece by piece, until I've ruined her, and she becomes exactly the woman I want.

I slide my fingers between her legs to find her clit. She freezes for a second, then relaxes, whimpering as I toy with her until her fingers squeeze my shoulders and her breath starts to come in soft pants.

'Cillian,' she murmurs as I move my hand, circling the entrance to her pussy before sliding a finger inside her. She quivers, her muscles clamping down around me, and my cock swells even harder as I imagine what it'll feel like to fuck her. She's so bloody tight and I'm not a small man. A thought strikes me, and I pause my movements.

'Cillian?'

I pull out of her and look down at her face.

'You've really not done this before?'

'This?' she asks, chewing on the corner of her lip and trying to avoid answering. Her cheeks flush, however, giving me her answer, even if she doesn't say it. Her pain at thinking men didn't want her was unfortunate, but if it gives me this precious gift, then I'm not sorry.

'Are you a virgin, Niamh?'

Her mouth widens in shock, but she nods. 'Yes, I mean, as you well know men just disappeared... It seemed like no one wanted to—'

'Okay, okay.' I close my eyes and blow out a breath, part of me angry for hurting her like this, the other triumphant that she's only ever going to be mine.

She draws back, and I open my eyes to find her refusing to meet my gaze.

'Niamh,' I whisper. 'I want you. But we don't have to ... I mean, there are other things we can do tonight ... *Gléigeal.*'

I look up at the monastery. It must be almost midnight now and as dark as it's going to get, but there might still be some visibility. Not that I care too much. There's no one outside. And if any of the Brothers value their lives, they'll keep their eyes off what's mine.

Niamh shivers in my arms, and I can see a blue tinge on the skin around her lips.

'Out,' I say, lifting her off me and setting her back down. We've been in the loch for too long, my thoughts of finally having her taking away any consideration of time. I boost her out of the water before I climb out after Niamh. I can't help smiling at the sight of her rolling awkwardly onto the planks.

'Not exactly the sophisticated impression I was hoping for,' she says ruefully. She starts to sit up, but I kneel over her and press her slowly back down. 'Cillian...'

I slip my tongue inside her mouth, and she opens easily for me, whimpering as I claim her for myself. I hold myself above her, running my hand down her side, loving the feel of her delicate curves under me. When I reach the bottom of her T-shirt, I pull it upwards, pushing it roughly over her breasts.

'Off,' I say, gripping her T-shirt with both hands and waiting for her to half-sit up so that I can pull it up over her head. I lower my head and take her nipple in my mouth, the chill of her skin warming quickly as I gently suck on one, while teasing the other with my fingers.

'Cillian,' she moans, her back arching and pushing more of her flesh towards my mouth.

'Lie back.' I instruct her and wait, holding my breath to see if she obeys. Anxiety flashes across her face, but it's only for an instant, and I can almost see her body relax as she does exactly as she's told. My cock jerks at the sight of her submission. Every interaction I've ever had with her leans towards her being beautifully submissive, and after the last year or so with Vittoria and her incessant demands in the bedroom, the thought of that is so welcoming.

'Good girl,' I whisper. 'Let me take care of you. Let me make this good for you.'

'But ... but what if someone sees?'

'They know better than to look.'

I lie on my side beside her, looking down at her naked body beautifully spread out for me under the moonlight. I trail my fingers over her, chasing them occasionally with my mouth to make her shiver again, but not from cold this time. She only occasionally meets my gaze, and I try to remember when I last felt shy about sex. I'm not sure I ever did, or maybe I've just forgotten. That I'm going to be the first person to do this with her ... it makes me want to make it perfect. She moves towards me, seeking my heat, and we press our bodies together, our mouths fusing as we each try to devour the other. She's growing more confident, and it makes me desire her even more.

'Hands above your head.' I instruct. A split second of hesitation, then she obeys, moving her hands above her head and grasping hold of the edge of the jetty.

Her mouth opens on a gasp as I lower my mouth to her nipple again, circling it with my tongue, before moving to her other breast. She shudders and arches towards me as I suck hard. I blow gently on her puckered skin, smiling when it tightens further. She arches up, a low moan of pleasure leaving her lips.

I had intended to wait until we were inside, but seeing her here laid out for me like this, I can't wait to see her surrender to me completely. I capture her mouth with mine once more as I slide my hand down her stomach, until my fingers brush through her neatly trimmed curls. She gasps as I find her clit once more, and I push her legs apart, giving myself space for when I slide one, two, three fingers inside her. I want to feel her stretch – she'll need to if she's ever going to take my cock inside her. I gather the wetness already pooling at her entrance and circle her clit, slowly increasing the pressure as I alternate between fucking her with my fingers and rubbing her. She's slick and ready as I toy with her, feeling her body ready itself for me.

'Tell me you want this,' I demand. 'I want to hear it.'

'Yes,' she whimpers as I curl my finger round, teasing the entrance to her body. 'I want this.' Her hands grip my arms, and the bite of pain as her nails dig into me for a moment, makes my cock even harder, but there's no way she's interfering in this. I slide my finger inside.

'Cillian,' she gasps, her eyes are staring at me, but I'm not sure she's really seeing me. I pull out, placing a second finger beside the first, and tease her clit before sliding them both inside her. I move them in and out, loving the tiny noises she makes as I do so. Her hips grind with my touch, her body growing taut, her neck arching back as she holds her breath for a long moment. She whimpers, opening her eyes when I remove my hand.

'Relax,' I whisper, kissing around the line of her jaw until I reach her ear. Then, I gently bite down adding a third finger, and she cries out as I angle my hand differently and start to really push her towards an orgasm. 'Just let yourself fall.'

'What ... what if ... what if someone...' she pants.

'No one is watching, Niamh. Come for me, little one,' I say as I bite down on the skin between her neck and shoulder.

She cries out, clasping her inner muscles around my fingers as I work her clit faster with my thumb, a little more roughly than before.

'You're so wet and ready for me, aren't you?' But she doesn't respond. 'Tell me,' I demand.

'Yes,' she hisses. 'Cillian! Please...'

I curl my fingers inside her, finding the spot that takes her breath away. With every movement she's getting closer to coming, but she can't seem to reach it, doesn't seem to know how to...

'Niamh, tell me you've given yourself an orgasm before.'

'Yes,' she whispers. 'I'm not that innocent, Cillian.'

I move between her legs, and lower my mouth to her entrance, watching as her eyes go wide. I flick my tongue over her clit as I slide my fingers back inside her, and her head falls back. I lick her, tasting her pussy, devouring her like I've never been satisfied before. She cries out my name as I continue to work her clit, forcing her towards that orgasm. And I watch her as she comes apart in my arms, her body's movements uncontrolled and erratic until she finally settles.

She shivers as I remove my fingers from inside her and, as her tremors subside, I lift them to my mouth, sucking them, tasting her release as she watches me, the flush on her cheeks deepening as I lick every drop. Wanting her to taste herself, I lean down and kiss her, plunging my tongue inside her mouth, taking what's mine.

'That was...' she says, her voice thready as her breathing slowly returns to normal. 'That was...'

'The first of many,' I promise her, her words releasing a coiled knot of tension inside me. 'Now, where's your room?'

'Upstairs,' she says. 'One of the rooms that overlooks the jetty.' Her face pales as she sits up, covering herself with her hands.

'No one saw,' I assure her. 'No one is looking now.'

'But there are windows, Cillian.'

'Someone will only have seen what I wanted them to see, *Gléigeal*. Trust me.'

'Trust you?' She lifts an eyebrow.

She's right to question me. I have a lot to prove to her after the way I've behaved around her the past four years. But I will earn her trust eventually.

I use my Glamour to dress me in robes, like the monks, and pull the hood down low over my face, hiding my identity. Although I'm allowed into the sanctuary, I don't want to advertise my presence.

'Be wary of the people here,' I tell her. She's still human and despite the fact she's shown how strong she can be, the Underworld is a dark and dangerous place. And she's surrounded by people who would break her if they were allowed.

Under the clear night sky, the bright moonlight, we creep our way through the cloisters and down the flagstoned corridors of the monastery. Niamh leads the way to her room and at the door, I stop her, no longer able to wait. I push her roughly against the cold wall, putting my hand behind her head and bringing her lips up to meet mine. I kiss her hard, our faces hidden by the hoods of our robes, lost in the desperation to have each other. She angles her hips up, grinding against me, feeling the solid length of my cock, which has been teased for too long. I want her on her knees in front of me, taking me into that sweet mouth of hers. The thought of fucking her mouth in the corridor of the monastery, knowing that any of the Seven might come out and find us, sends a low groan through me. I can feel the pre-cum on the tip of my cock and I know I'm going to corrupt every essence of her innocence.

'You're mine,' I whisper.

'But you're not mine,' she dares to say before I make contact. I stop, breathing heavily, my heartbeat pounding inside me and drop my forehead to hers. She tries to step to the side, but I don't let her, keeping her pinned in place and cupping her chin with my hand.

'Yes, I am.'

'But—'

'You think I am going to go back to my fiancée after this? I've tried so long not to want you, not to think about you, but now I have you and I've tasted your sweet pussy I am never letting that go. You're mine.'

'I thought that maybe you planned to keep me here...' She slowly raises her eyes to mine. 'Does Vittoria know I'm alive?'

'Not yet.'

'You lied to her?'

I smile at her as I stroke her cheek with the back of my hand. 'No, I just didn't tell her the truth. I gave her a deer's heart, and let her assume.'

Niamh's eyes widen. 'She asked you to cut out my heart and give it to her?'

'Yes.'

'So, last night. In the woods. That's what you were planning to do?'

I keep hold of her, my arm winding around her waist, keeping her flush to me, and push open the wooden door to her room, backing her inside. The room is small and simple, furnished with the basics that someone might need for a quiet life. I notice the bed, a single narrow frame, made for one person not two.

'You know I'm the Huntsman, right?' I look down at her.

She nods.

'But I could never have...' I draw in a breath 'I want you, Niamh. So much.' I guide her hand under my robes to show her just how much. She gasps as her fingers tighten around my length, and I show her how to stroke me. My lips curve into a lazy grin. Her eyes widen, but it's with lust as much as fear. Her fingers stroke the top of my cock, a drop of pre-cum coating them and I moan, letting her know how good this feels.

'But you didn't take my heart,' she says, her hand reaching down to squeeze my heavy balls. She's teased me enough that I don't think I can hold on much longer, I need to find my release and an image of her desperate to please me, swallowing my cock until her breath comes in desperate, broken gasps, tears sliding down her cheeks as her throat works around me, makes my need almost painful. The thought alone nearly undoes me.

'I couldn't.' I push on her shoulders, watching as she sinks to the stone floor, and I remove my robes. Her breath catches as her gaze roams over my body, lingering on the chiselled lines of my abs, the powerful curve of my thighs. For a moment she looks as if she's unsure whether to worship me or surrender. Tentatively leaning forward, she grips me with both hands, her eyes wide as she takes in the full length of my cock. I step closer, lining myself up with her perfect pink mouth as she opens it slightly, her tongue flicking out to lick across my tip then closes her mouth around the tip of my cock and sucks. I let out a guttural moan of pleasure as her tongue toys with me, the sensation of her warm wet heat enough to make me worry about spilling down her throat like a virgin. She runs her tongue around me as she draws me deeper, licking and sucking, as her hands grip my base, working up and down, finding a steady rhythm.

I place my hands either side of her face and thrust, gently at first but then harder and harder, needing to feel her take me all. She blinks up at me as I force myself deeper, feeling her throat pulse as those tears I imagined spring to her eyes.

'Are you all right?' I check in with her, relieved when she nods. A moan escapes her mouth while her tongue works my length, her hand falling to her side as she angles her head to take me deeper.

I've imagined this moment in so many ways, but never did I expect it to feel this good. My orgasm is building fast, and I don't think I can hold out long. Chasing her the other night, kissing her, feeling the tightness of her pussy around my fingers – I've wanted it all for so long and with every new sensation she's bringing me closer to the edge. With one last thrust, I spill down her throat. Her eyes widen as she struggles to swallow, but she does, then looks up at me, eyes bright as she lets me slip from her mouth then licks her lips.

Her eyes are full of a knowledge she didn't possess before, and there's a satisfied smile on her lips. My innocent angel corrupted by my dark desires. And she loves it.

'One day, soon, we'll go back to the woods. Recreate the hunt.'

Her breath hitches, desire sparking in her eyes. I help her up, and wrap my arms around her.

'And this time when I catch you, I'll make you submit willingly to everything I want to do to you.'

'But you definitely won't try to kill me next time?'

She's teasing me. I shake my head. 'I never wanted to kill you but I never thought you'd be granted sanctuary. And the alternatives are far, far worse.'

She shudders against me. 'I heard them. Just as they reached the causeway. Howling.'

I close my eyes, thankful that she got here on time.

'I think you were always going to be safe. The white stag appearing when it did was a sign.'

'A sign from whom?'

I shrug, desire cooling as reality makes a fast and an unwelcome return. 'Hopefully, from the power behind The Unseelie Court itself. Vincenzo's rule is twisting that, and I can't allow it to continue any longer. It was the main reason I was marrying Vittoria.'

'For the power?'

'For the chance to make changes that might allow our world to recover. But my sister is right. I can't do that with Vittoria by my side.' My head drops back, and I sigh before shaking my head. The events of the evening and my orgasm have drained me. 'I can't do it without her either. If I'm with you I can't become king.'

She frowns as if she's only just realised what we've done. 'So, you're not marrying Vittoria?'

I shake my head. 'It's over. Tomorrow I'll make it official. Then I'll be back to take what's mine.'

'But you're staying tonight?'

'I am,' I promise.

She nods. 'I'm glad, I don't want to be alone after—'

I kiss her.

'We should shower. Alone.' Otherwise I'll be taking her virginity in the small en suite, and that's not where I want her, not the first time, anyway.

'What is it?' she asks me when I come out after my own shower, wrapped in a towel.

'What?'

'You're smiling.'

'Just thinking that we'll both be having firsts tonight.'

'Really? What can you possibly be doing for the first time with me, Cillian Hunter?' she asks, clearly puzzled.

'Sleeping in a bed all night with a woman I haven't just fucked.'

She makes a face. 'Lucky me. You know I don't mind *not* creating that first for you.'

I shake my head at her. 'Our first time, I want us both to be free.'

'Okay,' she murmurs, relaxing in my arms. 'I'll give you that.'

CHAPTER 25
NIAMH

I wake alone, with only the thin sheet pulled up over my body. I'm still on my side, and even though he was only here for a few hours, I miss Cillian's presence behind me. I keep my eyes closed for as long as I can, replaying the events of last night. The feel of him pressed against me. My eyes flash open at the memory of what I did to him, the feeling of his cock in my mouth, swallowing his cum as he found his release. I'm not sure I can ever face him again – except that I want ... more.

Part of me is rightly pissed off about the way Cillian's been manipulating me over the years, watching me, keeping other men at a distance, 'dealing' with them. But at least he looked a little shamefaced after he'd told me.

He's returned my phone to me, leaving it on the bedside cabinet and I tap in my pin. There's a post it on it instructing me not to contact anyone but him, and for a moment I can't work out if that's him being ultra-controlling or keeping me safe. There are so many red flags flying around him, this could easily be just a way of controlling me. But, I decide to give him the benefit of the doubt, this time, and wait until I've spoken to him.

I switch off my read receipts as a precaution and then read through all 141 messages that Rose has left since she woke up on Saturday morning. Tears pool in my eyes as her messages show that she's losing hope.

> I hope Cillian is lying to me and that you're not dead. I will never forgive him if he hunted you down.

I smile at the message, which would have made no sense before Friday, but now explains so much. And proves that my friend, despite her faults, truly cares for me. It seems to run in her family. Although I can't help worrying that the way Cillian cares for me, might destroy me.

I expect him to return that evening, or at least to come back after he finishes working at the club, but he doesn't.

Days pass, giving me far too much time to think. On the second day, a parcel of my clothes arrived, including a swimsuit. I looked for a note in the bundle, but there was nothing – although the fact that there were so few matching outfits in it tipped me off that it was Cillian who packed for me rather than Rose.

I wonder why he hasn't told Rose I'm alive. Maybe because the more people who know, the more likely it is that Vittoria might find out. And he also won't want Rose to come here and find Matt. And she would come here, I was sure of it. She wouldn't just abandon me here.

Today is another beautiful day, the eighth since Cillian left me. Despite having messaged him several times, I've had no response. Matt has assured me that time can pass differently between the worlds and that Cillian may only have been gone for a few minutes. But even this does nothing to help my growing anxiety.

The lazy summer days have made an otherwise dull and miserable existence more bearable. When I first arrived, I discussed helping the Seven with their cases should they decide to face The Unseelie Court, and now I while away my evenings discussing the details with them and using the practices I've learned at law school over the past four years. It's hard to come up with a defence when the Underworld laws don't seem to exist in written form, and much seems to be decided by either Vincenzo or The Unseelie Court's magic, which means I'm often at a loss for what they think I can do. Matt's case is the most clear-cut – put the ball in the Rialis' court and ask them to present evidence of motive and a link to the weapon used.

I notice that, despite my offer, neither Declan, Dominic nor James has come to ask for help. With his personality and obnoxious behaviour, I'm pretty sure that Sal must be a serial killer, and I can't realistically see any court letting him walk free. But he's determined that his motivations should exonerate him. I am less convinced, but it's not my job to judge, so I listen – and mostly regret having done so. There's been several times I've had to ask him to stop talking and give myself time to come to terms with some of the things he's done – not that any sane person could ever fully justify them and I'm realising that I will need to learn to accept that sometimes my actions might help to set a villain free – if I ever get back to that life.

∼

My afternoon ritual is to swim with Matt. He's started wearing boxers to swim, which has made the whole situation a lot less embarrassing. Twice, we've swum to the opposite shore but, just as Matt told me, as soon as we reach the beach on the other side, we find ourselves right back on the island again.

'This is ridiculous,' I complained the first time. 'The monastery was all the way over there, and now it's right here.'

Matt laughs. 'Welcome to the Underworld, where the laws of nature are more suggestions than actual laws.'

I roll my eyes and set off again, checking the position of the far shore and the monastery on a regular basis until my feet touch the shore and, bam, I'm right back on the island looking up at the buildings along the shore.

'Look on the positive side,' Matt tells me.

'What positive side?' I snap.

He shrugs. 'The sun is shining, and we don't have anything else to do until the delivery gets here?'

'Yeah, that really makes up for everything.'

Today, we're all waiting for a delivery to arrive. The Brothers will all need to pass through to the human world to collect it, and all I'm expected to do is put anything arriving for the kitchen away once someone else has brought it to the Underworld.

I can see why Matt needs to be positive, though. He's been here a long time and is fully aware that his life is passing him by. He's four years older than when I last saw him, and what I notice most is that he seems to have given up. Whereas I'm still determined that I'm not going to stay here any longer than necessary. With the weather being so warm and having nothing to do once the cooking and cleaning is finished, I've been trying to persuade myself that the rest is simply an unexpected holiday. Hopefully when Cillian returns...

'Stop it,' Matt says, swimming over.

'Stop what?'

'That smile, that's a sex smile.'

'What? No, it's not.'

He just grins at me, and I flush deeply. I guess maybe it was a sex smile.

'So, you and Cillian.' He shakes his head. 'Maybe if I ever get out of here, there might actually be hope for me and Rose.'

'Will I need to get out of here for there to be any hope between me and Cillian?'

'How much do you know about The Unseelie Court and how it operates?'

'Not much. All the Kinfolk I've met have seemed basically human, I've never noticed anything different unless it's been pointed out to me. Declan showed me his true form.'

'Most will have been using Glamour to hide their true physical selves – like Declan and Lachlan, obviously. And humans are easy to fool. No offence. You'll see more and more the longer you're here.' He pauses, as if trying to decide whether to explain that further or not. 'So many of us hide in plain sight.'

'What about Cillian? Is he hiding ... something?'

Matt chuckles. 'Lots of things, I'm sure, but his physical appearance isn't one of them. Not in his case. Or any of the Hunters for that matter.'

'But—' I pause. It's going to sound crazy, but I really need to know. 'Sometimes I see Cillian with antlers.'

Matt nods, as though that's perfectly normal. 'Cernunnos. Dressed in the leathers and adorned with the antlers of the mightiest deer in the Caledonian Forest. You see him like that when he embodies the Huntsman. Each of the families represents one of the old gods. Family representations can change if a bloodline dies out, or is ... well, let's just say that, similar to in the human world, sometimes people want to take what rightfully belongs to others and are willing to kill to get that.'

'Like the Rialis?'

'Like the Rialis. They came here nearly a century ago from Northern Italy. They are Kinfolk, as you know, and rose to power here very quickly. Vincenzo's grandfather was ruthless and ambitious – just like his descendants. And so good at obtaining information about their rivals ... well, about everyone, really.'

'So Kinfolk exist all over the world?'

Matt shrugs. 'Wherever there are humans, there are Kinfolk. The Underworld exists everywhere, although it has its own borders and boundaries. The two of them impact on one another, though, even if humans don't always know it. There are so many different magics that I'm sure I'm not even aware of them all. The longer you're here, the more you'll understand.'

Then his expression falters. He takes my hand in his and squeezes it tightly, looking earnestly into my eyes. 'You shouldn't be here. We need to find a way to get you back home. Humans pass through into the Underworld for a variety of reasons...'

'And?' I prompt.

'And it usually doesn't end well.'

'Oh.' I frown and try to work out what he means. It doesn't feel different being here. My daily life is different, certainly, but I'm not sure what would be different if I'd ended up in these circumstances in the human world.

'I don't really know how you got here, or why. You implied Cillian sent you here, but ... but I saw him here with you and I know that isn't the whole truth, is it?'

'No,' I confirm, but I'm learning not to volunteer more than is asked, so I stop there.

'The longer you stay, the less likely you are to ever get home. Time can pass very differently when you step through a thin place.'

'How long have you been here?'

'How long have I been gone?'

'Almost four years,' I tell him.

'It feels longer,' Matt says.

'But—' I stare back at him. When I last saw Cillian, it felt as if ... as if he was telling me that we could be together. I'd foolishly imagined that meant living back home, in the city

I'd grown up in. Moving on with my life. What if too much time has already passed? What if I've missed starting my professional training? What if I'm going to be stuck here cooking and cleaning for the Seven forever?

'I need to go back, Matt. I have a life, a future.'

'Then you need to find a way to get there as soon as possible.'

I swallow, suddenly realising the significance of this. Is this what Cillian really meant. That he wanted me stuck here, at his mercy? It didn't seem like that, but honestly, I wouldn't put it past him.

'I'm beginning to wonder,' I say, 'that ever since I met Rose, I've been slowly being drugged, manipulated...' I frown remembering that the night I first met Cillian was right after I had a drink at the party. Maybe that's not the only hallucinogenic device the Kinfolk have used on me.

'No, you're Rose's friend, she wouldn't—'

'And ... what about my feelings?'

'What do you mean?'

'Are ... are my feelings even real? I've been living with Rose for nearly four years now. Being around her, the food and drink I've shared with her ... could that be influencing me? Making me think I have feelings for someone, when I don't really.'

'You're worried that you don't really care about Cillian?'

'Maybe,' I admit. 'And...' I don't know how to choose my words. I can see Matt loves Rose. How will he react to my uncertainty? 'I suppose I'm worried that Rose has been manipulating me, too.'

He smiles sadly at me and shakes his head. 'If Cillian

didn't care, he would simply have killed you during the hunt. And I know Rose loves you, Niamh. When she met you, she defied Cillian to invite you to that party, defended her choice of you as a friend more than once. And it wasn't just to stick it to her brother. I know we didn't know each other all that well, and I'm sorry that she was with me rather than you when your parents were killed. But I'm glad you've been there for her. It's made me being here so much easier to bear.'

'Matt—' I stop, more unsure than ever about what to say to him, but really sure now that he needs to know. 'About Rose...'

'What?'

'I'm worried about her.'

'Why?' He's turned to face me, his face tense, concerned. Maybe I shouldn't have said anything.

'She just ... she's changed so much since you've been gone from her life. She never settles for any guy, she's wild, reckless. You were the only one for her, and she won't accept a replacement. She's miserable without you.'

Matt's face falls, and he shakes his head. 'No, tell me that's not true. All I've wanted, hoped for, these past few years, is that she's been living a normal life, or as normal as a Hunter's can be. But, Niamh ... you know I can't leave. Because of Vincenzo, I'll be found guilty. I have no chance of a fair trial. And even on the off-chance the Court exonerates me, Vincenzo would still hunt me down.'

'He'd get away with that?'

'He'd find an excuse. Vincenzo gets away with anything, nowadays.'

'How can you be so sure?'

'Because it already happened to my father. That's why I was such a convenient patsy. The son of a traitor? Who would even bother to defend me?'

'Then how did you get here?'

'Cillian hunted me. He caught me, but for some reason he believed me. And then he let me go, gave me the chance to come here. He sees it as a sort of test, I think. Only those who deserve to, find sanctuary before the dawn. I know he sees through Vincenzo but the rest either don't, or don't care.'

'Cillian saved your life?'

'He did.'

I smile, as I cling to this knowledge. I'm not deluded. At the core of his being, Cillian Hunter is a good man.

'I'll defend you,' I promise Matt. 'If Cillian thinks you're not guilty, then neither do I.'

But he drops his head forward, his shoulders sagging as he sighs. We both sit in silence for a minute, then the monastery bell tolls and he groans.

'Finally. I need to go and help with the bloody delivery.'

'Is there food in it that comes from the human world?'

'Should be. Oh, right. Yes, why don't you come and make sure you know what's what. It might help you ... last longer here.'

We exchange wry smiles, pull on our robes and head for the monastery.

'I can hear an engine,' I say to Matt. 'How?'

He frowns. 'The delivery.'

'Yes, but how did it get to the island, does the causeway reappear?'

Matt notices the glint of hope in my tone. 'There's no way to escape anyway, I'm sure Declan will have warned you.'

'He did.'

'The landscape in the human world is very different,' he says. 'The loch has been mostly drained and a road leads right up to St Marnox. You should stay here in the Underworld. The deliveries all arrive in the human world, but we'll bring the food through and leave it in the kitchen for you to put away. Just go and wait there.'

'Okay.'

Matt heads towards the sound of the lorry, while I head for the kitchen. I've only just reached the walled garden when I notice that the door in the wall leading towards the front of the monastery is open.

As I walk past the beds of herbs, I see a woman in a uniform with a clipboard standing beside one of the benches. Strange, Matt didn't say anything about anyone coming through to the Underworld but I guess someone has to bring the food through.

I smile at her. 'Can I help with anything?'

'I'm Ulla.' The woman smiles at me and looks at the information on her clipboard. 'You could take this?'

'Sure,' I say and reach for the box she gestures towards. It's a small box, but heavier than it looks.

'We have a regular delivery scheduled here. It's nice to get the chance for a wee day trip into the countryside. We all argue about who gets to come.'

I laugh. 'I'd love to be heading back to the city if I'm honest.'

'Why? Have you seen the guys who live here? Although...'

she looks around and then leans in closer to me. 'Sometimes they're a bit odd. Intense. You know?'

'I...' I break off, as a frisson of unease slithers down my spine.

'There's not a single one of them that I'd turn down for a ... date, mind.' She grins at me. 'If you know what I mean?'

I nod and laugh, hoping it doesn't sound as forced as it feels. 'None of them are my type,' I say. 'So, don't let me stand in your way.'

'Oh, I won't. Now, I'm off to get a signature and try my luck.' She waggles her eyebrows at me, and indicates the box. 'You should try one. Specialist apples Declan wants to experiment with for a cider. But I threw in a couple of extras we had. They're delicious.'

'Thanks,' I say. 'I will.'

She smiles a broad smile, and I brush off the uneasy feeling I got from her just a few minutes ago.

'Of course, no problem. I'm Eve, by the way.' I smile sweetly at her, hoping she'll not suspect I'm being untruthful. But really, what does it matter? She's just here to drop off a delivery. It's not like I owe her anything.

'Eve. Nice. Biblical, even. Oh, and appropriate,' she says, gesturing to the box before heading towards the door to the brewery itself with a second box.

I take a moment to choose an apple. They all look delicious, huge and shiny, and the sight brings back a memory of my mum handing me an apple, one just like these, at our kitchen table. I smile as I remember her polishing it and handing me the large shiny red fruit. For once, I'm grateful for my robe as I polish the apple on my sleeve and stare at my face reflected in the mirror-like surface.

Above me, birds chirp in the trees, and several are hopping in and out of a stone birdbath at the centre of the planted beds. I wander closer to them, slowly so as not to scare them away. I can afford to take a break from chores to eat one apple. I'm safe here, aren't I? Looking up at the cloudless blue sky, I lift the apple to my mouth and take a large bite.

I grimace. The taste is sickly-sweet, not the crisp freshness I expected, and when I go to swallow, the apple sticks in my throat. I cough, or at least try to, but I can't dislodge it. I look at the apple and see a face staring back at me from the polished surface. It's Ulla, and she's laughing. Something is happening. It's like … like that fateful night in Sussurri. I feel exactly the same. I fall to my knees, then crumple onto my side, my muscles frozen, although right now I can still see and hear. Whatever drug this is, it's much faster-acting, and I'm already beyond being able to call for help.

'Don't worry, Niamh,' Ulla says, coming into view. She's kneeling beside me. 'Oh, did you not understand? It's only the walls of the monastery itself that count, not the garden ones. Shame. Now just relax and you won't feel a thing. Close your eyes and fall asleep like a good little girl, and then everything in my world and Cillian's world can go back to exactly the way it's supposed to be.'

I'm not sure whether I'm hallucinating, until she leans forward lifting my necklace from around my neck. I try to stop her, but I can't move a single muscle. My eyes are still open, so I watch her stare down at my necklace as her face and hair and body slowly morph into Vittoria's. She lets out a blood-curdling scream and rips my necklace from me. *No!* I try to scream but nothing comes out, my voice trapped inside me.

'Vittoria!' I hear Matt calling to her as my eyes slowly close. I sense him rush up to me, kneeling down beside me and taking my hand in his. 'What happened? What did she do?'

With my last breath, my fingers release, and the bright red apple falls to my side, a single bite mark visible.

CHAPTER 26
CILLIAN

When I return to the human world, it's been two days since I last set foot in my businesses, and I'm grateful that the teams that manage them are as competent as they are and can manage without me when I have other priorities, usually hunting, but this time at St Marnox.

An update from Sean informs me that Rose hasn't left her flat since the incident, and I make a mental note to visit her as soon as I can.

As I drive into town, the Necropolis comes into view, perched on a hill just east of the city centre and next to Glasgow's medieval cathedral. It's a sacred spot for a great many people, including the Kinfolk, as it's the site in the human world of The Unseelie Court.

A Court session hasn't been called for many months – they're becoming more and more infrequent as time passes, and I don't like it. But until I become king, this won't change. I close my eyes, knowing full well that my decision to choose

Niamh over Vittoria may mean that never happens. Despite the challenges, however, I'm determined not to give up. My rightful place is on that throne – I can feel it – and I will stop at nothing to get what I want. After all, my sister is correct. The Unseelie Court, with Vittoria as its queen, cannot be anything but corrupt, even if I am king by her side.

Knowing the conversation I need to have, I call Vittoria.

'Cillian? Where have you been? We've been concerned.'

'We? Really?' I challenge her. 'You haven't called or texted.'

There's a pause. 'Should I have to? Surely my future husband understands that I worry about him.'

I turn a laugh into a cough. 'Is that so?'

'Of course.'

'I had business to attend to. I didn't expect to be away so long.'

'In the Underworld?'

'Yes.'

'I see, well, I must have missed you. I had business there, too.'

'And did it go well?' I don't know why I ask. I barely even care, but there's something about her words that makes me think that she's saying one thing and telling me something else.

'I certainly did. And it was utterly delightful,' she says. 'My father is calling a meeting of The Unseelie Court.'

I swallow, strange that suddenly Vincenzo is doing things that align so closely with my intentions. 'When?'

'As soon as everyone arrives. I'm sure you'll find it very informative.'

Her voice drips with sarcasm as she ends the call, and I roll my eyes, looking in my rear-view mirror. But instead of seeing the road behind me, I find myself looking directly into Vittoria's face. I swerve as I blink hard at the sight.

Scrying. My heart hammers loudly in my chest. It's a power that hasn't manifested in generations. So long, in fact, that it has practically passed into myth. But... I mentally go through all the places I've been recently that had smooth shiny surfaces that she could have...

'Fuck.' I slam my hand onto the dashboard. Realistically, I realise too late, she could have been watching me just about anywhere. And the reason the Rialis always seem to be a couple of steps ahead of the rest of us, is likely due to this. How have they kept this a secret for so long?

Glasgow's Necropolis – the city of the dead – lies close to the place where the city was founded. It's only been a human cemetery since Victorian times, but it's been a site of great importance in both the human world and the Underworld for far longer.

I cross the Bridge of Sighs, reaching the thin place and whispering the words my father taught me long ago to part the veil. With no physical door to pass through, entry is different, and I feel the strange vibration of a shimmering doorway around me, the sensation as it parts, granting me entrance into the Underworld. As I travel, the rumbling of the brewery trucks passing under the bridge is replaced by the burbling of the Molendinar Burn. Once upon a time, a member of The Seelie Court was the embodied spirit of that water, just as I'm the embodied spirit of the Wild Hunt. Now, the burn flows mostly underground, covered with streets and bridges until it pours out of an ugly pipe into the river Clyde. Most barely know of its existence, and The Seelie Court is just as lost.

Growing up, the tales my father told me made it sound as if it was the innate goodness of The Seelie Court that somehow led to their demise, that somehow, they deserved it because they didn't fight back hard enough against the Blight. But The Unseelie Court is fading now, too. Blight corrupting more and more of the chamber, and that's certainly not being caused by our goodness. I glance up towards the hilltop, where the great Tree of Life once stood, but it's empty.

Could pollution and the destruction of the environment be a cause? It's a possibility, and might explain why the dark Unseelie Court has survived longer than The Seelie Court of light.

Once across the bridge, I enter the Necropolis itself. Facing me is the grand entrance to The Unseelie Court. More than a century ago, the humans planned to hollow out the hill and turn it into a catacomb. Eventually, they gave up, leaving the small space they had already dug out covered by an impressive doorway. Some say these attempts precipitated the Blight. But the two co-existed for almost a hundred years, so it seems unlikely.

As I approach, the heavy doors open for me, and I go through a torchlit corridor before emerging into the circular

Court chamber. Its ceiling is so high that it can't be seen, and is simply a deep, dark, unending blackness.

I take my place in one of the thirteen alcoves around its circumference, each formed by the graceful arch of the tree's roots. Every remaining Kennard and any member of the eight ruling Kin are allowed to be present when the Court is in session, but I'm surprised to find that Rose has arrived before me. She's sitting on one of the carved wooden seats in our alcove, high carved panels on each side mark our territory as separate from the Kin on either side. I nod to her as I approach, and she gives me a reluctant smile. Sean is already seated behind her, Aiden beside him.

My tattoos tingle, and I look up at the carvings of Cernunnos on the alcove ceiling. Each alcove has a different one, relevant to the god represented by whichever Kin holds that seat. The Hunters have always represented Cernunnos's Kin, while the Rialis are a more recent addition to The Unseelie Court, now representing the sea god, Llyr. Vincenzo's alcove also contains a carved wooden throne fit for The Unseelie King.

I expect to be one of the first to arrive, given how close I was to the Necropolis when Vittoria informed me of the Court session, but in addition to Rose, Vincenzo Riali is already seated on the throne. Vittoria, beside him. A momentary regret washes through me. If I were to marry Vittoria, that throne would most likely be mine, eventually. But while everything about her looks perfect, all I can see is the evil I saw as she held the deer's heart.

I stand tall beside my sister, waiting for the other Kennards, knowing that no matter what happens here I am sure of two things: the first is that I'm not going to bow to the demands of The Unseelie Court and lose my position as Kennard without a fight, and the second is that I will not be marrying Vittoria.

When Chris was alive, it was expected he would simply take up the mantle of king when his father died. I had no particular wish to rule the Court – the responsibility for my own Kinfolk seemed like a solemn enough responsibility. But now that I'm convinced that Vincenzo's inaction is allowing the Blight to continue to spread and destroy the Underworld I can't simply sit back and let it continue.

I watch the remaining Kin arrive, one by one – the MacGowans, the Kelsos, the Websters, the Macphersons, and then Alec Carruth, alone as usual – while there are a handful of family members from the other Kin. We're only missing one now, the McLoughlins, who may well all be working at this hour, but they will attend; they always do.

'Are we classing this as a late night or an early morning, Hunter?' Alec Carruth asks.

'Whichever you prefer, Carruth. It's an early morning for me.'

'Moving from being a country bumpkin to a city boy, I'm still finding that it's easier to think of it as early mornings,' he confesses ruefully. 'But I doubt I have as much to entertain me at night as you do.'

The Kelsos and the MacGowans laugh, but the rest of us remain stoic.

While we wait, I glance at the five alcoves in the chamber that will remain empty – four Unseelie Kin who simply disappeared, leaving no trace and barely any memories, and the alcove containing the doorway to The Seelie Court. All are covered in signs of Blight, and the creeping black spores are showing signs of spreading even further in the chamber. I wonder if I'm allowing the Blight to ultimately destroy us if I choose Niamh? The Hunters are just one Kinfolk family – surely, we're not powerful enough to do that? Am I the only Kennard left who truly wants to stop the Blight? None of the others have shown many signs of standing up to Vincenzo. In fact, most seem to benefit from his decisions, however, given the fact that I was supposed to be marrying his daughter, most of the others probably believe the same of me. Finally, the door opens and Robert McLoughlin wanders in, swaggering towards his seat without a word of apology.

'Are you going to tell us why we're here, Cillian?' Vincenzo asks when no one makes a move to call the session to order, and I stare at him.

'You called this meeting, not me,' I reply.

There's a low murmur around the room. Clearly, I am the only one to whom Vittoria told the truth.

'My apologies, Kinfolk,' Vittoria says, standing gracefully. 'There was little time and I didn't want there to be any delays or risk any of the Kin being missing.'

'*You* called the meeting?' Carruth turns to her.

'I did,' she says calmly, but doesn't elaborate, forcing Carruth to press her.

'And?' Alec Carruth asks. 'Why are we here, *Vittoria*?'

If the emphasis he places on her name bothers her, she doesn't show it. But I make a mental note to watch him. There's something about him I just don't trust.

'I called this meeting because Cillian Hunter is

considering backing out of a deal with my family,' Vittoria announces. I clench my fists as I fight to retain a neutral expression.

'You haven't dragged us all here simply to inform the rest of the Court that a deal between the Rialis and the Hunters has gone south, have you? I don't have time for this.' Carruth pushes to his feet and takes two steps towards the exit.

'It is relevant if it has an impact on the future Unseelie King,' Vittoria states. 'Something that affects all of us, surely. Plus, you were all happy to accept our hospitality to celebrate the making of the deal, which makes you all a part of it.'

'Your engagement?' Carruth says, now staring at me. 'You're ending an engagement that's taken you, what ... four years to finalise ... after four days? Or is it three? What the actual fuck are you playing at Hunter?'

I don't miss the fact that his gaze slides to Vittoria and then to Rose, and I shift forward so that my body blocks his view of my sister.

'It's true. Since last week, certain things have come to my attention, and it will no longer be possible for me to—'

'Please, Cillian. You really should let me speak – before you make a complete fool of yourself.' Vittoria's voice is dripping with hate, and there's a sharp intake of breath around the room.

'Very well, as long as you don't actually think I'm going to change my mind, then by all means, speak.'

'For the past four years, my fiancé may have done his best to keep his infatuation with a human secret. But on Friday, that infatuation caused him to betray his duty to The Unseelie Court in the worst way possible.'

I stare at her. Who would have guessed that Vittoria was such a master at pretending to care? But looking at the other faces, I can see that most are thoroughly engrossed in her performance. There are actual tears pooling in her eyes as she continues.

'Last Friday night, after our engagement party. When Cillian and I were ... celebrating ... we were interrupted by a message from this human – his sister's friend. She claimed that Rose had been attacked at Sussurri – of all places.' Rose shifts in her seat beside me.

'Vittoria—'

'No, Cillian, I am allowed to finish, am I not?'

Her father nods and gestures for her to continue.

'We arrived at the club, where it appeared that we were rescuing Rose and her friend. In fact, it was a clever set-up. Three Kinfolk lost their lives all due to a misunderstanding, engineered by this human.'

'That's not—' I start, but Rose places a hand on my arm and shakes her head.

'Let her finish,' she whispers. 'You need to find out exactly what you're dealing with before you can form a rebuttal.'

I nod, impressed by her wits and maturity.

'Of course, I immediately tasked our security with investigating. Rose had, indeed, been drugged as the human claimed, and we prevented her removal from the premises. We also located and tended to her bodyguard who had been attacked. There was a confrontation, but we were not in possession of all the facts at the time and mistakes were made.'

Fuck, it's like listening to a high-ranking politician who's been caught red-handed in a blatantly compromising position but who is going to simply style it out and assume she'll get away with it. Fear grips me that she might actually be right, she might *actually* fool them.

'Security footage shows that the drinks that were drugged were, in fact, only handled by one other person. Rose's friend. The human. The human who then stabbed one of the Kinfolk in the neck. Francis MacEadailt, who we have since discovered was a loyal member of the Riali Kin, although sadly not well known to those of us at the top. He only meant to help Rose, as did his friends. Video footage from earlier in the evening shows them dancing. Happy together.' Vittoria pauses, her gaze sweeping around all the Kennards in the room. Every single one has their attention fixed on her, including Carruth. I shake my head as Rose slips her hand into mine and squeezes.

'I can't contradict anything she's saying, Cillian. I'm sorry,' Rose says. 'I don't remember them doing anything bad. They brought us sealed drinks, did everything right. And... and I can only imagine how the way I'm dancing with them will look.' Her gaze moves down to the floor, and I hate that she's ashamed.

'It's all right,' I tell her. 'You have nothing to apologise for.'

She frowns. 'I got her killed.'

'Does this human have a name?' MacGowan asks, slapping his closed fist into his palm. Rose notices, but though she rolls her eyes, I can see real fear in her face at Vittoria's next words.

'Niamh Whyte. The same Niamh Whyte that I have on good authority Cillian Hunter didn't successfully hunt and kill, as he claimed. Instead, he presented me with a deer's heart – one from a sacred white Underworld stag.'

I slam my hand down on the barrier in front of me. 'I did not lie. You asked for a heart, and I informed you that I had brought you one.'

'Cillian…' Rose shakes her head.

Vittoria pauses for a moment to think, nods reluctantly.

'Very well, we can agree to disagree on that point,' she says. And I can see that I've played into her hands. Now she looks magnanimous while I look petulant. 'There is still no excuse for why she isn't dead. She's human. And she killed Kin. The punishment is clear… And not only that, but he's'—she drops her head, sniffs delicately, whispers—'he's been spending time with her, using his ability to access St Marnox to visit a murderer, and ignoring me.'

I sit there in shock, she is twisting everything – and she has clearly seen far more than I ever imagined. But of course she has. I recall the eyes in the mirror. She's been using an ancient power to follow me. Watching my every move over the last four years, seeing the decisions I've made and the internal battle I've fought with myself. It seems madness that she would do such a thing, but I know Vittoria and I know that she will stop at nothing to remove any threat from her path. And it makes me wonder … is this the first time she's tried to kill Niamh?

Vittoria smiles at everyone and then sits down next to her father's throne. He reaches out and pats her hand, pleased with her performance. The silence that follows echoes around the room, then, all of a sudden, everyone seems to be talking at once. Accusations and questions are thrown around, demands are being shouted asking what punishment Niamh should receive for her actions. No one asks what should be done about me. Yet. But watching Vittoria's and Vincenzo's reactions to all this, I know that's where we're headed. And I will not let them succeed.

Vincenzo calls for order, and the chamber falls into an uneasy silence. The majority of eyes fall on me, and they are far from friendly.

'Perhaps I should appeal to the Court to allow Vittoria to become queen in her own right after my death,' Vincenzo says. The others are hesitant – except for Carruth, who looks positively murderous – but no one dares to outright disagree, and Vittoria smiles. 'Well, Hunter, what do you have to say for yourself?'

'For myself? What about on behalf of Niamh Whyte? Are we just going to take Vittoria's word for all of this?'

'She claims to have footage,' MacGowan points out, and Vittoria nods. 'And who would lie to the Court, Cillian? Would you care to share your version of events?'

'My *version*? The truth is that the Rialis allowed this attack on my sister to happen in one of their clubs, not interfering, or even noticing the danger she was in until Niamh contacted me for help and I informed them about the situation.

'Three men died in that lane on Friday night. Vittoria and I each killed one, perhaps mistakenly, but I don't think so. Eduardo Conti attacked me directly, as did Roberto Gallo. All three men are Riali Kin. Does Vittoria not even know the men who work for her? The men that are willing to die for her and her father? If so, then I find them unworthy of ruling our Kinfolk. We deserve a ruling family who know their people, who trust their people and who can protect those around us. From every danger that we face. Not use their positions to protect their own interests.'

'They were trying to assist—'

'Bullshit, Vittoria. *You* killed Roberto so that I couldn't interrogate him. I took Niamh into the woods at your request, and as my duty to this Court as Huntsman, because I did see Niamh kill Kin – in self-defence. However, I hunted her down as I would any accused, and it wasn't me who let her escape. That night, there was a more powerful magic at work than neither I nor any member of The Unseelie Court possess. It was that magic that helped Niamh escape, that magic that sent the white stag, that magic that gave her the words to enter the sanctuary. She's safely at St Marnox, where none of you can reach her. There is no need for this session of the Court. But seeing as we're here I wish to bring up another matter—'

'This isn't the time, Cillian,' Rose whispers urgently. 'Whatever you're about to say, you'll be starting at a disadvantage. It can wait.'

'It can't,' I whisper back, then face the Court. 'It has come to my attention recently that the Rialis, or more specifically, Vittoria Riali has been scrying. The King's family could have been watching any of us, even in areas we considered secure using this magic.'

There's another flurry of gasps and murmurs around the chamber as Vittoria stands again.

'It's not illegal.'

'When did that change?' Carruth asks. 'In the past scryers were hunted as soon as their magic was discovered. No one should have the ability to spy on other Kinfolk like that.'

'Oh, please. We all spy on each other in different ways. This is no different.'

'It very definitely is,' MacGowan interjects. 'Vincenzo?'

But even as he turns to the King for help, he realises the futility of it. Vincenzo will never rule against his daughter. Not when it could lead to her being hunted and killed.

Vittoria smirks as she pulls an apple from her pocket and gazes at the shiny surface.

'You know, we have always been told that all those criminals are safe within the walls of St Marnox, haven't we?'

There's a general murmur of agreement.

'The Hunters wield a great deal of power in being able to essentially pardon the guilty, allowing them to live out their lives in peace, while we are left behind, dealing with the aftermaths of their crimes. They visit them, ensure their safety, provide for them.'

'I don't have the power to pardon anyone. They have to reach sanctuary, if they weren't meant to—'

'In fact,' she continues, ignoring me, 'the man who murdered my brother is also there, living each day of his life while Chris rots in his grave, the line of inheritance of this Court forever altered. A guilty man caught by the Huntsman, and subsequently allowed to go free and reach sanctuary. Very convenient, don't you think? After all, Christopher's death opened his path to become king.'

'That's not—' I begin, but a sharp gasp beside me stops

me in my tracks. I turn to face Rose, a look of utter betrayal on her face. A look that will haunt me for the rest of my life.

'Cillian?' she whispers.

'You have to understand, Rose. I couldn't tell you. He—'

But Rose turns and runs from the chamber before I can finish.

Vittoria preens.

'Poor Huntsman, all alone with no allies. No family, no fiancée and no future.'

She turns the apple towards me, using magic to make it appear much larger than it is. Reflected in the surface I see a scene at St Marnox. The seven monks stand around the stone altar in the old church, and on it, deathly pale, her chest unmoving, lies Niamh.

CHAPTER 27
CILLIAN

The one advantage of finding out about Niamh's fate in the Court chamber is that from here there is direct access to the thin place in St Marnox. The only way for the seekers to leave there, also allows the Hunters, but no one else, to enter. Grateful to not have to take the time to drive to the monastery, I'm out of my seat and passing through the thin place as fast as I can, arriving in the centre of a small side chapel that overlooks the altar.

Some time has passed since the vision in the apple, and the seven monks are no longer gathered around Niamh, keeping watch. Only Matt sits beside her, holding her wrist, his fingers on her pulse. He looks over at me.

'Let her go.' Now that Niamh is mine I'm not going to tolerate any other man touching her.

'You took your time,' he says, dropping her hand as I hurry across the chapel.

My stomach drops. 'How long has it been?' I ask, cursing the unpredictability of time when using thin places.

'Eight days,' he says.

I swallow as I take the last few steps towards her slowly.

'She's not breathing?'

'No, she's ... stuck. Trapped between life and death. We've tried everything we can think of to wake her, but—' He gestures at her body. She's so still that it feels as if the chapel itself is holding its breath along with her.

'Why didn't you tell me?'

He shrugs, 'We've been trying. Check your phone.'

'Tell me exactly what happened,' I say, but he shakes his head.

He swallows. 'She should have been safe. She didn't leave the monastery. She's barely been outside alone. We had a delivery, just the usual two guys who bring the supplies to St Marnox every week.' He looks down at her. 'They often bring fresh fruit and veg for the kitchen with them but someone had already taken it in. None of us thought anything of it. We had no idea that there was someone else there.'

'Who?' I ask, even though I already have the answer.

'Vittoria. She must have followed the delivery truck in her car. All Kinfolk can reach St Marnox in the human world, which is how the deliveries arrive.'

My fists clench as I curse myself for not dealing with Vittoria before I left the chamber. Rage burns as the snake on my wrist tightens its coils.

'But Niamh should have been safe here,' I insist. 'It's in the rules and even the Rialis can't break those.'

'From what we can work out, Vittoria didn't break any rules,' Matt says. 'We all thought that "within the walls" of St

Marnox meant the outer wall, but it must mean only the walls of the monastery itself. The Rialis always find a way around the rules, don't they? Some way to twist everything to fit their own needs.'

I nod. 'It's how they've stayed in power so long. It's why I want to be king. To change that.'

I take a deep breath, regretting my decision to give up my chance at the throne just for a second. But to rule alongside Vittoria would only give her access to my family's power as well as her own. And I know the Court wouldn't survive that. Not to mention that sooner or later, one of us would be dead at the other's hand.

'Anyway, it wasn't until we'd finished unloading the van that I found them in the kitchen garden. But by then it was too late. Cillian, I'm sorry.'

'It was definitely Vittoria?'

He nods. 'I saw her. She'd used Glamour to disguise her appearance to Niamh, but afterwards...' He frowns in confusion. 'She did something, I'm not sure. It was like she grabbed something away from Niamh ... and her Glamour just ... faded and we all saw her true self. How do you think she knew Niamh was here?'

'Well, either someone from here told her—'

'No one here would tell the Rialis anything.'

'You worked for them. As did your father,' I point out.

'My Kin come from the water. Vincenzo is the embodiment of the sea god, Llyr. I don't hunt, Cillian, or I would have worked for you. But I definitely wouldn't tell them anything. No one here has any love for them. I know these men, Cillian. They're far from perfect, but I'm sure of that. Rightly or wrongly, Vincenzo is responsible for most of them being here.'

'Are there mirrors here? Reflective surfaces?'

He frowns. 'In the kitchen, yes. All the units. And mirrors around the place. Why?'

I curse and rub my forehead with my hand, regretting for the first time the lack of attention I paid to my fiancée. 'Cover them all. Everything. Vittoria's been scrying.'

Matt lets out a low whistle. 'You're sure?'

'Very. She showed me Niamh lying unconscious, surrounded by the seven of you, in the surface of an apple in The Unseelie Court chamber.'

'But ... but we thought that magic was lost, intentionally wiped out. No one has been able to—'

'It seems, we were wrong.'

'So, she might have been watching us ... via any reflective surface...'

I nod grimly. Avoiding scrying is a challenging task, especially with someone powerful wielding the magic which is why historically those who held this power were hunted down and killed. Scryers wield a power virtually unsurpassed by any other, and my ancestors were responsible for their scourge, as it fell to the Huntsmen to hunt them down and kill them. After all, knowledge is power. And the Rialis already have enough power. It's not a gift that is passed down through generations, so how has Vittoria come to be in possession of such power? The irony that I was hunting the wrong woman is not lost on me.

I stare down at Niamh, wondering just how long Vittoria

has been watching her. With all the technology we use nowadays, not least our phones, there are surfaces everywhere that can be used for the magic. The antique mirrors in Cernunnos, including in my bedroom, the windchimes Vittoria encouraged me to buy my sister... Dammit, I put those in the flat Rose shares with Niamh – gave Vittoria a way to watch her. That ancient mirror in Vittoria's flat – it must be what she's using to scry. I pull my phone from my pocket and look at the screen. I need Aiden's hacking abilities to find a solution that will save Niamh and prevent Vittoria from bringing her more harm.

'What do you think she took from Niamh?' Matt asks.

'Her necklace,' I say, leaning over and running my fingers around Niamh's delicate bare neck.

He frowns. 'I don't remember her wearing one.'

I stare at him. 'You don't?'

'No.' He smiles slyly at me. 'But then I've never paid attention to her the way you have.'

'She always wears it. Her mother gave her that necklace, and Niamh will be devastated if it's now in Vittoria's hands.' I rake my hands through my hair and then realise something odd. An urge to forget about Niamh's necklace forms in my head, and for the first time I recognise this for what it is. Magic. But from where? We need to find it. 'Search the area thoroughly and see if you can find it discarded in the kitchen garden or grounds. It's a gold pendant, with a heart-shaped dark red stone at the centre. A garnet. Get the others to help – and can you send James in here?'

'Got it.' Matt nods and hurries off casting one last look back at Niamh.

I close my eyes and focus my thoughts on Niamh's necklace. How have I not given it any significance before? The magic within it is more powerful than anything I have access to. I search her face for any sign of Kinfolk magic, but there's nothing.

~

'How is she?' Brother James asks, taking a seat opposite me. I fight the urge to rip his hand away as he places it on Niamh's brow, then lifts her delicate wrist to check her pulse.

'Do you know what's caused this coma she's in?' I ask.

'She's been poisoned with *Crateagus aetheria*.'

'Celestial hawthorn? That—'

'—only grows in certain places in the Caledonian Forest. Areas of the forest that only exist in the Underworld,' James confirms. 'There's no known antidote. It induces this coma-like state – she's essentially frozen in time. And I have no idea what to do. I've looked through every text that mentions it. And nothing on how to reverse the effects. In fact, it should have simply worn off, it's as if there's still a source poisoning her constantly but we can't work out how.'

'Have you ever noticed the necklace she wore?'

James looks at me, frowning. 'No, she wasn't wearing one when we removed her robe to examine her.'

I somehow contain my rage at the thought of him touching her. He's a doctor, he would have needed to examine her. Plus I can't kill him within these walls.

'But before that. Did you ever notice it?'

He shakes his head. 'I never saw her without her robes.' That helps to calm me a little.

There's something my mind is trying to piece together, but as soon as the pieces begin to fall into place, they suddenly drift apart again. All I know is that the necklace is key. I need to focus on that, despite the urge to forget.

I run my fingers around Niamh's neck, tracing the path the chain has lain on for all those years. I rest my hand flat on her chest exactly where the pendant would have lain and ... and I can feel a slight tremor, like that of long-term magic. I stretch my hand out into a V, and move my hand closer to her throat. My thumb lying where the chain would have been on one side, my index finger on the other.

I nearly pull my hand back when power suddenly rushes through me. My fingers tighten on Niamh's throat. And for the second time, my serpent tattoo embodies.

James's chair clatters as he leaps to his feet. He's about to grab my wrist to attempt to pull me off her, but the snake lunges for him, hissing a warning before it slithers from my hand and wraps itself around Niamh's neck and starts to squeeze.

'No!' I yell. Is this the Court informing me that I did the wrong thing, that I should have hunted her down and killed her? I can't move my hand – magic stronger than my own is holding it in place, my own fingers squeezing as tightly as the snake is. Niamh's head tilts back as the snake's coils tighten still further until suddenly it rears its head back and strikes. Its fangs lodge front and centre in her throat and then it's gone and only my hand remains.

Niamh's body convulses as I loosen my grip, pulling my

hand away. She sits up and coughs. A chunk of apple flying from her throat as she holds her throat and blinks.

I almost laugh in disbelief as James reaches for the piece of poisoned fruit. He holds it up so that I can see the two clear puncture wounds that go deep into the apple.

'What the…' I whisper, looking at the serpent, which has now returned to my wrist. I close the gap between us, pulling her against me.

'Vittoria…' Niamh whispers hoarsely.

'It's all right. We know what happened, and we'll work out the rest when you're better. Don't try to talk yet.'

'I'll get you something to drink,' James says. 'One of our medicinal brews.'

'Not Stox,' Niamh rasps, and I smile. I lift her off the altar and carry her through to a lounge area, sitting down with her cradled on my lap. I don't know how long we sit there, until James brings her the drink.

'I'd really like to check you over, Niamh,' he says.

'She's fine,' I snap, not wanting to let her go even for a second and definitely not ready to let another man put his hands on her.

'Cillian, it's probably a good idea,' Niamh says, attempting to climb off my lap, but I hold on tighter, before finally accepting that she's right.

I keep hold of her hand, though, as James checks her blood pressure and the puncture wounds on her neck.

'How does it feel?' he asks.

'Rough and sore. Like a bad sore throat.'

'The wounds are almost healed. While there was a physical aspect to the manifestation, it's essentially a magical wound, so it's healing much faster than normal. I still can't quite—' He shakes his head. 'I've never seen anything like this. Powerful magic like this – it's only heard of in stories.'

'Maybe not anymore,' I say. My Huntsman senses are peaking, and I can sense something in the area. 'There's something stirring. I'm sure of it. Old magic.'

James rubs his stethoscope on his robes moving to put it down the front of Niamh's robes.

'No!'

'But—'

'No,' I insist. 'She can hold it herself, or I'll do it.' Niamh makes a face at him and laughs. Sensibly, James doesn't.

Niamh turns to me, and although I can see that she needs to rest, she puts one hand on either side of my face.

'He's my doctor, Cillian. You will let him do what he needs to do without him having to worry about you losing your temper.'

I frown as James keeps his gaze firmly on his stethoscope, then finally I nod.

'Fine, but I'm taking you upstairs right after this and only calling him in an emergency.'

'Okay,' she says. I don't miss her rolling her eyes at James, wisely he doesn't respond.

I fold my arms as I watch James listen to her back and then her chest. Smiling when I see his hands trembling.

'She's as well as can be expected,' he announces finally. 'Get some rest and I'll check you over again in the morning.'

He's barely finished speaking when I scoop her up into my arms.

'Keep everyone working in the other building as much as possible today.'

I ignore James's laughter and march through the monastery to her bedroom, kicking the door closed behind us before I finally put Niamh down.

'Cillian,' she whimpers, as I hold her way too tight, rocking her against me, reassuring myself that she's still here, that she's breathing again, alive again. I let her go a fraction, only to thread my fingers through her hair, holding her head in place so that I can kiss her. She kisses me back just as desperately, and finally I accept that she really is all right.

'I want you. I need you,' I say. 'Vittoria knows it's over.'

'Good. Then I want you, too,' she whispers, her smile still a little shy. I search her face for any sign that she's not okay. But she seems to be fine.

'I thought I'd lost you,' I say, as I grab hold of her robes and pull them over her head. 'Let me see you.'

She pauses for a moment and bites her lip. I look around, and deciding to play safe, I draw the curtains, and make sure there are no reflective surfaces in the room. Satisfied, I look back at her. She's toed off her shoes and is waiting for me, her hands on the waistband of her shorts. I watch as she pushes them down her long, toned legs, then steps out of them.

She takes hold of the hem of her T-shirt, then with a deep breath she pulls it up and over her head, dropping it to the floor at her side. She's not wearing a bra, but she immediately covers her breasts with her arms, and turns her head to the side.

'Look at me, Niamh,' I say. 'You're beautiful, don't cover yourself.'

It's almost painful to watch as she slowly drops her arms. As soon as she does, I move closer, running my hands over her body, feeling her soft, smooth skin beneath me. I pull her to me, angling her face to mine and kissing her slowly. She deepens the kiss as our tongues tangle together, greedily devouring each other more and more. I circle her nipple with my thumb, teasing it as it puckers beneath my touch. I pinch it hard and she cries out at the pain. Breaking the kiss, I bend to blow gently on it, before I run my tongue over and begin to suck. First one nipple, then the other.

I bite again, quickly soothing it with my tongue. 'Don't ... please ... again...' Her back arches and she sighs.

I want more from her, but once I start, I know I won't stop.

'Are you sure?'

'Yes.'

'And you feel all right?'

'Better than all right. I feel ... different somehow. But in a good way,' she adds when I'm about to step back. 'I want this. *Please*. I need this.'

Teasingly slowly, she pulls her white cotton panties down, and I moan as I see the dark hair that forms a small triangle between her legs. Her confidence grows under my approving eye, and she drapes her arms around my neck, making no attempt to cover herself. I kiss her again and again, desperate to show her how sorry I am for leaving, and she pulls my shirt from my waistband, undoing the buttons with nimble fingers. She discards it on the floor as she runs her hands down my taut back, her fingers seeking to touch every part of me.

'Should we—'

'You think you're in charge, *Gléigeal*?'

'I ... I...' she falters. 'I thought you'd want...' When she takes a step away from me, clearly unsure, I smile as my predatory instincts take over.

'One day I'll take you back to the woods and have you run from me again. And when I catch you...'

She shivers but I see the excitement in her eyes.

'But here and now, we're not going to do that. We *are* doing this my way, though.' I drop my hands to my belt buckle pushing the strap through and loosening it slowly. Then I slide the thick strip of leather from around my waist, one belt loop at a time. She licks her lips as she watches, then looks up at me.

'What?' She swallows. 'What are you going to—'

'Lie on the bed.'

'Not until I know...' She hesitates, rightfully so, but she will do what I want.

'This isn't for punishing you. *This time*. Your safe word is apple,' I say.

She wrinkles her nose. 'Really?'

'I think we can safely say we both now associate apples with something deeply unpleasant.'

'Apple,' she confirms and after taking one single deep breath, and looking back at me, she obeys.

'Put your hands out, wrists together.'

I thread the end of the belt through the buckle and back up to make three loops.

'Hands in.'

She does as she's told, shivering when I pull the belt tight around her wrists and I can sense the fear run through her.

'Relax and put your arms above your head.'

There's a brief hesitation before she does as I asked, and I kneel on the edge of the bed, leaning over her as I fasten it to the headboard. She pulls at the restraints and while there's some movement, it's clear she can't get free.

Cillian,' she whimpers. 'I can't—'

'You can, *Gléigeal*. Just look at me and breathe.'

I lock my gaze with hers as I move around to the end of the bed and kneel between her parted thighs. She's sprawled out before me, her pert breasts decorated with small bite marks, my bite marks. Her body is flushed and aching for me as I grip her knees, easing them back until her pussy is revealed, pink and wet, waiting to be claimed. The scent of her arousal fills the air, intoxicating and impossible to resist. She whimpers and I know she's ready to be taken.

'Cillian...' she swallows, her voice trembling.

'You've done this before. You have the safe word.'

She nods and I lower my mouth to her, licking greedily at her pussy. Her hips gyrate as I tease her clit with my tongue, and I have to hold them firmly in place when I start to suck. Her body is so responsive that when I press a finger to her entrance, it slips in easily. I know she can take more of me, so I insert two more fingers, seeking out the spot I found before and bending my fingers to rub it.

Small gasps and moans fall from her lips, interspersed with my name and a series of prayers. And all too soon, her demands follow.

'Cillian!' she cries out finally as I work her body with my fingers and mouth. Her inner muscles clench around my fingers, but I don't stop and as soon as her body softens and relaxes, I start again to push her over that edge a second time. And I know I will never grow tired of hearing her screaming my name.

CHAPTER 28
NIAMH

When I open my eyes, I'm staring up into Cillian's – piercing and blue. He drops a kiss on my lips and smiles.

'Are you all right?'

I nod, my smile broad. I expect him to loosen the belt now, but he doesn't. He lies down alongside me, still half-dressed. I shiver as he cups one breast with his hand.

'You look more beautiful this morning than you ever have before,' he says, looking up at me, checking I'm all right as he slides his hand down my body, leaving its warm weight splayed over my stomach for a moment before moving lower.

'Cillian?'

'Mmm?'

'Don't you want to—' I stop when I can't work out what words to use. 'Aren't you going to—'

'There's no rush.'

'No, I suppose not,' I say, gasping as his fingers reach my clit again. 'I want to return the favour...'

He smiles down at me. 'Not today. Your throat.'

'It's fine. And I want to.' I pull at my restraints, frustrated that I can't touch him. 'Please, Cillian, I need to—'

'You need to know what it feels like to have a man inside you, oh so slowly, stretching you out until he fills you completely. Then, when he starts to move, he makes you feel so good, so full and...' I writhe beneath him, his words igniting something deep within me. I pull harder at the restraints, desperate to touch him.

'Please, Cillian. I've told you I want this. Why—?'

He shakes his head, and I wish I could read his mind.

'Let me go,' I say.

'Why?'

'Because I want to touch you.'

He frowns. 'I suppose... But some of the things I want you to do—'

'I might want to do them, too. If you don't let me try, how will I know. Please, set me free.'

Reluctantly, he reaches for the belt and loosens the straps, freeing my wrists. I can see marks where the straps were tight and I pulled against them as he fucked me with his tongue and his fingers.

'Sorry,' he says, tracing them with the tip of one finger.

'Are you?'

'Not really,' he grins. 'I like seeing the marks I've left on you.'

I kiss my way down his chest, feeling his rock-hard abs, and lick his skin gently, hungrily. When I put my hands on his waistband, he covers them with his, stopping me.

'I don't want to hurt you,' he says.

'But I don't mind if you do.' I lean forward and bite down on his nipple. He gasps, then flips me onto my back, pinning me down with his body.

'You need to be sure, Niamh.'

I roll my eyes. 'I'm not saying it again, Cillian.'

He raises his eyebrows and looks pointedly at the belt. Then he stands up and pulls off his trousers and boxers, taking something out of his pocket and placing it on the bedside table. I can't keep my gaze off his dick. It's even bigger than I remember from last time, and for a moment, I doubt my decision. Then, I reach out and wrap my hand around him. Cillian groans.

'It's so warm and thick.'

'It is. And if you don't stop doing that, I'm going to come before I get anywhere near doing what I want to do with you.'

I pull my hand back and smile up at him coyly. 'We definitely don't want that.'

'After watching you take me in last time,' he says, a little breathless, 'the way the tears slid down your cheeks as I sank into your mouth, I thought about taking you all night. Imagined how you would feel, what noises you would make as your pussy stretched around me.'

'Hmm.'

'And now I get to find out if I was right.'

I'm surprised at the sense of wonder I see on his face, and I reach for him and draw him down over me. 'Will it hurt?'

'I don't know. This is a first for me, too. But I promise I'll do my best not to hurt you. I want you to enjoy it, I want you to want me to take you again and again and again. And you will.' He presses his cock against me with every repetition and I part my legs, letting him nestle more comfortably between my thighs.

I nod. 'Okay.' I place my hand against his tanned chest, the tattoo of Cernunnos dark against his skin, but still and silent. Then he rolls to the side and grips his cock with one hand.

'Get me ready,' he says. At first, I'm not sure what he means, but then I sit up and lean over him, knocking away his hand and replacing it with mine. He doesn't need me to do this, he's giving me time. Time that I don't need.

I stroke up and down his shaft, smiling in satisfaction at his moans of pleasure. He threads his fingers though my hair as I lean over him, preventing me from changing my mind. Not that I'm going to. Tentatively, I lick the pre-cum from his tip, and when he groans, I lick around him, tracing the vein on the underside up and down before I cover him with my mouth and take him in. He watches me in awe, and I wonder what I must look like, naked, and desperate to please him – in whatever way he chooses. I angle him down my throat as deep as I can take him. He groans, his fingers loosening in my hair and I smile around his cock, loving the fact that I can affect him so deeply. But I want to do more, make him feel more. Give him the same pleasure he gave me. I frantically circle him with my tongue, sucking him, pushing him towards his release.

I can hear his breath getting shorter as his orgasm builds, until suddenly he's no longer there in my mouth and I whimper in disappointment. He sits up, tipping me over on to my back as he reaches for a condom, unrolling the thin rubber over his thick, hard cock, his eyes never leaving mine. My pussy clenches as I wonder how he's going to fit inside me. He's stretched me with his fingers, but I know it's not going to compare.

I expect him to lie on top of me, but he doesn't. Instead, he sits back, stroking his cock, as he watches me sat here, transfixed.

'Show me what you do when you think of me,' he whispers.

I look at him in shock. I've never masturbated in front of anyone before, and I shiver. But it's Cillian, the one man who's shown that he's attracted to me, and it's enough to overcome my nerves.

I spread my legs and reach down, slowly parting my lips with my fingers and rubbing my clit. I gasp, as I dip one finger inside myself, stroking back and forth, his gaze fixed on where it enters my body. I've never felt so vulnerable but also so powerful. I have a man – a god – transfixed on me, Niamh Whyte, and just the thought alone might send me over the edge.

And then he fists his cock, his own movements keeping pace with mine. 'You can change your mind, you know?' But I shake my head, the wetness that pools between my legs a sign that I'm more than ready. I'm close, so close, my breath coming in shallow gasps, when he reaches out and pinches my nipple with his fingers as my body reaches a peak, my muscles clenching as my hips buck and writhe.

Smiling, he moves over me, pushing my hips apart with his and settling between my legs. 'Wrap your legs around my back.'

His cock presses against my core, nudging at my entrance and he rubs over me, coating himself in my wetness. I take a deep breath; my insides clenching again at the thought of him sliding inside me, a mix of fear and anticipation.

His eyes meet mine, a darkness clouding his usually bright blue eyes and I try to smile.

'I'll be gentle,' he promises me. 'The first time, anyway.' He notches his cock against my opening, and I feel him start to push.

'Cillian, I can't ... I...' But my words are too slow, and he's already inside me. Only the tip, though. I have the horrible feeling that what feels huge to me right now, is in fact a tiny fraction of what's to come. I tense at the unfamiliar sensation.

'Stop,' I choke out as the discomfort becomes too much. He pulls back a little, watching me until I release the breath I'm holding. He kisses me again, his fingers finding my clit, rubbing it with slow circles. There are so many sensations flooding me as my body softens, and he resumes pushing just the tip of his cock in and out of my sensitive opening.

He's slow, careful and as I relax, another orgasm starts to build until I can't keep track of what I'm feeling anymore. I know only that I want more, that my body wants something more. That one orgasm wasn't enough. How could it be? I'm empty, and my body needs to be filled. And not just by any man. By one man. Cillian.

'Better?' he asks, and when I nod, he pushes further, gently at first, but as my body softens for him, ready to be taken, he presses more insistently inside with a few shallow thrusts. It hurts a little, but not as badly as the last time.

Again, he pulls back and I shift on the bed as he enters me again, and this time, he buries himself to the hilt.

I cry out as he thrusts harder and faster. Each movement more forceful than the one before, my legs are wrapped tightly around him, every stoke stimulating my swollen clit. We find our rhythm, and he fucks me with a wild desperation. Until I can't keep up anymore. My back bows as another orgasm sweeps through me, and I cling to him, his arms around me, as I let him fuck me without any restraint. My body collapses onto the bed, unable to function any longer, my entire being narrowing to simply being his to use. His pace quickens and his fingers move between us, returning to my clit. It doesn't take him long to make me come, and my orgasm must trigger his, as he throws his head back and, with an animalistic growl, spills inside me.

As our racing hearts slow, he reaches down, wiping a loose strand of hair from my face and kisses me as if it might be our last time. Eventually his cock softens, and he slips out. We lie side by side as we fight to catch our breath. I'm sore, a delicious ache reminding me that I'm no longer a virgin. It's a good feeling, and I'm already excited about doing it again. There's a strange emptiness with him no longer inside me. I reach for his hand, interlacing his fingers with mine and squeezing. And nothing has ever felt better than him squeezing mine back.

I glance down at him and see a small streak of blood on the condom and feel instantly light-headed. It must show on my face because Cillian says, 'You all right?'

I nod at him, my thoughts whirling as I try to get my head around the fact that my body has changed.

'Yes, it was just...'

He reaches for me, pulling me in against his body. The bed is small and cramped but there's nowhere else I'd rather be. Cillian disposes of the condom as I lie there utterly spent.

'Was it ... was it okay?' I ask.

'You were perfect, *Gléigeal*. Just perfect.'

'Maybe you just liked the novelty of me being a virgin.'

'I can't say I hated it,' he admits. 'But...'

He takes my hand and presses it against his rapidly swelling cock. 'I'm going to want you more than once. You're going to be far from being a virgin by the time I've finished with you, Niamh.'

He kisses my hair, his fingers stroking my body. 'From now on, you'll never think of doing that with any man but me.'

I smile, the thought filling me with a bubbling sense of joy. 'I never have.' But a sense of uncertainty clouds my vision as I wonder what hope there is that this might last.

'Are you sore?'

'A little,' I admit. 'An ache rather than anything else. It was ... perfect. And I'm glad it was you.'

His smile is smug until his expression falls.

'You should hate me for what I did. Before. For the way I made you feel. Thinking that—'

'For making me think that I was repellent to all other men? That I was doing something wrong. That I would never have anyone to hold me, or love me, or—'

He winces. 'I wanted to be the only one,' he says. 'The only man to take you, to hold you, to love you.'

I sit up, emboldened perhaps by the change in me, and I lock my gaze with his.

'Cillian. I'm giving you this one chance because I want you, too. But if you mess this up, I won't give you another one.'

He looks momentarily astonished at how assertive I am being, before smiling.

'Okay.' He kisses my neck, sending tingles down my spine. 'I promise to spend the rest of our lives making it up to you.'

'Even if I'm stuck here forever?'

'You won't be. I'll fix this. I promise.'

'You can't promise that.'

'No.' He strokes my hair.

'You're not going to stay for long, are you?' I say, as he kisses me, his hand on the side of my face comforting me.

'I can't. I have to go back tomorrow. It's too dangerous for now.' He sighs. 'But I'll sort it out. Somehow. I just need some time.'

Staring into his eyes I can see the truth in his words and I'm even happier when he spends the next half an hour proving that this was not just a one-off. And that my virginity was not the reason he wanted me. As his body ploughs into mine, I know I'm no longer a needy, wanting mess. Now I have him and he's giving me exactly what I want without any more holding back.

'Look at me,' Cillian demands. And suddenly it's easy. I can't move, can't get away. He's giving me more pleasure than I ever thought possible, and it seems so simple. The only thing I have to do is look at him, so I lift my gaze to stare into his milky-blue eyes.

I expect this orgasm to hit me harder and faster, but instead it's like a slow wave rolling over me. I cry out, the way he moves inside me, slow and relentless, building my pleasure to a cresting peak. Every heated promise he whispers fuels the fire building inside me and no matter how deep he is, how connected we are, I can't seem to get enough. His fingers circle my clit, again and again, until my back arches off the bed, bringing my breasts closer to his mouth, and he leans down and sucks as I fall apart. Finally, he slams home, finding his release for a second time as he fills me once more.

'Niamh,' he whispers as he moves, letting me turn on my side. I'm facing away from him, a little raw and exposed, and he pulls me back against his hard body, wrapping an arm around me and holding me close.

'Cillian...' I murmur.

'Shh. Just sleep,' he whispers.

CHAPTER 29
CILLIAN

I haven't slept. Sleep was impossible after I made love to her for the first time. But I don't want to push her too fast, so I let her sleep through the night, kissing the back of her neck to wake her only when the sun is fully up. There's still half an hour before she needs to get up, and selfishly I want her again before I leave.

She turns in my arms, blinking up at me as I move over her easily, settling between her thighs, my cock nudging her entrance. She smiles sleepily.

'Niamh?' I ask, and when she nods, I slide easily into her. Her lips form a surprised 'O' as her legs wrap around my waist. I keep my thrusts slow and deep, our lovemaking sleepy and apparently spontaneous. Though I've been planning this for hours.

I don't stop kissing her as we move together, bitterly regretting my choices over the past four years. Why did I push her away like I did? Vittoria was constantly telling me how selfish I was, always choosing my duty to the Court over her. But that wasn't the reason. All along I've been stalling in the hope that... I don't know. That something would change, that having Niamh wouldn't mean I had to give up everything else. But that's where we are now. And I'm not sure I'm going to regret it. I will never be king if I choose Niamh, and yet the sacrifice is worth it. On a personal level, at least.

I have to go back and face the Court again. They might even have made a decision in my absence. Without uttering any words, I've chosen Niamh with my actions. But there is no way out of here for her, apart from through the Court, and Vittoria has already made her guilt appear to be the only sensible way to interpret the events of that night.

I realise that if the Court takes my position as Huntsman from me, then I will no longer be able to visit Niamh here, if she stays. I must fight to remain the Huntsman. And persuade her not to risk facing a trial in a Court corrupted by the Rialis.

'Cillian?'

I blink down at Niamh, who is staring up at me. Her hands are on my hips, holding me still.

'Come back to me.'

I nod. 'I'm sorry. I was just—'

'Worrying about what the Court will decide?'

'Yes.'

I lean my forehead against hers and start to move again. This time determined to focus on her. She winces as I thrust a little harder, and I stop.

'Don't stop,' she says. 'I'm just—'

But I pull out and sit up, reaching for the pillows. 'Turn over.'

She frowns but does as she's told, and I push the pillows in under her stomach.

'Head down,' I say, running my hand down her spine. 'Cillian,' she murmurs, a little confused, but a hand on her back keeps her in place as my cock nudges her entrance and she groans as I sink inside her, my hands gripping her firm arse. I want to do this every morning and every night from now on. I will never get enough of the way this woman makes me feel. She circles her hips and pushes back, my cock sliding in deep.

I watch my body move easily in and out of hers, loving seeing her spread in front of me for the taking. Her echoing gasp makes me smile as she gives me what I need, without needing to be taught anymore. I lean over her, sliding one hand around the soft skin of her thigh to reach her clit and continue to thrust slowly in and out of her welcoming body as I feel her excitement build, her body tensing, reaching for an orgasm she's not yet ready to have and I'm not ready to give her.

'Relax,' I say, kissing the back of her neck, then biting into the soft flesh where it meets her shoulder. 'And just enjoy.'

She gasps as I take my time, pushing deeper inside her than I have before with this new angle. I stroke up the length of her spine with my hand.

'Cillian,' she whispers, reaching back towards me. I move then, taking both her hands and leaning over her, interlacing my fingers with hers, pinning her hands to the bed beside her head. Inside her pussy, my cock is moving over and over that sweet spot, and her pleasure builds.

'Please,' she whispers, shifting her hips, trying to escape the intensity of the sensations, but I don't let her. She cries out, a long, low wail as her whole body peaks and shudders. I hold myself still for a moment as her body practically strangles my cock, then she collapses spent onto the pillows.

But I'm far from done with her. I lift her hips with my hands and pull her back to meet me, thrust for thrust. I watch as her fingers grasp onto the duvet for a moment, then let go as another orgasm crests. There's no resistance left in her as I keep up my pace until, finally, I collapse on top of her as I reach my own peak.

We lie together until all I can hear in the room is her breathing as it slows.

Her body under mine, comforting rather than passionate, is unlike anything I've experienced with other women, and it's this I want more of. This sense of peace and ... joy. Having nearly lost her, I'm sure now that I would be willing to give up anything to have this woman by my side forever.

But as it stands, there is no way to get her out of here – unless she's willing to face The Unseelie Court for killing Kin – the outcome of which is both predictable and fatal, and not an option.

I move off her, adjusting the pillow so that we can lie spooned together once more, and we lie there for a while. I wonder if this will be the last time we're together. Would fate actually be that cruel – to wait until we've finally got together then force us apart?

'You're thinking again, aren't you?' she asks.

'Just that we're going to need a bigger bed,' I say, and she laughs, tracing invisible patterns on the backs of my hand.

'Let me come with you?' she whispers.

'Absolutely not.'

'Cillian, please. How can I defend myself if I don't even go to the trial?'

'If you don't go, then there won't be a trial. And if you do go... You didn't see them the last time. The way Vittoria presented the evidence...'

'Yes. Even you started to believe I was guilty?'

I smile against her shoulder, and she shivers. 'She twisted everything. It all sounded so plausible.'

'Cillian?'

'What, *Gléigeal*?'

'Do you trust me?'

'Of course.'

'Then trust me to come with you. This is what I do, this is who I am.'

'Rose said... Rose said she didn't remember enough to contradict any of what Vittoria said.'

'You saw Rose?'

'Yes.'

'So, she knows about Matt?'

'Yes.'

'Oh, Cillian. Just tell her the truth this time. And trust me, trust us. Please. I shouldn't be condemned for what I did. And the knife ... what if that ending up in my hand was someone else's magic? Let me challenge this and fight to get my life back.'

'I'll think about it,' I say, and her face falls. She knows I mean no. Not wanting to ruin this morning with a pointless argument, I get out of bed and head for the shower.

∽

Declan clearly doesn't expect Niamh to be back on catering duty so soon after her brush with death, so I leave her sitting on the jetty after a brunch cooked by Brother Duncan. She has a book in her hand, but I know she hasn't actually turned a page since she sat down half an hour ago.

'You'll come back?' she asks, standing up to hug me, but refusing to make eye contact.

'As soon as I can,' I promise, but we both know I might not make it. I kiss her, hating that I have to prise her fingers from my jacket so I can leave. But she doesn't say another word. Doesn't ask again to come with me – or ask for promises I can't keep.

∽

I shake my head when I push through the thin place in the chapel and emerge into the Court chamber. I look around realising that I've come back at virtually the same time as I left. Right in the centre of the Court with every eye on me.

A door thuds, and I look towards it, surprised to see Rose enter. She frowns at the door, opens it and peers back into the corridor, and I suspect that the Court chamber is playing tricks on her and that she thought she was getting to leave.

'Dammit,' she curses, stomping across the floor back to her seat.

'You're back?' Vittoria fixes her cold eyes on me, 'Is there anything about your previous statements that you'd like to change, Cillian? The Court can be very forgiving when it wants to be.'

We observe one another across the chamber. There's a hum in the atmosphere that I don't think was here when I left, and I look around, trying to work out the source of it. I notice Alec Carruth looking around, too, as well as MacGowan, so I know it's not just me who can hear it.

'What have I missed?' I ask.

'Nothing at all,' says Vincenzo. 'Looks like the Court is very keen for you to speak on this matter, and for the rest of us not to have our time wasted.'

'I'm sure Cillian has some new information to consider since he left,' Vittoria says smugly. 'He may even have had a change of heart, in which case, once we resolve the small matter of why my brother's murderer is still breathing, we can all go home.'

'Matt didn't kill Chris!' Rose states, standing up.

'He was found desecrating the body,' Vittoria states. 'Drenched in his victim's blood. If you had seen it, Rose, then you'd never trust him again.'

'He was trying to save him,' Rose says through gritted teeth.

'Christopher was immersed in water when he died. It was instrumental as a cause of his death. Matt is water Kin.'

'And? So are a lot of Kinfolk.'

By this time, I've reached our alcove. I put my arm around Rose's shoulder and kiss the side of her head, realising I've not shown any affection towards my sister since the night

Matt died. The knowledge adds to my burgeoning sense of regret.

'We will deal with this,' I tell her quietly. 'But not yet. After this, you should go to St Marnox and talk to Matt.'

'Why, Cillian? I could have been going there all this time. Seen him. Not ... not lived my life the way I did, mourning him every single day, thinking that I could never have ... never have the life I wanted. You kept me from him.'

'He asked me to, Rosebud. He wanted you to live your life fully, not spend it visiting him like a prisoner.'

'But—'

'Rosebud...'

'This is all very touching, Cillian, but can we please get on with the case in hand,' MacGowan says. 'Vittoria?'

'In the light of these revelations, it should be clear that there is significant doubt about Cillian Hunter remaining as the Huntsman.'

'For trying to save the life of an innocent?' Rose scoffs but even as she speaks, the humming in the chamber gets louder. Rose and I both look around our alcove, which has started to glow.

'Is the Court ... is this it coming back to life?' Rose whispers.

'I don't know.'

The other Kin are whispering amongst themselves. Vittoria, who had looked unsure for a split second, squares her shoulders and resumes her speech.

'This may well be a sign.' Vittoria gestures around her. The lights in each alcove are just a little bit brighter, the atmosphere a little more positive. 'Could this be The Unseelie

Court itself, affirming what we are saying? That Niamh Whyte was guilty of killing Kin and should have been punished accordingly? In sparing her life, allowing her to reach sanctuary, Cillian Hunter has proven himself unworthy of his position and should be removed.'

The lights flicker, going out briefly before starting to build in intensity once more. There's more muttering, and it's hard to tell whether the others are in agreement with Vittoria or will back me. Again, Rose stops me when I try to speak and looks up at the source of light in our alcove. 'No, wait. The Court. She's misinterpreting. And it will put her right itself, that will be far more effective.'

'You're not rushing to defend yourself, Cillian?' Vittoria asks. 'No attempt to deny your deception or justify your actions. Even if they're moot now.' Her smile is wicked, but I ignore her goading.

'I didn't want to be rude and interrupt. After all, you appear to know a lot more about me and the decisions I've made as Huntsman perhaps even than I do.'

My statement is met with a low murmur of laughter from around the chamber.

The hum stops abruptly. There's silence for a long moment, then Carruth laughs loudly.

'Do you want to continue with this nonsense, Vittoria, or simply present your evidence from Sussurri?'

'Fine.' She's furious. I can see it in the set of her shoulders. For the next ten minutes, she projects footage into the centre of the Court. The Court's magic ensures that we can all watch it easily, always at the right angle for our position around the chamber. Rose sits stoically, watching herself dancing and flirting with the men. I notice Carruth glancing over more than once, and several of the younger men — although many of them I'm sure already know my sister intimately. She's allowed to make whatever choices she wishes about the men she spends time with, but guilt gnaws at me. If I had told her about Matt, things might be very different. But I'm so fucking proud of her for sitting through it, not reacting to any of the whispers I try not to hear. None of the men whispering behave any differently themselves.

Security footage shows Sean heading down a corridor, followed by Niamh a few minutes later, but only Niamh returns. The dancefloor footage also shows that no one else touched the drinks after Niamh bought them.

'There doesn't seem to be much doubt about her guilt,' MacGowan says, but I know him. He's wanting this to be over so that he can get back to propping up one of his failing bars. 'But if she's already at St Marnox, surely there is nothing else to be done? The Court has seen fit to grant her sanctuary.'

Vittoria is watching me, waiting to see how I react.

'Have you nothing to add, Huntsman? No further information about the human? Something that may make the Court reconsider your suitability for the position?'

I shrug. 'You can try and force me out, Vittoria. But I will never go willingly. For any reason. Including my choice of bride.'

The hum must have been gradually building again, unnoticed, but now it suddenly screeches as if there's interference. Everyone in the chamber winces at the discordant sound.

'Bride?' She laughs. 'But—'

MacGowan pushes himself to his feet. 'Everyone is talking in riddles. Tell us what we are here for.'

Carruth laughs. 'They are fighting about who gets to be the next King of The Unseelie Court. And whether Cillian remains as Hunter.'

'But Vincenzo isn't even dead yet,' MacGowan points out.

'Quite. And yet these two Kin continue to think that it is somehow their right to rule the rest of us,' Carruth says. 'But heredity only plays one part in the decision. And in the end, the Court itself will decide.'

'From candidates I put forward,' Vincenzo insists.

'Only if you are prepared for your death, Vincenzo.'

'I'm preparing now.'

Carruth takes a moment, to look around the chamber, then stands. 'With all due respect, you have held the position of King for the past ninety years, mostly because no one else really wants it. It's a poisoned chalice with a lot of responsibilities and very few benefits. And during that time, the Court has faded. I will not support any Riali's claim to the throne after Vincenzo.' Carruth motions to the others of his Kin that it's time to leave.

'Cillian wants it,' Vittoria responds instantly. 'And the only way he can be assured of the position is by marrying me. We all agree on that.'

I clench my fists. She's right. I do, if only because I know I could do a better job than Vincenzo. I know that given the chance, I could reverse the decline. Push back the Blight. The Rialis were incomers when they arrived here little more than a century ago. A Kinfolk family powerful enough to replace one of the Kin at The Unseelie Court within a decade of arriving, but since they took the throne, only they have thrived.

'I do,' I admit finally. 'Or I did, at least. Maybe then, the Kinfolk would stop fading out of existence, the Blight would stop spreading through the Underworld and the Court. Then we could begin to re-establish the Kinfolk as true powers in both worlds.'

Carruth chuckles, and Vincenzo moves as if he's going to rise and challenge me for my impudent statement, but Vittoria stays unnaturally calm, putting a hand out to calm her father. I watch her for a long moment. She sits there so composed, and yet when her eyes meet mine, I can see the hatred burning deep in them. She wants to be queen for her own gain, to carry on her father's work. With her by my side, I will never be able to tackle the Blight.

'Tonight, Vittoria told us a very plausible tale, about a human plotting to kill Kin, successfully, I might add. During my brief interlude in the Underworld, I discovered that Vittoria has taken matters into her own hands. She broke the sanctity of St Marnox by poisoning one of the seekers on the grounds.'

'A murderer,' she spits. 'And the rules state that seekers are only guaranteed safety within St Marnox walls.'

It's funny how so often we take words and phrases for granted without thinking about exactly what they mean. As Kinfolk, we should know better, but as St Marnox is an island, I have always assumed the seekers were safe at all times, not just within the literal sanctuary walls, and so I'm relieved that Niamh survived.

'She deserves to suffer for what she did. She drugged your sister, put her in danger, killed three of my Kin.'

But I shake my head. 'No, Vittoria. I don't believe that. Niamh would never do anything to hurt Rose. You've not shown us everything about that night. You're intentionally deceiving the Court.'

'How can she be worth it, Cillian? I could have offered you so much more.' Vittoria sounds the closest to desperate that I have ever heard her. 'Are you really willing to give up everything, your position, your future, just to have her?'

'You're really in love with a human?' Carruth scoffs, and all around the Court there's laughter. 'Then Vittoria has a point. Not only will you not be king, but you'll also forfeit your position as Kennard if you marry her.'

'I will *not* step down,' I announce.

'There is no other option,' Vincenzo says. 'You cannot marry a human and remain Kennard of one of the Kin. You will marry my daughter, and together you will control both the Hunters and the Rialis, as well as The Unseelie Court. It has already been agreed.'

'No.'

'I tried to give you a chance to keep your position as Kennard of the Hunters, your chance at becoming king,' Vittoria responds.

'No, Vittoria, you are trying to ensure that you retain your chance at becoming queen. But everything that has happened over the past few days has taught me that I can't marry you.'

'You still want a dead woman?' Vittoria screams. Rose leaps to her feet and stares at me, her hands over her mouth.

'She's not dead,' I say. 'You failed, Vittoria. There is so much wrong in our world, and that starts at the top.'

'How dare you!' Vincenzo stands up. 'I have given everything to ruling this Court. The Blight—'

But whatever Vincenzo is about to say doesn't get said as a light starts to glow in the centre of the chamber. The glow expands, forming a column of light. It grows wider and wider still, and, inside the thin place to St Marnox, begins to open. Two figures step through, and I close my eyes, praying that I'm not about to see what I think I'm about to see. I don't want her to have done this. I don't want her to die trying to save me.

CHAPTER 30
NIAMH

'I'm thinking of going through,' Matt says as I make my way down the central aisle of the old church and into the side chapel.

'Even if it means they'll kill you for what you did?'

'Even if,' he says. 'But I didn't do it. At least then she'll be free.'

'Matt—' I take his hand, and he squeezes mine.

'Are you going to follow him?' he asks.

'He'll not be happy.'

He turns and looks at me. 'So, that's a yes.'

I inhale, then stop and sit down in the front pew and look at the decoration around the windows. Carvings done by stonemasons, long dead. Perhaps for a thousand years or more. I'm struck by a sudden thought.

'Are the Kinfolk immortal? Do you age like humans?'

'Those of us who appear or can appear human, yes. Pretty much,' he replies. 'Why? Worried you're dating a much older man?'

I laugh. 'Cillian is definitely old enough. But that's good to know.'

'What do you think you can do at the Court, Niamh?'

'I'm not sure,' I admit. 'I mean, I have no idea how your legal system works.'

'Legal system,' he scoffs. 'It's not so much a system as something determined by the whim of an old man – and some rather unpredictable and ancient magic.'

'When I was coming here'—I pause, not sure what to tell him—'I think there was magic helping me to get here, keeping me safe, but also preventing Cillian from killing me.'

'What sort of magic?'

'No idea. Whatever it was, it all seemed to be working in my favour. There was an old washerwoman who gave me directions, a thick mist that shrouded me from Cillian's hunt and a white stag that gave its life so that Cillian would have a heart to present to Vittoria. All of them led me here to St Marnox. And the only place we can go from St Marnox is back to the Court.'

'Hmm.' He regards me. 'You seem different today.'

My cheeks heat at the thought of why that might be, then I lift my hand to my chest and pause, feeling the emptiness around my neck. I'm shocked I haven't noticed it before, but I suppose I've been focused on other things.

'My—' I look around me, as though my necklace just dropped off me somewhere here.

'Your necklace,' Matt says, and I turn to him. 'It wasn't in the garden,' he adds, 'I think Vittoria took it.'

'She stole my necklace?' I grind my teeth. 'My mother gave me that.'

I get up, determination gripping me.

'We should go. I don't want my fate to be left in the hands of those who wish to condemn me. I should at least present my version of the events.'

'Aye.' Matt nods. 'And I want to see Rose. If I can't be with her, then I want to let her move on. Properly.'

'She loves you, Matt. It's only ever been you.' I wish I could fix this for him, and for Rose. And maybe with me to defend him, there's a chance.

He smiles sadly. 'Do you need to take anything with you?' he asks.

I shake my head. 'No. But ... how do we know *when* we'll arrive.'

'We don't. Let's just hope that wild, unpredictable magic that got you here, is ready to take you back there at exactly the right time.'

'I hope so,' I murmur, though I don't feel confident.

'If it's meant to be, it will,' Matt says. 'So let's find out.'

I get up and he puts his arm around my shoulders and, side by side, we step up to the thin place. Matt lets go of me, and presses his hands on an invisible barrier, whispering strange words as he pushes through. I stick as close to him as possible, closing my eyes at the odd sensation that touches my skin as we move between the worlds—

And emerge into the middle of an underground cavern.

'Welcome to The Unseelie Court,' Matt whispers as our new reality takes form around us.

We're surrounded by a column of light that reaches upwards from the floor. I put a hand out to touch it, and it repels me with a buzz of energy. I pull my hand back and look around the strange room. It's definitely underground, a large circular cavern surrounded by small intricately carved wooden alcoves. I look up to see how high it is, but the chamber seems to go up forever into the darkness.

Looking back at the alcoves, I spot Vincenzo in one, sitting on a large throne. 'So, he really is a king?' I whisper.

'He really is. And chances are, Cillian will be next. Except that—' Matt stops, and his brow creases. 'Oh.'

'What?'

'If he's with you, he'd have to give up that. Maybe even being the Huntsman. Dammit.' Matt kicks at the floor. I put out a hand to stop him when I see the way the Rialis are watching him.

'You need to behave like you're on trial,' I say.

'Niamh. We *are* on trial.'

Cillian walks towards us, placing his hands on the wall of light surrounding us. I echo his movement, prepared for the energy zap this time, but although our hands look like they're touching, I can't feel his. He smiles at me, then shakes his head.

'You shouldn't have come,' he says.

'We had to. We both had to.'

'Matthew Muir,' Vincenzo says, drawing our attention to the throne. 'Isn't this convenient? Are you ready to pay for your crimes?'

Matt looks at Rose, then smiles a gentle smile at her before he faces Vincenzo directly, meaning that I can no longer see his face. 'I didn't murder Chris, Vincenzo. I think you know that.'

'I don't want to hear his name pass your lips,' Vincenzo

snarls. 'I should never have given you another chance. You, and your father, you're scum. Traitors.'

'No,' says Matt calmly. 'I'm ready to stand trial, Vincenzo, because I'm not guilty of the crime I was accused of. I won't have any more of my life stolen from me in that place and to do that I have to place my trust in the Court.'

Vincenzo scoffs. 'I am the Court, and I already know you are guilty. The evidence I presented before was enough to instigate a hunt. The Court—'

But Matt ignores Vincenzo and turns his gaze back to Rose and then he's simply gone.

'Where did he go?' Vincenzo lurches from his seat but is pulled back down by Vittoria, who whispers to him.

'We're not here to discuss your son, Vincenzo,' a younger man says, looking to the others for support. A couple nod in agreement, while yet another leans back in his seat and gives me a thumbs-up, clearly loving the spectacle.

'You tried to kill me,' I say, addressing Vittoria. 'It should be you on trial and not me.'

'Ridiculous! We've just watched the evidence. I had every right to seek vengeance for the deaths of my three Kin.'

'So, you admit it, then?'

'What?'

'That those three men were Riali Kin. They worked for you?'

'Yes. Low-level employees. I didn't recognise them in the alley. It was dark.'

All around the chamber people mutter, and chairs shift.

'See, those of us who were there'—I indicate Cillian standing next to Rose and Aiden, with Sean behind them—

'we know that's not true. One of the men, Ed, recognised you at the time. Implied you'd been lovers – yet you claimed not to know him.'

'I didn't remember him,' Vittoria snaps.

'It's funny, Cillian knows everyone who works for him, even the humans. He remembers their names. Rewards loyalty. And yet you—' I pause and smile at her. 'Well, I can understand why Cillian doesn't feel you'd make a good queen, don't you?'

The man who spoke earlier laughs, and the one who gave me a thumbs-up leans forward almost gleefully.

'None of this changes the fact that in that lane you lifted a Kinfolk knife from the ground, held it up and stabbed a man, Kin, right through the throat with it.'

'Kin who were attacking me. Kin who had drugged us earlier and planned to rape and kill me.'

There's an energy in this place – I can feel it in the way the ground trembles under my feet, in the way the torchlight around the walls is growing incrementally brighter with each passing minute.

'You're human!' Vittoria yells. 'You cannot be allowed to kill Kin!'

'I did not intentionally kill anyone, Vittoria,' I state calmly. With every passing statement, I feel more sure about myself. 'I can't be guilty of murder if there was no intent to kill. Four years ago, you told me that you would never need a lawyer like me. But I think perhaps, you do.'

'The videos show you buying the drink that drugged Rose.'

'Buying them from *your* barman. In *your* establishment,

Vittoria. I was not the only person to touch those drinks and you know it. There was another man, too, behind the bar. The one sitting behind your father now, in fact. I'd recognise that smile anywhere.'

I regret my words as soon as they leave my mouth. Mocking a scar is not something I'd normally condone but standing here, facing the woman who tried to kill me more than once – well, I suppose anger is a very normal, human response.

Something shifts in my head even as I think it, and a memory flashes into my thoughts. The washerwoman by the stream. A feeling I had then of familiarity. I spread my hands out in front of them and look at them, and for a moment they don't really look like my hands. I shrug off the ridiculous thought and catch Rose's eye. She's staring at me, her lips parted, her brow furrowed.

'It's funny, that in the alley, I don't even remember picking up the knife. I looked at it, it was lying on the ground, just out of my reach. Then Frank attacked me, and it was just suddenly in my hand – like magic.'

Vittoria smirks. 'And how are you going to prove that?'

'It's a pattern, though. Isn't it? And you said it yourself—'

'What are you talking about?'

'When we arrived. You said that it had been four years of you trying to kill me.'

Cillian's head jerks towards her, and he glares at her. 'What?'

'What did you expect?' Vittoria snaps at him. 'From the very first moment you set eyes on her, you didn't want me anymore. Me? When I have so much more to offer.'

'The night my parents died,' I go on, 'a car followed them. *Your* car.'

'I wasn't anywhere near the accident.' She sounds so sure, so confident, I almost believe her. But she must be lying. I know she's behind it. 'And all it did was push him closer to you. Until the next day, at least.'

'You made a mistake, Vittoria.'

'Don't be ridiculous. The only mistake I made was in not killing you myself. But you always seemed so inconsequential and pathetic. So easy to forget about until... Until something would happen, and then he'd notice you again. Even a few weeks ago, when he finally proposed, it was the night he saw you at your graduation party. He asked me because he wants so very much to be king that he can't allow himself to be tempted by you. And I knew that even if I was his wife, he would still want you more.'

'You think you have so much, Vittoria, and yet you keep taking from me. My parents, Cillian, my necklace.'

'This?'

She pulls it from her pocket and flings it at me. It hits the column and explodes in a storm of bright red light. Those outside the column of light cover their ears, cowering from the explosion and the noise that follows. A cacophony of voices all screaming, but the screaming fades until all I hear is many voices holding a single note in a beautiful harmony.

The light in The Unseelie Court grows brighter, and one of the dark alcoves starts to gently glow as the room begins to spin. There's still no sign of Matt, so I'm alone, spinning inside a column of light. The faster I spin, the more the lights fade until the chamber falls into pitch darkness. I feel cool air on my face, the gentle touch of rain and look up to see that the hill above my head has opened to reveal a night sky full of stars.

Power prickles across my skin. It passes over me and through me. In front of me, I see my mother's face. As she smiles at me, her eyes grow brighter, her hair deepens into a richer shade of chocolate, and her cheeks take on the colour and texture of the most delicate of pink roses. My father puts his arm around her shoulders. He smiles at me, then kisses my mother's cheek. They are both glowing – the same glow I have seen all around me here in The Unseelie Court. No, not the same. Not quite.

I reach out and touch the column, feeling the pulse of power within it. So much of what I've witnessed around the Kinfolk and in the Underworld has been all about deception. Glamour. Truths that cleverly masquerade as lies, and vice versa. They all consider themselves experts in deception, but none of them has seen the truth that was right in front of them. None of them has truly seen me.

I place my palms flat against the light, and its power flows into me. My awareness increases. I can hear the creatures moving in the earth that surrounds us, sense the millions of people's lives in the city. Feel the two worlds hovering, side by side, see the thin places where the veil between those worlds stretches and tears and allows people to pass through. It moves through me, finding all the magic placed upon me by my parents. And with the untangling of that magic, I remember the stories my mother whispered to me in the dark, everything she taught me about The Seelie Court in the hope that one day, one day we could return.

Voices speak in a language long forgotten, telling me how they hid me, how they had no choice. Until the Blight is reversed, they will not be the only ones who are safer in hiding. But for me there will be no more hiding. I cover my face with my hands as the column stops spinning, feel the pulse of Glamour slide from the surface, revealing my true nature. Drawing the last of the concealing magic from my face, I shake it from the tips of my fingers as I look up into Cillian's confused face.

He reaches for me, and I step into him, lifting my face as he lowers his, his lips finding mine and breathing life back into my every fibre of being. The power flows, swirling between us. From me into him and back and when I see myself reflected in his eyes, they are no longer merely human.

'Niamh,' he whispers.

I am Kin.

CHAPTER 31
CILLIAN

This changes everything.

The chamber erupts into chaos, everyone talking, shouting, at once. Carruth is furious, MacGowan is yelling. And then there's silence. A silence only achievable using magic. Niamh and I remain exactly where we are. I can't take my eyes off her. I thought I knew her; I do know her. I've watched her for four years. How could I not have seen ... seen what she truly is?

It's broken when Vincenzo scrapes his chair back to stand.

'Well, Cillian. It would indeed seem like we did not fully understand the situation. Your choice of bride, it seems, will not preclude you from remaining as Kennard, nor from potentially becoming king. After me, of course. Vittoria?'

Vincenzo sounds utterly despondent, and now he looks around and frowns.

'Where is she?'

With no answer, the Kin search the chamber, until it's

established that she's no longer present. Vincenzo grows more and more frantic, before he's finally persuaded to return to his throne. 'What have you done with them?'

'Them?'

'Don't act ignorant with me, Cillian. Matthew Muir has gone, too.'

'One minute he was there, and the next he was gone,' Niamh says. 'You saw as much as we did.'

Beside us, there's a soft tinkling sound, and Niamh crouches down to pick something up.

'My necklace,' she says, standing. 'The remains of it, at least.'

The chain is broken, and little of the gold surround remains. The garnet heart is still intact, however, pulsing gently with light. The plain gold oval now a delicate filigree of symbols and knotwork reminiscent of the designs in this very chamber. Similar, but different. And suddenly I understand – this is Seelie magic. I touch the hard red stone and feel the beat of a heart within it. Low laughter echoes through my head. Niamh closes her fist around it and smiles.

'You ... you're Kin.'

'It would seem so.'

'You didn't know?'

'No.'

'Your parents?'

'They hid me. They were in hiding, too. I think the whole Seelie Court is. But they told me stories, and I'm slowly remembering them now the magic has been undone.'

'But they're still out there?'

She turns to look at the alcove that used to house the

entrance to The Seelie Court and, for the first time, I see the light above the door is glowing. It's barely there, but even as we watch, it grows a little stronger.

'I think so.'

'There were times when I sensed magic around you that I didn't fully understand,' I tell her. 'And this explains it.'

'I had no idea,' Niamh says, shaking her head. 'Although ... perhaps it was one of the things I sensed when I met Rose. One of the things I sensed when I met you.'

'Huntsman!'

We turn to face Vincenzo. One of his men is beside him, the man Niamh identified as having been in the bar that night.

'I have a job for you. Two, actually.'

I take a deep breath, knowing what he's going to say. 'Vittoria and Matt.'

'Not as stupid as you look,' he says, but although his words are clearly intended to wound me, there's no avoiding the defeat in his posture.

'If Niamh is correct, your daughter killed Kin with no justification. And she has admitted to attempting to kill Niamh more than once. There is a price to pay for that, Vincenzo.'

His shoulders slump, then he whirls on me. 'I expect you to show her the same leniency that you showed—'

'Look,' Niamh says, gesturing at a spot above The Seelie Court alcove. She opens her palm and looks down at the necklace in her hand. On the wall, I can see the same oval shape, only much larger, the size of a person, covered in the same filigree design formed of earth and tree roots. And behind them is a figure. Vittoria. Her eyes closed, her face the most peaceful I have ever seen it. Trapped by her own actions in the Court chamber. Maybe forever.

'Get her down!'

'I can't,' Niamh states calmly. 'It wasn't me who put her there.'

'Then, who?' Vincenzo demands.

'This Court? The Seelie Court? I really don't know, I'm sorry.'

Vincenzo lets out a cry of anguish, stumbles as he crosses the chamber, never taking his eyes off his daughter. For a while, no one moves or makes a sound. No one dares. Until Vincenzo turns. As he stalks towards us, his posture straightens, an aura of some large creature shimmering into place behind him.

'I won't rest until I find a way to free her. She didn't know you were Kin, you can't blame her for merely trying to secure her future,' he says, and I move between him and Niamh, determined that she won't suffer any more at the hands of this family.

'Her not knowing doesn't change anything,' Niamh says, stepping around me to stand beside me. I reach for her hand. 'Perhaps the Court is deciding her fate. Perhaps there's more to her story and it's waiting for it to be revealed before making a decision.'

'She can't be blamed for something she didn't know she was doing!'

Niamh smiles. 'Then neither should I.'

Vincenzo looks up at Vittoria again, his shoulders

slumping. It's as if he ages years in a few seconds before he glares at me.

'I deserve to see the one who took my son from me punished,' Vincenzo demands. 'Bring me the heart of Matthew Muir.'

'But—' Niamh starts, but I put a hand on her arm and stop her.

'The Court let him go,' I tell Vincenzo. 'Do you think that would have happened if he had been guilty?'

'It's likely one of you who helped him escape,' Vincenzo says. 'You've claimed to be our allies, but it was all a lie. Consider our alliance truly severed. You will not allow him sanctuary a second time, Cillian Hunter. It's the least that you can do. He must pay for his crimes.'

'He's not guilty,' Rose insists coming to stand beside me. 'At the very least he deserves a fair trial in this court.'

'Is that even possible with you as King, Vincenzo? So many of the people I hunt down are your personal enemies. So many now plead with me, assuring me of their innocence.'

'The Court instigates the hunt—'

'Based on evidence provided by you,' Rose points out. 'And we have all just witnessed your daughter presenting the Court with strategically altered evidence. Why should anyone trust in its decisions anymore.'

'I agree.' Alec Carruth stands up and makes his way forward, ending up standing altogether too close to Rose for my comfort. 'Perhaps the Blight is affecting the Court in more ways than we have realised. Cillian called for us to work harder to eradicate it a few weeks ago, and I agree.'

'The Court is fine,' Vincenzo insists. 'The Blight is here to stay. We must learn simply to work around it. With it, even. We don't have the resources to destroy it.'

'One day, Vincenzo, I will be The Unseelie King, and I will ensure that the Blight is eradicated, whether that means I profit or not.'

'Such idealism,' Vincenzo sneers. 'But you'll learn. And one day you'll be just like me. Now, excuse me while I go and try to find a way to free my daughter from whatever you have done to her. I will not lose both my children. There must be a way...'

He glances at Niamh, his face twisting in disgust, before he heads for the doors, followed by the rest of his Kin.

And with that, most of the other Kin follow. All glancing worriedly at us and up at Vittoria before they go.

Niamh places her hand on my arm and when I look at her she smiles and shakes her head. No, I will never be like them, I will be ruthless but fair, and the Underworld will prosper. I just need Vincenzo to die – and that is something I can arrange.

'Where does this leave us?' MacGowan asks, coming towards us, although I notice he doesn't come too close.

'You should bring the King what he wants,' Carruth says, joining us. 'He's within his rights to ask.'

'But Matt is innocent,' Niamh says.

Carruth looks her up and down, then smiles. 'As you well know, Miss Whyte, no one is truly innocent. Somehow Matt needs to prove that he's not guilty and in the end, that'll be for the Court to decide.'

'The Court set him free tonight,' Niamh argues. 'Perhaps we should see that as a sign.'

'Perhaps,' Carruth concedes. 'Time will tell.' Then he and MacGowan leave together and only myself, Niamh and Rose, remain.

'Where did Matt go? she asks. 'He was right there with you and then— What have you done with him?'

'I didn't do anything with him,' I say gently.

'Are you really going to do that?' she asks me. 'How can you, when you know it's wrong.'

'Rose, I—' I stop. Rose doesn't expect me to answer. She's looking directly at Niamh.

'Did you know?'

Niamh shakes her head, tears pooling in her eyes.

'I'm so sorry, Rose.' She reaches out, but my sister bats her hand away.

'Nothing beats family, they've always got your back, right? They never lie to you about anything important.' Her voice chokes off, even though her face remains calm, stoic. She never cries, but I can see she is desperate to.

'You know I'd never want to hurt you—' I start.

But she covers her ears with her hands and runs out of the chamber, Sean in her wake. With a final glance up at Vittoria, I offer Niamh my hand and lead her from the chamber.

'Come on,' I say. 'We'll fix things later. For now, I'm taking you home. For good.'

'But what about Rose?'

'I'll give her some time, then talk to her.'

'Will you really hunt Matt?'

'Yes.'

'But ... Cillian.'

He puts his hands on my upper arms and gives me a slight shake. 'I have to, Niamh. Don't you see Vincenzo has given me no choice? But until his name appears on my palm, it won't have a time constraint, nor will it need to end in his death.'

'What if a hunt is never called?'

'I don't know. But if I don't find him, Vincenzo's men will. And I don't think that will end well for Matt.'

'But if you can't send him back to St Marnox—?'

'I never said I had all the answers. Why don't you let me do my job, and—'

'And in the meantime, I'll do mine and work on finding a legal solution to present to the Court. Force them to provide evidence of Matt's guilt,' Niamh says, a new authority clear in her tone. 'And maybe together, we can find something that resembles justice.'

I stare at her, and I suspect this will not be the last time Niamh surprises me like this. Or maybe now that our two worlds are far more similar than I ever imagined, I'll stop being surprised by her.

'How do you feel?' I ask as we make our way past the torches to the exit.

'I'm not sure yet. Surprisingly normal.'

'Are you sure?'

'I'm sure.' She kisses me, pulling away with a wide smile on her face. 'How did I not know who I was? It all seems so clear now. Although, I'm not sure what changed. Was it Vittoria taking my necklace, or when we...' She blushes, charmingly.

I laugh and hug her, loving that even after all we've done together, that she still retains some of her innocent charm.

'You know, several times in the past four years, I have meant to ask Aiden to investigate you further. I meant to ask him to look into your parents' lives in more depth, meant to ask him to get copies of the accident reports about their accident. To find out more about your necklace.'

'So why didn't you?'

'You parents' magic was good, Niamh. Thorough. I think I just kept ... forgetting. The easiest way to hide, after all, is if no one is really looking for you in the first place.'

'My mother's magic. It was her magic that hid me.'

'How do you know?'

She shrugs. 'Just a feeling.'

We walk out the main doors into the Necropolis.

Niamh smiles as she turns her face up to the summer sunshine. 'We're in the Underworld?'

'How can you tell?'

We laugh as we cross the bridge, and she stops to look down into the Molendinar Burn. I stand behind her, wrapping my arms around her and pressing her against the sandstone parapet. She twists her head around to kiss me, then turns back, placing her hands over mine.

'What I don't really understand is why Vittoria kept coming after me? You were going to marry her, you stayed away from me, she was getting exactly what she wanted.'

'I don't think that was enough for her.' I kiss the nape of Niamh's neck. 'She knew there was something between us, knew I would never ... yearn for her, the way I yearned for you. She wanted to be the fairest in my eyes. And I just couldn't give her that.'

She nods and is quiet for a while. I can see her looking over the Underworld's city landscape – ironically, it's far more idyllic than the one in the human world.

'What are you thinking?' I ask her.

'That there's a lot of open space for running.'

My lips curve into a smile.

'And lots of places to hide.'

'There certainly are.'

'I love you, *Gléigeal*.'

'I love you, too, Huntsman, and if you can catch me, I might just show you how much.'

She winks at me, ducking under my arm and running far away from me, her long dark hair streaming behind her, leaving only the sound of her laughter dancing in the wind.

I smile as I count to ten, giving her a chance before I commence my hunt.

Acknowledgments

Here in the west of Scotland, both our past and our present is a fascinating mix of cultures and languages, and I have drawn from a range of traditional fairy tales, myths and legends when creating the world depicted in *Fairest* and acknowledge the inspiration provided by these – I've tried to combine them in my own unique way.

There are so many people without whom this book simply wouldn't exist – especially in the form it is now. To my family for putting up with the messy house and the disorganised cooking schedule – although most other things were done with varying degrees of success! To all the members of Procrastination Begone! who encouraged me to submit *Fairest* to the Romantic Novelists Association conference in 2025 and encouraged me at every step. To Ali Henderson for organising the 121s at that event and later putting me in touch with my editor, Jennie Rothwell, from One More Chapter. To Jennie for all her suggestions, large and small, which have helped to make this book what it is now. To Lucy Bennett and Koti Komori for the amazing artwork. To Sue Cook, Julia Chalkley, Rachel DeBrave, Sasha Green, Victoria Finnigan, Carol MacLean and Skye MacKinnon for your regular chats, encouragement, comments and for generally keeping me sane. And especially to Marguerite Kaye for all the coffee, chats and advice about navigating the world of publishing. Finally, a huge shout-out to all the local libraries (primarily Helensburgh and Dumbarton) which have provided me with a space to write where no one expects me to do anything except sit at my computer and type. Thank you!

The author and One More Chapter would like to thank everyone who contributed to the publication of this story...

Analytics
Imogen Wolstencroft

Audio
Fionnuala Barrett
Ciara Briggs

Design
Lucy Bennett
Fiona Greenway
Liane Payne
Dean Russell

Digital Sales
Laura Daley
Lydia Grainge
Hannah Lismore

eCommerce
Laura Carpenter
Madeline ODonovan
Charlotte Stevens
Christina Storey
Rachel Ward

Editorial
Janet Marie Adkins
Rosie Best
Kara Daniel
Charlotte Ledger
Jennie Rothwell
Sofia Salazar Studer
Emily Thomas
Helen Williams

Harper360
Emily Gerbner
Ariana Juarez
Jean Marie Kelly
emma sullivan
Sophia Wilhelm

International Sales
Ruth Burrow
Bethan Moore
Colleen Simpson

Inventory
Sarah Callaghan
Kirsty Norman

Marketing & Publicity
Chloe Cummings
Grace Edwards
Katie Sadler

Operations
Melissa Okusanya

Production
Denis Manson
Simon Moore
Francesca Tuzzeo

Rights
Ashton Mucha
Alisah Saghir
Zoe Shine
Aisling Smyth

Trade Marketing
Ben Hurd
Eleanor Slater

The HarperCollins Contracts Team

The HarperCollins Distribution Team

The HarperCollins Finance & Royalties Team

The HarperCollins Legal Team

The HarperCollins Technology Team

UK Sales
Isabel Coburn
Jay Cochrane
Leah Woods

And every other essential link in the chain from delivery drivers to booksellers to librarians and beyond!

ONE MORE CHAPTER

YOUR NUMBER ONE STOP FOR PAGETURNING BOOKS

One More Chapter is an award-winning global division of HarperCollins.

Subscribe to our newsletter to get our latest eBook deals and stay up to date with all our new releases!

signup.harpercollins.co.uk/join/signup-omc

Meet the team at
www.onemorechapter.com

Follow us!

@onemorechapterhc

Do you write unputdownable fiction?
We love to hear from new voices.
Find out how to submit your novel at
www.onemorechapter.com/submissions

Mairi MacMillan lives on the wet and windy west coast of Scotland, brewing dark tales and even darker cups of tea – despite her son's advice that five minutes is the maximum steeping time required. After an intentionally dramatic time at university, she left Glasgow's urban sprawl many years ago, and now spends her days weaving romances containing characters that may or may not be inspired by some of her quirkier kinfolk.

When not corrupting perfectly good characters with morally grey choices, she can be found wild-swimming in a sea-loch described locally as 'baltic', ice-skating, or nose-deep in books with heat levels to compensate. She's currently plotting her escape from the everyday grind in a yet-to-be-acquired camper van, much to the amusement of her nearly-grown children. Her husband remains hopeful that one day she'll get around to sorting out her clutter – and that he might be invited along on any trips!

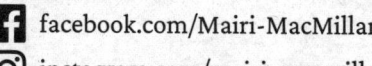

https://substack.com/@mairimacmillan

facebook.com/Mairi-MacMillan-Author
instagram.com/mairi_macmillan_author